FUGITIVE

FUGITIVE

Paul Fraser Collard

HEADLINE

First published in Great Britain in 2020 by
HEADLINE PUBLISHING GROUP

1

Cataloguing in Publication Data is available from the British Library

ISBN 978 1 4722 6343 8

Typeset in Sabon by Avon DataSet Ltd, Arden Court, Alcester, Warwickshire

Printed and bound in Great Britain by Clays Ltd, Elcograf S.p.A.

HEADLINE PUBLISHING GROUP
An Hachette UK Company
Carmelite House
50 Victoria Embankment
London EC4Y 0DZ

www.headline.co.uk
www.hachette.co.uk

For Debs

Glossary

―――◆◈◆―――

amba	flat-topped mountain peak
Bendigo Thompson	English bare-knuckle boxer
bemouti	villain, thief
bint	British army slang for a girl or woman
chokey	cholera
Falasha	Abyssinian Jew
farenj	foreigner
footpad	robber who targets pedestrians
glacis	a slope in front of the walls of a fortress
griffin	nickname for an officer newly arrived in India
havildar	native rank of sergeant
jezail	type of native flintlock musket
John Bull	personification of Great Britain
Koh-i-Noor	'Mountain of Light' – Indian diamond now part of the British Crown Jewels
lembd	cape or tunic
loophole	hole or slit cut into a wall through which a weapon may be fired
Maria Theresa thalers	silver coin originally minted in 1741 and named after the Empress Maria Theresa

mudlark	child who scavenges in river mud for items of value
Mussulman	Muslim
nabob	corruption of nawab (Muslim term for senior official or governor), used by the British to describe wealthy European merchants or retired officials who had made their fortune in India
pankha-wala	servant operating a large cooling fan
particular	London fog
pagdi	turban, cloth or scarf wrapped around the face
prantara-durga	fortress built on the summit of a hill or mountain
puttee	leg binding worn below the knee
ravelin	triangular fortification outside a fortress's walls
rhino	money, cash
Rupert	British army slang for an officer
sepoy	an Indian infantryman serving in one of the armies of the three Indian presidences
shamma	large cotton shawl
shekel	money, cash
sola topee	light tropical helmet – forerunner of the pith helmet
specie	gold and silver coins
slumming	visiting impoverished areas of a city for entertainment
subadar	native infantry officer, equivalent to captain
Tayib	good (arabic)

THE BRITISH EXPEDITION TO
MAGDALA, ABYSSINIA 1867-1868

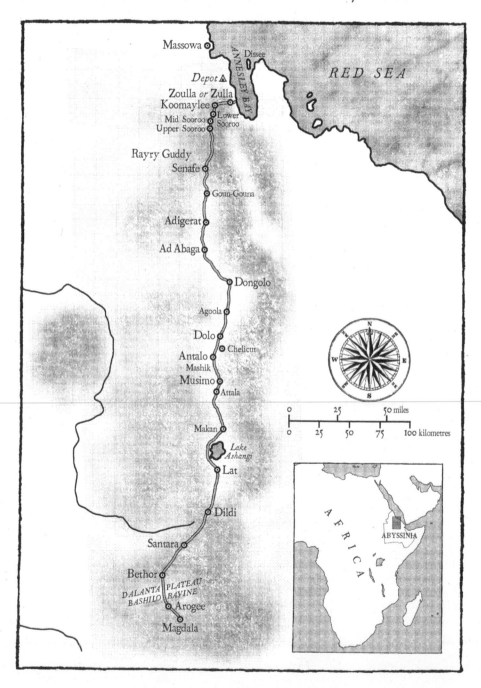

Massowa
Dissee
ANNESLEY BAY
RED SEA
Depot
Zoulla or Zulla
Koomaylee
Mid Sooroo — Lower Sooroo
Upper Sooroo
Rayry Guddy
Senafe
Goun-Gouna
Adigerat
Ad Abaga
Dongolo
Agoola
Dolo
Chelicut
Antalo
Mashik
Musimo
Attala
Makan
Lake Ashangi
Lat
Dildi
Santara
Bethor
DALANTA PLATEAU
BASHILO RAVINE
Arogee
Magdala

N
W   E
S

0		25		50 miles
0	25	50	75	100 kilometres

AFRICA
ABYSSINIA

To the Governors, the Chiefs, the Religious Orders, and the People of Abyssinia.

It is known to you that Tewodros, King of Abyssinia, detains in captivity the British consul Cameron, the British envoy Rassam, and many others, in violation of the laws of all civilised nations.

All friendly persuasion having failed to obtain their release, my Sovereign has commanded me to lead an army to liberate them . . .

When the time shall arrive for the march of a British army through your country, bear in mind, people of Abyssinia, that the Queen of England has no unfriendly feeling towards you, and no design against your country or your liberty . . .

Signed: Lieutenant General Sir Robert Napier,
Officer Commanding, Abyssinian Field Force

Prologue

---·•·---

Plateau of Wegera, Abyssinia, October 1863

The sun rose. It cast long shadows over rocks and distant mountains, and coloured the sky with great streaks of fiery orange that pushed back the grey of night to bring light out of the darkness. Warmth was returned to the barren lands; life and illumination replacing the blackness and cold of the night.

'Only God could create such beauty in such a place as this.'

'I beg your pardon, master?' The servant who led the small party of three men turned in the saddle.

'I said that this is God's work, Negusee.' The man who had broken the silence spoke again, his voice louder as he addressed the servant for the second time. It was a good voice, a strong voice, the kind that could fill every inch of a church's nave. Yet that day it echoed off rocks, with no one to listen to it save for the pair of tired and chilled servants borrowed from Consul Cameron's retinue, and three dust-shrouded mules.

The Reverend Henry Aaron Stern had not chosen the easy path. He served his God in a different way; one that would see him spend his days not in the quiet tranquillity of an

English parish, but on the dusty hillsides of the chaotic land of Abyssinia. Now, as he watched the sun rise, he marvelled at the splendour of the wild country that had been his home for so long, and which beguiled and terrified him in equal measure.

He rode on, his body swaying to the movement of the mule beneath him, savouring the peace, the only sound the mesmer-ising scuffle of hooves on the stony ground. These lands were majestic in their lonely beauty. Mountains filled the distant horizon, their tops shrouded with clouds formed from a beguiling palette of greys now that the sun was rising. The road he followed was well used, the armies that traversed the land trampling the dust and rocks of its surface into a fine powder. It was a good road, solid, built on strong foundations, and it followed the undulations of the land, weaving past boulders too large to be blasted out of its path.

Ahead, the first rays of the sun glinted off the slab-faced wall of a monolithic mountain, the light concentrated into a single, dazzling beam that conjured the image of a star fallen to earth. The notion made Stern smile. For a moment he was not a dusty missionary, but a king following a glittering star; his journey not to witness the birth of the son of God, but along a winding road that would see him returned to the city that had taken him in, clothed and guided him. London had provided a future for the poor Jew from Hamburg, who had arrived into its grasp some twenty-four years before with nothing but rags on his body and hope in his heart. Now he longed to return there. His time in the wilds of Abyssinia was over.

His mule stopped moving, then raised its tail. The sound of shit splattering onto the ground was loud in the early-morning quiet. It was enough to make him laugh, the noise, and the stink that followed, a reminder that he was still bound to this hard land of rock and granite, for a while longer at least.

Bowels emptied, the mule resumed its slow, hypnotic gait. Stern let it take its time. There was no point hurrying, the journey he was on too long and too arduous for anything other than an easy pace. He did not mind that it would be months before he would see London again. He was quitting Abyssinia with a full and righteous heart, for he knew that his work here was done.

The rising sun caught the water of a distant lake. It was as smooth as glass and reflected the line of mountains that surrounded it, a perfect mirror image caught upon its surface. It was beautiful, yet Stern felt nothing but sadness. For despite the untamed beauty of its landscape, Abyssinia was an ugly place, coloured not with the splendour of its natural bounty, but with the blackness of anger and the dirty taint of blood.

He shivered at the thought. He had been drawn to this land and its people, his life as a missionary for the London Society of Promoting Christianity amongst the Jews giving his existence the purpose it had needed. His service had brought him here over three years before, to the shores of a country that needed Christ's teachings like no other he had found. Christianity had been his own saviour and he had wanted nothing more than to bring its teachings to others. He had first heard tales of the lost Jews of Abyssinia many years before he had arrived there. The country was Christian, but there were still great swathes of the place that clung to their own, false faiths. He had wandered the country, spreading the word of the one true God amongst the Jews, the Mussulmen and the pagans he had found. Two years earlier, his funds had run out, so he had returned to London to raise more, even publishing an account of his time amongst the heathens to help finance his return. That book, *Wanderings Amongst the Falashas*, had earned enough money to return him to Abyssinia the previous year.

Now he was leaving for a second time.

'My work here is done.' He spoke the words aloud. He liked the way they sounded.

'Master?' Negusee rode in front of Stern and now twisted in the saddle to look back at his temporary master.

Stern caught a hint of disdain in the retainer's expression. 'I said my work here is done, Negusee, and it has been a success. I say that without pride.'

'Yes, master.'

'How many have I converted to the Christian faith? Why, I believe I have lost count.' Stern chuckled at his own words, taking comfort from hearing them. '*The Return to the Falashas*, I think that is what I shall call it.'

'Master?'

'My next book, Negusee. It will be the perfect companion to *Wanderings*. The title has a suitable ring to it, I believe.'

'Yes, master.' Negusee turned to face the direction of travel once again.

'Or perhaps *The Return to the Land of the Mad King*.' Stern spoke quietly, as if frightened of being overheard. It would be an accurate title, although not one he would dare speak of until he was far from the lands of the great Emperor Tewodros. For Tewodros, or Theodore as he was more commonly known in England, was indeed a mad king, a quixotic and dangerous mystery of a man if ever there was one. Stern had never been formally presented to him. Still, he had heard and seen enough to have a firm opinion of the man's character.

At times Tewodros was said to be great company, welcoming

European missions into his pavilion, quizzing them on matters of politics and asking a thousand questions about the countries of Europe. He was known to be both humorous and generous; an affable, scholarly man who thirsted for knowledge of the world in which he wanted his newly conquered land to take its place. Then there would be a sudden change. Stern had heard it said that there was never a time when the catalyst for that change had been obvious. But the swift anger and raging temper that had followed was said to be terrible to behold. It was a temper that inevitably led to death.

Stern knew Tewodros's story as well as any man; the tales and legends that detailed his rise to power were told in every village across the land. Little was known of his early years, other than that he had emerged around twenty years before as a petty chieftain called Kasa Haylu in the lowlands to the west of the country. Early victories over local rivals set him out as a man to be feared. His power grew, as did his reputation as a leader touched by the hand of God himself. That reputation earned him the hand of Tewabech, daughter of Ras Ali, regent to the Emperor Yohannes III. Yet Kasa was not yet done. When the Empress Menen left the capital of Gondar undefended, he struck, taking the city as his own. Many battles followed as the armies of the fiercely independent regional nobility sought to retain their power. Kasa won them all. The more he won, the more warriors and chieftains flocked to his banner. When, eight years before, in 1855, he defeated his last opponent, the Dejazmach Wude, he proclaimed himself emperor, taking the title of Tewodros II.

Yet his reign was not to be a happy one. He defeated the last independent region, Shewa, shattering their army and leaving himself as the only power in the land. Yet the patchwork of

provinces that made up Abyssinia, so long independent, rose
one after the other, forcing the new emperor to put down a
string of rebellions as his rule was challenged from every
quarter. His army crushed each and every show of resistance
with a ruthlessness that would shame even the great Khans of
the East, yet he never succeeded in achieving a lasting peace.
Instead he was forced to kill again and again, slaying any who
stood against him.

And he had been driven quite mad by the process.

Stern shivered, not just from the chill in the morning air. He
heard the sound of a shepherd's reed pipe coming from far off
in the distance and concentrated his mind on it, seizing on the
distraction to divert his thoughts away from the brutality of
Tewodros's reign, brutality that he had seen with his own eyes.
The gentle melody echoed off the rocky ground, the sound
fluctuating and undulating so that he had to concentrate to
hear it clearly.

As he rode on, he thought about the changes wrought
on Abyssinia. So much had changed in the eight years since
Tewodros had risen to power. The long years of bloody decline
had started with the loss of the emperor's wife, the beautiful
Empress Tewabech. Each year that had followed had seen at
least one more rebellion. All were quashed without mercy, the
perpetrators, their followers and their families executed.
Tewodros's land was filled with blood, his throne held up by a
foundation of corpses. Invasions had followed, the Egyptians
raiding the Abyssinian lowlands without pause. Betrayals had
become almost constant, even men Tewodros had appointed
himself turning against him. For now, he clung on to his
power, but he was having to fight harder and harder to retain it
as each year passed.

Stern had witnessed the emperor's reaction to such a betrayal at first hand. He had been part of an audience attending the trial of one of Tewodros's own senior commanders. The man, once trusted to lead one of the emperor's armies, now stood accused of plotting against him. For once, Tewodros had been icy calm, his temper contained. Yet that had not stopped him from ordering the man's right hand and foot to be cut off before he was left as food for the hyenas. Blood and mutilation. Torture and death. Such was the currency of Tewodros's reign.

Stern felt a rush of bile surge up from his gut as he relived the moment of dismemberment. The memory of the events he had witnessed haunted him. He had prayed for guidance and for the strength to remain in Abyssinia to do God's work. He had heard nothing by way of a reply. That silence had been drowned out by the screams of the emperor's victims that resonated in his head, and had left him bereft. So he had made the choice to leave while his own limbs were still attached to his body.

The small party rode on in silence. The plateau of Wegera stretched away from them. The great expanse was coloured with earthy tones, the browns of the soil and the greys of the rocks broken by great swathes of stunted bushes that bore a smattering of tiny leaves alongside hundreds of huge thorns. The only sign of the hand of man was the great road they followed, which would take them northwards to the coast. It was another legacy of Tewodros's reign, the emperor's obsession with cannon and all other artillery leading him to construct the beginnings of an expansive network of roads that criss-crossed the country.

Ahead, spread across the plateau, was a collection of tents. All were black, except for one. That single red pavilion stood out like a beacon. Stern's heart sank. Only one man had a tent the colour of blood. Tewodros. Emperor of Abyssinia. Descendant of Solomon and his wife Sheba. Murderer. Killer. And master of all.

'God is our refuge and our strength, an ever-present help in trouble.' Stern muttered the words under his breath as he pulled back on his reins and brought his mule to a stand. 'We will not fear, though the earth give, and the mountains fall into the heart of the sea, though its waters roar and foam and the mountain quake with their surging.'

He looked around. Silence surrounded him. No one else was on the road save for his little party.

'I think we shall divert to the east.' He shifted in the saddle and made a play of searching for another route. He did not look at Uttam, the second servant from the consul's staff, who had been ordered to accompany him on his long journey to the coast. The old man had plodded dutifully in his wake for days without uttering a single word. Now he looked back at Stern with doleful eyes that spoke more eloquently than any words.

'Master, that is not possible.' Negusee still led the three. Now he turned his mule around to face his temporary master, a forced smile plastered across his face. 'We must pay our respects to His Majesty. To not do so would be to treat His Majesty with the utmost contempt. Men have been put to death for much less.'

'Come now, Negusee, I do not imagine he would mind. We have a long journey ahead of us and I am not sure we have the time to delay.' Stern hummed and hawed, hoping that the servant could not hear his fear.

'No, master.' Negusee's smile faded. None of it had reached his eyes, and now they betrayed their owner's disdain. 'We must pay homage to the emperor.'

Stern made no attempt to move. Fear was flooding into his gut, then heading lower so that he could feel it squirming into his bowels. He knew Negusee was speaking the truth. To pass the emperor by would be a dreadful insult, one that could earn its perpetrator a brutal death. His mind conjured the image of a man being held down. Once again he heard the screams as first a hand, then a foot was sliced from the man's body. He saw the blood – there had been so much blood – pouring out of his wrist and ankle like water from a jug. He had screamed the whole time, even as he was dragged from the tent, a great snail trail of gore left in his wake.

The image gave Stern the heaves, and he gagged. The burn of vomit hit the back of this throat, acrid and sharp. He swallowed it down with difficulty, then burped, the foul taste of bile filling his mouth.

Negusee was watching him, his face expressionless.

'We shall pay the emperor our respects.' Stern spoke the bitter words. His throat still burned, so he reached for his canteen. It took a while for his shaking hands to remove the stopper. He drank the water, relishing the cool liquid as it ran over the scalded flesh at the back of his throat. He swallowed it down, then drank again, scouring away the taste of fear.

'Lead on, Negusee.' He gave the command in a firm voice. The water sat heavy in his stomach. He burped again, yet it did nothing to relieve his biliousness.

They saw the first of Tewodros's warriors as they rode closer to the tents. These were not soldiers, not as Stern knew them. They were wild men, hewn from this harsh land, their spears and swords carried with the casual expertise of men well versed and practised in their use. They did not know him, these killers. But they saw his white face and they knew that their master's hatred of the Europeans had been growing stronger with each passing day. So now they mocked Stern as he rode towards the great red pavilion. They cursed him and spat at him, spears shaken and pointed as if about to strike him down.

Stern forced his spine to straighten. He tried to think of Christ shuffling through the crowd on the way up the hill at Calvary. He himself carried no cross, yet his fear was just as heavy as any wooden spar, and it took all of his strength to make himself sit straight-backed on the mule and hide that fear away.

Tewodros's warriors pressed closer. He felt hands scrabble at his arms and legs, fingers like claws digging and jabbing. All the while he was bombarded with abuse, words he did not understand bellowed at him. The clamour increased with every step his mule took. Shouts. Jeers. Hatred unleashed.

He reached the red pavilion. Still the crowd pressed around him. At any moment he expected to feel the sharp stab of a blade slicing into his flesh. Inside his belly, fear was taking hold. Muscles that had trembled now shook. Bowels that felt filled with water almost gave way, and he had to clench his buttocks tight lest he void them there and then.

More soldiers lurched out of the pavilion. He saw at once that they were drunk. They staggered towards him, anger flaring as they saw a white face in their midst.

'We must find some shade.' Stern blurted the words. He had to shout to make himself heard, such was the furore that surrounded him.

'Master?' Negusee was close enough to hear, yet still he questioned the white man he had been ordered to serve.

'We need shade!' Stern shouted, desperation and fear revealed without a care. He did not know what to do. Never before had he faced such hatred directed at him and him alone. He looked around. All he could see were angry faces. All he could see was their loathing. All he could see was danger.

The outcry stopped in an instant. It was replaced by silence so complete that the air suddenly felt heavy, as if a violent thunderstorm was about to break.

With dread in his heart, he turned to face the pavilion. Around him, every man was falling to his knees. The crowd, which had seemed so close to frenzy, was still.

He saw why, and his heart froze.

Tewodros stood in front of his pavilion. He looked just as Stern remembered him. As ever, he was dressed simply in the same white shamma as the lowliest of his men. He was barefoot and wore no gold or jewellery. He did not need to. For his eyes were black and full of fire, and they lit his face better than any precious stone ever could.

'What do you want?' Tewodros saw a white-faced farenj in front of him and so spoke in English.

'I saw Your Majesty's tent and came hither to offer my humble salutations and respects.' Stern slithered from the back of his mule. To his relief, his legs did not fold beneath him as he hit the ground. As soon as he found his footing, he bowed low.

'Where are you going?'

'I am, with Your Majesty's sanction, about to proceed to Massorah.' Stern was proud of his even reply.

'And why did you come to Abyssinia?'

'A desire to circulate the word of God amongst Your Majesty's subjects prompted the enterprise.' Stern heaved down as deep a breath as he could manage. He felt his gut spasm and shifted his weight, clenching his buttocks tight lest they let loose the torrent of terror.

'Can you make cannons?'

For the first time since Tewodros had strode out of the tent, Stern did not know what to say. It was an odd question at the best of times, and he was not prepared for it. 'No, Your Majesty.' He tried to smile, but his mouth would not respond properly.

'You lie!' The two words were bellowed.

Stern took half a pace away from the mad king standing in front of him. He realised that Tewodros was as drunk as his commanders.

'Where are you from?' Tewodros roared the question at Negusee. Stern's servants were lying a yard apart behind their temporary master, their faces turned to the dirt in front of them. 'You,' he jabbed a finger towards Negusee, 'are you the servant of this white man?'

'No, Your Majesty. I am from Tigray. I am in the employ of Consul Cameron and only accompany this man down to Adowa, whither I am bound to see my family.' Negusee spoke without lifting his head.

'You vile carcass! You base dog! You rotten donkey! You dare to bandy words with your king.' Tewodros's rage was immediate. He could not keep still and hopped from foot to foot, arms gesticulating wildly. 'Down with the villain and bemouti, beat him till there is not a breath in his worthless carcass!'

Stern could do nothing but stand and stare as one of

Tewodros's guards stepped forward, a club the length of a man's leg in his hands. He was still staring when the club was pulled back then smashed down violently onto Negusee's head.

'Your Majesty.' Stern tried to intervene, but the words came out in nothing more than the quietest whisper. Events were happening too fast. It was as if what he was seeing was somehow not real; a night terror come to life. Never before had he felt such complete dread. It consumed him, paralysing his body.

Tewodros's guard battered Negusee without pause. The servant was helpless, but still he tried to defend himself. He lifted an arm, attempting to ward off a blow. The stick smacked into it, the bone shattering with a loud snap. Negusee screamed then, pain and fear released. Blow followed blow. After a dozen, he no longer moved. Still the stick came for him. Blood flew, the wooden shaft of the stick running thick with it, slathering the hands of the guard.

Stern watched on, frozen with fear, as Negusee was beaten to a pulp, his head shattered and his limbs flattened. The only sound was the thump of the heavy stick into flesh and the grunts and gasps of the guard who wielded it without thought of mercy.

'There's another man yonder!' Tewodros was not done. He stood behind his guard, face twisted with relish as he watched Negusee die, the front of his white shamma speckled with bright red blood. Now he pointed at Uttam, who just lay there, shaking in abject terror as his fellow servant was beaten to death in front of his eyes. 'Kill him also!' Tewodros shrieked the words, his rage heightened by the blood spilled at his command.

Uttam looked up in horror as he saw his fate approach. He was given time to do nothing more before the bloodstained stick came for him. The first blow smacked into his head, shattering his skull. The battering started again. It was slower this time, the guard tiring of his gruesome task. Yet still the club did its bloody work.

Tewodros turned away, drawing a pistol from beneath his shamma. He aimed it at Stern. 'You insult me!'

Stern opened his mouth. No sound came out. He could do nothing but stand there, terror freezing his very soul.

'Knock him down!' Tewodros screamed. 'Brain him! Kill him!'

Stern went ice cold. At the last, he felt his bladder give way, a sudden warm rush of hot piss soaking into the front of his trousers.

Then the guard came for him.

Stern came back to life. He did not want to. With life came pain. It consumed him, the white-hot torture like nothing he had ever experienced. He did not know how he still lived. There were few memories of the beating he had received. God had been merciful and had taken away his consciousness to spare him the horror. Now he awoke to agony and to the iron touch of shackles clasped around his ankles and wrists. He knew he was a prisoner of the Mad King, one of the hundreds of souls incarcerated for a hundred different unnamed crimes.

He cried out then, his body racked by great heaves and shudders as terror engulfed him. He raged into the darkness, fear and pain mixed into an intoxicating cocktail that took away every part of his true self. He did not know for how long he screamed, but it went on until he was utterly spent, his cries losing their power until they were little more than a pathetic whimper. Only then did he try to move, but the chains around his wrists and ankles were too heavy, and he could do nothing more than writhe on the ground.

He lay still. A great feeling of nothingness overwhelmed him. He was utterly powerless. He was beaten. He was broken. He was alone.

'Fear not, for I am with thee,' he whispered into the darkness, seeking his God. 'Be not dismayed, for I am thy God. I will strengthen thee, yea, I will help thee; yes, I will uphold thee with the right hand of my righteousness.'

The words echoed in the gloom. Stern fell silent. He was a prisoner of the Mad King, but he would never be alone.

For his God was with him.

Chapter One

———◆•◆•◆———

London, January 1868

The darkness wrapped itself around the streets of Whitechapel like the remorseless fingers of a murderer tightening around a victim's throat. The particular was bad that night, the fog thick, choking, cold. It had been the same all week, the lifeless, breathless air filled with the cloying tendrils of smog both day and night, the dense haze making it impossible to see more than a couple of yards ahead. For some, that was a good thing. There was little beauty on display in the narrow, forgotten streets of the East End, and many would say the filth and squalor was at its best when hidden from sight. But it was not the lack of aesthetic qualities that made some favour a fog-filled night such as this. For in the particular, anything could happen. And it frequently did.

'Where is he?' The voice was overly loud, as if a deliberate attempt to hide the fear of its owner was being made.

'He will be here.' The answer came immediately. It was hissed, the sound pitched low. 'And keep your bloody voice down.' Only the foolish brought attention to themselves in such a place as this. Especially when their accent betrayed their status as clearly as any open display of wealth.

'I said that slumming was a terrible idea,' the first voice replied, although this time the advice had been heeded, the words spoken with reduced volume.

'Then you should have stayed at home.' There was little pity in the second voice.

'Maybe I should.'

'Then go.'

'Good grief. Not on my own!'

'In that case, shut up.'

'You are being cruel, Charles.'

'And you, my dear Bertie, are worrying about nothing.' Charles Worthington, son of a lord and owner of the largest collection of silk handkerchiefs in all of London, spoke quickly and smoothly.

'How on earth can I be worrying about nothing? I thought the whole point of this exercise was to go somewhere that is absolutely not safe. Is this place not dangerous?' Albert Moncrieff, known to all as Bertie, no longer attempted to hide his concern. He came from new money, his grandfather a small-town businessman from the fringes of London who had made his fortune investing in canals. That one fact had dominated his life, from his first day at prep school to this evening in the gloomy streets of the East End.

'The point was to have some fun.' A third voice entered the discussion. 'And we cannot have even an iota of that if you insist on whining, old man.'

'I am not whining, Johnny. I'd just feel better if this man of yours could damn well be on time.' Bertie lacked the silver-spoon swagger of his two companions and his trembling tone belied his concern.

'He will be here, I assure you.'

'How can you be so sure?'

'Because he won't get paid if he does not appear.' John Arbuthnot Brown was the son of a politician. He was certain of himself and his place in the world, and he showed that constant confidence in the snap of his tone and the terseness of his words. 'He is a businessman, after all. I very much doubt his enterprise will survive if he does not take care of his guests. My cousin was here just last week, and he has yet to stop talking of the larks he and his gang had. He said that it was the best night of his life, a veritable trip into Babel, and I for one fully intend to experience that for myself. Besides, the man we await lives on his reputation, and that reputation will count for naught if he allows us to be molested or interfered with in any way.'

The three men had dressed for the occasion, and their long plain black overcoats did a fair job of not drawing attention as they waited, just as instructed, at the corner of Great Prescot Street and Mansell Street, a short stroll from the omnibus station at Aldgate. Despite the hour, the fog and the darkness, they were surrounded by a great crowd. In Whitechapel, life was conducted on the streets. Those streets teemed with people both young and old; men, women and children mixing together as they spent another night doing all they could to avoid returning to the overcrowded tenements where they would pass a miserable, cold night before starting another merciless day attempting to survive.

Many of the barrows and stalls that catered to the throng had closed for the day, but those that served the night-time crowd were still very much in evidence. A baked-potato man, a great cloud of steam billowing from the chimney built into the lid of his tin oven, was busy on the other side of the street. Two young girls, neither much more than ten years old, were selling matches from tin trays held against their small tummies by knotted string worn around their necks. Both shouted for attention, their high-pitched voices competing with one another for the punters passing by. Next to the girls, a glove seller, a woman well wrapped in heavy woollen shawls, her face barely visible between a thick muffler and a trilby hat pulled low, was doing a brisk trade, with plenty of customers for her wares. To her side, a man sat forlornly on a stool next to a great tin bath filled with ice. He was roundly ignored by the crowd, who were already chilled to the bone. A man selling pea soup was doing a much better trade, his bucket already nearly emptied and ready to be refilled from the local chop house.

'I am cold and hungry.' Bertie broke the silence. He shuffled from foot to foot as he spoke.

'Do shut up, old man.' It was John who answered, his tone betraying nothing but annoyance. 'And try to stand still.'

'I am quite certain that someone has defecated near here.' Bertie ignored the advice. He sniffed to emphasise his observation. 'Can you not smell it?'

'Be quiet.' This time it was Charles who answered. 'You are drawing attention.'

Bertie quickly scanned the crowd. Most were moving along, the chill in the air incentive enough to keep from standing still. But a group of shadowy figures on the other side of the street were looking his way, faces barely discernible in the fog. None attempted to hide their scrutiny of the three young men loitering on their turf.

'Oh my.' He turned to tug at his friend's sleeve. 'Do you see those men, Charles?'

'I do.' For the first time, someone other than Bertie showed a trace of fear. 'I think it might be better if we left.'

'I agree.'

'We need to wait.' John's answer left no room for negotiation. 'The instructions were quite clear.'

'But do you see those fellows over there, Johnny? Oh Lord, they are moving towards us even as I speak.' Bertie's eyes were riveted on the group of men, who had suddenly started to advance towards them.

'He said he would be here,' John insisted, but there was no hiding the tremor in his voice. Bravado only lasted so long on the streets of Whitechapel.

'Perhaps we should move along.' Charles reinforced Bertie's suggestion. He reached out, placing a guiding hand on John's arm.

'Fine.' John glanced across at the sinister figures and finally gave in. He began to move down the street towards the dubious security of the Aldgate omnibus station.

The three men did not get the chance to take more than a single step.

'I say, look out!' Charles called out in warning as a thin, dark-faced man slipped out of an alley no more than ten yards away from them. He was dressed in a long tan trench coat that was pockmarked by a thousand stains. A brown pork pie hat, several sizes too small, was perched on the very top of his head, his hair cropped close to the scalp.

There was little time to do more than take in his appearance before the man was just a foot in front of them.

'Stay back, you hear.' John stood his ground, his feet moving to take up a fighter's stance whilst his fists rose. He had read of bare-knuckle fighters and had even seen an image or two in

Punch. He knew how to stand, if perhaps not how to actually fight.

'All right, Bendigo fucking Thompson, stand down before you do yourself a mischief. Now then, are you fine young gentlemen here to see the captain?' The man had strutted straight up to the group, his feet moving fast and his shoulders swaying in a confident swagger. Now he stood with his chin raised, a wide smile plastered across his ferrety face.

'You're late.' John dropped his fists.

'And you're already making too much of a fucking ruckus, chum.' The man gurgled phlegm, then spat out a fat nugget. He was not much to look at. At a little over five feet tall, he was dwarfed by all three of the men who had come slumming. He was as slight as a chimney sweep's brush and just as grimy. Snot trickled from one nostril before he hawked it back inside his nose, swallowing it noisily. 'So, are you boys ready for some larks or what?'

'We're here to see the captain.' John made no attempt to hide his disdain of the short, grinning idiot standing before him.

'And so's you will, chum, and so's you will. But all in good time.' The man made a play of looking around him, his small, beady eyes darting back and forth.

'And just who the devil might you be?' John's mouth curled in distaste.

'Me? You can call me Cooper, same as everyone else round here. I'm here to make sure you gets where you're meant to be going. Now look alive-o and let's be on our way.'

John turned to his friends. Neither looked impressed.

'I say, are you really the captain's man?' Charles voiced the doubt all three were feeling.

'Course I fucking am. Me and the captain, why, we're like that.' Cooper lifted a hand, linking two blackened fingers together to indicate quite how close he was to the man whose enterprise the three had come to experience. He grinned at them before glancing over at the cluster of shadowy figures, who had now paused halfway across the street. 'I see you almost met Davy and his boys.'

All three heads turned in unison to stare at the footpads, who had just been thwarted of their prey.

'All right there, Davy lad. These boys are here to see the captain.' Cooper raised a hand and waved cheerily. 'Fucking Welsh twats,' he muttered, hiding the words under his smile. 'Now then.' He turned back to his three guests. 'You lot ready to get a-going?'

'That *is* why we are here.' Some of the confidence had drained from John's voice. He was still staring at the footpads, who were lingering as if reluctant to leave the scene.

'Then all's well and fucking lovely. Now at this stage in the proceedings, I am obliged to give you all a little bit of friendly fucking advice.' Cooper took hold of his lapels as he gave what could only be a prepared speech. 'Have any of youse met the captain before?'

'Of course not.' John answered for all three.

Cooper sniffed, then gurgled snot as he nodded at the answer. 'Then you listen fucking carefully to what I is about to say.' He grinned, enjoying his moment. 'And what I have to say is this. Whatever you do this night – and I promise you is going to do a lot of good fucking stuff this night.' He paused to wink at his guests. 'Whatever you do, do not fuck with the captain. The captain, why, he's killed so many men he's lost fucking count. That's why no one messes with him. Not fuckwits like

Davy and his boys. Not the peelers. Not even them fucking detectives over at Scotland Yard. No one, and I mean no one, fucks with the captain. Do you all get what I is saying?'

'We do.' John spoke again.

'Then let's be off. No sense dilly-dallying round here. Not when we have places to be.' Cooper gave his guests one last grin, then swiped a hand across his grotty nose before turning on his heel to lead them to the evening's entertainment.

Chapter Two

———◆◆◆———

Cooper gave the three gentlemen no time to dawdle. He led them at a smart pace down the alley he had emerged from, then through a network of smaller streets and narrow back ways. He said not another word as he swaggered along, arms swinging, the three taller men in the long dark coats trailing in his wake.

'Here we are then.' He brought them to an abrupt halt.

'Where the devil are we?' John was the first to speak. The words rasped out, the fast pace stealing his breath. They were standing midway down an alley that ran between the backs of two long rows of tenement houses.

'I have no idea, but I think I have just trodden in something rather noxious.' Bertie wrinkled his nose in disgust.

'Shut your muzzles,' Cooper snapped. He dug a hand into the pocket of his verminous trench coat, producing a small flask that he lifted to his lips. He took a sly nip, then slipped it away again. Refreshed, he grinned at his three charges, but said nothing.

The three did as they were told. They waited, listening to the shouts and cries coming from the squat tenement nearby.

More than one baby wailed, the pitiful cries at odds with the angry voices that came from the end of the building, where a man and woman were engaged in a slanging match at full volume. In another part, a woman sang, her voice quite without melody or rhythm.

'Do you think—' Bertie started.

'Hush now.' Cooper was quick to interrupt. 'He's coming.'

The three men looked down the alley as one. Sure enough, a figure was approaching. The fog wrapped around him like a ghostly shawl, so that he was little more than an apparition, a dark shadow shrouded in mist.

'Is that him?' Bertie whispered.

'That's the captain all right,' Cooper answered softly, the words barely audible.

The figure came closer. It did not hurry. It did not swagger or strut. It simply moved with purpose.

'Have you got the rhino?' There was no greeting. Just five short words, delivered staccato. Little could be seen of the captain's face beneath a dark-coloured pork pie hat pulled down low. He was tall, just a shade under six foot, and was wearing a tightly buttoned overcoat.

'Are you truly the captain?' Oddly, it was Bertie who spoke for the three. He stared at the man, his eyes as wide as those of a child seeing a bear for the first time.

'I'm the captain.' The words were spoken softly, but every man heard them. 'Now have you got the rhino?'

He lifted his chin as he repeated the question. For the first time, the three gentlemen got a good glimpse of his face. A scar ran down the left-hand side, the lower half disappearing into a heavy beard. But it was not that that drew their attention; it was the hard grey eyes that stared back at them as if the captain could see right down to their very souls.

The confirmation of identity was enough. Charles fished into his overcoat and pulled out a thick wedge of banknotes, which he held out in front of him.

The captain took the bundle swiftly. He did not check it. Instead, he carefully unbuttoned his coat and tucked the notes deep into an inside pocket. It was artfully done, every gesture sharp and controlled, the coat pulled open just long enough to give the three men a glimpse of the stout oak cudgel hooked into the captain's belt.

'Follow me.' The captain turned on his heel and walked back down the alley, setting a rapid pace. He did not bother to see if they followed.

'Evenin', Captain.' The boy standing by the back door of the Black Griffin stepped forward as the small group approached. He was less than eight years old, but he knew the captain. Everyone did.

'Jimmy.' The captain returned the greeting. 'Has it started?'

'Not yet. They're waiting for you.'

'Good.' The captain turned on his heel. The three men who had followed him stood there, breath condensing in front of their faces in the chill night air. 'Take them in, Cooper.'

'Right you are, Captain.' Cooper's chest puffed up as he was given the order. 'Look alive-o, gentlemen,' he called over his shoulder as he strutted forward.

The captain stood back as the young gentlemen filed through the doorway and up a darkened flight of wooden stairs. He could smell their fear as they passed him, the scent as clean as the cheap perfume of a whore. The three were far from the parts of London where they would feel comfortable, where they were known, and where their money and their families' reputations gave them power. Here, in his London, they were like lambs brought fresh to Smithfield. They were defenceless, their lives placed in his hands in exchange for a few small sheets of thin paper.

It was not the first time he had had power over men's lives. For years he had led soldiers on the battlefield, stealing a place that was not his then flourishing in his deceit. And in the chaos of battle, he had thrived. There amidst the blood and the slaughter, he had become the man he was that day; one who was certain of what lay in his soul: the good and the bad, the dark and the light, the shadow and the shade.

He could smell something else in the air that night. Something almost strong enough to hide the scent of the men's fear. He could smell their excitement. They had come to him for debauchery. They had come for drink, for visceral, bloody entertainment and for sex. He would provide all three and he would provide them in such quantity and quality that there would be a queue of people from their privileged world asking for the enigmatic captain and the chance of a night spent in his care.

'Come here, Jimmy.' He gave the command.

'Yes, Captain?' the small boy squeaked as he reluctantly shuffled closer.

'You not going to ask us for payment?'

'Not from you, Captain. You get in gratis.' The boy stopped well short of the tall man. His eyes did not once look up from the ground.

The captain grunted at the remark. It was not what he wanted. He brought the men, these walking pocketbooks, into these filthy streets so that they would part with their money and share it with the folk for whom this place was home. He looked at the lad tasked with charging everyone who went up the back stairs of the Black Griffin a shilling for the privilege, waiting to see if he would look up. He didn't.

'How many men just went in, Jimmy?'

'Four.'

'And me makes five. That's five shillings, Jimmy. Five whole shillings.'

'I can add up, Captain.' The remark was said so softly that the captain barely heard it.

'What's that you say, boy?'

'I said I can add up.' For the first time the lad looked up. This time he spoke clearly. 'I ain't bottle-fucking-head stupid.'

The captain saw the flash of defiance in the boy's expression. It was what he had been waiting for.

'Good.' He dipped into his pocket and pulled out some coins. 'Come here and hold out your hand.'

The lad did as he was told. Slowly and carefully, the captain counted out six coins, looking at each one in turn before placing it carefully on the lad's palm.

'How many is that, Jimmy?'

The boy looked at the coins. Then he looked at the tall man who loomed over him. He hesitated.

'Come on now.' It was a command, not a request. 'You told me you can count.' The captain smiled at the delay. The boy would know who stood in front of him. He would have heard the tales. Some elements in those tales were true, or at least they were somewhat close to the mark. Most were not. The captain did nothing to confirm or deny any of them, leaving the whisperers to tell them without interference. None knew the truth. No one did.

'Six.' Jimmy gave the answer.

The captain's left hand clipped the boy sharply around the ear. 'Try again.'

Jimmy looked up into the captain's face. The blow had not stung. He had been punched and beaten enough in his short life to know real pain.

'Five?' He gave his second answer, then flinched, expectant of another clout, harder than the first.

'You learn quick, lad.' The captain laughed as he got the answer he wanted. He said nothing more as he entered the doorway and began to climb the simple wooden stairs that led to the first of the entertainments he had arranged for his guests.

Chapter Three

———◆———

The captain paused on the top step. The air in the upstairs room of the Black Griffin was ripe. The room was heated to the point of suffocation, the two fireplaces both filled with roaring flames. Body pressed against body, every inch of space taken. The room smelled earthy, the stink of too many hard-working men pressed together in too small a place. Underscoring the earthy tang of body and sweat was the odour of beer, gin and cheap wine.

He stood surveying the crowd, checking all was as it should be. He had learned to be cautious, to never take anything for granted. The streets he had made his home were filled with men looking to do him harm, or failing that, to get paid for making sure that harm was avoided. He had faced down a number of protection rackets in the last few months, and he was sure he would likely have to do so again before long. But for now, he saw nothing that concerned him, the great press of bodies just as he expected.

In the centre of the room was a white-painted wooden ring, the walls elbow-high, the whole affair around six feet across. The white paint was old enough to have turned a putrid shade of yellow, the wood scuffed and battered from the crowd that thronged around it twice weekly. Men were pressed close, impatient for the night's entertainment to start, beer tankards clutched in sweaty hands. Those towards the back of the room stood on chairs or tables or anything they could find that would allow them to see over the heads of those closer to the ring.

On the far side of the room was a simple slab of wood set on two sturdy trestles. Behind it were a dozen kegs of ale and a set of shelves filled with tankards, bottles of gin and cheap wine. Two barkeeps were stationed there, both working hard as they did their best to satisfy the needs of the punters shouting their orders and thrusting coins towards them.

The atmosphere was raucous. Every man had to bellow to be heard. Whoops and yells came almost constantly, with great peals of laughter adding to the racket. But there was something else present, something subtler than the dozens of bellowed conversations and the bawdy tomfoolery. There was the taint of expectancy in the overheated air. The captain could sense it like it was a physical thing, as real as the stink of beer and gin. Yet he himself felt nothing. It took more than the prospect of blood to excite him.

There was not enough space to swing even the skinniest of cats, but still the throng did its best to step back as he walked in. Even men well in their cups eased out of his way. It was almost enough to make him smile.

He slipped through the crowd, heading to the area that had been kept free for his guests on the far side of the ring. The three of them were drinking the first of that night's ales, laying a base for what was to come. It was all planned. From the length of time the gentlemen had waited on the street corner to the moment Cooper had arrived to greet them. Even the presence of Davy and his three sons had been part of the night's scheduled events. Nothing was left to chance. Nothing.

'A good evening to you there, Captain,' a voice called out as the captain pushed his way close to the ring.

He recognised the speaker at once. Harlequin Billy had been organising these evenings in the East End since the captain had been a boy. Dog-fighting was his speciality, but he could turn his hand to most things that involved entertaining a crowd. Bare-knuckle fighting had been a favourite for a while, but that had stopped when his best fighter had been beaten to a bloody pulp by an Irishman, the shame of losing to a Paddy enough to put an end to Harlequin Billy's enterprise. Now he organised dog fights and ratting at half a dozen venues across the East End. Most were fair fights, with only a few ringers thrown in to keep Billy in a decent style, something that endeared him to his public, who packed out every event he arranged.

The captain nodded a greeting to the old man. As ever, Billy was dressed in his distinctive coat, decorated with a hundred or more scraps of coloured cloth. Like its owner, the gaudy garment was old and threadbare, with rents in the fabric and patches where the decoration had been torn off to reveal the tatty brown material that lay beneath. Yet the effect worked. Harlequin Billy stood out as the showman he was.

'Now that you're here, we can be making a start.' The old man grinned at the captain, then turned to clamber into the ring. The crowd hushed as he took his place in the centre of the small arena. After the boisterous hubbub, the silence that followed was as reverential and respectful as a Sunday-morning congregation hushing at the arrival of the vicar in his pulpit.

'Now then, gentlemen, now then.' Harlequin Billy raised both arms, palms held towards his crowd. 'You all has your fancy, I know that, and you all knows me. There'll be fair fights here tonight, the most vicious vermin we can find and the best ratters in all of London!'

The crowd growled its assent. Most had been there for a good hour or more, enough time for them to have sunk plenty of ale, wine or gin and to be ready for blood.

'Now, you all know Honest John.' Harlequin Billy pointed across at a fat man seated on a stool just outside the ring. 'You know he ain't about to get up to nothing untoward. As fair as fucking fair, he is, and that watch of his ain't ever missed a second, ain't that so, John-o, my lad?'

Honest John grinned, then held aloft an enormous pocket watch the size of a man's fist. He brandished it at the crowd, who applauded in approval.

'So, who's ready for the first bout?' Harlequin Billy bellowed.

The gathering roared in approval.

'I said, who's ready for the first bout?' Harlequin Billy grinned from ear to ear as he worked his audience.

This time the response was deafening. It was the feral snarl of the mob, the sound of men lusting for blood.

'Then here we go.' Harlequin Billy twirled on the spot, swishing his fancy coat around him so that it billowed away from his body. The crowd cheered, then surged closer to the ring, elbowing and jostling to be able to see.

Throughout Harlequin Billy's display, the captain had said nothing. He stood apart from the three toffs, his back pressed against the wall of the crowded room. Not one man encroached on his space, leaving him a fair view of the pit.

To his front, his guests pressed close to the white wood wall. He caught glimpses of their faces as they turned to laugh and cheer at one another. All were flushed, the heat and the beer colouring cheeks and necks. Their excitement as they waited for the first of the things they had come for was palpable.

'And now, gentlemen, we have for your delectation the main bout of the evening!' Harlequin Billy once again stood in the centre of the ring, his arms raised as he worked his audience one last time. 'You've all heard of the dog, and I promise you he's a fucking killer, you have my word on that. He's going at fifty rats in two minutes, and I reckon tonight he'll be faster still!'

The crowd greeted the announcement with a raucous bellow of delight. They had lost none of their enthusiasm for the ratting, despite the half-dozen bouts that had gone before. Most were half cut now, the drinks coming as quickly as they could be served.

Only the captain stood apart, watching over his guests closely. They were already drunk, or at least close to it. That was the important thing this early in proceedings. Get men like this drunk and they were putty in his hands.

Two of the toffs – he had not bothered to learn their names, and neither did he care to do so – were shouting in each other's faces, their skin flushed and sheeted in sweat. The third was arm in arm with a man the captain knew well. A hat maker, notorious for beating both his wife and his only son. Tonight he was making friends with a man who likely carried more money in his pocketbook than the hatter would make in his lifetime.

The captain scowled. The presence of the man was not part of the plan. He lifted a hand, beckoning Cooper to his side.

Like his master, Cooper had not taken a sip since they had arrived at the Griffin. He obeyed the summons instantly.

'Get him away,' the captain whispered into Cooper's ear.

Cooper licked his lips, then nodded. He would not gainsay the captain. Not ever. He turned away, quick, short steps taking him to the side of the cruel hatter. It took a moment to whisper in the man's ear, and another to stand aside whilst the hat maker turned to glance at the captain. A moment later, and he shuffled away, head bowed. Cooper stepped smoothly into the gap he had vacated, beaming at the toff as if they had been separated for too long.

The captain almost smiled at the display. Cooper was proving to be as loyal as any soldier he had commanded. It was unexpected. He had not thought to find such devotion here, in these tough, lonely streets.

Harlequin Billy's assistants were busy. They circled around their master, tossing fresh sawdust onto the floor of the ring, covering the worst of the spilled blood so that the arena was fit for the evening's finale. The captain watched them as Billy played to his crowd, his familiar patter encouraging the wagers that were being shouted around the room before the final bout got under way. Another assistant followed the men with the sawdust, a rank rag smearing the blood that had sprayed onto the inner walls of the ring.

The last dog was brought out. Its owner, a man with hollow cheeks and great grey bags under his eyes, carried the animal in a cage, which he set on the floor at one side of the ring. Inside, the animal was going berserk, its small body turning around and around as the stink of blood drove it into a frenzy.

The captain watched as the dog's owner pulled on a huge leather gauntlet that stretched almost to his shoulder. From a pocket he produced a short club, the stout oak shaft capable of braining a terrier with a single blow. Only when he was ready did he gesture for one of Billy's men to open the cage.

The terrier went wild. It darted forward, throwing itself against the door, teeth bared as it snarled and snapped. Before it could leap out, its owner reached in with his gauntleted hand and grabbed it deftly around the scruff of the neck, then stepped back, the snarling, writhing animal held far away from his body.

The captain watched the terrier. The animal bit and snapped, its small, powerful frame contorting as it fought to be free. It wanted nothing more than to kill. The urge consumed it. It *had* to kill. The captain knew the emotion well. He had felt it himself.

Harlequin Billy's assistants cleared the ring, leaving just the owner and his raging beast. There was a pause, the air filled with the final wagers being shouted, then a great jeer as two men lifted a wide wooden chest to the edge of the ring. They held it there whilst a third man stepped forward with an iron crowbar, which he rammed into a gap between the lid and the box. He held his pose for a moment, smiling at the crowd. Then he levered the crowbar, splintering wood and tearing the lid away.

Dozens of tiny black bodies tumbled from the box. The captain recoiled, as did anyone close to the ring, as the dank, fetid air of the sewer was released. More bodies followed, a second crate emptied as quickly as the assistants could manage.

As if driven by a hidden signal, the rats surged around the ring in one great mass. They flowed across the sawdust, hot, lithe bodies clambering over one another. They squealed as they moved, the sound unearthly. As one, they hit the far side of the ring, bodies thumping hard into its solid sides, claws scratching and gouging at the wood. They started to swarm up the side, clawing and climbing on one another in their desperation to escape. They got halfway up, then fell back, bodies tumbling and jumbling together.

In their midst stood the hollow-cheeked man and his dog.

The terrier smelled the damp odour of the rats. It writhed harder than ever, twisting and snapping, desperate to get to its hated enemy. It was all its owner could do to hold it, such was the force in its small body. Rats surged around his tall boots, so that he paddled amongst them, yet he paid them no heed, his attention fully focused on the deadly ball of fur in his grasp.

The crowd pressed forward yet again. There was a wall of sound now. It crashed over the ring, cheers and shouts intermixed, the cacophony of sound like nothing that had gone before.

'Let him loose!' Harlequin Billy roared, just as the frenzy around him reached fever pitch.

The hollow-cheeked man threw his dog downwards, then darted to the ring's side and clambered over.

As soon as it was released, the animal went wild, teeth snapping, body twisting as it started its longed-for orgy of killing. It tore into the rats. Blood flew, splatting across the fresh sawdust. Small black bodies were tossed this way and that, necks twisted and broken, limbs and flesh torn ragged by the dog's teeth.

Some of the rats fought back, the dog's white fur quickly dotted with specks of blood. One jumped up to sink its teeth into the soft flesh of the terrier's nose. It hung there for a moment like some ghastly decoration, before a toss of the animal's head threw it away.

Through it all, the dog went about its task with brutal precision, teeth and head working in perfect unison. It was a killing machine that left broken bodies in its wake just as a threshing machine threw out stalks of corn. It never slowed, never tired, the little animal bred for this moment.

The crowd cheered, bellowing the number of the dead. Still more wagers were shouted back and forth, money changing hands almost as quickly as bodies tumbled onto the sawdust.

'Time!' The fat timekeeper shouted the word.

The terrier's owner swung his leg over the ring wall and stepped amongst the carnage. He cared nothing for the small bodies that he crushed under his boots. His gauntleted hand reached for the dog, but the animal was lost in its lust for blood and its lips drew back in a snarl as it saw the hated leather glove coming for it.

The owner did not stand on ceremony. He pulled out the small oak cudgel, delivering a short, sharp blow to the animal's head, knocking it sideways. Dazed and stunned, the terrier was powerless to resist as it was once more grabbed by the scruff of the neck. For the second time that night, it was held aloft. Blood dripped from its muzzle like rain. The crowd roared its approval, yells and cheers filling the room with sound.

The captain watched the spectacle. Not once had he called out, the bestial emotions that were being released washing over him. Now, as the fight drew to its bloody conclusion, he was overwhelmed by the urge to get away. It surged through him like a rush of vomit spewing up from his stomach. Unstoppable, violent, sickening.

He started to move immediately. He would not wait for the count of rats killed by the dog, or for the settling of the wagers that had been placed on the bloody tally. Instead he pushed through the crowd, working his way to the stairs, desperate to be away from the stench of blood and from the men who revelled in its presence.

Chapter Four

———◆·◆·◆———

The captain waited for his guests in the shadows by the stairs. It was cold outside, yet the chilly air was refreshing after the fetid atmosphere inside. Even the touch of the particular was welcome, its clammy tendrils cool against overheated skin.

The gentlemen came down the stairs noisily, staggering into the cold night air. One reeled to the side as the chill breeze smacked him around the chops. He would have fallen had Cooper not been ready to catch him.

'I only damn well won!' Another of the toffs turned to his friends, cupped hands held out in front of his body. They were full of coins. 'What on earth will I do with all these damned things, Charles?' The coins represented a fortune to many of those who lived close to the Black Griffin, but were nothing but an amusing encumbrance to a man more used to paper money and the credit of his name.

'Damn your eyes, John!' laughed the third man. 'You might have made yourself a veritable fortune, but I lost ten whole shillings!'

'Good Lord, how will you stand it!' John guffawed, unable

to keep a straight face. 'Here, Bertie, take these.' He offered his treasure to the man who had nearly fallen. 'Give them to your good old grand-pater to invest! I certainly don't want the damned things in my pocket. They'll ruin the cut of my coat.' He and Charles laughed as only the drunk could laugh, overly loudly and without concern for how they appeared.

'Perhaps we can use them.' Charles peered at the pile of coins as if he had never seen such things before. 'I've heard you can buy a tuppenny whore around these parts. For the amount you have there, you should be able to get yourself a whole damn harem.'

The remark set the pair off again. It was all John could do not to fall as he doubled over, his body convulsing with laughter.

'Stow it.' The captain put an end to the farce. He stepped out of the shadows as he spoke, his voice not much louder than a whisper.

'Good Lord, there you are, Captain!' John's eyes widened theatrically. 'We quite wondered where you had got to. Was the sport not to your taste?'

'Now, now, gentlemen.' Cooper interceded before anything more could be said. 'Time we was moving along.' He stepped between his master and the man holding the coins. 'Here you are, sir. Let's be putting those lovelies in here, shall we?' He produced a small cloth sack from his pocket, holding it open in front of John's cupped hands. 'They'll be right as rain with me. I'll hold on to them for now, and give them back later on.'

'You can keep them for all I damn well care, old man.' John tumbled the coins into the small sack.

'No, no, no, I wouldn't hear of it, sir. You won these fair and square.' Cooper made a great play of carefully folding the neck of the sack closed before concealing it somewhere in the folds of his coat. The lie was delivered smoothly. The man would not be heading home with a single one of the coins. 'Now then, if you fine gentlemen are quite ready, we can be on our way to our next venue.' He grinned at the three men, then turned to his master.

The captain gave the briefest of nods to acknowledge the work. Then he turned on his heel and led his guests into the darkness.

The captain knew these streets as well as anyone. He had first learned their twists and turns as a child, his formative years spent living in a gin palace run by his mother. That palace had been burned to the ground, his mother dying in the blaze. He had been back there just the once since he had returned to London. The palace was long gone, its burned-out shell replaced by a new public house.

A lot of time had passed since that bitter day nearly nine years before, but the pain of the loss still burned just as brightly as it had when he had stood there on that fateful night and stared at the wreckage of his mother's life. His mother had never held him close, or smothered him with love. But she had taken care of him, sheltering him from the dangers that were so common in the dark streets of the East End. She had given him a home, and a chance at life, even when his father had abandoned them both. He had much to be grateful to her for, but that gratitude could never now be repaid. For she was gone. Like so many others, she was lost to him.

He had looked for the man who had taken his mother's life. It had been scant consolation to discover that man, a brute called Shaw, had been killed by another gang leader called

Finch who had taken his patch. Shaw had largely been forgotten in the streets he had once terrorised, just as the captain's hatred and desire for revenge had faded with time. These days the captain was a very different man to the one who had returned to his childhood home. But his knowledge of the streets lived on, even if the new factories, warehouses, roads and railway lines that had come to the East End had altered the appearance of some of them.

He set a brisk pace, taking his guests on the quickest route to their next place of entertainment. Speed was all now. The men were buoyed by beer and blood, but that could quickly fade. The captain knew from experience that fear, so quickly banished by the first of an evening's drinks, could return tenfold if the real world was allowed to take hold of a man's soul.

He sent Cooper on ahead to prepare for their arrival at the next establishment, then led the gentlemen down a series of alleyways, never giving them time to dawdle. It was only when he stepped off one of the main thoroughfares and into yet another darkened alley that he saw the three men in his path. They stood in the shadows, loitering with intent. Even in the gloom, there was no mistaking the shape of the cudgels they held. It was the weapon of choice in the streets of Whitechapel. In the right hands, it was deadlier than even the sharpest knife.

The captain stopped on a sixpence, halting those who followed him with a single raised hand.

'I say, what the devil—'

'Shut your muzzle.' He snapped the command, then stepped forward. He did not fear the footpads. He had faced worse. Much worse.

'I know you.' The words came out flat and level, his tone calm. He pulled back his long overcoat as he continued to advance towards the three men, moving it back over his hip just enough so that they could see his own cudgel. 'You're Finch's boys.'

'This here is Mr Finch's manor, and it's ten shillings to pass this way, Captain. That's ten shillings for each of you.'

The captain shook his head slowly. He knew enough of Finch to be wary. The man ran a protection racket that was about as subtle as a hammer to the noggin. Pay and be left in peace. Refuse to pay and face violence and retribution. The captain had refused to pay, and he was not about to start now.

He turned to look back at his customers. The three toffs stood transfixed, eyes wide so that the whites were bright in the darkness. In his head, a clock was ticking. If they lingered here, the effects of the ratting would be lost. He could not allow that to happen. He needed the gentlemen to be swept along on the crest of a wave of debauchery and sin, so that when they were finally dumped on the beach of reality the following morning, they would remember only the juiciest morsels. Finch's three foolish footpads were putting all that at risk.

'Gentlemen, I apologise for the delay.' He spoke quietly so that only the three could hear. Then he turned fast, right hand dropping to his cudgel and drawing it in a heartbeat.

'I said no.' He spoke the three words in the same even tone. And then he charged.

He hit the first footpad before the man could react, darting the cudgel forward, driving its end into his gut with a thud. The blow doubled the man over. As soon as his head came down, the captain swung the cudgel in a short arc, clipping it smartly against the crown of the footpad's head. He fell without a sound.

The captain did not linger. He spun to one side, body

moving fast. The second man lumbered forward, slashing with his own cudgel. The captain saw the blow coming and stepped aside, letting the club swing past. It was easy then. He chopped his own weapon down, cracking it smartly against his attacker's forearm. It was a sharp blow, delivered with force, and it broke the man's arm like a twig. The cudgel fell from his hand, clattering noisily onto the cobbles. Unarmed and defenceless, the man could do nothing as the captain stepped forward, weapon raised and ready to strike. Yet he held the blow back. He did not want to kill. Not if he could help it.

The man stepped back smartly, moving out of the cudgel's reach, hands clasped to his broken forearm. The third man still stood at his side, his body curled and taut as if about to fight. His face betrayed his confusion at the sudden climax to their attempted ambush.

'Tell Finch he is not to cross me again.' The captain delivered the words calmly and evenly. Not even the short fight had caused him to lose his breath.

The man with the broken arm looked at him, his face contorted with pain. 'I'll tell him all right. But he won't let this lie, so you'd better watch your bleeding back.'

'Is that meant to be a threat?' the captain scoffed. 'Now pick up your mate and fuck off.'

The two footpads did not linger. Together they hauled the man the captain had knocked over to his feet, then moved away as quickly as they could. Neither one looked back.

'Well, I say.' Bertie breathed the words into the silence that followed their departure.

The captain held his ground. The fight had awoken memories in his mind, images of the battles he had fought sneaking past his defences. For a fleeting moment, he stood again on the blood-soaked battlefield of Solferino, the bodies of the dead carpeting the grassy plain around him.

Voices shouted in the tenements nearby. At least one baby screamed, its rest broken by the sound of the scuffle.

'Did you see him?' Bertie whispered to his pals. 'I've never seen anyone that fast.' His tone was reverential.

The words penetrated the captain's mind. Forcing away the images that threatened to overwhelm him, he took a moment to hang the cudgel back on his belt. Control returned to his mind, barriers re-erected against the memories of all that he had been.

'Follow me.' He did not look back at the three men he had defended. He knew they would follow.

Chapter Five

———•◦•———

They reached their destination no more than two minutes after they left the alley. It waited for them at the end of a covered passage that ran down the side of a tenement block. The purpose of the passage might once have been to access the rear of the building, but that night it led to a different place. It led to Babylon.

The establishment was not much to look at. There was just a single lantern at the end of the alley. It was no beacon, just enough to light the way and nothing more. A narrow flight of stairs led down to a basement level, a second lantern hanging outside a simple wooden door. There was no sign to announce the building's purpose, no garish facade or ornate decoration to entice a passer-by to step inside. It was as far away from a gin palace as a drinking den could be, but it was the captain's place, and he felt a prickling of pride as he saw it emerge out of the gloom.

'Look alive there.' The captain noticed his guests starting to dawdle, so called on them to follow. He did not stop, taking the stairs quickly and nimbly.

The gentlemen's faces betrayed their hesitation and their

distaste at the lingering smell of mould and piss that permeated the air of the stairway. But still they did as they were told and followed him.

Two heavyset men waited for them in the shadows. Both stepped forward the moment the captain arrived, knuckling their foreheads in a gesture of respect before turning to the three toffs.

'Just a moment there, my lord.' One of the men stepped in front of the first guest. 'Arms up.' He reached forward, hands moving quickly to pat down the gentleman's pockets with a deft touch before repeating the process with the next. The second of the door's guardians simply stood by as the check was completed, his hands balled into fists and held ready should he be called into action. All three gentlemen were frisked in the span of a single minute. Task complete, the doormen stood back, a simple nod to the captain confirmation that none was carrying anything they shouldn't.

The captain stood at the door with his hand on the latch. He looked at each of the three men in turn, making sure he had their full attention.

'Welcome to Babylon,' he said, then he turned and pushed it open.

A great wave of light and sound rushed out the moment the door was opened. It flooded the small space at the bottom of the stairs, filling it with life. The contrast with the mouldy air and the darkness was complete.

The captain did not linger. He stepped inside, his face already starting to flush as the heat of the room touched his chilled skin. The familiar aroma hit him immediately. It was smoky and warm; beer and spirits mixed with a touch of perfume and sweat. It was the smell of his place, the smell of home.

'Welcome, gentlemen, welcome.' He turned to sweep his arm in an exaggerated gesture of greeting. All three toffs grinned as they followed him inside the establishment they had all heard so much about.

They entered a small vestibule lined with heavy dark blue curtains to keep out the cold. It was brightly lit, both side walls bearing heavy gas burners that were going at full tilt. The floor was covered with simple red quarry tiles and the walls were painted dark blue to match the curtains.

They were given no time to linger. As if they had been waiting for the three men to arrive, two young women stepped through the curtains. Both were dressed tastefully in pretty scarlet dresses with collars buttoned high under their chins and full skirts that skimmed the tiled floor. They were beautiful, their cheeks artfully painted with subtle colour and hair bound tightly behind their heads, where it was held in place by a number of small silver clips that flashed as they caught the light.

'I say.' Bertie could not hold back the exclamation as one of the women pulled his coat off his shoulders. 'Steady on.' He played up to the moment, widening his eyes as if something inappropriate had just occurred.

'Hold fast there, old man.' John tittered at the display. 'Don't fire your first broadside too damned early.'

The two women paid the ribald remark no heed. They busied themselves around the gentlemen, flashing smiles as they removed coats and hats that were then whisked away.

'This way, gentlemen, this way.' The captain waved his guests forward, diverting their attention from the women. He pulled back the curtain opposite the door, ushering the men through another doorway that led into the Babylon's main salon.

They were not the only men present. At least two dozen others were scattered across the room, some standing in small groups, others sitting at one of three long tables lined with benches. A few more lounged in heavy wingback armchairs in leather the colour of walnut, which were arranged in two tight circles to one side. The room was large enough to house a good fifty people in comfort, and there was plenty of space left for the newcomers.

The Babylon's decor was simple and unfussy. There were no pictures on the dark mulberry walls. Heavy mahogany panelling ran around the lower half, the dark wood lightened by brass gas lamps. The floor was bare, the wooden floorboards left untreated, but there was not a scrap of dirt to be seen.

The room's main attraction was the bar that was arranged along one wall. It was not large, perhaps no more than ten feet from end to end. It was made from a single great slab of mahogany, the surface polished so that it gleamed, and was tended by two young men. Both were dressed in crisp white shirts with wide, loose cuffs left unbuttoned, and gaudy scarlet waistcoats. They looked uncannily alike; both sported a neatly cropped beard and moustache paired with short-cropped hair.

In one corner of the large salon, an old man played a fiddle, his fingers dancing across the instrument's strings as he filled the room with an up-tempo jig. Jimmy the Fiddle was ancient, his face so lined and craggy that it was hard to even discern his features. Yet he played well, and he played fast, the notes coming clearly and quickly, the jaunty music filling the room with life. In the opposite corner was a single long red curtain that hung from ceiling to floor, its weight supported on a thick brass rod. A man guarded whatever was hidden behind it, his jowly, heavyset face betraying a complete lack of emotion as he stood like a living statue, the only indication that he was alive the slightest movement of his turnip-shaped head as he surveyed the crowd.

'Whisky!' The captain made the pronouncement as he led his three guests to the bar. Both of the men working there reached below the counter at the same time, one producing a bottle, the other four short glasses. The captain nodded in approval, then stood back so that his three charges could take their place at the bar.

'It's nothing like I expected.' Bertie looked perplexed as he made a play of looking around the room.

'What *did* you expect?' The captain's face was impassive as he stood watching the two barkeeps at work. The whiskies were poured swiftly, each measure judged to perfection so that the liquid sat just below the rim of the glass.

'I'm not really sure.'

'Yes, you are.' The captain reached for one of the glasses. 'You expected it to be full of scantily clad women just waiting for you to arrive.'

'Well . . .' Bertie coloured as the captain saw straight through him. 'That *is* what is said. This is all rather . . .'

'Respectable?' The captain finished the man's sentence.

'Yes, that's it.' Bertie grinned, then picked up one of the glasses, moving it carefully towards his nose so that he could smell the liquid inside.

The captain looked around the room. It was his place, the space just as he wanted it. It was classy, or at least he believed it to be so. He had seen a lot of the world, and had lived in all manner of places, from the simplest farmstead to a maharajah's palace. He had cared little for any of them, but now, here, he had found a place of his own. He answered to no man, or woman, and he should never have been happier.

'To Babylon.' He lifted his glass as he proposed the toast to his three guests. 'May you all find what you desire.'

'Hear, hear!' The men greeted his words with a cheer.

The captain drank first, tossing the liquid down his throat in a single gulp. The others followed his lead.

'Goodness!' Bertie gasped and spluttered as the whisky hit the back of his throat, much to the delight of his two friends, who whooped and hollered at his reaction.

The captain gestured for the glasses to be refilled. He did not smile.

'It's behind the curtain, isn't it?' John leaned forward. 'What we came for.' He whispered the words in a conspiratorial tone.

'Perhaps.' The captain would not be drawn. He reached to the bar and took up the freshly refilled glasses, handing them round. 'Drink.' He gave the command, then tossed a second measure of whisky down his throat.

His guests did the same. This time Bertie managed not to splutter. Glasses were returned to the bar. A sharp gesture from the captain made it clear that only three were to be refilled.

'So, *is* it behind the curtain?' Bertie sounded like a small boy confronted with a parent who would not reveal a secret, no matter how hard he begged.

'You want to find out?'

'Of course we bloody well do.' It was Charles who gave the tetchy answer. He knocked back his whisky, then plonked his glass on the bar.

'Well then.' The captain finally smiled, yet none of it reached his eyes. 'I'd better show you.'

He led the three toffs across the room. The doorkeeper's expression was unaltered as they approached. But he did nod to the captain before he stood back, a thick right arm reaching out to pull back the curtain. It revealed a simple dark wooden door with a round brass handle.

'Are you ready?' The captain looked at each of his three guests in turn.

'Yes!' the three answered as one. Their whisky-fuelled excitement was palpable. They had all heard the tales. It was time to discover what they had come for.

The captain pushed the door, which opened easily on silent hinges. It revealed the heart of his enterprise and the reason why these rich young fools had paid handsomely to come so far from the safety and security of their homes.

For inside was Babylon itself.

Chapter Six

———◆◦◆———

The captain sat in one of the wingback armchairs and closed his eyes, savouring a moment's peace. A pale ale in a cut-crystal glass waited on the table in front of him. He had never acquired a taste for whisky. He would drink it when he felt he had to, and he knew of no other tipple that could get a man drunk as quickly, which was why he made sure his guests were filled with the stuff as soon as they arrived. But he himself preferred good, simple beer.

'You taking it easy there?'

He opened one eye. A tall woman with red hair looked down at him. Like the pair who had greeted his guests when they arrived, she was dressed respectably, in a dark green dress, the crinoline skirt cut in the latest fashion so that the bulk was behind rather than to the sides. The high collar of the bodice she had left unbuttoned to reveal the delicate flesh at the base of her throat, a daring decision that would have created a scandal in the drawing rooms of the elite, but which here in the Babylon was somehow quite fitting. Her hair was untamed by clips so that it cascaded over one shoulder, the thick, vibrant tresses curling together. He had smelled her arrival before she had spoken, the French perfume she wore both delicate and fresh.

'It's been a long night, Bella,' he answered, sitting up straighter in his chair and reaching for his beer. 'I'm knackered.'

'Well, it's far from over.' She perched on the edge of another chair nearby, her hands placed neatly on her knees.

The captain nodded in agreement and sipped at his beer. 'Are they having a good time?' he asked.

'What do you think?' The answer was sharp.

'And your girls are looking after them?'

'Of course they are.' She bristled a little at the question. 'My girls know what to do. Just make sure those ruffians you employ do their job right.'

'They will.' The captain drank more of his beer. The warm liquid slid down his throat like nectar.

'Are you going to check everything is set?'

'When I'm ready.'

'Well, don't leave it too late, not like last time.'

'I won't.' He drained his glass, then set it back on the table. He would have sat back for a moment's more rest, but Bella was watching him like a dog waiting for a walk.

'I know you, Jack Lark, and I know what you're like. You're lazy.'

Jack sighed. He was not to be allowed to rest. He did not mind that Bella had used his real name. 'The captain' was for the benefit of his punters and his growing reputation. She knew his given name, as did all those who worked for him. But she did not know his story. None of them did.

He had met her three years previously, when she had been leading punters to the whores working on Hanbury Street in

Spitalfields, and he had been guiding his first guest through the hidden streets of the East End. They had come a long way in the years that had followed. His business had grown. He had started out as a one-man enterprise that catered to a single guest on a night of slumming. Now he owned and ran the Babylon, employing a dozen staff and entertaining the best part of fifty guests a month, along with a regular clientele of men he trusted enough not to mess up his more lucrative evenings. Bella had stayed with him, and now ran a dozen whores. Their two businesses were intertwined and growing, making them both richer by the day.

'That's why I like to have you around, love,' he mocked. 'You keep everyone in line.'

Bella shook her head in mock-exasperation that did nothing to hide the glint that crept into her pale green eyes. 'Get on now, Jack. My girls will be tired by now. It's time to start the fireworks.'

Jack knuckled his forehead. 'Yes, ma'am.' He pushed himself to his feet, grimacing as he moved. He had sat still for too long, and now his back made its protest at such inaction known by sending a shooting pain from the bottom of his neck all the way to the tops of his legs. 'Jesus fucking Christ.' He hissed the words as the pain caught hold. It was getting worse by the year, and he knew few ways of easing it.

'Is it bad today?' Bella had risen with him, and now she reached out to place a hand on his arm, her face betraying her concern.

'It's all right, love. It'll pass.'

'I'll have one of the girls rub you down later.'

Jack grimaced. 'I'm not a bloody horse.'

'No, you're a man. That means you're twice the trouble and

half the use.' The answer came back with a wink.

Jack shook his head at her sharp tongue. But he would take her up on the offer. Bella would let one of her girls rub his back, but she herself would come to his room. She always had, right from the start. It was not love, for either of them. It was something else, something almost the same, yet they maintained a distance from one another. They would sleep together and they would have sex, but they would never be truly intimate. Their minds they kept apart and separate. They both knew what it was. And what it wasn't.

'Jack.' Bella nodded towards the entrance vestibule. Two men were standing by the curtains that screened the small room. They had removed their hats, which were clasped to their bellies. One of the Babylon's two door guards was with them, his face creased with worry.

'I see 'em.' Jack recognised the men. 'I'll deal with them.'

He left Bella and went over to the two men, who were surveying the room as they waited, eyes taking in every detail.

'They wanted to see you, guv.' Jack's doorkeeper made the introduction. 'They say they work for—'

'It's all right, I know who they are.' Jack cut him off. 'Go back outside.' He dismissed the man, then focused his attention on the two newcomers, who had both stiffened and stood a little straighter as he approached.

'I've told you before that I don't want you here.' He looked at them coldly. 'So either your Mr Finch is bloody forgetful or he's plain bottle-head stupid.'

Neither man's face betrayed any emotion at the greeting. 'You should show Mr Finch respect.' The words were uttered in a flat tone devoid of all emotion.

'I'll show respect when your governor comes here himself

rather than sending a pair of bloody monkeys like you in his place,' Jack replied mockingly.

'Take care there.' The man who spoke was not young. What little hair he had left was completely grey. He had let it grow long on one side of his head so that he could fold it over his balding dome, but it was thin and raggedy-looking. Removing his hat had caused the flap of hair to twist, so that much of his scalp was left on display. His face showed the ravages of the years, his skin decorated with the cracks and fissures of a hard life. His nose was misshapen and lumpy from where it had likely been broken a dozen times. Half of one ear was missing, and a scar ran across the left-hand side of his mouth, twisting it out of shape. To Jack's eye he looked like a bull mastiff that had been in one too many fights, but that like all such dogs wanted to fight once more.

'This is my place and I'll do whatever I bloody well please.' Jack held the man's gaze. 'So, are we done here?'

'No.' The man swept a hand over his head, smoothing his hair across his scalp. 'Mr Finch has a message for you.'

'Then tell me and be quick about it.' Jack was tiring of the conversation.

Finch had been trying to get his claws into Jack's enterprise for some time now. Whether it be footpads like the ones he had encountered that evening, or men sent to the Babylon, Jack had ignored them all. Extortion and robbery were Finch's main occupations, along with anything else that offered an opportunity to make some ready cash. Jack had heard that the man was trying to turn to more respectable trades, a clear sign that he was making far too much money and needed a front for his illicit activities. There had even been a rumour that he had rented a warehouse near the docks and had started to run a legitimate business importing tea and other goods from the colonies in the East. Yet the presence of the two men at the Babylon tonight confirmed that he still intended to maintain his hold over the streets where he had started his fortune.

'Mr Finch is a very fair man. He don't take kindly to you knocking 'is blokes about, but he's still going to make you a fair offer.'

Jack made sure his expression revealed nothing. He held the man's gaze, his eyes never once moving away. 'Let me guess. Mr Finch is going to offer me protection. Is that right?'

The man smiled, or at least the unscarred side of his mouth moved upward at the corner. 'You're a sharp man, Mr Lark.'

'You know my name?' Jack was not surprised.

'We know all about you, old son.'

'Then you'll know that I don't pay for protection I don't need.'

'Oh, I think you'll want to pay us. You see, Mr Finch can be very persuasive.'

'I'm sure he can.' Jack searched the older man's gaze for a shred of something other than mute obedience. He found nothing. 'Who are you?' He wanted to know more about the man he was soon to make his enemy.

'You don't need my name, old son.'

'I like to know who I'm talking to.'

'All right then. Swan. My name is Swan.'

'Well then, Mr Swan, I'm going to give you the same answer I've given every other fat-headed prick who has come here looking for an easy shilling.' He saw a flicker of anger as the man absorbed the insult. 'You can tell your Mr Finch that I'm not paying him a single bloody penny. If he wants to come here

to discuss that, then he's welcome. Until then, you can walk
your chalk and leave me the fuck alone.'

'I don't think Mr Finch will like that; he won't like that
at all.'

'I don't give a fig what he likes.' Jack stepped closer so that
his face was just an inch away from Swan's own. 'I'm not paying.' He spoke the words slowly, just to make sure they were
understood. 'You look like a clever man, Mr Swan. I reckon
you've seen something of this world, but I promise you that
you've never met a man like me. So hear what I say and tell it
to Finch.'

Swan glowered, his lips quivering. Then he nodded. 'I'll let
Mr Finch know. But . . .' he paused and winced, as if in sudden
pain, 'I reckon that's not the end of it. Not by a long ways.'

'Just give your master the message, Swan.' Jack held his
position, his eyes riveted on the other man.

Swan laughed dismissively, as if he found the warning
pathetic. The sound died as Jack continued to stare at him, his
gaze level, his face expressionless. It left an awkward, uneasy
silence. Finch's henchman was used to making threats, and he
clearly had no idea how to deal with receiving one.

Swan said no more. He nodded to his partner and they left
quickly and quietly, leaving Jack looking thoughtfully after
them.

'Trouble?' Bella had come close enough to hear the short
conversation.

'Maybe.' Jack was not foolish enough to believe for even
one second that his refusal would be heeded. There would be
consequences for saying no. Finch would come for him, or
he would come for the Babylon. Whichever it was, Jack would
be ready. There would be a fight, but he had been in so many,

he did not fear another, especially not one that would take place on his own turf.

'Well, I reckon your guests have had their share of fun for one night,' Bella announced. 'Why don't we finish this off now, then we can talk.'

Jack nodded without looking at her. It was good advice and he would heed it. The night had gone on long enough. It was time for its finale.

Chapter Seven

———◆•◆•◆———

J ack did not linger at the threshold to the Babylon's back
room. His man held the door open as he approached, a
simple nod the only greeting given.

The room was brightly but softly lit. Gas lamps burned
merrily on every wall, but most of the illumination came from
a great chandelier that was still lit the old-fashioned way, a
hundred candles giving a purity to the light that was enhanced
by the whitewash on the walls. The furniture was more deca-
dent than in the main room. Chaises longues were dotted
carefully around, the seat fabric of the palest cream, the legs
and frames decorated with gilt. There were four marble-topped
tables, all with gilded pedestals and frames. Arranged around
these were chairs in the French style, the seats and backs made
from the same cream fabric as the chaises, the legs and arms
gleaming with more gilt.

It was a stylishly and expensively decorated space, but it
would be a rare man indeed who walked in and had his eye
drawn by the decor. It was the people that took the attention
here. A few men were present, the clientele similar to that
found out in the main room, though no more than half a dozen

were allowed entry at any one time. They offered the one splash of colour, their dark clothes making them stand out against the palette of pale whites, creams and golds. They looked wholly out of place, their large, clumsy bodies and heavy boots standing in stark contrast to the ethereal ambience of the room.

Then there were the women.

What little clothing they wore was white in colour. Their underclothes were covered in delicate lace woven into intricate patterns and enhanced by golden thread that ran sparingly through the design. Most wore simple white slippers, and many sported silken shawls, also in white, that billowed back from their shoulders as they floated around the room.

To a guest arriving for the first time, it would be as if they had slipped into another realm. But that would be to misunderstand the space that Bella had created. For this was a place firmly rooted in the earthliest of pursuits. It was a room that sold sex. And it did so at a high price.

Jack stepped into the room. It reminded him of another time, its passing similarity to the simple chambers of a maharajah never failing to make him feel out of place, just as he had all those years before when he had fled from the British cantonment at Bhundapur to take refuge in the fortress of a man who would soon rebel against the ruling British and force him to pick a side as diplomacy gave way to violence. He was not in his world. Bella's Babylon was too clean, too contrived and far too splendid for him ever to feel comfortable here. He had found his niche in the shadowy corners and dark places where few chose to go, and where only men like him could thrive.

'Good evening, Captain.' A girl sashayed past carrying a bottle of French champagne and two crystal flutes. She was heading towards the chaise longue where one of Jack's guests reclined, a daft smile plastered across his face as he gazed at the beautiful vision heading towards him.

Jack ran his eyes around the room. He knew all the men here. Many men wanted to return to the Babylon. A rare few were given permission, only those with the deepest pocketbooks and the best behaviour allowed repeat visits to the back room. The rest were turned away, no matter how much they offered to pay. For Jack and Bella, reputation was all. The Babylon was a place for men to escape the harsh reality of the real world. A place where they could enter a realm of decadence laced with debauchery; a domain of beautiful women, drink and sex. No one would be allowed to spoil that illusion.

As he surveyed the room, one of the side doors opened, and Bertie staggered out through the white netting that framed it, his hand held out behind him. A willowy brunette, her hair rumpled and disordered, emerged a moment later. Bertie led her a few steps forward before turning to pull her towards him. She looked over his shoulder as he clasped her to him, her eyes fastening on Jack. She smiled, then made a face of mock exasperation.

Jack did not return the smile. He kept his distance from Bella's girls. Many of them tried to gain his favour, and it was not always easy to say no to their less than subtle advances. But he did his best, remaining resolute despite the temptation.

Whores did not offend him. They had always been a part of his life. The trade was as old as time itself, and he did not imagine it would ever end, no matter how far the world advanced. But he made sure the girls were treated fairly, and he knew Bella was inundated with requests to join her entourage. He did not get involved in any of it. They were her girls, not his, and he did not earn a penny from any of them. He knew that Bella treated them better than any other madam, and she made sure they kept a fair share of their hard-earned rhino.

'My goodness me, Captain.' Bertie had released his partner and now stumbled his way closer to Jack, a fresh glass of champagne in his hand. 'My goodness me.' He staggered to a halt grinning from ear to ear.

Jack grunted as he saw that his guest was a dozen sheets to the wind and then some. 'I'm glad you are enjoying yourself.'

'Enjoying myself!' Bertie spluttered. 'I am not just enjoying myself! Indeed I am not! I am in heaven, sir. In heaven! And I do believe I have found an angel fallen straight from God's own lap.' He turned to stare longingly at the girl he had recently released, who now sat at a nearby table, a small mirror in hand as she checked over her face and its layer of paint.

Jack barely noticed the younger man's enthusiasm. He kept looking around the room. He had two of his three guests placed. He just needed to know where the third was.

'I have never, ever been to such a place,' Bertie continued, only pausing to guzzle champagne.

At last Jack spied the third of his guests. Charles had been lying on the floor on the far side of the room. Now he got unsteadily to his feet before staggering to the corner, where there was a screen that hid a large chamber pot. Jack did not know if he was desperate to piss or to puke, but whichever it was, it was urgent.

Guests located, he turned back to face the door that led to the main room. Cooper was loitering there, leaning against the wall, hands thrust deep into his pockets as his eyes lingered on one of Bella's girls. Judging by the activity in his trousers, poorly masked by their fabric, it was clear his mind was else-where. But it was not busy enough to completely distract him from his master, and he stopped his fiddling as soon as Jack's eyes turned upon him.

Before Jack could summon Cooper to his side, the crash of a falling table came from the Babylon's main salon. The sound of a dozen glasses smashing as one was loud enough to be heard over the jaunty notes of the fiddle that still filled the room with music.

Another crash followed as a second table went over. The first bellows of sudden rage came hard on its heels.

'What the hell is happening out there?' Jack yelled at Cooper.

'The bloody dockers are having a barney!' Cooper gave the dramatic news, his expression revealing his shock.

Yelps of fear, and of sudden and unexpected pain being inflicted, half drowned out Cooper's voice, along with the roars of men starting to fight. Out of nowhere, violence had erupted in the Babylon.

Jack held his position. The girls were all on their feet, their first shrieks of fear ringing out as they hastily rearranged their clothes. Their punters stood with them, and Jack made sure to note the position of all three of his guests.

'You!' He pointed at John, the gentleman closest to him. 'Look alive! Collect your things. I'm getting you out of here.'

'What the devil is going on?' John stumbled towards him, words slurred.

'It's a bloody brawl,' Jack snapped. 'Let's get you gone.'

The sound of the commotion in the main room intensified, the first thump of bodies tumbling to the floor coming through clearly. Jimmy the Fiddle played on, the tempo of his music increasing to match the furore that had erupted around him.

'Who is fighting who?' John was slow to comprehend, the

combination of whisky, champagne and sex addling his wits.

'I've haven't the foggiest,' Jack snapped. 'Quickly now, all of you, unless you want to be on the wrong end of a good thumping before you go!'

John's two friends were lumbering towards them. Jack gestured to them to hurry. Speed was all now. He needed to keep them moving, and moving fast.

'Right, come with me!' He gave the command, then turned to plunge into the bedlam that filled the main room. The three gentlemen followed, pressing close to their host as they ploughed through the confusion.

Men fought all around them. Punches were thrown this way and that whilst other men wrestled, their bodies stumbling and tumbling and filling the room with violent motion. A young lad reeled past, his face a mask of blood from where his nose had been smashed. Bertie took one look and shrieked, recoiling from the boy, who fell away, crumpling to the floor at their feet.

Jack exhorted them to hurry. A tall fellow in a dark green suit blocked his way, so he ducked a shoulder and thumped into the man's back, barging him out of their path.

They moved as quickly as they could, the four huddled together. Jack did his best to skirt the worst of the fighting, but the brawl swirled around them and he could not spare them completely.

A man sporting a flash claret and gold waistcoat grabbed at Bertie as the group hurried past. He shouted in triumph, then pulled hard, tugging Bertie almost from his feet.

'Hold fast!' Jack shouted, then turned to confront the man. With Bertie doing his best to break free, his attacker could not defend himself. Jack saw the opening and thumped his fist into the side of the man's head, knocking him sideways. Still it was not enough to break the man's hold.

'Hit the bastard!' Jack barked at his guest.

Bertie twisted in the man's arms. From somewhere he found the space to extract a fist, and lashed out as he had been commanded. It was not a strong blow, a slap more than a punch, but his hand connected with his assailant's face, the sound clearly audible.

The man fell as if his legs had been cut away from under him. Bertie went down with him, a sudden squawk of fear escaping his lips before he landed on top of the man.

Jack gave him no time to dwell. 'Get to the door!' he bellowed at the other two toffs, who were gaping in surprise and delighted horror at the sight of their friend knocking a man down, then he grabbed at Bertie, hauling him back to his feet. 'Go! Go! Go!'

The group moved on, stepping over the body of a man who lay comatose on the ground. Around them men were lashing out at anyone they could find, their shouts, grunts and groans filling the room with noise. Through it all, the fiddler kept up the fast tempo, the music raucous and loud.

When they reached the curtains that screened the main entrance, the three gentlemen paused for a moment, looking back at the scrummage that had engulfed the room.

'Get out!' Jack shouted. His hands moving from shoulder to shoulder, he ushered his guests through the curtains and on through the door beyond that was being held open for them by the two doormen.

The cold hit them as they burst outside, and they came to a breathless halt, all three sucking down lungful after lungful of the chilled air.

'My goodness me.' Bertie spoke first, the air condensing to form a cloud around his face.

'Bloody hell, old man.' John was bent double. 'You knocked that fellow onto his backside.' A mixture of awe and surprise underscored his breathless comment.

'I did!' Bertie hooted with unrestrained glee as he realised what he had done. 'I knocked him down!'

Jack took control of the situation. His voice was the only one that was not slurred by drink. 'Now come on, let's get you away before trouble comes out to find us.'

Three anxious faces turned his way. None of them had considered the fact that the brawl might escape the confines of the basement rooms.

Jack pushed past them, then took the steps two at a time.

'What about our coats?' It was Charles who called after him. They were the first words he had managed to string together since he had left the back room. He had paused at the foot of the steps and now peered up at Jack.

Jack turned to look down at his charges. 'You want to go and get them, then be my guest.' He gave no sign of being prepared to come back down the steps.

'Let's just get out of here, old man. We can replace a damn coat. We can't replace our faces.' John gave the advice as he pushed past his friend to start ascending the steps, which he did at a much slower pace than Jack had done. The sage advice was enough to make the other two follow his lead.

Jack smiled. The fight had served its purpose, rounding off the evening in memorable style. It had also put an end to the night's entertainment. He had learned that his guests needed a spectacular climax just as much as they needed the fearful opening. It was all part of the experience.

'Come on, look alive, you three,' he exhorted his guests as they came up the stairs. All were breathing heavily, as if they had just climbed a mountain rather than a mere dozen steps.

'Thank you, Captain.' Bertie came to stand in front of Jack, a strange drunken grin plastered across his features. 'I shall not forget this night. Not ever.'

'I'm glad to hear it.' Jack did his best to smile at the inebriated soul wobbling from one foot to the other in front of him. 'Just be sure to tell your friends. Now come on. It's only a short walk to the omnibus. Let's get you on your way home.'

He said nothing more as he led his guests back into the alleyway for the short stroll to Aldgate. The cold tendrils of the particular wrapped themselves around him, and he savoured their cool touch. It had been a good night. One that was even better now that it was almost over.

Chapter Eight

Jack returned to the Babylon and was pleased with what he found. He had not been gone for much more than ten minutes, but already the broken glass had been swept up, the tables and chairs that had been overturned in the ruckus had been returned to their normal positions and the floor had been scrubbed clean. The girls from the back room, along with the two ladies who had greeted Jack's guests as they arrived, were mingling with the remaining punters. It made for a sociable scene. Jimmy the Fiddle had not moved from his corner perch. He continued to play, the tunes he now selected more sedate than the wild screeching cacophony that had accompanied the earlier free-for-all.

'I want a bloody word with you, Jack my lad.' A man harangued him the moment he stepped through the curtain.

Jack recognised him immediately. It was the fellow wearing the flashy claret and gold waistcoat. He was a regular, one of the few invited to return to the Babylon as often as they wished. Such clients, rare as they were, were expected to join in the staged altercations when they occurred. 'What's wrong, Tom?'

'Did you have to bleeding whack me so hard?' The man

gave an exaggerated wince and held his hand to the side of his head.

'I'm sorry, but you know it has to look realistic. Here, have a drink or two on me.'

Jack grinned at the expression on his customer's face. Tom Brown ran a gang of dockers. It was a good job, one that paid him enough to enjoy the Babylon's delights once a week, and Jack knew him well. He was a sound man, one who looked after his lads, even helping them when they were sick or fell on hard times, unlike many of the other dockers' masters, who would make the devil himself wince at their stinginess.

'I won't say no to that.'

Jack gave the lads behind the bar the instruction before leaving the docker with a firm squeeze to the shoulder. He ran his gaze around the room, looking for anything left out of place. He saw nothing. The men and women who worked in the Babylon knew he had a keen eye, and they did not shirk from getting things back just so.

He spotted Bella sitting in one of the wingback armchairs, so went to join her. On the way, he nodded to one of his younger employees, a lad they all called Sunny because he was always smiling, no matter what he was doing. Sunny was sitting at one of the tables in front of a bowl of water. With the help of one of Bella's girls, he was wiping blood from his face and neck. It was not his own, but was bought from Smithfield by the barrel and carefully stored in little glass vials that were smashed during the staged brawl. It added a realistic flourish to the dramatic fight, and it was always Sunny who had the task of smothering the stuff across his skin, then making sure that the night's guests got a good eyeful of the gory sight before they left.

'How are we looking?' Jack asked as he took a seat. Bella was tallying the night's takings, a healthy heap of coins and banknotes on the small table in front of her.

'Not bad.' She made an entry in the red leather ledger. Everything was recorded there. It was not the first such ledger. The previous ones were stored away in the rooms above the Babylon where Jack and Bella lived, a record of the successful growth of their enterprise. Bella's girls lived in the garret rooms on the top floor, whilst the rest of the Babylon's employees found their own lodgings in the streets nearby.

'Not bad?' Jack lifted an eyebrow as he looked at the money on the table. 'Looks better than that to me.'

Bella glanced at him and shook her head, then returned to her tally. 'It's been a good week.' She spoke softly, her concentration on the numbers she was writing into the ledger.

Jack had the sense not to say more. From what he could see, there was a good amount to be shared out between them; enough for him to make another deposit into one of his accounts, even after all the Babylon's employees had been paid.

'Esmeralda didn't show up again.' Bella carefully closed the ledger, then slipped the pencil into her hair.

'Any of the others tell you why?'

'No.'

'She got a man of her own?'

'Maybe.' Bella reached for a glass of red wine that was on the table, then sat back in her chair. 'Though I reckon one of the others would've dobbed her in if that was the case.'

'You going to give her another chance?'

'She's had plenty.'

'But she's a looker.' Jack sat back too, making sure he was comfortable.

'You think that gives her the right to mess me around?' Bella snorted, then drank from her glass.

'I thought that was important.'

'Doing what you're told is important. Men will tup anything that flashes its tits at them.'

'Are you saying our clientele aren't discerning?'

Bella was spared having to reply by the arrival of one of the two barkeeps with a glass of beer for his master. He placed it on the table without a word.

'You want me to talk to her?' Jack reached for his beer. The action of bending forward sent a sharp pain rushing down into the pit of his spine, and he could not help grunting with the sudden pain.

'No. Then she definitely won't come back.'

'I'm that terrifying?'

'To them, yes. It's your scar. It makes you look like something from a nightmare.'

Jack's fingers lifted to trace the raised flesh that ran down the left-hand side of his face. 'I sometimes forget I have it.' He spoke quietly, as much to himself as to Bella.

'That's because you've got so many of them. You're fair covered.'

He smiled. It was true. His body carried the story of his life, his scars a map of his history. Bella's body was flawless, her pale skin decorated only with a few freckles. Her scars were hidden away.

Jack sat back with his beer. Neither said anything further as Bella finished her tally, then bundled the paper money into a small hessian sack.

'I'm going up.' She rose to her feet. She looked tired, the skin under her eyes greyed and puffy.

'I'll finish this and follow you.' Jack watched as she crossed the room towards the door that led upstairs.

When she was gone, he lifted his beer and drank it slowly, taking his time. He closed his eyes, savouring the simple pleasure of beer and comfort. His mind did not dwell on the evening. It was unremarkable, save for the appearance of Finch's goons. Yet even that was an issue for another day. He had long learned to live in the present. Fate would dictate his future, just as it had from the moment it had presented him with his first opportunity to take on a life that was not his own. He was a lot different to the young man who had stolen a British army officer's scarlet uniform over ten years ago, and there were times when he could scarcely credit the path that had led to this moment of quiet comfort and warmth, no more than a quarter-mile from the place where he had been born and raised. The journey that had brought him here had covered thousands of miles, from the battlefields of India and Persia to the war-torn United States. He had loved and he had lost. He had saved lives and he had killed more men than he could recall. The price he had paid to become this man sitting with his beer had been high.

He drained the last of his drink, then carefully placed the glass back on the table. He took his time getting to his feet, moving gingerly so as not to jar his aching back. There was no need for him to linger. Others would lock up and close the bar down.

No one stopped him as he walked to the back room. The last punters would soon be on their way, then the Babylon would fall silent until the next evening. One of Bella's girls smiled at him as he passed her by. Annabel had only been with them a few weeks, yet she already knew not to bother him. He did not return the smile, so as not to encourage her. She was beautiful in an ethereal way, her blonde hair and pale, delicate features setting her apart from the rest of Bella's girls. She was tall, her arms and legs long and slender. He knew some men would pay well for a night with those long limbs wrapped around them, yet he also knew it would never be him. She was a pretty girl, for sure, but she was still just a girl.

He reached the door in the corner. It had been left ajar, and he went through and up the stairs it hid from view. At the top of the first flight was a long landing. Another flight of stairs led directly up to the rooms on the floor above, whilst a series of doors waited at the landing's far end. It was towards these doors that he headed, treading as lightly as he could so as not to disturb Bella should she be asleep already.

The landing was lit by a single gas lamp placed on a table halfway along one wall. The decoration here was much simpler than in the downstairs rooms, the floorboards painted grey whilst the walls were panelled in a dark mahogany.

He approached the door on the left, the one that led to his own room. He paused at the threshold as he saw the warm glow from within that escaped beneath the door. Bella was not asleep. Not yet.

He opened the door slowly. The room was simply furnished, the space dominated by a large wrought-iron bed that sat in the very centre of the floor. On top of the mattress was a pretty embroidered counterpane, the type a girl would make with painstaking care over many years, then save for her marriage bed. But fate had had other plans for this counterpane, just as it had other plans for girls like Bella.

'You didn't stay down there long.' Bella spoke as she saw him in the doorway. She was standing to one side of the bed, carefully folding her dress.

'I'm tired.' Jack gave the honest answer. He made no move to come further into the room. He had eyes only for the beautiful woman who waited for him.

'You want me to go?' Bella's hands paused, the dress held still.

'No.'

She said nothing more. There was no need to. She finished folding her dress, then placed it carefully on a steamer trunk near the bed, beside the hoops of her skirt, which she had already removed. Then she turned to face him, reaching behind her back to untie her pale blue silk corset. She kept looking at him as she removed the corset and then the rest of her underclothes. Only when she was naked did she look away, sliding onto the bed and under the covers.

Jack had watched her the whole time. Bella was no skinny girl, and he reckoned she was as beautiful as any of the women who had crossed into his life. Not that he would tell her that. She did not need the whisperings of a lover. She was from the hard streets of London, where a kind word was as rare as gold in horseshit.

He strode into the room, closing and locking the door behind him. He undressed quickly, his clothes tossed carelessly into a pile. There was no shame as he removed his clothing. She had seen him before; the scars and the welts and the burn marks. He had nothing to hide from her. At least not on his body. His secrets he kept to himself. Those he shared with no one.

Chapter Nine

———◆—◆—◆———

The dining room at Bentham's had been recently refurbished, and was still fashionable enough to be filled to capacity even at luncheon. It occupied the entire second floor of the elegant Georgian building a stone's throw from St James's Park. It was brightly lit, filled with a dozen chandeliers paired with matching wall lights. The decor was as elegant and sophisticated as the clientele, the fixtures and fittings covered with enough gold to make a maharajah wince at such a vulgar display of opulence. The tables were a vista of white cloths, porcelain plates, crystal glasses and silver cutlery. There was a constant hum as the diners conversed, underscored by the booming laughs of the male diners and the delighted squeals of their female guests, the sudden bursts of sounds announcing to all the pleasure and fun that was being had.

The room smelled of spring despite the year being stuck in the dog days of January, and every table was decorated with a small bouquet of winter flowers. Their fragrance competed with the perfumes of the ladies present to create a heady miasma, enriched by the heat coming from the room's many fireplaces. Dozens of waiters in smart white uniforms bustled back and forth in the narrow gaps between the tables, their white-gloved hands carrying huge silver platters. Their uniforms stood in stark contrast to the sombre morning coats worn by the male guests and the myriad colours of the ladies' dresses.

Jack sipped at a flute of crisp champagne, doing his best not to wince at the sharp taste. He did not understand the attraction of the drink. It was devilishly expensive and about as palatable as vinegar. He swallowed his sip, his face betraying no hint of his distaste, then set the tall crystal flute back on the table, taking care to place it in exactly the same spot it had come from.

'You must tell me more.' One of his three companions, a widow whose husband had died of an unspecified disease whilst serving with the East India Company, waved her own champagne glass in an airy gesture in front of her face as she made the demand. Jack judged her to be in her late thirties, but she claimed to be a decade younger. She might have lied about her age, but there was no other fault on display that day. Eliza was beautiful. She knew it, and she basked in the attention she received from every man who spoke to her. Her blonde hair was styled artfully on top of her head. She wore a dress of violet silk, its bodice cinched tight. The gores that made up the skirt were of the most modern style, the crinolines a fraction of the size they would have been just a few years before, when enormous skirts had been all the rage. Amidst the dark clothing of the gentleman diners, and the pale oranges, yellows and whites of the other ladies' gowns, the bold, bright colour of Eliza's dress stood out, something clearly much to her liking.

'Now, I have told you before, Eliza my dear.' The man

seated opposite Jack spoke in an overly loud voice. 'A gentleman does not speak of such things.'

'But I wish to know.' Eliza leaned towards her escort. 'You *will* tell me.'

The man who had been allowed to take her to luncheon sighed in an exaggerated fashion. He was dressed in a navy morning coat that sat perfectly across his broad shoulders. There was no denying that George Macgregor was a fitting companion for the striking Eliza, for he was as handsome as she was beautiful, with a square jaw and a fine pair of mutton-chop whiskers that bore just the first brush of silver. Tall and narrow-waisted, he looked every inch the hero, and he was well aware of that fact.

'Very well, although I shall not tell it all.' He looked directly at Eliza, as if she were the only person in the world. 'It was in the Crimea, when we were in the trenches around Sevastopol.' He paused and gave the slightest of winces, as if just the touch of the story on his lips pained him. 'It was a ghastly business. My regiment had been stuck in the same damned spot for weeks, and let me tell you, it was about as unpleasant as soldiering can get.'

Jack paid little attention as Macgregor continued his story. He had heard it many times before. They had first met when Macgregor had engaged Jack to show him the dubious delights of the East End. After that memorable night, they had repeated the experience many times before the roles had been reversed and Macgregor had treated Jack to a night at the best clubs that London could offer. Their friendship had grown from there. It had taken time, and Jack was still not really sure why or how it had happened. It usually suited him best not to allow anyone close. But somehow he found himself looking forward to spending time with the rake who never took himself too seriously.

Macgregor had been born into a fortune. His father had convinced him to purchase a commission. He had served in the Crimea, but like so many others, he had resigned his commission when the war had come to its gritty and protracted conclusion. He had not done much since, but he had a hundred tales of women chased and virtue despoiled. He was a rogue, a wastrel and a scoundrel, and Jack liked him immensely.

It was not just the opportunity to enjoy fine living that attracted Jack to the world of the capital's wealthy elite. It was something much subtler and harder to define. It gave him access to grace and calm; to places where a man did not have to fight to keep what he had, or for what he wanted to achieve. The life he shared with Macgregor was filled with fun, laughter, elegance and refinement, and he savoured every minute of it.

'After seeing all that, well, I must confess I couldn't eat my dinner at all!' Macgregor finished his tale, then guffawed loudly, the sound growing as he saw the faces of nearby diners turn his way, lit by smiles, as if they too were somehow joining in the fun.

'Georgie, you shouldn't tell such tales, not at the table.' Eliza smiled as she rebuked him gently, her blue eyes sparkling in the candlelight.

'You did insist, my dear.' Macgregor leaned in close, his face no more than an inch from Eliza's.

'You shouldn't.' Eliza moved a fraction closer. The words were whispered.

'Oh, I do apologise,' Macgregor breathed. 'But I have only told you the half of it. You see, when we got out of there, I was thinner than a half-starved cat . . .'

Jack's mind drifted away once again. He had no desire to see Macgregor flirt with the beautiful widow. He was still hungry, despite the six courses he had consumed. Bentham's was famous for its cuisine, the newly engaged French chef feted across the city for his ability to create the most delicate of dishes, the ingredients carefully combined then presented so that each course was a work of art. It was also served in portions so small that at first Jack had thought they were being taken for a ride. Not for the first time, he wondered at the sanity of the rich and their desire to spend a small fortune on a meal that would leave a mouse famished. He had seen a number of schemes and scams in his life, and had run a good few himself, but he had never found one that was as efficient at fleecing the pockets of the rich and foolish as a London dining room.

'I take it you have heard this tale before, Mr Lark.'

He was brought back to the moment by the fourth guest at the table, one of Eliza's friends whom he had not met before that day. He had paid her scant attention thus far, and he felt a prick of shame at his negligence. The two of them were there to make up the numbers, nothing more, but that did not mean he should have been so rude.

He sat up straighter and focused his attention on her. He had not ignored her because she was unattractive. Far from it. Ruth was an elegant woman, with long, dark hair set against pale skin. But she was far too slim for his taste, as if she avoided food too frequently for her own good, and her eyes were dull, lifeless even. She looked like a porcelain doll and was just as animated. There was little difference between her and the many other women he had entertained at Macgregor's request. It was enough to make him wonder if there was a factory hidden somewhere in the better parts of London that churned out a sad procession of suitable young women who knew how to act quite properly at all times, with never a hair or a word out of place.

'I have.' He had to clear his throat as he began to speak.

'And does it improve with its retelling?'

'It does not.' He smiled as warmly as he could manage.

'But Mr Macgregor tells it so well, does he not.' Ruth lowered her voice, the words for Jack alone.

'He does.' Jack was already tiring of the polite chit-chat.

'Do you not have tales of your own to tell?' The question was asked rather pointedly, as if his companion suspected he was already becoming bored.

'Some.' Jack reached for his champagne, using the action to hide his discomfort. He had more tales than he could tell at a lifetime of polite luncheons. Few were suitable for a lady's ears.

'Will you tell me one?'

'Perhaps another time.'

'But you have served.'

'Yes.'

'And you have fought?'

'I was just a humble soldier, ma'am.' He tried his best to charm.

Ruth did not fire off another question. Instead she sipped at her own drink. But her attention did not waver and she looked at him over the rim of her glass. He wondered if she knew that he was dissembling.

'My dear Ruth. Do not believe a single word Jack says. Why, he is one of the bravest soldiers that ever wore scarlet.' Macgregor tore his attention away from Eliza for long enough to interject.

Jack shook his head at the words. Macgregor knew all

about the Babylon and how he made his living, but he was
privy to little of his past. He knew that Jack had fought in the
battle at the Alma river in the Crimea, where he had led a
company of redcoats for the first time. But Jack had never once
spoken of Bhundapur or of Khoosh-Ab. He had told Macgregor
something of his time in India, but he had never shared the full
horror of being the first man into the breach at Delhi, or hinted
at what it had been like to stand in the ranks of the French
Foreign Legion as they endured the wholesale slaughter at
Solferino. He had never spoken of his time in America beyond
a few oblique comments, and he had revealed nothing of
marching in the blue of the Union as they had tried to turn the
Confederate flank at Bull Run, or of what it had been like to
fight in grey at Shiloh, where the Union army had somehow
snatched a victory from the jaws of certain defeat. The only
part of his life that he had talked of was the last weeks of his
time in Mexico, and the acquisition of the money that had paid
for his passage back to London. Even then, he had held back
much of the truth.

'Is that so, Mr Lark?'

'No.' Jack attempted to deflect Macgregor's claim.

'I do not think you are telling me the truth. I can see you
have been in the wars.' Ruth smiled, looking him dead in the
eye even as she rather tactlessly alluded to his scarred face.

'I have a few scars, that is true.' He moved his hand to touch
his left side. 'I took a bullet here. It went clean through me.'
He let his fingers dwell for a moment before he moved his
hand up to his shoulder. 'I took a sword cut here, slashed me to
the bone. I bled like a stuck pig.' He held her gaze, waiting
to see her reaction. 'I have dozens more. I cannot even remember
how I got them all.'

Ruth said nothing, but her smile had faded.

'And then there is this one.' He touched the scar that ran down his cheek and into his beard. 'I took this just outside Delhi. It's from a sword and it's as close as I ever came to death. I killed the man who did it.' The words came out shrouded in ice. The memory was old now, the events that had led to the bitter skirmish outside the walls of the city far away in his past. Yet time had done nothing to lessen their power to hurt.

Ruth had visibly recoiled, sitting back in her chair as if to try to get as far away from her luncheon companion as she could. He did not know if it was the gruesomeness of his tales that repelled her, his cold tone or simply a topic that was so unwholly suited to a luncheon table. He found he did not care.

'What say you to a jaunt to the Crystal Palace? I have not been for ages.' Eliza made the suggestion loudly, blithely unaware of the tension that had suddenly arrived on the other half of the table.

'I think that sounds a lovely idea.' Ruth replied enthusiastically, seizing upon the suggestion like a drowning sailor clutching at a floating spar.

'And you, Mr Lark?' Eliza turned her attention to Jack.

'I would be delighted,' Jack answered smoothly. He looked at Ruth, but she would not meet his gaze.

'Would you indeed!' Macgregor guffawed at his reply. 'The Crystal Palace, how pathetically damned parochial!'

'George, your language!' Eliza exclaimed.

'I apologise, my dear. But really, Jack should be coming with me to Abyssinia, not gadding about town on some damn jaunt.'

Jack sighed. Macgregor had been planning a trip to Abyssinia for the past year. Tales of the distant land had filled the newspaper columns ever since its ruler had dared to take some Europeans hostage several years before. Jack had followed the story, but the tale had fired Macgregor's imagination, and he was forever asking Jack to go with him on his adventure.

'Abyssinia?' Eliza gave a delighted squeal. 'How very outlandish. Why don't I come with you instead?'

Macgregor guffawed at the very idea. 'I really do not think you would enjoy it, my dear. The place is riddled with every form of pestilence and disease known to man. It is said that there are flesh-eating insects just waiting to eat you alive. Then there are the fearsome native warriors. They stand at least seven feet tall and think of nothing but killing. The papers say they take a trophy from every one of their victims. Each one of them wears a ghastly necklace made from ears or fingers and toes.' He clearly relished his own descriptions, and Eliza hung rapt on every word, her hand clasped to the base of her throat in horrified delight.

'The terrain is said to be fearsome. Mountains taller than Mont Blanc, narrow gorges so deep that they are cast into an eternal night, and a hundred gullies where the locals are just itching to tumble rocks down onto your head. Then there is the great Gorilla King himself.' Macgregor paused to look around his small audience. 'His name is Tewodros, and tales of his cruelty are legendary. He thinks nothing of having men, women and children beaten to death. He throws priests into the flames and does not hesitate to enslave people by the thousand.' He sat back in his chair, as if exhausted by the picture he had painted of the remote land that he planned to visit.

'Remind me why you want to go there again?' Jack cut through the hush that had followed the bluster.

'Oh Jack, you should hear yourself. You sound like an old

man.' Macgregor was not in the least offended by his friend's lack of support. 'If the daring of the adventure is not reason enough to join me, then I would urge you to think of something more tangible. The Emperor of Abyssinia has subjugated the whole damn country, collecting anything that caught his eye along the way. It is said that he has taken the treasure from a dozen kingdoms. Gold, specie, jewels, he has it all. You mark my words, there are fortunes to be made there. A king's ransom in treasure is just waiting for men like us to take it. If we don't, then others will, and I am not of a mind to let that happen.'

'You already have a fortune.' Jack noted the way Eliza's eyes narrowed slightly at the revelation. 'You don't want for anything.'

'But think of it, Jack. It is not just the value of the treasure. There is fame to be won too.' Macgregor said the words in a reverential tone. 'Imagine being the man who brings home the emperor's golden crown, or steals away another Koh-i-Noor.'

'Ah, there we have it.' Jack shook his head. 'You yearn for glory.'

'Do you not want to be the talk of the town, Jack? Do you not wish your name to be plastered across every newspaper in the country? Do you not desire immortal renown?'

'No.'

'Truly? Tell me then that the idea of being invited to the palace to regale our queen with the tales of your valiant deeds does not stir your passion.'

'I can think of few things worse.'

'Come now, Jack. I know you. You want more than this.' Macgregor waved his hand airily.

Jack held his peace, keeping his expression neutral. He would not be drawn.

'Do you not crave to return to the wilds? I know you have travelled, that you have fought, just as I have. Do you not want to experience that life again, even if just for a short while?'

'No.' Jack left no room for discussion. He had thought of it often enough to have convinced himself that he was not lying. He had had his fill of war and campaigning. There had been too many nights when he had lain on the hard ground, chilled to the bone, his body near broken from the wounds it had taken, his mind cast into darkness by the events he had witnessed. He did not want to return to that life. Not now. Not ever. Or at least that was what he told himself. For to admit to wanting it would be to deny everything he had built.

'You are such a sourpuss, my dear Jack.' Macgregor shook his head in mock despair, but he still reached out a hand and clasped Jack's shoulder, the action a reassurance of the friendship between them.

'Are you really going to go?' Jack asked. For the moment, their two guests were ignored.

'I have the preparations fully in hand.'

'Then you're a damned fool.'

'And you're a miserable curmudgeon who should be coming with me.'

'No. I'm the sane one. And I'll be here waiting for you when you get back with God knows what manner of bloody disease.'

'And I shall bore you with a thousand tales of my adventure and force you to listen to every single one.'

'I will listen to them all with pleasure.'

'Good.' Macgregor squeezed Jack's shoulder. 'You really will not go with me?'

'No.'

He held Jack's gaze for a moment longer, then nodded. 'So be it. I shall make my name without your assistance.'

Jack let the remark pass and glanced at Eliza. She was looking at Macgregor through hooded eyes. It was clear she saw him as a hero, his adventurous spirit only adding to his appeal. Yet no matter what he said, and no matter how compelling a picture he painted, Jack would not go with him. He could not leave the Babylon, not yet, and he felt no lure to try to make a name for himself. He had done that, and it had cost him more than he could ever have imagined. So he would settle for what he had, and try to be happy with that.

His days of chasing fate were behind him.

Chapter Ten

━━━◆◆◆━━━

Jack jumped out of the hackney carriage and ran across the street. He was late.

It was a week after the luncheon at Bentham's. Jack had passed the afternoon playing billiards with Macgregor and two of his associates. The game had gone on too long and he had wasted another half an hour trying to locate a carriage – there were never enough around during the day. Now he was late, and he hated being late.

He galloped into the first alley, boots skidding on the muddy ground, and powered down its length before turning left, his body moving without thought. Five minutes of madcap running and he was there.

'Then you listen fucking carefully to what I is about to say.'

A familiar voice reached his ears. He was just in time.

Ahead, he saw six shadowy figures standing together at the entrance to the alleyway. He recognised Cooper's slight frame easily enough. The other five men were there for an evening at the Babylon. A profitable night lay ahead, and he offered a silent prayer of thanks that he had not arrived a few minutes later and let a handsome amount of money slip from his grasp.

'And what I have to say is this. Whatever you do this night – and I promise you is going to do a lot of fucking stuff – whatever you do, do not fuck with the captain.' Cooper pressed on with his regular patter, unaware that his master had only just slipped into place.

Jack forced as deep a breath into his lungs as he could, trying not to pant. It would not look good if he made his entrance gasping for air.

'The captain, why, he's killed so many men he's lost fucking count. That's why no one messes with him.' Cooper finished his lines, his audience hanging rapt on every word.

It was Jack's cue. He sucked down a last breath, turned up the collar of his greatcoat, then pulled his pork pie hat down on his head, dropping his chin as he did so, hiding his face in shadow. Only when he was set did he begin to approach that night's guests. He kept his pace measured, as always, and felt the gaze of his customers fall upon him. This first impression was everything.

'Is that him?' a strident voice sang out as he approached.

'That's the captain all right.' Cooper made sure to speak in a hushed voice.

'He doesn't bally well look like much.' The man's voice came back at once, loud and clear.

'Hush yourself now. He won't like you boys making a ruckus, he won't like it at all.'

'What utter rot,' the same voice replied. It was rewarded with a short peal of laughter from his companions.

Jack heard the words clearly as he approached. He had come across men with the same arrogant tone before. Not every guest was cowed by their surroundings. Some retained their sense of entitlement even here in the dark alleyways of the East End. There was no boundary to arrogance and stupidity.

He took his place, making sure to keep his face hidden.

'Have you got the rhino?' He delivered his line, voice steady and level.

'Have we got the what?' The same voice he had heard before barked a short, staccato laugh that was immediately echoed by his companions. 'What on earth is *rhino*?'

Jack sighed. It was going to be a long night. He stepped forward, placing himself four-square in front of the man doing all the talking. He was taller than Jack, but he was lanky and thin, with a prominent Adam's apple and small, beady eyes that darted back and forth as they examined the man now standing in front of him.

'Have you got my money?' Jack pitched his voice low, the words rasping.

'Oh, now I understand. You want your consideration. Well, why didn't you bally well say so, old man.' The tall man guffawed at his own words, then fished in his pocket and withdrew a thick sheaf of banknotes. 'Do I pay it all now?'

'Yes.'

'But what if it's no good? What if you're taking me for a chump?'

'Why would I do that?' Jack stepped closer, lifting his chin so that he could stare straight into his guest's eyes. 'What's your name?'

'Fleming. Thomas Fleming.'

'And *are* you a chump, Mr Fleming?' His tone did not change as he asked the pointed question.

'How damned rude.' Fleming was clearly not scared of Jack.

'If you want to leave, then leave.' Jack took another step closer. He could smell the man in front of him. He reeked like a cheap whore. 'Take your money and be off with you.'

'Now I hardly think that is the way to speak to one of your customers.' Despite his manner, Fleming still took a half-step backwards. He turned to look at his friends for support. They grinned, some even nodding encouragement. It was enough for him to turn back to face Jack once again, a leering smile plastered across his face.

Jack sighed. Money bred arrogance as easily as a bitch on heat attracted a dog's attention. He was not in the mood for this. He looked one last time at the man being so damned difficult, then shook his head. It was not worth the trouble. It might also play to his advantage. His guests found him through recommendation. It would not hurt that some had failed to secure his services.

'Be off with you.' He gave the command without raising his voice. 'I'm not serving the likes of you.' There was nothing more to be said, so he turned on his heel and began to walk away, pace slow and steady. After a moment, he heard the scurry of footsteps behind him.

'You sure 'bout this, Jack-o?' Cooper hissed as soon as he was at Jack's side. 'There's five of the fuckers. That's worth a fair bit.'

'Let 'em go, Coops. We don't need pricks like that.'

'The girls do!' Cooper ducked his head away as Jack glared at the glib remark.

'I say, stop!' Fleming called after them. 'You there, Captain, wait.'

Jack turned. 'I thought I told you to be off.'

'Look, we don't want to go.' Fleming spoke quietly, so that

his cronies wouldn't hear him. 'Here's your cash, your rhino.' He thrust out the wad of notes.

Jack stared at it. There was a lot there. But every instinct was telling him to turn the man away. Some people were trouble, and he could smell it there and then, just as easily as he could smell Fleming's cologne.

'Look, chum, the captain don't need your fucking money, all right.' Cooper did his best to fan the flames, just as he was meant to. 'I told you not to mess with him.'

Jack lifted a hand to silence his man. 'Are you going to cause me a problem, Mr Fleming?' he asked, voice quiet.

'No, we won't. I promise. Here.' Fleming pushed the money towards Jack.

Jack looked at the notes and thought of all the men and women waiting back at the Babylon. He could not let his ego get in the way of them putting food on their family's table, or keeping a roof over their heads.

He took the money, despite his misgivings, and pushed it deep into a pocket, his eyes still fixed on the man who had given it to him. Yet there was only one thing left to be said.

'Follow me.' He turned on his heel and began to walk without waiting for the others to catch up.

They left the King's Head just over an hour later.

'That was stupendous!' One of Jack's gentlemen guests hooted with delight as the small group stumbled outside. His face was speckled with blood, but he either did not know or simply did not care. 'Did you see that bitch's head come off!' He staggered on as if his brain no longer retained the power to control his feet.

'Steady now, Arthur.' Fleming, the man who had made such

a song and dance when Jack had arrived, reached out an arm to steady his friend. All five gentlemen were three sheets to the wind.

'But did you see it?' Arthur continued. 'Good God, I think I'm going to be sick.' He turned away, then bent double. A moment later, vomit splattered noisily across the cobbles, much to the delight of his four friends, who whooped and hollered in mock disparagement.

Jack said nothing. The stink of the man's puke caught the back of his throat so he turned to spit it away. The dog-fighting had been vicious that night. It was not often that the animals were left to fight to the death, but the crowd had been smaller than usual, quieter too, so Harlequin Billy had allowed the last fight to go on longer than was normal, leaving the two dark-haired terriers to tear each other apart, much to the delight of Jack's five guests, who had pressed close to the pit's walls, roaring with delight as the blood splattered across the ring.

'Let's go.' He did not raise his voice as he gave the command. The five men obeyed without hesitation, falling into line behind him like pissed ducklings.

'I'm looking forward to this,' Fleming cooed with anticipation as he followed Jack away from the King's Head and into the darkness. 'I heard the whores are up for anything.'

'I bloody hope so,' one of his fellows chimed in. 'I'm as randy as hell now.'

Jack closed his ears to the bombast. He had heard it all before. He knew Bella's girls could take it. Every single one of them was tougher than the pricks that trailed behind him. The five gentlemen would behave themselves one way or another. They always did.

Chapter Eleven

hey reached the Babylon without altercation or interruption. All were cold by the time they arrived, the crisp night air stealing their breath and leaving any bare skin feeling like it was covered in ice.

'Get on with it now.' Jack stood impatiently near the entrance as the lone doorkeeper frisked the men one at a time. He was ready to get inside and out of the cold, and even keener to escape from his five guests. It was not often that his customers got under his skin, but that night their crass bluster was irking him. 'Where's Thomas?' he snapped.

'Tommo's sick, guv,' the doorman grunted as he squatted to run his hands up one of the toff's trousers.

'Bad?'

'Might be the chokey.'

'Bugger.' Jack spat out the single word, thinking as much about the hassle it would cause him to find a new man to stand guard as he was about the dire fate faced by the fellow who had stood there every night for the last year. 'That'll do.' He gave the command before the doorman had even finished his search, and pushed open the door, relishing the wash of heat on his skin. The noise of the place assailed him. It was a good sound, to his ears anyway; the sound of a larger than normal crowd, which boded well for his takings.

'Welcome to Babylon.' He gave his customary greeting, then stood back as the two hostesses came forward to remove hats and coats. He did not linger. As soon as the coats were taken, he pulled back the inner curtain and stepped inside.

His ears had not been deceiving him. The place was packed. Many of the men there that night were dockers, the familiar hooks tucked into their belts. He smiled. It was payday, and from the looks of things, a good proportion of the dockers' wages would be finding its way into his and Bella's accounts.

He summoned Cooper to his side.

'Captain?'

'Give them whisky. Lots of it. Then take them through.'

'Don't you want to do it?'

'No. You've earned it.'

Cooper grinned from ear to ear. It was the first time he had been allowed to take charge of this moment. 'Right then, gentlemen, let's get you set up,' he called out to the five men, who were lingering by the curtain. They all sported rosy cheeks from the sudden heat, and to a man they looked like hounds eager to be let off the leash.

Jack did not wait to see them served. He stalked across the room, nodding at a few of the regulars who looked his way. His favourite chair was occupied by a docker at least a foot taller than him, but the man saw him coming, and was on his feet and moving away before he even got close.

With a sigh, Jack sank deep into the chair. He could still feel the night's chill in his bones, and he pulled his woollen jacket close around his body, waiting for the cold to disperse. No sooner had he been seated, however, than he heard the sounds of a scuffle behind him. The Babylon saw its fair share of fisticuffs, but it was rare this early in the evening. Still, he did his best to ignore it, hoping it would pass, or that Cooper or another of his men would stamp it out quickly.

The sound of the ruckus grew. Voices were raised and he heard the smash of a glass hitting the ground.

'For fuck's sake,' he growled as he forced himself back to his feet. He wanted nothing more than a moment's peace, and now he was denied even that.

He saw the source of the fuss immediately. The troublesome guest, Fleming, was squaring up to a docker. The toff might have been the taller by a good few inches, but Jack knew the man he had chosen to confront, and he was sure that in a matter of moments, Fleming would be knocked on his arse. He could not let that happen, as much as he would like to see it.

'Enough!' he bellowed as he strode forward.

The docker's cheeks were flushed with anger, yet he did as he was told and took a step back.

'This man insulted me!' Fleming stepped after his foe. 'He called me a prick!'

Jack caught the docker's eye and nodded. Only then did he turn to Fleming. 'Have you had a drink, Mr Fleming?'

'I rather think I dropped it.' Fleming looked from Jack to the docker and back again. His righteous fury was fading fast.

'Then let me get you another one.' Jack stepped between the two men.

'What about him?' Fleming pointed behind Jack at the docker.

'I'll talk to him. Let me sort him out for you.' Jack raised an arm and clasped Fleming's shoulder, turning him around and steering him away from the altercation.

'He was damned rude.'

'I am sure he was.' Jack had to grit his teeth as he applied what charm he could muster. 'Some people just don't have the manners they're born with, do they now?'

'They damned well don't. I want him punished.' Fleming tried to raise another accusatory finger, but Jack was forcing him back to the bar, where one of the barkeeps had a fresh whisky waiting.

'Leave it to me.' He picked up the glass and handed it to Fleming. 'Now drink up and enjoy yourself.'

Fleming opened his mouth as if to say more, but whatever he saw reflected in Jack's gaze was enough to halt the words before they were fully formed.

Jack gestured to the barkeep to pour more whiskies, then approached the docker who had attracted Fleming's ire. 'Sorry about that,' he said.

'That man is a fucking prick, Captain.' The docker glowered over at the bar.

'Of course he's a prick. That's why he's here.' Jack reached out and patted the docker's shoulder. 'Leave it be, you hear me?' He smiled even as he gave the warning.

'He's still a prick.'

'And you know better than to cause me any trouble.'

The docker was no fool. He knew who he was talking to. He nodded his assent, then turned to rejoin his companions.

'Shall I pop 'em through now, Captain?'

Jack turned to see Cooper hopping from foot to foot behind him. 'I'll do it.'

Cooper's face darkened. 'I thought I was going to look after this lot.'

'That was before you nearly let one of them get the shit kicked out of him.' Jack glared at Cooper, pushing past him. It was time to hand the men into the care of Bella and her girls. Then he might get a few minutes' respite.

'Gentlemen, would you please come with me,' he called, beckoning to his guests.

All five grinned. The dog-fighting and the drinking had been fun. But they had come for more.

Jack wasted no time on speeches or preamble, instead leading the men straight to the hidden door.

'For the love of God.' Fleming was the first to speak as they entered the bright white room. He sounded like a pilgrim finally arriving in the Holy Land.

'Good evening, gentlemen.' Bella spotted their arrival and came across to greet them. She raised a single eyebrow at Jack, noting their somewhat early entry into her world. 'Welcome to Babylon. I hope you enjoy your evening.' She gestured to where her girls were waiting.

Jack's guests needed no more invitation. They stepped inside, heads turning this way and that as they took in the delights of the Babylon's inner sanctum.

Bella came to Jack's side. She watched the gentlemen carefully as they moved across the room, just as she watched for her girls' reaction.

'You're early.' She spoke out of the side of her mouth.

'That's because one of them is being a pain in my arse,' Jack answered honestly.

'Which one?'

'The tall one.'

'He looks like he'd blow over in anything more than a strong breeze.' Bella scowled as she made her own judgement.

'Doesn't stop him acting like a dolt.'

'If he hurts any of my girls, it'll be your fault.' She looked away from the five men long enough to glower at Jack.

'If he hurts any of your girls, I'll break both his arms.'

Bella tutted the remark away, treating it as the empty threat that it was. They both knew the truth. The gentlemen could do whatever they wanted, and still Jack would walk them to Aldgate to make sure they got home safe.

'Who's that?' Jack sought to divert the conversation, using his head to indicate a young girl he had not seen before.

'That's Josephine.'

'Josephine?' All Bella's girls took a new name when they joined her stable. Old identities were forgotten, and the girls were given a clean slate, a rule that both Jack and Bella upheld rigorously. It did not matter what you had done before. Once you joined the Babylon, you were given the chance to start afresh.

'She likes it.'

'It doesn't suit her.' Jack ran his eyes over the girl. She was skinny to the point of looking starved. Bella had dressed her in a loose shift decorated with lace. It was tightly laced around the chest and belted around the waist. The attire did little to hide the fact that she lacked any sort of curves.

'You don't like her?'

'She's too thin.'

'For you maybe.' Bella knew Jack's taste as well as he did. 'But it's the fashion these days. God forbid a woman should have tits or hips.'

'She looks more like a boy than a woman.' Jack gave his opinion.

'That's why some men prefer girls like that. It lets them

have their fun as they like it, without having to ask themselves some damned hard questions.'

Jack grunted in acknowledgement of her remark. For his part, he didn't care in which direction a man's taste ran.

Fleming had taken an immediate liking to Josephine. He was the first of the five to give his attention to one of the girls, and he was starting roughly, pulling her towards him, his hands grasping her tightly around her bare upper arms. He held her there and thrust his head forward, his mouth on her neck, snuffling and snorting as he sucked at her skin. To the cheers of his friends, he pulled back, smacking his chops as if he had been feasting on the finest beef. He released one hand, then shoved it up Josephine's shift.

'Oh, she's a hot one!' he cackled as he groped away, one hand busy whilst the other gripped her tightly.

The other four clapped and cheered as their leader showed them the way. Already they were looking around the room and licking their lips as they leered at the girls around them.

'You want me to stop him?' Jack hissed at Bella.

'No. She has to learn.' Bella's answer was quite without emotion.

'He'll hurt her.'

'They haven't had their fun yet.' She made a play of deliberately looking away.

'It's your call, love. No skin off my nose.' Jack was lying, but he knew better than to interfere between Bella and her girls.

'Just make sure your boys are ready outside. We'll give them an hour. Then I want them out of here.' Bella had the measure of Jack's guests.

'Fair enough.' Jack would not argue.

He was about to leave and return to the main room when he saw Fleming push Josephine into the arms of one of his cronies then make a play of looking around the room as he sought another target for his attention. His eyes fell on Bella and he lurched into motion, pushing past a chaise longue then using the back of a chair to steady himself as he came towards her, his lips curling into something that might have been meant as a smile, but which looked more like a cruel leer.

'Now then, aren't you lovely?' He slurred the words as he came to a stop in front of her. 'I like my women with a bit more meat on them, and I think you will do rather nicely.'

Bella laughed. 'My girls will look after you, sir. If Josephine is not to your liking, then I'm sure one of the others will be happy to oblige.'

'I don't want a bloody child.' Fleming stepped towards Bella, his tongue flickering over his lips, wetting them so that they glistened. 'You're what I want.'

'The girls are here for you, sir.' Bella's tone was unchanged. She had dealt with men like Fleming a hundred times.

Fleming glanced once at Jack, then stepped closer still, reaching out to take hold of Bella's right hand. He cradled it in both of his, as if it were a precious object.

'You don't mind, do you, old man? I mean, she isn't your filly, is she?' He looked Bella up and down, his eyes lingering on her chest, then pushed himself closer so that he was almost pressed against her front.

Jack took a half-step forward. He was stopped in an instant as Bella lifted a hand to ward him away, the gesture hidden behind Fleming's head.

'Now then, sir. Let's find you someone to look after you.' Bella twisted elegantly to one side so that Fleming was against her hip and not her front. It was artfully done, but the toff would not be so easily denied. He stepped after her, pulling her to him then pressing his groin into her back, crushing her skirts. His hands dropped hers and slipped around her body to grope for her breasts.

'Where do you think you're going, missy.' There was malice in his tone now, cruelty and lust mixing together. 'I said I wanted *you*, not one of your damned whores.'

Jack had seen enough. He started forward again, his only thought to beat the man mauling Bella to a pulp.

He had not taken more than a single step before it was made plain that he was not needed.

Bella twisted in Fleming's grip, tearing herself free and swinging round to face him. Her hands moved fast, pushing Fleming in the chest and forcing him away.

'You prick-teasing bitch.' Fleming staggered, but kept his balance and came for her, his bulging trousers visible evidence that his blood was up.

Bella was ready for him. Her knee came up sharply the moment he was in range. It connected swiftly and surely with his cock and balls, the blow driven with enough force to double him over.

Fleming lurched forward. Bella lunged, nails raking at his face. They caught his cheek, gouging deep as she drew them across his skin.

He reeled away, a short, sharp shriek of pain turning to a roar of anger as he raised a hand to his face and discovered blood pouring from the wounds.

'You bitch!' He balled his fist and punched out, the blow rising from down by his hip.

It would never land. Jack grabbed the fist in mid-air with

one hand, then took firm hold of Fleming's collar with the other, hauling him backwards away from Bella.

'What the hell do you think you're doing?' Angry words spluttered from Fleming's mouth as Jack dragged him towards the door, his arms windmilling around him as he fought to stay on his feet.

'You've had enough fun for one night,' Jack grunted as he fought to control the man, who was now fighting to be free. He stepped back, dragging Fleming with him, but had taken no more than three steps before an almighty crash came from the main room. Shouts and bellows followed.

'What the hell?' Jack hissed as the sound stopped him in his tracks. It was too early for the staged fight that would finish the evening.

'Jack, come quick!' Cooper was in the doorway between the two rooms, his pale face filled with fear.

'What is it?'

'Finch's boys!'

Jack understood in a heartbeat. Finch had ignored the message Jack had sent his way. The evening's plans had just been thrown into chaos.

Chapter Twelve

———•—◆—•———

'Stay right there. Move so much as an inch and I'll brain you.' Jack threw Fleming into a chair, then snarled the command into his face. Fleming could wait. Finch's men could not.

He rushed to the door between Babylon's two rooms, where Cooper waited for him. Finch had sent at least two dozen men to create pandemonium.

Their initial rush was unstoppable. The first of them charged to take the bar. Jack's two young barkeeps did their best, vaulting over the bar, hands balled into fists. Yet Finch's men were well prepared and well armed, and they lashed out with cudgels, the short oak clubs battering the two young men to the ground with a series of vicious blows.

The rest of the men surged through the room, feet and clubs sending chairs, tables and glasses crashing to the floor. Every act was intended to subdue any thought of resistance, the storm of violence designed to shock. At least one of Jack's men tried. The man charged with guarding the door to the Babylon's back room stepped forward, heavy fists battering one of Finch's thugs to the ground. Yet one man could not stand for long. Other attackers swarmed towards the lone doorkeeper, surrounding him then lashing out. They made short work of it, a dozen short, sharp blows knocking him over. The clubs were joined by heavy iron-toed boots that kicked out as the man fell to the floor, the blows coming without pause.

Finch's men knew what they were about. They had gambled everything on a quick, brutal attack, and it should have worked as intended. But they had forgotten the dockers that Jack allowed into the Babylon. And they had forgotten Jack himself.

'Shit, shit, shit,' Jack muttered as he plunged into the turmoil. The dockers were fighting back, many brandishing the heavy carrying hooks that were the essential tools of their trade. It evened the odds, but it would still be a hard-fought affair.

To his front, a docker swung his hook, clattering it into the head of one of Finch's men, knocking him down. Around them, others bellowed as they fought, the hard men from the docks relishing the chance to scrap.

Jack grabbed another of Finch's men, spinning him round, a rising uppercut launched the moment the man faced him. His fist made contact with enough force to flatten his opponent's nose and split open his upper lip.

'Get the fuck out of here!' He gripped the half-dazed man by the hair. With a sharp jerking motion, he dragged his head down hard and fast, crashing it into his rising knee. The two came together with a sickening crunch. He didn't even bother to watch as the man fell away, already looking for the next target.

He saw Cooper being knocked to the ground, his face smothered in blood from where a cudgel had caught him on the crown of his head. He fell hard, lost from Jack's sight in the press of bodies that littered the room in a confusing melee.

'Come on, boys!' yelled Jack, stepping further into the fray.

He grabbed a man whose face he did not recognise, swinging him around then pushing him hard in the back so that he sprawled over a table before tumbling to the ground. Another of Finch's men reeled past, nose pouring blood. Jack seized him as he passed, turning him around to face him. As soon as the man stood square, Jack butted his head forward, smashing his forehead into his opponent's already bloodied face. It was a brutal blow. Finch's man fell away, hitting the floor with a thump. The moment he landed, a docker swung a heavy hob-nailed boot that caught him on the temple, finishing the job.

'Fucking end them!' Jack jumped over the prostrate body. He was knocked sideways as he landed, one of Finch's men turning to barge him with a shoulder. He staggered to one side, only just keeping his footing as the man came for him, punching hard, driving a fist into his stomach. Another blow followed, a wild swipe that would have connected with Jack's face had he not seen it coming. Even as he found his balance, he swayed back, letting it sail past the end of his nose by no more than an inch. It was the closest the man would come to landing a second punch.

Jack thumped the man in the gut as soon as the blow went by, half doubling him over. As soon as his head came down, he punched again, smashing his fist into the back of the man's head, following it with another jab that landed in the exact same spot. A third followed, the swinging strike catching the thug on the side of the head with enough force to send blood flying from his face.

Jack gave the man no respite. It was easy enough to grab the lapels of his jacket, then pull him forward into the vicious punch that hit him full in the face. No more blows were needed, Finch's man falling away as if his legs had been turned to so much mush.

Jack spun around, trying to read the pattern of the fight. He spied Cooper back in the fray, his face a mask of blood, the little man tussling with an attacker a good foot taller than he was. He made a rough tally. Half a dozen of Finch's men were sprawled on the ground, whilst those still standing were being driven back towards the main door, where they huddled together, their bloodied cudgels held out to ward off any of the dockers who came close. It was almost done. Finch would receive the lesson he needed. He would know not to mess with Jack again.

Then Fleming strode into the fight and everything changed.

Jack's warning had clearly not had the effect he had intended. Fleming paused at the doorway between the two rooms, his face still covered in blood from where Bella had clawed his cheek. There was a wild glint in his eyes as he surveyed the fracas. Then he charged forward, hitting one of Finch's men in the side, driving hard with his shoulder, knocking the man half off his feet.

But Finch's man knew how to fight. He found his footing, then lashed out, flailing at his attacker. The first punch missed, Fleming somehow lurching out of the way. He even launched a blow of his own, his fist swinging at his opponent, but it was poorly aimed and it bounced off the hard muscles of the man's shoulder. Fleming cried out as the impact drove it wide.

Finch's man counterattacked. His right fist was driven hard, cracking into Fleming's already bloodied cheek. It snapped his head to one side, leaving him powerless to defend himself from the second punch, which hit him on the opposite cheek, spinning him around and knocking him down so that he thumped onto the floorboards on his arse.

He sat there, a bemused expression on his face. He lifted a hand to his mouth, staring at the blood he saw on his fingers, eyes wide in shock.

Then he drew his gun.

None of Jack's guests should ever be armed. It was one of his rules, enforced rigorously. He paid men to stand at the door and search everyone who came into the Babylon for hidden weapons. Yet that night it had been cold, and only one man had stood guard. Jack had given him the hurry-up, keen to get out of the chill. It had been a mistake.

He moved, rushing across the room. Time slowed. He saw Fleming raise the pistol, a tiny pepper-box revolver no bigger than his hand. A heartbeat later, it fired.

The bullet hit Finch's man square in the chest. At such close range, even a tiny pistol could be deadly. The man crumpled to the ground without a sound, blood pouring from the wound.

Heads whipped around, eyes alive to the sudden raise in the stakes. Fleming was already staggering to his feet, his arm outstretched, his mouth stuck open in a silent scream. He fired again, the tiny gun spitting out a second round. The bullet struck the shot man, his jacket twitching as it buried itself deep in his body.

The fighting stopped, the brawl coming to an abrupt end as the sound of the shots pierced the roar of the melee. Those closest to the door rushed to get out, those nearby elbowing and shoving as they tried to follow. Men nearer to the shooting did their best to get away from it, flailing this way and that as they fought to escape.

Only Jack ran towards the gunfire, his sole thought to reach Fleming and stop him before he could kill again.

Fleming turned away. Jack knew what he was doing. He had been shamed, and he was about to exact revenge on the woman who had dared to show him such contempt.

He turned the pistol on Bella.

She stood in the doorway to the Babylon's inner sanctum, a thick-shafted cudgel in her hand. She had held her ground throughout the fight, guarding the entrance to the back room where her girls hid away and striking out at any man who tried to enter. But there was nothing she should do against a man with a gun.

She saw the tiny pistol aimed at her. She did not flinch or twist away. Instead she stared back at Fleming, her mouth moving as she called out to him.

Jack did not hear the words. Men running in the other direction blocked his path. He fought past them, battering his way through with elbows and fists. But he could not close the distance fast enough. He was only three yards away from Fleming, but it might as well have been a thousand.

'You bitch!' Fleming screamed, his mouth contorting with rage.

The little pistol fired. The bullet flew across the room, hitting Bella just under her right breast.

Fleming was not satiated. He pulled the trigger again, firing another bullet that hit no more than an inch away from the first. He laughed manically then, his mouth stretching wide. He was still laughing when Jack charged into him.

They went down hard, arms and legs entwined. The impact with the wooden floorboards was brutal, but Jack did not feel a thing. He pushed down with his hands the moment he hit the floor, levering himself up and on top of Fleming's prostrate body. A heartbeat later, he drove his fist down into Fleming's unprotected face. More blows followed, pounding relentlessly into the man beneath him, his eyes seeing nothing but the red mist of an all-consuming rage. There was no thought of mercy. No respite. Just punch after punch, the blows coming without pause even as his knuckles came away covered in blood and scraps of flesh.

He did not know what stopped him, but his bloody fists lowered and he pushed himself to his feet, his chest heaving with exertion.

He was surrounded by silence.

The Babylon was near empty. The men from Finch's gang had fled, along with the dockers. The room was in ruins, tables overturned in every direction, chairs splintered and broken, smashed glasses littering the floor.

Jack turned on the spot, looking around him, searching for danger. He stopped when he reached the doorway to Bella's room. The other four gentlemen he had brought to be entertained were staring back at him, faces twisted in horror. Behind them he could see the terrified expressions of some of the girls as they gazed down at Bella's body lying in an ever-expanding pool of blood.

He forced himself to look at her. She appeared small to his eyes, frail even. The skirts of her dress were rucked up, her pale ankles revealed. The bodice was decorated with great red splotches, the tears ripped in her flesh by the pepper-box's bullets pouring blood like water from a broken dam.

There was no need for him to check. He knew that she was dead.

He glanced at the four gentlemen. They were watching him

as if he were Lucifer himself. He knew why they stared as they did, but he looked down to confirm it. He could barely recognise Fleming now. The man's face had been beaten to a pulp, what remained little more than a bloody pile of offal and bone.

Bella was gone and he had killed a man.

And yet he felt nothing.

'Come on, Jack.'

Hands pulled at his elbow, a voice pleading with him to move. He shook off the grip on his arm. He wanted to look at the man he had beaten, the man he had just killed.

He squatted down, peering into the bloody ruin of Fleming's face, searching for the human being that had been there just a few minutes before. He did not find one. There was nothing but blood and gore.

With a grunt, he stood, his chest heaving as he sucked down as deep a breath as he could manage. He wanted to feel something. Hatred, remorse, fear. It didn't matter what it was, he just wanted to sense something other than the dreadful nothingness that engulfed his soul. It was as he remembered. Time had not changed it. Absence had not altered it. He had killed a man, just as he had killed so many men before. And just as before, it meant nothing.

'You killed the fucker, Jack.' The voice tried again. Hands tugged his sleeve. 'We've got to go.'

Jack turned slowly away from the man he had murdered with his bare hands. Cooper was there, the blood from the wound to his head already blackening on his skin.

'It's murder, Jack. Murder.' Cooper spoke the words slowly and clearly so that they could not be misunderstood. 'Those bastards over there saw it all. If you stay, you'll swing, you hear me. They'll hang you for this.'

This time Jack did not resist as Cooper pulled him towards the door. A single word resonated in his mind – *murder* – and for a moment he wanted to laugh aloud. Was he a murderer? Was a man who had killed a hundred men anything else? The idea was funny, ridiculous even.

Then he glanced back at Bella's body and coldness engulfed him again.

His life here was done. Another chapter ended suddenly in blood and death. Just as they always did.

Chapter Thirteen

———◆———

Jack stood on the street corner as dawn broke. He pulled up the collar of his greatcoat so that it kept out the chill wind that whistled down the narrow street, then wiped a bandaged hand across his face, trying to smear away the tiredness that left his eyes gritty and sore. There had been no sleep that night, and he did not know where or when he would rest again. The hours of darkness had been spent on the street, watching and waiting.

'They're here.'

Cooper had stayed with his master, never straying more than a yard from his side. It was his shirt that had been torn into the strips that had been used to bandage Jack's hands, which were swollen and sore after the beating they had delivered. Not once in all the long, cold hours had either man spoken. Until that moment.

'I see them.' Jack muttered the words. He leaned on the corner of the building twenty yards down the narrow street from the Babylon, watching the arrival of the officers from the Metropolitan Police who had to come to deal with the aftermath of the fight that had left the drinking den with three corpses inside.

'Peelers.' Cooper made the unnecessary identification.

Jack said nothing. He stayed where he was, lingering in the shadows, watching the first two policemen disappear down the steps that led to the Babylon. He was still there when more arrived a few minutes later.

There was no need to move. None of the men who came and went in the next minutes ventured down the street. There was enough inside the Babylon to keep them busy.

An hour later, two more men arrived. Unlike those already in the Babylon, they wore coats and suits instead of the high-collared blue uniforms and custodian helmets of the Metropolitan Police officers. He knew who they were, their reputation preceding them. It was a dubious honour that was being afforded to him. There were only twenty-seven detectives in all of London. Now two of them had arrived at his place. It was the first indication of the importance of one of the corpses, for detectives like these did not concern themselves with the death of a madam or a back-street thug. But the murder of a gentleman, now that would draw their attention, and it confirmed what Jack had known.

He had killed a young man of importance, a man from a family with enough wealth to ensure that London's finest detectives were going to investigate the sudden death of one its members. He did not doubt they would be successful. Plenty of folk had seen who had killed Fleming, and he was sure the four other gentlemen would be all too keen to tell the sorry tale. Not that the truth mattered to men such as these. The detectives had a reputation for being ruthless and quite without mercy. They never failed to find a perpetrator for the crime they were investigating, even if they did not concern themselves with discovering the truth at the same time.

The first body came out. It had been placed on a stretcher and covered with a thick brown woollen blanket. Four of the policemen carried it, the men taking their time to manoeuvre it up the tight flight of stairs and then away. Two more bodies followed, neither treated with the same level of care and attention.

Then came the living.

Jack knew he should move away. He did not need to see any more. Yet he stayed, his eyes locked on the small procession of women who trailed a policeman up the stairs. He had watched the four gentlemen leave. They would have raised the alarm, their tale of a violent murder enough to secure the services of the peelers and then the pair of detectives. Bella's girls moved slowly, their bodies wrapped in blankets and shawls, their heads bowed. Only Josephine spotted Jack. Her face was puffy and blotchy, her eyes raw from weeping. They found Jack's gaze and held it, even as she followed the other women as they left the Babylon for the last time. There was time for him to register the accusation in her stare before she looked away.

He knew what was to come. Like all the girls, Josephine would be taken to Scotland Yard. There, in a quiet back room, she would tell the detectives everything. It would not likely spare her from whatever her interrogators wanted to do, but it would confirm the gentlemen's story, and it would seal Jack's fate.

It was time to leave. He slipped away, sliding into the shadowy streets without a backward glance. The Babylon was abandoned.

From that moment on, he was a fugitive.

Chapter Fourteen

———◆•◆•◆———

'Follow me, sir.'

Jack did as he was told, doing his best to ignore the distaste in the man's tone. Macgregor's ageing and grumpy valet clearly did not appreciate being disturbed so early in the morning.

'Good morning, Jack!' Macgregor greeted Jack warmly as he was escorted into a chamber that appeared to serve as both drawing room and dining room.

The suite of rooms near Charing Cross station was not the finest, but it was a dozen leagues better than any to be found in Whitechapel. Macgregor was resting in a comfy-looking brown leather club chair, that morning's *Times* folded in his lap, the remains of his breakfast and a silver teapot on the low table in front of him. A small bone-china cup was held in his right hand, his little finger curled just so, the tea inside fresh enough to still be steaming.

The suite was decorated like a comfortable gentleman's club, and it certainly smelled like one, the lingering odour one of cigars and spilled port. The walls were painted a warm green, and were decorated with a series of anonymous gold-framed hunting scenes. The furniture was dark, heavy and clearly expensive. It was the home of a gentleman, one more concerned with comfort and familiarity than style.

'Stoke that bloody fire. It's as cold as a parson's heart in here.' Jack made the terse suggestion as he crossed the room, going straight to the meagre coal fire burning in the grate.

'Of course.' Macgregor seemed delighted to have Jack disturb his breakfast. He tossed the folded *Times* onto an empty chair, then stood, his tea still held carefully in his hand. 'Do as he asks, would you, Benson,' he said airily. 'You look bloody awful, Jack. Did you get caught in bed with someone's wife?'

Jack grunted. The remark was typical of Macgregor, whose mind worked in almost only one direction. 'Is that tea?' He stared at the cup in his friend's hand.

'How remiss of me.' Macgregor looked aghast. He turned with alacrity and pointed to the low table. 'Another cup, Benson, look lively there, man.'

The valet was poking half-heartedly at the fire, stirring it to life. His sigh at the second command was audible. He took his time, carefully returning the poker to the companion rack that stood on the hearth before going to do his master's bidding at a pace that would put a snail to shame.

Macgregor ignored his disgruntled servant. 'So, do tell. What on earth has happened?'

'Wait.' Jack followed Benson's slow progress across the room. Macgregor sipped at his tea, his eyes alive with excitement as he waited with bated breath for whatever scandalous tale Jack was about to share.

'I need to get out of London.' Jack spoke in an even tone as soon as Benson had moved out of earshot.

'How wonderfully dramatic!' Macgregor's face lit up at the first scent of gossip. 'Will you tell me why?'

'I killed a man.'

Macgregor spluttered his tea. Jack did not react. He simply looked back at the other man and waited for the display of astonishment to be over.

Benson returned with a second cup and saucer held out in front of him. If he wondered why his master was red in the face with tea dripping down his chin, he made no remark of it. As before, he took his time, moving slowly to the low table. He poured a measure of tea from the silver pot, the sound of the liquid hitting the cup loud in the silence that had followed Jack's announcement. He added milk, then, at the same leisurely pace, crossed the room to hold out the cup and saucer to Jack, his expression perfectly neutral.

Jack took the small cup, leaving Benson holding the saucer, much to the valet's obvious annoyance. He looked pointedly at Jack's bandaged hands and the smudges of blood that had seeped through the cheap cotton, then glanced up, a single eyebrow raised and a knowing look in his eyes.

Jack held his gaze, then smiled. He intended it to infuriate the man, and from the sour look that spread across Benson's face, he had clearly succeeded. He maintained the expression until the valet sniffed and turned away.

At last Jack turned his attention to the tea he needed so badly. The cup was light and delicate in his bandaged hands, and it contained a paltry amount of liquid. As Benson left the room to do whatever a disgruntled valet did, Jack drained it in two gulps, relishing the heat but caring little for the milky concoction that bore little resemblance to the thick soldier's tea he preferred.

'Look, I need your help.' He got straight to the point. His life had involved its fair share of lies, and he would not add to the tally now. 'I need to get out of the country.'

'You expect me to aid a murderer?' Macgregor tried to sound incredulous, but he was unable to disguise his delight at the intrigue that had landed in his lap.

'It wasn't murder. The fucker deserved it.'

'You do not sound the least bit remorseful.'

'I'm not.'

'I would suggest changing your tone when you stand in front of a judge. Why, you could be hanged.'

'There won't be a bloody judge. Besides, the man I killed had just murdered two other people. It's him who deserved to swing, not me. I just saved the nation the bother of the trial and the cost of a rope.'

'He deserved it, you say?' Macgregor sipped at his own tea. The saucer rattled as he replaced the cup on top of it, his hands shaking.

'Yes.'

'Then let's find you a lawyer to sort all this out. If it's as clear-cut as you say, then I am sure you have nothing at all to concern you.'

'No.'

'Why?'

'Because it was Lord Tosspot I killed, or whatever the bastard was called.'

'He was a gentleman?' Macgregor did not grimace at Jack's turn of phrase. They had spent enough time together for him to have experienced Jack in more than one shade.

'He wasn't gentle, and he wasn't much of a man, but he was a toff, if that's what you mean.'

'My God.' Macgregor looked horrified.

'What?'

'You're a killer.'

'No shit,' Jack scoffed. 'You were a soldier; you did your fair share of killing.'

Macgregor turned away. 'That was on the battlefield.'

'You should have seen the Babylon last night. If that wasn't a battlefield then I don't know what is.' Jack was watching Macgregor closely. 'And there's something else.' It was time to reveal all.

'Something else?' Macgregor sounded as though he could not take any more.

'One of the others that was killed worked for a fellow called Finch. He's a powerful man, in my part of London at least. Let's just say we aren't exactly friends. He won't be happy one of his own got topped.'

'Oh dear God.'

'So he'll be looking for me too.' Jack spoke the words deadpan.

'But you didn't kill that man?' Macgregor found it difficult to form the words.

'No. That was Lord Tosspot. But men like Finch don't ask questions. They do whatever they think they have to do to protect their reputation. In this case, that'll mean slitting my gizzard before dumping me in the Thames.'

'So you are truly a wanted man. The authorities are looking for you on a charge of murder, and this Finch fellow is after you for what he thinks you did to one of his men. If either of them captures you, you'll be killed.' Macgregor offered the quick summary.

'Something like that.' Jack watched his friend closely.

Everything hung on what he said next. He held Jack's life in his hands.

Macgregor said nothing. He looked into the distance, his mind clearly whirring as he considered the situation Jack had dumped in his lap.

'Do you remember that girl? The one you fell for?' Jack broke the silence. He spoke slowly and carefully. It was not a kind question, but it was time to remind Macgregor of their history.

Macgregor's face fell. 'Of course.' The words came out in barely a whisper.

'You remember what you said?'

Macgregor did not answer. Instead he walked to the window, where he stood in silence staring out at the rain that pattered gently against the pane.

'I thought I was doing the right thing.' When he spoke again, there was pain in his voice.

'You were. Didn't stop you getting in the shit.'

'And you fixed it.'

'I did.' Jack did not have to add more. It was enough to remind Macgregor of what had happened in the early days of their fledgling friendship. Macgregor had become besotted with a young whore, and had insisted on setting her up in her own rooms, where only he could see her. It had been Jack who had found out the truth. The girl had kept working, using the rooms Macgregor paid for to entertain other clients. He had revealed the sad tale and had then been the one to make the girl leave. Threats of blackmail had followed, and Jack had sorted them too, his growing reputation in the streets of the East End enough to find the girl a place where she could no longer cause trouble. Macgregor had promised to return the favour one day, whenever Jack needed it. Neither had spoken of that time in their lives since. Until now.

Macgregor inhaled deeply, composing himself. 'There is no need to hark back to what happened. Of course I'll help you.' He let out his breath, taking his time doing so. 'But I warn you, I am leaving within the week.'

'Abyssinia?'

'Yes.'

'I thought you were bullshitting.'

'You have a charming turn of phrase this morning, Jack.'

'Just being me.'

'Have you not always been so?' Macgregor was looking at him quizzically, as if really seeing him for the first time.

'I have always been me, at least to some extent.' Jack smiled wolfishly. 'I am a man of many parts.'

'As I am learning.' The shock was gone, and Macgregor's usual ebullient manner had returned. 'Come with me to Abyssinia. I've asked you a dozen times before and you've always said no. But given your somewhat straitened circumstances, perhaps now you will answer differently.'

Jack looked at Macgregor. He had to give his friend credit. For a moment he had feared he had misjudged the man standing in front of him, but he need not have worried. Macgregor was as solid as a rock.

'There's two of us.' He would not leave Cooper to face Finch's retribution alone.

'The more the merrier! We shall make a fine party of four.' Macgregor seemed genuinely delighted at the prospect of adding men to his venture.

'Four?'

'A friend of mine, a fellow called Watson. We were at school together. Watson works at the British Museum. He will be providing the expertise. If anything, he is keener to go than even I.'

'Fine. Whatever. Like you said, the more the bloody merrier.' Jack spoke the truth. He didn't care who was on the expedition, just so long as they were ready to leave London sharpish.

'Capital!' Macgregor hooted in delight. 'So you'll come?'

Jack held his breath for a moment. Bella's face sprang into his mind's eye, the life force that had sustained her stolen away by Fleming's bullet. Her death mask looked back at him, eyes glazed and lifeless. It was a reminder that his time here was done. The thought did not upset or intimidate him. He had made a fresh start before, and he had always known he would have to do so again. Everything in his life was temporary. People came and went. It was why he never allowed himself to become attached to anything or anyone for long. He knew they would always be taken from him in the end, no matter how hard he wished for it not to happen.

'Yes. I'll come.' He spoke the words clearly and without a trace of doubt or sadness. When fate came to cast your life into ruin, there was nothing to do save to suck it up and find a way to carry on.

Chapter Fifteen

---

*J*ack stared out of the garret room's window. He could see something of the city beyond, despite the grime and mould that caked so much of the glass. It was not much to look at, just a long line of rooftops, the grey slates dampened by the rain that had been falling for hours. The sky was sombre, lousy with heavy black clouds. It was the London he would always remember. Dark, gloomy and shrouded with fog.

Not for the first time, he craved open spaces where he could see for more than a few yards. He wanted to be away from the grime and persistent damp of London, and the stink of other people. Life in the metropolis was cloying. It was holding him so tight that he could barely breathe, dank and stifling. And he was beginning to loathe it.

He remembered riding all day on an open prairie, taking in good clean air that did not taste as if a thousand other people had already breathed it. If he closed his eyes, he could see a boundless horizon, the sky an enormous bowl quite without limit. He remembered feeling small, his humanity lost in the great expanse that seemed to stretch on for ever.

He remembered feeling free.

He smeared a hand across his face, as if he could wipe away the soot and the grime. He could not. It was always there, etched into every pore. London consumed its citizens, worming its way under their skin until they became a part of the very fabric of the place. He could feel it even now, itching and scratching as it burrowed deeper and deeper. It would not stop until it had taken root in every part of him. He had to leave before that happened. Circumstances might have necessitated his departure, but that did nothing to hold back the first feeling of something he could only think of as excitement. He was returning to where he belonged.

He had told Cooper of the plan to join Macgregor and his friend Watson on their expedition to Abyssinia. For a man who had never ventured more than a few miles from the tenement block where he had been born, Cooper had been surprisingly phlegmatic at the idea of travelling halfway across the world to a country he had never heard of. It had been enough for him to know that he would be well away from Finch and from the Metropolitan Police.

Voices came from downstairs. Loud voices. Commanding and demanding. The cheap boarding house near Spitalfields market where he and Cooper had spent the night whilst Macgregor made the final arrangements for their departure was never quiet; there were just too many men living there for that to be the case. But this was different. The shouting increased in volume as doors slammed and boots thumped heavily onto wooden floorboards.

Jack went to the door and pulled it ajar, leaning forward so that he could hear better. The voices came almost constantly now. He placed four, maybe five different men demanding attention. More doors slammed, then came the thump of a body hitting the floor.

Footsteps approached. Fast boots on wooden treads. Jack eased away from the doorway, his right hand instinctively reaching for the revolver he had once worn on his hip. It had not been there for years, yet at that moment he wanted to hold a weapon and feel its power.

'Jack! Look alive-o!' a breathless voice shouted up the stairs.

'I'm here.' Jack stepped forward, door held wide open.

Cooper thundered up the final flight of stairs that led to the four rooms in the boarding house's attic. 'Finch's boys! Fucking loads of them.'

It was all the warning Jack needed.

He dived back into his room, heading for the window. There was no time to delay. There was no sense in fighting here. Not if they were outnumbered.

He threw up the window, grunting with the force it required. Cold air rushed in, the breeze flinging a misty rain into the room.

'Come on!' He paused to call to Cooper. Then he swung a leg up and ducked low as he clambered through the window. He had his escape planned. It had been one of the first things he had done when he had taken the room.

The air outside was cold and clammy on his skin, yet he paid it no heed and concentrated on his route, his eyes scanning ahead. He perched on the window ledge for no more than a single heartbeat, then dropped, his boots slipping and sliding as he fell, loose slates coming with him until he hit the gutter, stopping sharply. Slates fell past him, cascading over the edge of the roof and smashing violently in the yard four storeys below.

He was moving again moments later. He went left, moving across the roof, body crouched low, left hand pressing on slates made slick by the rain, the tiles icy and damp under his fingers.

'Fucking hell.' Cooper cursed as he took the same route down, his boots dislodging more slates.

'Come on, you dolt.' Jack had paused to make sure Cooper had managed to stop himself and not follow the slates over the edge. Now he spotted the first face at the garret window they had just left.

'Oi! You! Stay the fuck there!'

Jack recognised the fellow shouting down at them. It was Swan, the man who had come to the Babylon to deliver Finch's message. It did not matter to Jack who shouted the instruction; he had no intention of heeding it. He moved fast, keeping low, trusting his balance, reaching the far side of the boarding house in a matter of seconds. A line of similar roofs stretched away ahead of him. There was no way across. Instead, he turned, squatting low so that his backside almost sat on the tiles. Below him was the angled roof of the lodging house's back room, sticking out from the main building. It was lower, just two storeys high compared to the main building's four.

It would be a difficult jump. He would fall two storeys, then have to find a way to stop on the steeply angled roof. But if he made it, he would then be able to jump down into the yard below and make a break for the gate that led to the alleyway between two rows of terraced houses.

'Jack! Don't even fucking think about it.' Cooper was close behind. He had seen Jack turn and had worked out what madcap scheme his master was about to put into motion.

'You want Finch's boys to take us?' Jack snapped. He saw the terror on Cooper's face, and understood it. His own heart was thumping away in his chest, and he could feel the fear worming down into his gut. Yet there was no other way out, not if they wanted to avoid Finch's thugs.

He took a final breath, and jumped.

For one horrible drawn-out moment, he fell through the air, his stomach lurching up into his mouth.

He landed on his hip, an avalanche of broken slates sliding with him as he tumbled down the roof. He twisted onto his back, lying almost flat, and lashed out with his boots, digging the heels down, trying to find purchase. It did little to slow him, so he pressed both hands down as well, not caring that his palms were sliced and cut by the slates. He cared only for stopping and for avoiding a fall into the yard below.

Somehow, it worked. He came to a breathless halt halfway down the roof. For a moment he could do nothing but lie there, staring up at the grey-black sky, sucking down deep breaths. Yet he could not linger. Not with Finch's men so close. He pushed himself up and onto his haunches. He was still balanced precariously, so he moved carefully, bloodied hands reaching out to steady himself.

'Fucking hell!' Cooper was still on the higher roof, looking down. He swore one last time. Then he jumped.

Jack stopped to watch. He saw Cooper's arms flail at the air as he dropped. He hit the roof hard. Like Jack, he landed on his side, but Cooper was lighter, and he bounced, twisting around so that he fell onto his front. Then he began to slide. He tried to stop, the toes of his boots scrabbling at the roof and his hands stretched out above his head, palms pressing down in a vain attempt to get some sort of grip. He found nothing but slick slates, and slid on, clawing desperately at the slippery surface, accelerating towards the drop below.

For one agonising second, he looked across at Jack. There was no time to cry out before he went over the edge.

Jack heard the thump as Cooper's body hit the ground, the sound almost lost in the crash of a dozen slates smashing around him. He edged lower, fearful of losing purchase and following the other man over the edge, sliding down gingerly until he could see into the yard below.

He spotted him at once. He was spread-eagled on the ground, surrounded by shards of broken slates. He was not moving.

'Shit, shit, shit.' Jack hissed the words. Their attempt to escape was over before it had even truly begun.

'Stay right where I can fucking see you.'

The first man emerged from the door that led into the back room of the lodging house. It was Swan. More men followed him. They filled the yard.

Jack was squatting next to Cooper's unconscious body. He had jumped down into the yard to check that Cooper was still alive. There had been no question of abandoning the man to his fate.

He knew there was no point in fighting. Not one man against the dozen who had filed out of the lodging house. But that did not mean he would not try. He would not go easy.

'You led us a merry fucking dance there, old son. Shame it brought your chum nothing but a sore noggin.' Swan stepped forward. His face was twisted into something that on another man might have been a smile. On Swan's disfigured mouth it looked more like a snarl.

Jack ignored him. He checked Cooper one last time, his hand resting on his neck for a few moments to feel for the beat of a heart, then he stood. He winced as he straightened up, his back protesting from where he had jarred it jumping down into the yard. But it would not hold him back.

'Now are you going to come nice and quiet like?' Swan stood four-square in front of Jack, his men behind him. He held his hands out at his sides, ready to fight if needed. 'Mr Finch would like a word with you.'

'Mr Finch can take a running jump.' Jack stretched his fingers, readying his hands for the battering that was to come. Every man in the yard knew how the next few minutes would play out.

Swan pouted, as if disappointed by the pithy reply. 'So be it. Don't say I didn't give you the option, old son.' He looked at Jack one more time, then stepped back.

His men surged forward at the signal. They knew what they were here for. All had done it before and would likely do it again before the month was out.

The tallest man was on the left of the group, and Jack made his plan in the second it took for the group of thugs to take their first steps towards him. He ducked a shoulder as they moved closer, feinting to his right. The men on that side tensed, arms bending as they reacted to the movement, readying themselves to attack. They would not get the chance. As soon as Jack saw them tense, he shifted his weight, pushing it from one foot to the other so that he sidestepped to the left. He spun around as he moved, right arm held low, and stepped into the punch, throwing his full weight behind his right fist. The tall man saw him coming, but Jack's feint had stolen him a second and the man was just too slow.

His right hand connected with his opponent's face. It was a fine blow and it rocked the tall man back on his heels, claret-coloured blood spraying from his pulped nose. Jack did not wait to see if he fell. Instead, he spun on his right heel, driving his elbow into the breast of the next-closest man. The impact was brutal, his whole arm jangling from the jarring impact. It was enough to double the man over, hands clasped to his heart.

Jack was not done. He lashed out, flailing his left fist at a bearded face that loomed into view. A punch came back at him, the group closing around him even as he launched his one-man attack. The blows came fast, heavy fists battering away at him, but he barely felt a single one. He thought of nothing but fighting. He was finding his speed now, and he lashed out, slamming his fists into anybody within reach.

The fight descended into chaos. Jack had no sense of who was where, but he knew that every man was a foe, and so he thrashed around him, arms and fists wild. He landed a punch in a man's gut, then kicked another in the shins. A blow hit him on the jaw, snapping his head around. Hands clawed and grasped at his arms, but still he fought on, ignoring the pain, always moving, always punching, never giving in.

Another face came close, as one of Swan's men sought to grasp him in some sort of bear hug. Jack saw the movement and slammed his head forward, butting the man full in the face, knocking him down. Already other men were backing away, suddenly reluctant to tackle the madman who fought like a wild animal.

'Come on, you bastards,' Jack hissed breathlessly as he stepped after the nearest retreating man. He swung a bloodied fist. The blow landed on the man's jaw, snapping his head around before he crumpled, senses gone, his body tumbling to the ground.

'Enough!' Swan shouted, his voice dominating the yard.

Thus far he had stayed out of the fight, leaving it to the thugs who were paid to take the blows in Finch's name. Now he stepped forward, the six-inch shaft of a stout oak cudgel held in his right hand.

Jack saw him coming. He turned on the spot, bruised fists rising into a fighter's stance. His breath came in laboured gasps now. He had not fought like this for a long, long time, and he was tiring.

'Take the bastard down!' Swan snapped the command.

Jack had fought hard. Save for Swan, not one of the other men in the yard was unscathed. All were bruised and bloodied, and one was lying unconscious on the ground. But they still swarmed forward at Swan's command. This time they did not try to fight. Instead, they rushed at Jack, hands reaching out to grab him as they sought to wrestle him down.

Jack lashed out, fists flailing, but he could not keep so many hands at bay. They clasped at his arms, holding him fast. Still he tried to fight. He pulled an arm free, then slammed his fist into a man's throat, crushing his windpipe and taking him out of the fight. But the others pressed forward, hands keeping hold of him.

Swan picked his moment well. He danced forward, timing his rush for the moment when Jack was unbalanced. The oak cudgel he carried slashed through the air, aimed with precision, catching Jack cleanly on the temple. It was a short, sharp blow and it hit hard.

Jack's world turned black, and he fell like a sack of horseshit.

Chapter Sixteen

*J*ack awakened to darkness.

'Hey, Jack-o,' a voice hissed at him the instant he stirred.

He paid the words no heed, even though he recognised the speaker easily enough. He was lying on his back, stretched out across floorboards. The pain came then. He could feel the bruises deep in his flesh, and his hands felt like they had been pulverised by a hammer. But the worst pain was in his head, where something was pounding away so that it felt as if his brain had been cleaved in two and was even now oozing out of his ears.

'Jack-o?'

'Shut up,' Jack snarled. The words hurt his head. He wanted silence.

He was given a few moments' peace. It was long enough for him to finally open his eyes. The room was not as dark as he had first thought. A little light was filtering in around a closed door, enough for him to see he was in some kind of empty storeroom.

'You awake now, Jack-o?'

'Shut up, Coops, or I'll kill you.' Jack snapped the words then lifted a hand to nurse his jaw, his tongue running around the inside of his mouth as he checked for broken or loosened teeth. To his relief, he found nothing amiss. But that knowledge did nothing to lessen the pain in his head.

'Where are we?' He fired off his first question without making any effort to sit up. Lying there suited him nicely for the moment.

'No fucking idea.'

'Fat lot of good you are, Coops.'

'I ain't been a lot of use at all, have I now.' Cooper made the rueful admission. 'I let you down.'

'No, you didn't.' Jack heard movement outside the door. He sat up, taking it gingerly. The movement seemed to double the pounding in his head, but he was damned if he would be found lying on his back like a broken man. 'Help me up, for Christ's sake.'

Cooper did as he was told. He reached down, clasping his hands to Jack's forearm. Slowly and carefully, Jack got to his feet.

He stood there fighting the dizziness and nausea that surged through him.

'You all right there, Jack-o?'

'Give me a minute,' Jack hissed as he fought to control the pain.

'We're in the docks, I reckon.' Cooper stood at Jack's side, ready to catch his master should he fall. 'I heard Finch took a place down there last month. That's where we are, I think.'

'Maybe.' Jack had the pain almost under control.

Cooper looked at the ground and scuffed his boot across the floorboards. 'Sorry I fell.'

'It wasn't your fault. It was a damn-fool plan.'

'I'll make it up to you.' Cooper's reply was quick and eager. 'You know I'm your man. Now and always.'

Jack grunted. 'That fall must have scrambled what little brains you had.'

'Maybe.' Cooper grinned. He must have been hurting as much as Jack, yet he was not beaten. Not by a long way. 'We're a rum pair of coves and no mistake. Look at us.' He shook his head ruefully. 'You remember when I tried to pinch your pocketbook?'

'I'll never forget it. You were a shit pickpocket.'

Cooper grinned foolishly. 'Luckiest moment of my life, that was. Even though you fair broke my fucking hand, I reckon I still owe you for what you did for me.'

'You can start paying me back by finding us a way out of this bloody place.'

'Course I will. Ain't no place that can hold me. I'll get us out of here, I promise.'

The conversation was ended by the grating sound of a bolt being pulled back, the noise echoing around the cramped confines of the storeroom.

The door opened. Light flooded in, bright and glaring.

Jack blinked hard. The light hurt his head, but he would not show it, so he stood still and straight, facing the men who had come to fetch them.

'Well, there you are then. Nice and cosy in here, ain't it just.'

Jack looked back at the familiar face of Swan.

'This way now.' Swan stepped back and gestured for the pair to step out of the room. He was not alone. Four hefty goons stood with him, all armed with cudgels held ready for use. Finch was taking no chances, not this time.

Jack moved first. He had to clench his jaw tight as he tried not to stagger, the pain in his head almost driving him to his knees. For one grim moment he thought he was about to puke, so he swallowed hard, focusing everything he had on showing nothing to these men. There could be no sign of weakness. None at all.

Swan gestured for them to walk ahead of him. Jack looked at him, trying to discern something of the man behind the thuggish facade. He failed. There was no shred of empathy in Swan's flat stare. His eyes were lifeless.

He did as Swan ordered, Cooper behind him, following the curt directions that he was given. They were in a great ware-house, packed full of wooden crates stacked into tall piles so that they formed long aisles. He reckoned Cooper was right and they were somewhere down near the docks. But their location did not matter. They were in the heart of Finch's domain and a long way from their own world. There would be no one to come to their aid. They were on their own.

'In there.' The final command was given. They had reached the end of a long aisle of packing crates and now faced a door.

Jack stepped forward and pushed it open, entering a large office furnished with a huge mahogany desk topped with green leather. There was a second door on the far side of the room, and both it and the walls were panelled with dark wood, whilst the floor was covered with an expensive-looking Turkish rug. The office was neat and ordered, the desk bare save for an ink stand and a single steel pen. It was devoid of all other decoration, sparse and stale.

Jack wrinkled his nose. There was a strange smell in the room, one he could not place. It was like a lady's perfume, the fragrance delicate and flowery, yet there was something stronger beneath it, something earthier and woodier.

He turned to look for his guards. The four men with cudgels had departed. Only Swan had followed them inside, closing the door and locking it behind him. He stood in front of it, his hands clasped across his front, his face impassive as he stared into space.

A sound behind him caught Jack's attention. He turned in time to see the door on the far side of the office opening towards him. A young man breezed in and took a seat on the far side of the desk. He sat down heavily, pushing back in his chair so that he slouched away from the desk. He contemplated Jack and Cooper, then he smiled.

Finch had arrived.

'You pair have caused me no end of fucking bother.' Finch steepled his hands and looked at Jack and Cooper over them. 'And all to what fucking end?' He left the question hanging and rocked back in his chair, his eyes assessing his prisoners.

Jack did not react as he studied the man who had turned his life upside down. Finch could not be much more than twenty-five years old. To Jack's eye, he looked lean and strong, with the build of a prize-fighter. He was dressed in a smart dark pinstripe suit with matching waistcoat. A thick gold watch chain stretched across his stomach and his hands sported at least half a dozen gold sovereign rings, all oversized.

He finished his inspection of the pair, then sat forward. 'You want to tell me what the fuck this is all about, Mr Lark?' he asked.

'You sent your men to my place. They made me an offer that I declined. Anything that followed is on your shoulders, not mine,' Jack replied calmly. He was a fly stuck right in the middle of the spider's web. Struggling would only make his predicament worse.

'Fuck me,' Finch barked. 'You're a fucking clot and no mistake. I made you an offer, fair and fucking square. If you knew your fucking onions then you'd know you ain't got no choice but to pay up.' He shook his head, as if both saddened and disappointed. 'Now you'll have to be punished, cos I can't let a mutton-headed fuckwit like you set a bad fucking example to all the others.' He nodded to Swan. 'Take that silly little fucker away. He's just a bloody lacky. I want to talk to the high-and-fucking-mighty Mr Lark here on his lonesome.'

Swan did not need to be told twice. He grabbed Cooper's arm, tugging the slighter man towards the door.

'Don't give the fucker anything, Jack-o,' Cooper shouted, earning himself a clout around the head.

The door was unlocked and opened, and Cooper was handed into the care of the guards waiting outside. Jack heard the sounds of movement as Finch's men took him away. Swan returned and shut the door, though this time it was not locked. He took up his former pose.

It was now just the three of them.

'You said no to the wrong fucking man, Mr Lark.' Finch pulled his chair forward so that he could lean his elbows on his desk. 'There's a price to be paid for that.' He gave Jack half a smile. 'We won't meet again.' He made as if to get up. 'I reckon you're a clever fellow and all. You know what that means, I'll wager.'

Jack did. Finch was going to have him killed. He had no choice. He ran an enterprise that relied on fear. Jack had not done as he was told, and so he had to be punished.

'I'll find you, Finch.' Jack would not hold his tongue, just as he would not go meekly to his fate. He had once walked to his own grave and stood there as meek as a lamb as he waited for the end. He would not do that again. Not ever. He wanted Finch to know that – no, he corrected himself, he *had* to let Finch know that.

'What's that you fucking say?' Finch looked up, his face creasing into a smile.

'I said I'll find you.'

'And then what?' He pushed himself to his feet.

'I'll kill you.' Jack made the threat in a voice quite without emotion.

'You'll do fucking what?' Finch moved fast, stepping around the desk and coming to stand in front of Jack, his arms folded across his chest.

'I'll kill you.' Jack spoke in the same calm tone. Finch was taller than him, so he had to lift his chin. He had no doubt that the younger man was stronger too.

'Is that fucking so?' Finch contemplated him. 'You think you're a big man, Mr Lark?'

'I think I'm the man who's going to kill you.' Jack gave nothing away. He could smell Finch now he was closer. The cologne was almost overpowering.

Swan moved, as if about to intervene, but Finch stopped him with a raised hand. 'It's all right there, Swanny, Mr Lark and I is just having ourselves a little chinwag.' He pushed his head forward. 'You look old, Mr Lark, if you don't mind me saying so. Old and fucking tired.'

He was close enough for Jack to feel the wash of his breath on his face.

'I offered you a fair fucking deal, Mr Lark,' he continued,

'one that you weren't of a mind to accept. And then, as if that wasn't fucking bad enough, you killed one of my men.' For the first time, some real emotion entered his tone. 'I ain't about to let that go.'

He reached out, his hands caressing the lapels of Jack's jacket. He fussed with them, turning them over then laying them flat again.

'It'll be nice and quiet,' he said conversationally. 'Not quick, oh no, I reckon you've put me to too much fucking bother to let me make it quick for you. But as sure as eggs is eggs, it ends up with you having a little swim. They'll find you in a few days, what the fishes have left of you, that is.' He smiled. 'It's just business, Mr Lark, just fucking business. I hope you understand that.'

Oddly enough, Jack did understand. Finch had lost face. That had to be put right. It was no different from the British government ordering a hundred thousand souls to the arse end of nowhere to save its reputation on the world stage. The scale of their respective business might be a little different, but neither could afford to be seen to give an inch.

He sucked down a deep breath. Finch was still looking at him, the same odd smile on his face. 'Oh yes, I understand.' Jack nodded. 'It's just fucking business.' He gave a smile of his own, then slammed his head forward with every ounce of strength he could muster.

The headbutt landed exactly where he had planned. It crunched into Finch's mouth, the snap of breaking teeth greeting the wet thump of forehead on face. The force of the blow snapped Finch's head back, unbalancing him and sending him stumbling back.

Jack's head was in agony, but he ignored it. He whipped

round, reaching for the cudgel that he knew would be coming for him, blocking the blow that would have shattered his skull. There was a flash of panic on Swan's face, then Jack launched his right hand forward. It was a fine punch, one of his best, and it cracked into the point of Swan's chin with the force of a sledgehammer, slamming the back of his head into the door behind him. The twin impacts were too much. Swan's eyes glazed over and he slumped, his body folding over itself as he slid to the ground.

Jack moved fast, not caring that he trampled on the man he had just knocked down. As he made his escape, he took a moment to glance back over his shoulder. Finch was sitting on the edge of his desk, his face a mask of blood, his expression stuck somewhere between surprise, horror and fury. He held his hand in front of his mouth to catch the torrent of snot, phlegm and blood that was pouring forth. In the centre of the palm were at least two teeth, the white shards bright amidst the bloody slurry.

Jack enjoyed a moment's pride at the effectiveness of the single headbutt. Then he opened the door and ran.

Jack had no idea of the layout of the warehouse he found himself in. But it didn't matter. Not now. Escape was all that counted. If he was caught, then Finch would get his wish and Jack would find a watery grave in the Thames. He would not let that happen. Not whilst he still had breath in his body.

He ran through the long aisle of wooden packing crates as if the hounds of hell were hard on his heels, skidding around the first corner, then plunging on, heart and head pounding.

He reached the end of the aisle and staggered to a breathless halt.

He was surrounded by more aisles made from the ubiquitous packing crates. They stretched away from him in every direction. All looked the same. Not one showed a way out.

'Find him!'

The first shouts rang out, echoing through the warehouse. Other voices joined in as more men were summoned to the search. Cries and orders came from every direction now. Some close, some from the far side of the building. Jack stayed where he was, trying to place the men searching for him. He failed. There were too many voices and too many sets of boots to follow. He sucked down one last breath and plunged down the nearest aisle.

He had no idea where he was going. He rushed around a corner, then staggered into another aisle, making the choices without thought. He caught fleeting glimpses of men in other aisles as he ran, faces turning his way as he darted past. He ignored them all and kept moving, searching desperately for a way out.

The long aisles of packing crates gave way to hemp sacks heaped into great piles. The smell changed, the air dusty and dry. He ploughed on, his breath coming in great heaves.

Two men lurched into view, blocking his way. He turned without pause, forcing his body to keep going, and set off at a right angle, stumbling past more sacks, always moving, always running.

More men appeared, arms raised and fingers pointed as their quarry was sighted.

Jack skidded to a halt, then turned once more, trying to head back the way he had come. But he was slow, and the two men he had first spied had rushed after him, blocking his route back.

He was trapped.

'We've got the bastard!' a voice hooted in triumph.

The sounds of men rushing closer echoed all around him, the rest of Finch's thugs homing in on the area where the man who had knocked out their master's teeth had been cornered.

Jack tried to breathe, but his lungs were on fire. He looked around, desperate to find a way out, but saw nothing but the faces of the men sent to take him and the great heaps of sacks that hemmed him in.

'Fucking get him!' someone shouted. Obediently the two groups of men started forward. More were joining them all the time. There was no way through, not with so many men surrounding him.

He was the last rat in the ring. And the dogs were coming.

He charged, running back the way he had come. It was hopeless, futile, but no rat ever lay down and let the terrier's teeth take it. They fought, no matter that their death was already written. They fought, because at the end that was the only thing left to them.

Jack shouted as he charged. Once he had run with the rebels of the Southern states, and now he gave their banshee cry, the rebel yell that had been born on the battlefields of America echoing around the confines of a London warehouse. The wild yips and howls filled his aching head, lending strength to his tired limbs.

He threw himself at the first man coming towards him. He lashed out, punching his fist into the side of the man's head, knocking him to one side. Then he stepped into the gap he had made, arms flailing at the men surrounding him. He felt his blows land, his reward the sudden grunts and gasps of pain from the men he struck.

Fists battered back at him. First one, then another. The blows stung, but still he tried to fight on. He ducked his head, pumping his legs and forcing himself forward. He hit someone hard, forcing them back. But more punches came at him from every direction, thumping into his exhausted, aching body. One clattered across the back of his head, then another slammed into his gut, driving the last breath from his tortured lungs.

He lifted his head, shouting his rebel yell as loudly as he could. He tried to punch, but his arms had lost their strength and they failed him at the last. More blows came. Another fist smacked into his head and he went down.

They did not let him lie. Hands reached down, hauling him to his feet. He could do nothing as they dragged him away.

He had tried to flee.

And he had failed.

Chapter Seventeen

Jack lay on his back and stared into the blackness. The room Finch's men had dumped him in smelled damp. The stone floor he lay on was cold, and he could feel the chill seeping into his bones. Yet he made no attempt to move.

He did not know how long he lay there. But eventually, almost without conscious thought, his body levered itself into a sitting position. The pain moved with him, each new agony making itself known as a different part of his body came into contact with the cold floor.

He sat there then, letting his mind empty. There was no need to plan or to prepare. It was enough to endure. And to wait for whatever fate had in store for him.

If he were to place a wager, he would bet on Finch leaving him in this dark storeroom until night fell. Then his men would come for him. They would carry out whatever torture Finch was minded to deliver, then slit his throat before hauling his lifeless carcass down to the Thames. There it would be tied to rocks and thrown in the water. It was a common enough fate, the great river that ran through the heart of the metropolis a favourite dumping ground for the bodies that no one wanted to be discovered quickly. The mudlarks found bodies most days, the boys and girls who scavenged along the banks immune to the sight of bloated and putrid remains that they would search for anything of value, no matter the state of decay. It was a sad, ignoble end to any life. And it appeared it would mark the end of his.

The notion stirred something in his mind. He had faced this fate before. There had been times, too many to count, when he had escaped death by no more than a fraction of an inch. Every time there had been fear, even terror. Sometimes hatred and fury had mixed together to fuel a rage so intense that he had confronted his end snarling like an animal. There had been mute servility too, the approach of his death met with docile submission. Now he felt something else, something he could only call sadness. He would face death as he had faced life. He would do what he could, and no more.

He eased himself to his feet, stretching his spine and fighting against the pain. It was time to stand and force life into his flesh so that he was ready to face whatever was to come.

The sound of footsteps reached his ears. They came softly, stopping outside the door to his prison. The scratch of metal moving on metal came clearly, the bolts that secured him inside the room withdrawn with excruciating slowness.

The door opened cautiously. A thin light pushed away the darkness.

'Jack-o?' The name was hissed from the far side of the door. 'Jack-o, are you in there?'

Jack let out the breath he had been holding. As ever, fate was a capricious mistress. She had other plans to the ones he had conjured. Or at least a different path to the same end.

'I'm here.'

'Thank fucking God.' Cooper pushed the door wider. 'Well, come on then, for Christ's sake. We ain't got no time to waste.'

Jack stared at him. The other man looked unscathed save for a large bump that stuck out near his crown from his fall into the yard behind the lodging house. He stared back at Jack, his eyes flickering nervously around him, anxiety written into every pore of his pallid face.

'How the hell did you manage to get away?'

'Ain't no way those stupid buggers could keep me locked up.' Cooper hopped from foot to foot as he glanced around him, excitement and fear combining to keep him moving. 'One of them came in to give me some water. I knocked the stupid bastard out with his own fucking club. He's still lying where I left him, or at least I hope he fucking is. Now come on, before he wakes up and tells them I skipped out on 'em.' He turned, holding the door open, head never still as he checked for anyone approaching.

Jack stepped forward to grab the door before it closed. It hurt to move, but the pain would have to be ignored. He could look to his wounds once he was far away from Finch's clutches.

He slipped out of the room, glancing both ways as he closed the door behind him. They appeared to be in one corner of the great warehouse. The long aisles of packing crates stretched away from him, the rows silent and dark.

Cooper was moving swiftly at a crouch, his boots making barely any sound. Jack followed quickly and quietly until he caught the other man up.

'You know a way out of here?' he whispered.

'No.' The single word came back, barely audible. 'Let's just trust to luck.'

Cooper moved again, darting across an open aisle. Jack followed, crouching low so as to offer as small a target as he could. When they reached the end of the aisle, Cooper stopped suddenly. He stayed crouched low, but turned, a finger pressed to his lips, eyes wide.

Jack squatted down behind him. He heard the voices then, two men conversing quietly as they patrolled the aisles. He held himself still, his hearing focused on the sound. The seconds crawled past with excruciating slowness. The voices became more distinct as the men got steadily closer, and he knew that if they passed the end of that particular aisle, they could not help but see the two fugitives.

He braced himself, holding his muscles tight. If he had to fight, it would be a desperate affair. Every part of him hurt, and he did not know if he could find the strength to land a telling punch. But he would fight regardless.

The voices grew louder. The two guards had to be close now, no more than a couple of yards away.

Jack held his breath. He could hear the scuff of their boots on the floor and even the rustle of their clothing as they moved.

Then the sound changed. The volume of the voices started to decrease, the movements growing muffled. He cocked an ear, straining his hearing as he tried to place the men and understand what was happening. It was then that he heard noises on the other side of the nearest wall of packing crates.

He let out the breath he had been holding. The men had turned down the aisle that ran parallel to the one in which he and Cooper hid. Fate was looking down on them. She had chosen to keep them safe.

'Move.' He whispered the command.

Cooper did not need to be told twice. He set off again swiftly, leaving the aisle and turning away from the men who had come so close to discovering them.

Jack saw where he was going. A doorway was tucked into the corner of the warehouse. They scurried towards it, still keeping low. The door was bolted from the inside. Finch was concerned with ne'er-do-wells breaking in. He had not considered that one day a pair might be trying to break out.

'Thank fuck for that,' Cooper breathed, then turned to Jack, face breaking into a wide grin. 'Let's get out of here, shall we?'

'Wait.' Jack laid a restraining hand on Cooper's shoulder. They had found their way out. But that did not mean they had to leave. At least not yet.

'What are you playing at, Jack-o?' Cooper's voice trembled, his fear revealed.

'Let's leave a little gift for that toothless bastard.' Jack grinned as the idea formed in his head.

Cooper looked at him as if he was quite mad. 'Don't do it, Jack-o. Don't push our sodding luck.'

'Hush now.' Jack waved away his concern and began to search around for what he would need.

The corner of the warehouse was stacked with more of the same hemp sacks they had seen earlier. They were piled up to form dozens of high mounds. Jack approached the closest, laying a hand on the coarse fibres. They were as dry as tinder.

'Jack-o?' Cooper's voice wavered as he hissed the words. 'We need to get out of here before Finch's heavies find us.'

Jack ignored the warning. He was probing at one of the sacks. The contents shifted slightly inside, moving under his touch. 'It's tea,' he murmured. 'Perfect.'

'We don't need a fucking cuppa, Jack-o. We need to get out of here.'

'Shut up.' Jack was fishing in his pockets. He had been searched by Finch's men, but they had been looking for weapons. They had not cared about the nearly empty box of matches nestled at the bottom of one of his jacket pockets. He pulled out the box and shook it, smiling at the familiar rattle of matches moving inside.

'My eye. You ain't thinking to do that, are you now?' Cooper had moved to the door, but he saw what Jack intended. He started to pull back the heavy bolts, ready for their escape.

'I admit it's a terrible waste.' Jack laughed as he opened the box and pulled out a match. He loved tea. He had spent months in the United States without a single mug of the stuff. He had missed it badly, and he could not help feeling a touch of regret as he struck the match and cradled the flame that had sparked into life. 'Open the door, Coops,' he ordered.

Cooper did as he was told, peeking outside to check for anyone nearby.

Jack felt the wash of air rush in, the early-evening breeze chill on his skin. He stepped forward, cupping his free hand around the flame, protecting it from the draught. Then, slowly and carefully, he touched it to the corner of one of the sacks of tea. He held it there, letting the flame lick against the hemp. It caught almost immediately.

'Let's go.' Cooper was turning back and forth as he did his best to watch both Jack and the area outside the doorway. 'Come on now, Jack-o,' he pleaded.

Jack ignored him. He was working quickly now, striking one match after another, moving along the row, lighting one sack in each pile before going on to the next. Already whole sacks were alight, the flames flaring and jumping as they caught the dry leaves and the dust that surrounded them.

He struck his last match. With care, he took it to the pile of sacks closest to the doorway. He bent low, making sure to light the lowest sack in the heap. Only when he was sure that it had caught did he straighten up.

He surveyed his handiwork. Dozens of the tea sacks were alight, with more catching every second. The flames were starting to crackle and roar as they spread. He could feel the heat building.

Another heap of sacks went up with a great *whoomph*. It was enough to make him laugh out loud. It was a splendid sight. A fitting parting gift to repay the beating he had been given.

'For Christ's sake, come on!' Cooper was outside now and holding the door open as he beckoned for Jack to follow. 'You'll be the death of me, you will.'

This time Jack obeyed. As he stepped outside, he heard the first panicked shouts coming from deep within the warehouse.

'Jack-o, you're a fucking madman.' Cooper tugged at his arm, trying to get him to move.

'Oh no, I'm not mad.' Jack grinned. The pain of the beating was fading fast, the thumps and the welts melting away in the heat of the flames. 'I know exactly what I'm doing.' He laughed then, lifting his face to the darkening sky and whooping at the heavens. He had been beaten and threatened with a quiet death.

And he could not remember when he had last felt so alive.

Chapter Eighteen

Outside Cairo, Egypt, 13 February 1868

The train jolted from side to side as it crept along, just as it had done for the past few hours. It was moving at little more than walking pace, yet the locomotive hauling the carriages towards Cairo was making one hell of a racket, the sound reverberating through the entire length of the train. It made for laborious, juddering progress that would have tested the patience of a saint. And none of the four men incarcerated in the tiny compartment was anything close to being a saint.

'I won't fucking tell you again. Get your bloody elbow out of my side before I break your fucking arm.' Cooper shuffled in his seat as he snapped at the man who sat beside him.

'I am doing my best.' Watson squirmed, trying to make space where there was none.

'Then try fucking harder.' Cooper twisted around to lean his head against the dust-streaked window. 'I swear I'll rip your bloody arm right off and beat you to death with it.'

Watson did his best to move away from Cooper, but his progress was blocked by a stack of hardtack biscuit crates that took up the seat to his left. The six-berth space was crammed with luggage, every inch of the racks filled, with still more piled on the floor around their feet.

'Leave him alone, Coops.' Jack came to Watson's defence.

They had only met Macgregor's friend the day they had left London. He did not look like any adventurer Jack had seen before. He was around five and a half feet tall, and slender. He was dressed like a bank clerk, in a sombre morning coat with a pinstriped black and grey waistcoat and dark trousers. His dark brown hair was curled and lay flat against his scalp. Unlike most men of their age, he was clean-shaven, and Jack could see the legacy of a brush with some childhood disease in the pockmarks and scars on his hollow cheeks. His visage was pallid and grey, and his eyes were rimmed with red. It gave him the intense air of a scholar, one who saw little of the outside world.

A foul smell put a grim stop to his inspection of the academic. 'For the love of heaven. Was that you?' He glared at Macgregor, who was pressed close to his right-hand side.

'I cannot help it.' Macgregor's face was flushed as he glowered back at Jack. 'I swear my insides are in tatters.'

'I don't care if you have the fucking flux. Stop bloody farting. It stinks in here, and I am sick of breathing in the smell of your shit.'

'I wish I could stop, I promise you.' Macgregor grinned even as Jack's temper frayed. 'But it is quite beyond me, I'm afraid. I should never have eaten that spicy goat.'

'Then shove a bloody cork up your arse.' Jack turned his face away, burying it in the bandana he wore around his neck. He closed his eyes. There was nothing else to do but sleep and wait for the intolerable journey to be over. They were only a few days into their expedition, yet it was already taking all of his willpower not to commit murder.

They had left London on the morning express to Chatham and taken the boat train to Dover, crossing the Channel to Calais before boarding a train to Paris. They had spent a single day in the French capital, then taken another train to Marseilles. There they had embarked on the steamship *Pera*, arriving in the great port of Alexandria in Egypt that morning.

They had not lingered in Alexandria, going straight to the station, where they had boarded the Cairo train at ten minutes after three. It was scheduled to arrive late that evening. They had tickets for a train to Suez departing early the following morning. That leg of the journey, which once would have taken days of hard slog on a camel train, could now be completed in just a few hours, thanks to the railroad that had been laid between the two strategically vital cities.

Once in Suez, they would try to find passage to Abyssinia. It would not be easy; every ship heading there was under the control of the British army now that the campaign against Tewodros had started in earnest. It would be the first test of Macgregor's bona fides and letters of introduction. He had done well to secure them the very best, his contacts reaching to the highest echelons of the military hierarchy. Their travel papers and documents had been issued by General Sir Thomas Biddulph, Queen Victoria's private secretary, and Macgregor had received a letter of introduction from the Colonel of his former regiment, the 33rd Foot. He had even found them a place with Napier's Field Force, his contacts at Horse Guards securing him a role as an observer tasked with preparing a report on the performance of the new Armstrong guns that had been issued to the artillery batteries accompanying Napier's force, with his three companions listed as assistants. Yet, if all those documents failed to secure them passage, then the four of them would be marooned in Suez, still far short of their objective. There would be nothing else to do save to turn tail and head back home.

'I still think we could have won.' Macgregor was staring idly out of the window when he spoke, breaking the tense silence that had fallen over the compartment. The scenery crept past, a drab, sand-coloured monotone.

'We didn't stand a chance once His Nibs over there started crying,' Cooper pointed out without bothering to look at the man he blamed for the failure.

Watson at least had the decency to blush. 'I was not at fault. That . . .' he paused to select his next word carefully, 'lady was offering me her services and I simply did not want them.'

'You didn't want to fuck her?' Cooper did not beat around the bush. 'I would have. She was a good looker, for a Frog.'

'I am not you.' Watson's reply was haughty.

'No, we know that now, don't we fucking just.' Cooper was scathing. 'I still don't know what you thought was going to bloody happen. The whole point of going to that bloody brothel was to tup the birds.'

'I didn't know that.'

'And she only grabbed your cock, for Christ's sake.' Cooper glared at Watson.

'I was not expecting it.'

'You screamed like a fucking girl.' The verdict was damning.

'But you didn't have to punch her.'

'Of course I fucking did, chum.' Cooper leaned towards Watson. 'I thought she'd knifed you in the ball sack, the fuss you was making.'

'And we still could have won,' Macgregor's urbane tone cut through the discussion, 'if only you had not fallen so fast.' He raised his eyebrows as he looked pointedly at Cooper.

'She had a fucking mallet! I mean, who carries a fucking mallet under their bloody skirts.' Cooper was indignant.

'Well, you'll know for next time.' Watson was supercilious.

'Next time I won't be with you lot of fucking lightweights.' Cooper huffed, settling back against the window, his head banging on the glass as the train jolted. 'I ain't making that bloody mistake again. The next time I wants my comforts, I'll take myself off some place nice and quiet, without any of you bleeding lot getting in the way.'

'There won't be a next time.' Jack put an end to the matter. He was hot, and he stank to high heaven, but he did not mind the discomfort. He had started his soldiering as an infantry-man, and like foot soldiers the world over, he knew how to make the best of things, taking comfort when it was at hand and enduring when it was not. For now, there was nothing to be done. But that did not mean the time spent incarcerated in the tiny compartment could not be put to some use. He sought to divert their attention. 'So, tell me more about this place we're going to.'

'Ah yes, now that is a capital idea.' Watson seized on it with relish. 'I have a map that shows much of where we are going.' He got to his feet, reaching up into his valise, which was on the luggage rack above his head. 'I borrowed it from the museum before I left . . . Ah, yes, there it is.' He retrieved a rolled-up sheet of paper from his case, then sat back down, unrolling the map and spreading it across his lap so that the others could see.

'Here it is. Abyssinia.' He pointed with an ink-stained finger. 'It was once a great empire. Indeed, the current emperor claims to be the descendant of King Solomon and the Queen of Sheba, if you can credit such nonsense. Its northern boundary extends nearly to the Red Sea. By rights, it should have access to the sea, here at the port of Massowa, but that's been controlled by the Ottomans since the sixteenth century. The land runs south,' he moved his finger down the map, 'first across a great plain then into the fabled tablelands, a place of mountains and hidden dells. It is said to be one of the most beautiful places on this earth, but it is also damned dangerous.'

'Go on.' Jack sat forward, as did Macgregor, the pair interested to learn more of the land they were heading towards. Cooper, on the other hand, did not even bother to open his eyes.

'You said it was once a great empire. What happened?' Jack was keen to know more.

'It has long been in decline.' Watson seemed pleased to have an audience, and was warming to the role of lecturer. 'For decades it was nothing more than a patchwork of tiny independent provinces, each one run by a despot; in truth, they were little more than successful thieves and murderers. Then came Tewodros.'

'The Mad King.' Macgregor breathed the words.

'He has been called that, or the Gorilla King, if you prefer. His given name is Kasa Haylu, and he was chieftain of one of the main tribes in Kawra. Just like every chieftain before him, he fought his neighbours, but in his case, he won and then kept on winning. Soon he had a bigger army than anyone else, and he became powerful enough to claim the throne of the whole damn country. He assumed the title of Emperor Tewodros II back in fifty-five. His capital is here at Debre Tabor in the north-west of the country.' Watson pointed to the place on his map.

'It is important to understand that Abyssinia is a Coptic Christian land, although in truth it's a polyglot place. It really is an island in a sea of Musselmen, which suits Tewodros rather nicely as it earns him the attention of people like us. We sent him a consul, originally a fellow called Plowden, and we are not alone. Half the countries of Europe have dispatched an embassy of some description or another. The oddest of them all is the Bishop of Jerusalem, who sent a number of Swiss missionaries. It turns out they also happened to be rather fine gunsmiths. Tewodros set them up at a place called Gafat, not far from his capital, where he has put them to work making weapons. By all accounts, the fellow is absolutely obsessed with cannon, and now these men of God are building them for him.'

'God and guns?' Macgregor quipped. 'An odd mix.'

'Yes, it is rather.' The attempt at humour was lost on Watson. 'Tewodros has even had the missionaries build him an enormous two-foot-calibre mortar that he has called Sevastopol, of all things. Yet not all is happy in his kingdom. Ever since he came to power, he has been fighting to keep what he has won, and he has become utterly ruthless. There are tales coming in from Debre Tabor that quite chill the blood. If they are true, then good old Tewodros has killed hundreds of his own people in retribution for rebellion. He has been raiding into Mahdere Maryam, Karoda, Belessa and Jagur – all loyal heartlands of his kingdom – burning innocents alive and turning on his own in a desperate attempt to cling to power. He has even attacked the great monastery at Mitiraha, a place that he proclaimed to be a safe haven amidst the storm that has engulfed the kingdom for more than a decade. The story has it that he removed all of its valuables, then burned the monks alive in their huts.

'Of course, none of that matters to us. What the bloody savages do to each other is no concern of Her Majesty's government.'

Watson paused to assure himself that his small audience was following. They were. It helped that both Jack and Macgregor were fascinated, and were hanging on his every word.

'Except . . .' he interposed a dramatic pause and looked at them both in turn, 'that back in sixty-three, the madman took some of our people prisoner.'

Jack had heard of the prisoners. He had not had that much time for reading the newspapers – the Babylon had kept him too busy for that – but he knew about the distant despot who had sparked the ire of John Bull. The press had gone wild for it, damning the government this way and that, claiming Tewodros's actions were an absolute outrage, a heinous insult to Britain's status in the world and a threat to the country's reputation. Now Jack found himself caught up in the campaign that would bring the Gorilla King to justice. Only time would tell if the British public would get what they wanted, and if they would still care even if they did.

Chapter Nineteen

'This Tewodros fellow must truly be a mad bugger then.' Jack sought to extend the conversation. Listening to Watson was preferable to sitting staring at the shit-coloured sod-bloody-all that was passing by the window, or listening to Macgregor fart. 'Why on earth would he do that?'

'As I have it, the story is that he wrote to our dear queen in the belief that they were equals. God alone knows where these petty rulers get that sort of rotten idea from, but that's what I heard. He was asking for permission to send us an embassy, so that he could secure our aid in a campaign he was planning against the Egyptians, who continue to cause him all sorts of problems on the coast. I expect he thought it was a foregone conclusion that his sister queen, as he called her, would be only too willing to assist his Christian country in its quarrel against the Muslims in Egypt and the Ottoman Empire that controls the place. Naturally we ignored the letter, although there is a rumour that the blasted thing simply got lost somewhere – you know what civil servants are like.'

Watson rolled up his borrowed map. His small audience sat

back. Outside the carriage window, more of the same dreary scrub rolled past at barely walking pace.

'As I understand the affair,' Watson continued his lecture, 'our friend Tewodros didn't take into account that we are actually much more interested in keeping the Egyptians sweet, so that they continue to supply us with their cotton, than we are in some tinpot dictator in the middle of bloody nowhere. And of course, if we cosy up to the Ottomans, there is always the hope they will act as a bulwark against the damn Russkis. Naturally this put the Gorilla King's nose completely out of joint.

'We were not helped by the fools we have out there. The latest consul, a fellow called Cameron, spent far too long cosying up to the Egyptians, then decided to leave the country entirely without the emperor's permission. Tewodros clapped the stupid bugger in chains. To round things off, some idiot missionary called Stern decided it was a capital idea to call Tewodros's precious mother a whore – or words to that effect – in a book he had written. When good old Tewodros heard that, he rounded up every European he could find, along with their servants and families, and locked them all away. Naturally, we had no choice but to get involved. It took us an age, you know how long it takes to find out what is going on at the ends of the Empire, and of course the foreign office hummed and hawed as they do. But eventually we sent Tewodros an ultimatum. Some middle-ranking foreign officer called Rassam took it to him early in sixty-six, told him to release them or else. So what did the mad bugger do?' Watson offered the question, then answered it for them. 'Why, he took good old Rassam prisoner too!'

He sat back in his seat as if the news astonished him. Neither of the two men listening to him reacted, much to his disappointment. He eased forward again rather sheepishly.

'As I am sure you are aware, last year the decision was made to take the mad bugger out. The mission has been given to the army of Bombay and its commander-in-chief, Lieutenant General Sir Robert Napier. His field force is made up of the newly re-formed native regiments along with a solid core of British regiments. After that monumental cock-up in the Crimea, Napier hasn't spared a single farthing in equipping his army. He has assembled a force of some thirteen thousand fighting men, of which some four thousand are European. The whole field force numbers something close to sixty-two thousand souls in total, and he has collected around thirty thousand mules, donkeys, bullocks, camels and horses to transport them all. He even has forty-four elephants with him, if you can credit it.

'And that is not all. Napier wanted hard currency to purchase supplies and to secure the allegiance of those not loyal to Tewodros. The natives there won't accept anything save for Maria Theresa thalers, and the Crown's agents have scoured Europe buying up every single one they can find. Even that was not enough, and we had to persuade Austria to restart production in exchange for British silver. I have heard they made some two hundred thousand of the things a week to provide enough to satisfy Napier's demands.'

'And all that money will be out there?' Jack began to understand the opportunity that was unfolding in front of him.

'It will.'

'So let's try to get our hands on some of it.' Jack grinned wolfishly. You could take the lad out of Whitechapel, but you would never stop him looking for something to steal.

'It is, perhaps, an option.' Watson's eyes had opened wide at the mention of theft. 'Money is certainly being spent like water. Why, it is estimated that the entire expedition will cost over two million pounds, and some believe it will likely be double that.'

'How much?' For the first time, Cooper opened his eyes. 'Two million quid?'

'Two million pounds indeed. Can you even conceive of such a fortune?' Watson shook his head as if he was quite unable to do so.

'Fucking hell,' Cooper breathed. He sat up straighter, for the first time taking an interest in the conversation.

'The government even added a penny to income tax to pay for the whole thing,' Watson added.

'All for how many people?' Jack asked drily.

'There are four British officials in total. Consul Cameron, that man Rassam and the two men who accompanied him, a Dr Blanc and a Lieutenant Prideaux. Then there is the missionary Stern. I read something of his a few years ago. A book about his wanderings, as he called them.'

'Where is this Mad King holding them?' Jack tried to keep Watson on topic.

'Ah, yes, I forgot one of the finer details of this entire escapade. It is thought that he has taken all the prisoners to Magdala.'

'What is that when it's at home?'

'You have not heard of it? It is a mountain fortress. Impregnable, if the tales are true.'

'Bollocks.' Jack scoffed at the notion. No fortress was safe, not in the modern world of rifled cannon. 'So if I have this right, we've decided to send an army halfway across the globe, at the cost of millions of pounds, all to save a handful of idiots who were stupid enough to allow themselves to be taken prisoner?'

'Them dollar things?' Cooper tapped Watson on the shoulder to get his attention. 'Do you think we can find 'em?'

'There's more than just those to consider.' Macgregor twitched his eyebrows, as if what he was about to say was both daring and deliciously scandalous. 'This Tewodros fellow has accumulated more loot than Crassus.'

'Like what?' Cooper's reply was short and sharp.

'Gold and silver crowns, solid gold chalices, jewellery and religious vessels of every type, all decorated with precious stones; then there are rare coins, maps, books, antiquities . . .' Macgregor exhaled as if exhausted. 'There'll be no shortage of treasure just waiting to be claimed once the Gorilla King has fallen.'

Jack sat back in his seat. It sounded a decent enough plan. The general commanding the campaign, Napier, was clearly not sparing any expense, and it made sense that some of it might find its way into their own pockets. Then there was the native loot. Jack had been to India. He had seen the riches of the country, and he had seen the way most of those riches conveniently found their way into the hands of the officials and officers who were supposedly governing the place. He did not doubt that many men would become rich thanks to the campaign to teach this Tewodros character a lesson. All the four of them had to do was to make sure they were included in that distribution of wealth. The expedition could indeed make them rich. But only if they all played their part. He had no illusions about Watson and Macgregor's ability to fight. When it came to it, it would be down to him and Cooper to do what was needed.

'We should agree the split now.' He spoke softly, his eyes focused on Macgregor. It was time to get down to brass tacks. 'Quarters?'

'No. Half to me. The other half split between you three.'

'Is that fair?'

'Thus far I have paid for everything, so I deserve more than half, but I am inclined to be generous; you are my friends after all.' Macgregor's brow furrowed; for once, he was being serious.

'That's fair, Jack.' Cooper had been taking much more of an interest since the enormous sum of money had been mentioned. 'Means you and me get nearly half between us.'

'Half of nothing is still nothing.' Jack could not help smiling at Cooper's sudden enthusiasm.

'But it won't be nothing, will it? Not with that Napier fellow spending all them silver dollars, and not with all that other stuff just lying around.' Cooper looked at Watson for support. 'You really think there'll be lots of treasure out there?'

'There are fortunes to be made, I am certain of that. Tewodros has collected artefacts from all over the country and beyond. It is said there is an accumulation of wealth not seen since the days of the great pharaohs of Egypt.'

'Blimey.' Cooper was lost for words.

'There will be riches beyond measure.' Watson sat forward, something in Cooper's reaction infectious. 'And they will be ours for the taking.'

'So that's it?' Jack interjected. 'That's what all this is about for you? The money?'

'Need there be more? I need money, I am not ashamed to admit it. I want to further myself and my studies. I can only do that if I have sufficient funds. Just think of what I can achieve if

I am freed from the need to seek employment. I shall also be collecting material for an account of the campaign. It is important that such things are recorded and analysed.'

Jack grunted, unimpressed. But at least Watson was being honest. 'And what about you?' He looked pointedly at Macgregor.

'Is that important?'

'Yes.' Jack would not be denied. 'You don't need the money. He does.' He jerked a thumb at Watson. 'He just admitted that he hasn't got a brass fucking farthing to his name, so I can understand why he has to go, but why are *you* going?'

Macgregor did not reply. So Jack answered for him 'You need something to do. Am I right?'

'Why would I need something to do? I am hardly under-occupied.' Macgregor scoffed at the idea, then laughed as if it were the most preposterous thing he had ever heard. The sound fell flat.

Jack sighed. 'You need something to do because your life bores you.' He looked searchingly at Macgregor. 'This gives you what you want. It gives you purpose.'

For a moment, Macgregor held his stare. Then he looked away. 'You are right. In part, at least. But there is more to it than that.' He spoke earnestly, all trace of banter gone. 'I have never fought.'

'What?'

'I have never fought. I was a soldier, but I never saw a shot fired in anger.'

'But you were in the Crimea.' Jack had seen enough fighting at the Alma to last a man for a lifetime. It had only been the opening scene in the long drama that had been his life, but he was sure there were plenty of other men who had experienced all the action they would ever need on those bloody slopes.

'I arrived late. When it was all done.'

'You said you were in the trenches around Sevastopol.' Jack had left the theatre long before the protracted siege of the Russian Black Sea port, but he had heard of the dreadful fighting that had followed.

'I was.' Macgregor sighed deeply. 'But only afterwards. I'd been sick. Dysentery, would you believe. I missed the whole affair.'

'Lucky you.'

'No.' His denial was firm. 'I am something of a fraud, Jack. This is my chance to put that right. To do something real. To create a true tale for once, rather than all those lies I tell.' He hung his head at the admission. 'I have money, I admit. But nothing more.'

'You're bottle-head stupid.' Jack rolled his eyes. But he understood. He knew what it was like to want to prove your-self. He had changed the course of his own life to prove he could be as good an officer as any of those born with a silver spoon in their mouth. Macgregor wanted something similar.

'What about you, Jack?' Macgregor turned the tables. 'Why do you want to join our expedition?'

'You know why.'

'To escape? Is that all? You're a clever man. I believe you could stay one step ahead of even the finest detectives from Scotland Yard without giving it much thought. Why go all the way to Abyssinia to avoid them?'

'It's time to get away.'

'Ah, yes, there it is. You said I have no purpose in life, and that I need this trip to add something to my otherwise dull and meaningless existence. But isn't the truth of it that you are searching for something similar? You have told me something of your travels. Yet despite wandering from one side of the globe to the other, you have never managed to find a place you can call home.' Macgregor watched for Jack's reaction as he voiced the truth as he saw it. 'You crave excitement and so you create situations that give you a taste of what you are missing. That's why you play around town with me, and I should not be surprised if this horrible little situation you find yourself in now was really of your own causing, as you seek to end the boredom in any way possible.'

'You suddenly know an awful lot about me.'

'And you have said more these past days than you have in the whole of the last year.' Macgregor frowned. 'I think I am only truly getting to know you now.'

Jack wiped his hand across his close-cropped hair. 'Perhaps.' He could not deny all that Macgregor had said, and it was a truth that made him feel uncomfortable, for he had yet to fully admit it even to himself. He had not sought the disaster that had engulfed his life, but now that it had arrived, did he feel something that could be excitement? He was like a blind man given a momentary glimpse of light. It did not matter how that miracle had arrived. It was a hint of what could be, and that hint, no matter how fleeting, was everything.

'What of you, Cooper?' Macgregor wanted the last gap filled, and so he turned to look across at the man by the window.

'I'll go wherever Jack goes.' Cooper sniffed loudly as he gave the clipped answer. 'He looked after me when I had nothing. So now I look after him.' He shifted in his seat, clearly uncomfortable at being brought into the conversation. 'I'm his man. Now and always.'

'How very dedicated.' Macgregor looked delighted at the answer. 'What have you done to earn such unwavering loyalty, Jack?'

'He has nothing else. Not now. If he'd stayed in London, he'd have been back on the streets – if Finch's lads or the peelers hadn't nabbed him when they couldn't find me.' Jack glanced at Cooper as he spoke. They had met when the younger man had tried to pick Jack's pocket. Jack had broken three of Cooper's fingers for his trouble, but he had still offered him a job. Cooper was the first man he had employed. Not once in the three years of their acquaintance had they spoken of anything other than the matter at hand. Yet here Cooper was, declaring unswerving devotion. To Jack's surprise, he found it rather humbling. But there was something else, something much meaner of spirit, that had flashed across his mind as soon as Cooper had answered Macgregor's question. It was something akin to annoyance. He did not want another man's life in his hands, not Cooper's, not anyone's. He wanted to be beholden to no one but himself. He wanted to be free.

'So, there we have it.' Macgregor looked pleased with himself. 'A penniless academic seeking a fortune. A man with nothing, following his master to stay off the streets. A man with every advantage in life, seeking to make his own name at last. And a wanted man who has travelled the world and yet cannot find a place he can call home. Oh, we are a fine team, a fine team indeed.'

'We all sound rather desperate.' Watson spoke for the first time in a while.

'I do believe we are.' Macgregor laughed as soon as he said the words. 'The four desperadoes. I think that makes us sound quite splendid.'

Jack grunted to acknowledge the summary. It was a fitting description. The four men all had their own reasons to go to Abyssinia. Only time would tell if any of them would find what they were looking for.

Chapter Twenty

Suez, 16 February 1868

*J*ack sat comfortably in the rattan and cane armchair and shook out the previous week's *Times*. It was refreshingly cool in the hotel's lounge, the pankha-walas stationed around the room doing a fine job of moving the large sail attached to the ceiling back and forth. The breeze it created wafted around the half-dozen guests enjoying a leisurely morning in the bright, airy lounge with its open terrace facing towards the coast.

They had arrived in Suez hot, bad-tempered and stinky. All three discomforts had faded fast thanks to the grandeur of the Suez Hotel, where Macgregor had paid for a suite for each of them. The very next morning, he had secured them berths on the steamship *Koina*, which would sail on the tide the following day. They had been allocated two cabins by a British major called Stansfield, who was in charge of travel from Suez to Annesley Bay and the port constructed by an advance party of Royal Engineers on the Red Sea coast that had become the landing point for all men and material arriving in Abyssinia.

Stansfield had even managed to find each of them a horse, along with two mules for their supplies; all those animals were to be berthed on the *Sam Cearns*, a transport ship that would be towed behind the *Koina*.

Macgregor had not been content to rest on his laurels. He had hired a trio of servants to tend to the animals, or at least he had succeeded at the second time of asking. The first servants he had hired had run off with the month's pay he had given them in advance. It had been a chastening experience, and Jack had made sure that the second group of servants received nothing save for a stern warning of the fate they faced if they absconded.

Jack lowered his newspaper and reached for the white porcelain teacup that sat on the silver tray alongside the remains of his breakfast on the table in front of him. He lifted it to his lips and sipped at the pale gold liquid. It tasted insipid, but it was still a good way to start the day.

He had just settled back in his chair again when the sound of someone arriving in the lounge caught his attention. He looked up to see a red-faced Cooper slipping through the neat arrangement of chairs and table. He was trying to move briskly, but was managing to do little more than ricochet from table to table, the sound of the furniture being knocked and dragged across the floor capturing the attention of most of the lounge's clientele.

'You'd think they could leave a fucking path between the bloody tables.' He slipped into the chair opposite Jack's and stared keenly at his master.

'You'd think you'd know not to barge around the place like a bloody elephant.' Jack looked at his companion. Cooper's skin was glistening, his face running with sweat. 'Here.' He handed across a white linen napkin from his tray. 'You look like you've been for a swim.'

'I've been saving our bleeding lives, that what I've been doing.' Cooper took the napkin and wiped it across his face. It came away damp and streaked with dirt.

'What the hell do you mean?' Jack did not need such drama so early in the morning. With a sigh, he folded *The Times* and tossed it on the table.

'Finch is here in Suez.'

'What?' Jack sat forward at the news. It was not what he had expected to hear, not at all. 'Why the hell would he be here?'

'How should I know?' Cooper saw the expression on Jack's face and looked away.

Jack could scarcely credit the news. He glanced around the room. All was serene and peaceful, the other guests sipping at their morning tea or coffee. The only sounds were the gentle murmur of polite conversation alongside the soft scratching of the ropes on the room's sail as they moved back and forth. It seemed impossible that Finch was nearby.

He watched Cooper carefully. The younger man was shifting around on the edge of his chair. He was clearly anxious, frightened even, but there was something else, something more discomforting than mere concern. 'What have you done, Coops?'

'Nothing.'

'Cooper?'

'I ain't done nothing, Jack, I promise.' For a fleeting second, Cooper glanced across at Jack, then he looked away again.

Jack's mind was running fast. 'Why would Finch come all this way?' He spoke the question aloud, even though it was more for himself than for Cooper.

'Does it matter? He's here now and he's got half a dozen of his blokes with him.'

'But how the hell did they know where we were going?' Ideas were forming in Jack's mind. They were mean ones. Notions of treachery and betrayal. 'Unless someone told them.'

'Who knows? Maybe they found out for themselves.' To his credit, Cooper managed to meet Jack's glare.

'Or maybe you told them.' Half-formed ideas coalesced. 'You told him where we were going, didn't you, Coops?'

'I didn't think he'd fucking come after us, did I?' Cooper's defence fell faster than a whore's drawers. 'They was going to slit my gizzard back in that fucking warehouse. So I blabbed. I know I shouldn't have, Jack-o, but I told them all about what we was going to do. They didn't let me go, though, I promise you that. I escaped, just like I told you. I just bought myself some time.' He was babbling as he tried to tell the whole story at once. 'You know me, Jack-o. I'm your man. Not anyone else's. You took me in and gave me a chance. I ain't ever going to forget that. That's why I came for you. I could've run, could've got myself out of there. But I didn't, did I? I came and rescued you.'

'You bloody fool.' Jack shook his head, but he reckoned Cooper was telling the truth. It even made a sort of sense. Finch would have been apoplectic when he discovered that Jack and Cooper had got away. Worse, the man who had knocked his teeth out had then burned down his warehouse. The twin blows would have hurt and his reputation would have been badly damaged. The only way to redeem the situation and restore his reputation would be to find Jack and kill him. Jack could see how it could be worth travelling halfway across the world to do that.

'Did he see you?' He fired off the question.

'No, shit, at least I don't think so.' Cooper looked like he was about to bawl. 'I never thought for a bleeding second that he would come all this way.'

Jack sucked down a deep breath, controlling his emotions. 'What's done is done.'

'So what are we going to do?'

'Do? We're going to do nothing, save keep out of the bastard's way. At least you spotted him before he spotted you. He might know where we're going, but that doesn't mean he knows we're here right now.' Jack sat back in his chair. The alarm he had felt at first hearing Cooper's news was beginning to subside. If all that Macgregor had told him was true, it had to be highly unlikely that Finch would be able to get a berth for him and his cronies on the overcrowded transports heading to Abyssinia. 'We've just got to keep our heads down whilst we're here in Suez. Once we get out to the campaign, we should be fine.'

'What if he follows us out there too?'

'He won't be able to. He doesn't have any of the papers he'll need.' Jack felt his nerves settle. They were leaving Suez the following morning. 'We just keep off the streets until we head to the docks tomorrow.'

'So you think it'll be all right then?' Cooper sought reassurance.

'Yes, it'll be fine. Just stay inside. And no more telling anyone where we're bloody going, you got that?'

'Yes, Jack-o.' Cooper sighed with relief.

Jack picked up *The Times* and made a show of settling back in his chair. It was not good that Finch had come after them, not good at all. But it was not a disaster, far from it. All they had to do was avoid the man for the rest of today, then they would be on a steamer bound for Abyssinia. And there was nothing Finch could do to follow them.

'Order us some more tea, there's a good fellow. Oh, and see if they can rustle up some fried eggs.' Jack gave the instructions, then turned his attention back to his newspaper. It would be a long day sitting in the hotel, but he would do his best to make himself comfortable.

Chapter Twenty-one

—————•·◆·•—————

Annesley Bay, Abyssinia, 25 February 1868

It was still dark when they boarded the lighter. The small vessel bobbed up and down in the swell that surged around the side of the steamer, so that it made for a constantly moving target for the men clambering down the rope ladders towards it. The descent down the side of the steamer was a treacherous one. Jack took his time, placing his feet carefully. He could smell the rope, the damp stink of salty hemp filling his nostrils as he moved gingerly, the skin on his palms already burning from where he held the ropes tight.

They had left Suez just over a week before. It had been a dull, uneventful voyage, but at least it had got them away from Finch. Jack had seen neither hide nor hair of the man from the East End, and he began to doubt that Cooper had actually clapped eyes on him at all. It would not be the first time that Cooper had exaggerated a tale. Jack could well believe that he had seen a man who bore a passing resemblance to Finch and let his fertile imagination run away with him. Either way, the moment they had boarded the *Koina*, they had been safe. Finch could not follow them any further. Not without bona fides signed by someone of at least the rank of general. The thug would have his connections, but Jack doubted they stretched to the upper echelons of the British army.

He put all thoughts of Finch aside as he took his seat on the lighter, doing his best to quell the rush of nausea that surged into his stomach as the small boat wallowed in the swell. He had never been a good sailor, so he ignored the other passengers scrambling down to their places and looked up into the dark night sky, trying to fix on a point that was not moving around. Dawn was not far off, but the sky was still filled with a legion of stars that spread across the heavens, the hundreds of bright dots casting a serene light down onto the chaos of the British landings.

'Hold tight. We're casting off!' The midshipman charged with sailing the lighter to the shore called out the warning as his crew began to let loose the lines that held the little boat against the side of the steamer.

Jack took a deep breath and lowered his gaze. The bay was filled with ships, and every one was lit up, the illumination casting light across the water. The yellowish glow caught the waves that surged around the vessels, adding an enchanting touch to the scene, though it was totally lost on Jack, who was doing his best to hold on to the early breakfast he had consumed an hour before they had disembarked from the *Koina*. Yet it was still an impressive display, one that revealed the British Empire's ability to project its influence into even the remotest part of the globe. Jack had never seen so many ships in one place. They had assembled for one purpose and one purpose only: to demonstrate the power of the British and secure the freedom of the prisoners the foolish Gorilla King had dared to seize.

He held on to his seat for dear life as the lighter slipped away from the steamer. The motion was sickening, the boat rolling this way and that. It only steadied when the crew lowered their oars into the waves and began to pull, turning the bow towards shore.

Ahead, the shoreline was covered in mist. Some light filtered through the murk, the beacons set up to guide the ships towards shore taking on an unearthly quality as they burned through the ever-shifting fog. To the east and west, bright navigation beacons shone out from the islands of Shumma and Dissee, and more had been placed to mark out the dangerous shallows where coral reefs lurked to tear out the bottom of any ships that strayed too far from the main channel. The Royal Navy had been quick to bring order to this forgotten bay. They had stamped their mark on the place, filling it with buoys and light to ensure the safety of the hundreds of ships that had brought Napier's army to this deserted coast.

The lighter picked up pace as the crew warmed to their task. Jack could feel the power thrumming through the little vessel as it surged through the waves. For the first time, he felt some of his discomfort shift. The breeze washed across his face, salt already drying on his skin. The damp, piss-reeking air of the steamer was scoured away, replaced by the clean tang of the sea and by something else, something warmer and earthier. They were still far from shore, but he could already smell the land, and it drew him in like the landlubber he was.

The lighter altered course, heading towards a pier that stretched out across the shallows. A second was still under construction. To Jack's eye, they looked like a pair of long fingers pointing out into the bay, standing proud of the yellow surf that frothed along their length. Both were at least three hundred yards long, their bases made from the local coral, a hint of its former vibrant colour still just about visible. A double line of rails had been laid along the length of the fully constructed pier, and despite the ungodly hour, trucks were already moving back and forth, laden with stores and ammunition being unloaded from a transport ship docked there.

At the foot of the pier, he could see what looked to be a commissariat yard. Great stacks of pressed hay stood alongside packing crates arranged into mountains and grain bags heaped into tall piles. Behind them all, a White Ensign flew from a flagpole. To the rear of the commissariat yard were a dozen wooden buildings and storehouses, and behind them, hundreds of bell tents and larger marquees. The British were establishing a small town where there had once been nothing but sand.

Beyond the encampment, Jack could just make out the rest of the narrow coastal plain. The mist that shrouded much of the shore prevented him from seeing the first ridge of the plateau that he had been told was some twenty miles distant. Far beyond were the mountain ranges that would have to be crossed if they were to join the rest of Napier's army as it marched inland. For just a moment, he felt something akin to excitement as he thought of the wild lands that would have to be crossed on the way to Tewodros's fortress at Magdala. They had come a long way to reach this point. Now it was time for the anticipation to end, and for long-held plans to be put in motion. It was time to start their own campaign.

The little lighter slowed and immediately began to roll from side to side as the swell pushed against it. All notions of what was to come were forgotten as the urge to vomit surged through him. It took all of his willpower to swallow it down. The lighter wallowed where it was as the midshipman waited for his moment. The wait went on far too long for Jack's liking, but then the young officer gave the command and the boat surged forward, the men at the oars pulling for all they were worth. The lighter bucked and lurched, the sailors calling out the rhythm as their long oars dipped and pulled through the rougher water near the shore. The land came towards them in a rush, and for one stomach-lurching moment, the boat lifted as it rode a wave towards the beach, then crashed down, rushing forward at a breathtaking speed before the bottom caught the gravel at the shore's edge. The wild ride came to a neck-cracking halt, the lighter grounding with a great screech. Then it went mercifully still, the little vessel stuck fast.

'Out you get, you bloody landlubbers.' A burly matelot laughed at his pale passengers, who still clutched their seats in fear.

It took Jack a moment to force his hands to release their grip on the damp wood of his seat. Then he was up and away, grabbing his carpet bag and moving quickly, his desire to be back on firm land forcing strength into his shaking legs.

He went over the side and dropped into the shallows. The water surged around his ankles, cold and wet, and for a moment he thought his legs might give way completely. Then he found his footing and began to trudge ashore, lifting his bag high so that it would not get soaked. All around him, the other passengers were doing the same, staggering and lurching as they struggled to adjust to being back on land.

As Jack splashed his way ashore, dozens of men waded out to the lighter. The men, all natives of Bombay, swarmed around the small ship, hands reaching for the luggage that had come along with the passengers.

'Keep out of the way, gentlemen, if you please.' A British

soldier stood on the shore in his shirtsleeves, shouted the instruction at the lighter's passengers. His accent came straight from the Yorkshire Dales. It was a welcome reminder that though they might be hundreds of miles from home, they were still in the midst of a great British endeavour.

Jack staggered up the beach, boots digging great divots from the sodden sand as he went. Only when he was far from the water did he stop to set his carpet bag down. It was a relief to feel solid ground under his feet, even if his body still lurched this way and that as if he were still aboard the steamer.

Macgregor came to stand next to him, his own portmanteau dumped without ceremony. He was beaming with excitement. 'We made it.'

'Just.' Jack gave the one-word answer as he looked for the others. All four men had dressed ready for the campaign, choosing lightweight khaki jackets and trousers, with air pipe helmets covered with white cloth. He spotted Cooper easily enough as he waded through the last of the shallows, cradling his valise in his arms. Watson followed, his slight figure buffeted by the waves at the shore's edge so that he staggered in a meandering zigzag towards them.

'And so it begins.' Jack whispered the words as much to himself as to Macgregor. It felt good to be back on dry land. Yet any excitement he felt was tempered with something else, something darker. He had taken part in many campaigns, and here he was at the start of another. None had ever gone as he expected. Now he stood on the beach, his legs damp and cold, the mist clammy on his face, wondering which of them would see this bay again, and which would die, their body left forever on a foreign land so very far from home.

Chapter Twenty-two

———◦•◦———

'Good morning to you, gentlemen.'

Jack looked up sharply as their small group was greeted by a young officer in a scarlet shell jacket. The sight brought him up short. The officer was a reminder that he was with the British army again after so many years away from it. He might not be wearing a red coat of his own, but he was struck with a sudden feeling of being back where he belonged.

'All new arrivals need to report in,' the officer explained. 'So if you will follow me . . .' He gestured away from the shore.

Jack picked up his carpet bag, hefting the weight. The officer looked little more than a boy to his eyes. He was trying to grow a set of sideburns, but he was clearly struggling, the pale hair on his jaw patchy and thin. The sight was enough to make Jack smile. He was still two years short of forty, but the officer's youth make him feel rather old.

Nothing was said as the four men followed the officer away from the sea. The shore was filled with activity as more lighters came ashore from the other ships anchored in the bay. Each one was met by a reception committee. Naval officers controlled the first rush, their loud voices snapping the orders that saw their shore teams dash out into the surf to secure the newly landed craft. Then it was the turn of the army. Non-commissioned officers brayed orders to long lines of soldiers, who plunged into the churning waters to start the process of unloading the lighters. It was wonderfully organised chaos, the Royal Navy and the army bringing order out of confusion.

The young officer led them at a brisk pace into the encampment proper. Jack was struck by the sheer scale of the endeavour he had joined. Stores were piled everywhere, most of them hidden away under great sheets of canvas. Even though it was still not yet dawn, more men were hard at work. Red-faced British soldiers in their shirtsleeves worked alongside long lines of dark-faced sepoys as they began the herculean task of moving the supplies inland. Supervising them were a number of British sergeants and corporals, the NCOs looking smart in their red coats paired with grey trousers and white helmets. Their short, sharp shouts of command echoed off the piles of supplies, their accents coming from all over the British Isles. Alongside them were the subadars and havildars from the native regiments, their orders given in the same tone of command, even though they were delivered in a language Jack did not understand.

Underscoring the shouts of the soldiers were the noises of thousands of animals. Any inch of ground not taken up by supplies or tents was sectioned off into holding pens for the camels, horses, mules, ducks, geese, pigs and cockerels that had been transported here from all over the Empire. Every single one was making a noise as dawn approached, and the air resounded to the brays, honks, hisses and screeches of the beasts whose lives had been bound to the campaign.

'I wonder if we shall see Noah himself.' Macgregor made the wry remark as he walked at Jack's side.

Jack switched his carpet bag from hand to hand before he replied. 'I thought he only brought the animals in two by two. If he is here, it's clear he can't bloody count.'

'And I suppose he would need a pretty damn big ark to transport this lot. I have never seen so many animals in one place,' Macgregor sounded impressed. 'Or smelled them.' He wrinkled his nose as if disgusted by the ripe aroma of animal dung that hung heavy in the misty morning air.

'No. Me neither.' Jack looked across at Macgregor. For all his jokey banter, he could sense his friend's unease. He understood it. They were a long way from home. Their passage had taken days, and it had kept them busy, their minds always set on the next leg of the journey and on reaching their destination. Now they were here, and there was a feeling of anticlimax at having arrived, alongside an odd sense of unease.

'Don't you think it looks just like Varna?' Jack asked the question as much to distract as anything.

'A little.' Macgregor glanced around him. 'But I don't see any piles of corpses, do you?'

'If they're here, they're well hidden.' Jack kept his tone deadpan.

'I don't smell death.' Macgregor caught Jack's eye, then looked away. 'Perhaps we have finally learned our lesson. It really does not do to kill half the chaps before we even start the march.'

Jack said nothing more. The encampment at Varna had been the staging post for the troops on the way to the Crimea, and it had been a death trap. He himself had not been there long, but he knew Macgregor had spent some time there, and he had heard enough tales to know of the disgusting conditions that had decimated the army's ranks long before any regiment had taken the field. He had thought about Varna often on the voyage from Suez, wondering if he was sailing towards another hellhole where more men would die from disease than would be killed on the field of battle. So far he saw no sign of it, and Macgregor was right, there was no smell of death. Just the ripe stink of animal dung. It boded well.

'Right then, gentlemen, straight inside, if you please.' The young officer had brought them to a large bell tent, and now indicated that the new arrivals should go straight through the open flaps. 'Major Talbot will help you from here.'

'Thank you.' Jack nodded, then stood back, gesturing for Macgregor to go first. 'After you.'

'Thank you.' Macgregor turned to look back at Cooper and Watson. 'Do come along, you two, no damn dawdling back there.' The command was snapped before Macgregor plunged inside the bell tent.

Jack followed. The tent smelled of damp canvas, ink and sweat. It was brightly lit by lanterns and contained three desks arranged in a U shape. All three were covered with stacks of thick leather-bound ledgers and an inordinate number of papers arranged in chaotic swirls and heaps. At least half a dozen officers were hard at work, some seated at the desks, others working on crates spread around the periphery of the tent. As the newcomers entered, an officer bustled out, a thick sheaf of paperwork held purposefully in one hand.

'One moment, if you please.' One of the officers seated at the desks called out as the four men loitered near the tent's opening. 'I shall be with you directly.' He was poring over a ledger, a pencil quickly ticking a list.

After a moment, he signed his name, then tossed the pencil onto the desk before handing the ledger to an officer standing at his side.

'Now then.' He turned his attention to the waiting men. 'Good morning, gentlemen. My name is Major Talbot. I have the pleasure of welcoming all newcomers.' He smiled without any sign of pleasure in his expression. 'May I see your papers, please.'

'Certainly.' Macgregor fished inside his portmanteau and produced a small pile of letters, which he placed in front of Talbot.

'I thank you.' The thanks were given curtly, the officer already reaching for the papers. He studied them briefly, then glanced up.

'It says here you are to be attached to General Napier's intelligence department as observers.'

'That is correct.' Macgregor preened ever so slightly.

'Well, your paperwork is all in order, which is something of a rarity these days.' Talbot shuffled the papers together, then handed them back to Macgregor. 'Lieutenant Osborne will show you to a spare tent for today. There is a party leaving for Koomaylee tomorrow morning. You can join them.'

'Where is General Napier?' It was Jack who asked the question.

'He left a month ago. You will have the devil's own job to catch up with him; the old man is going to be moving fast, and he has a good head start on you.'

'What about the rest of the army?'

'Alas, they are not moving so quickly. The chaps in the Royal Engineers and the Bombay Sappers are working hard to make the route passable, but it is no easy task. They are labouring day and night to establish a railway line all the way to Senafe, with a field telegraph line to go along with it. Yet despite the difficulties of the terrain, the head of the main column should be past Antalo by now; that's over two hundred miles from where we now stand.'

'Two hundred miles?' Cooper could not hide his astonishment.

'It is the best part of four hundred miles to Magdala.'

'Bugger me.'

'Has there been any fighting?' Jack asked the question quickly, distracting Talbot from Cooper's choice reply.

'There has not been a shot fired, to my knowledge.' Talbot scowled at Cooper as he spoke. 'At least not at the enemy. The chaps are enjoying the sport, though. Plenty of game to hunt, if that is your bag.'

'How many sick?'

'None.'

'None?' It was Jack's turn to show his disbelief.

'Not a single one.' Talbot looked at him sharply, his eyes picking out the scar on his face. 'It beggars belief, does it not? But this is not the Crimea, or India, for that matter. We have not lost a single man.'

'Unbelievable.' Jack did not hold back his astonishment.

'It cannot last.' Talbot lifted a hand to ward off another officer who had come to stand at his side with a fresh ledger in his hand. 'But Napier is doing all he can to avoid being brought to battle. He is meeting the King of Tigre as soon as is possible. It is his land the column must pass through on its way to Magdala, where that devil the Gorilla King is holed up with the prisoners. If Napier secures an accord, the hope is that the column will be able to reach Magdala without having to fight at all.'

'Do you think he will be successful?'

'I see no reason why not. These petty kings have no love for

Tewodros. He has attacked them ruthlessly over the years, and they will likely believe they can only profit if he falls. If Napier can convince them that we are here merely to secure the release of our people, then I do not see why they should choose to interfere with our plans.'

'And then what?'

'Well, I cannot imagine Tewodros will give up the prisoners without a fight. Not after all this. They say the fellow is quite mad. He will want to try out all those bloody cannons of his, and the people he has with him are quite devoted to him. They must be, or else they would have abandoned him by now; they have had every chance.'

'So there will be a battle?' Jack pressed.

'Of course.' Talbot looked deadly serious. 'It will be no easy task. Tewodros's mountain fortress at Magdala is said to be impregnable. But Napier knows what he is about. He has said that he will not engage until he is absolutely prepared, and I do not doubt his word. Now, if you will excuse me, I'm afraid I must get on. I wish you all God's speed, gentlemen.'

Jack nodded and made to leave Talbot's tent, gesturing for the others to follow. It was the answer he had sought. One thing was now clear. The Mad King Tewodros would not back down, not now. So there would be a battle, and if the tales of the mountain fortress at Magdala were even half true, it would be a bloody one.

Chapter Twenty-three

———◆•◆———

*J*ack peered into the bell tent they had been allocated. It was filthy dirty and reeked. Worse, hundreds of small black insects scurried across the groundsheet that covered the floor. There were enough of them to make a soft scratching sound.

'Looks like this one is occupied.' He made the observation to his companions then ducked inside. The smell became worse – sun-warmed canvas mixed with rotten feet.

'Good Lord.' Macgregor followed Jack inside, then recoiled as the full force of the ripe aroma hit him. 'They expect us to sleep here?'

'It's just for the one night.' Jack looked around the tent, choosing his spot. He selected one furthest from the tent flap, away from draughts, where he would not be disturbed by anyone coming and going during the night, then dumped his carpet bag without ceremony. It thumped down hard, crushing a hundred small black bodies beneath it.

'What a horrible abode.' Watson had followed the others inside and now stood in the centre of the tent, turning around in a slow circle as he tried and failed to find a place that took his fancy. 'Do remind me what we are doing here.'

'Just think of the treasure we will find,' Macgregor answered glibly.

'It appears that all we shall find is lice.' Watson could not hide his feelings.

'Like it or lump it, chum.' Cooper was the last of them in. He made a quick survey of his new surroundings, then dropped his portmanteau opposite Jack's. 'I've slept in worse places.'

'I'm sure you have,' Watson observed, then sighed. 'It is not how I imagined it would be.'

'It's a damn sight better than *I* thought it would be,' Jack replied as he undid his bag and began to rummage inside.

'Truly?' Watson still refrained from placing his own bag on the groundsheet. 'I cannot imagine anything ghastlier than this.'

'Then you have a poor imagination.'

Jack's carpet bag did not look like much. Its sides were stained by salt and damp, and the whole thing was scuffed and battered from long, hard use. He had stored it away these past five years at a pawnbroker near Drury Lane, only retrieving it the morning they left London. A stale smell had been released when he opened it, one tainted with the stink of gun oil and grease. Now he reached inside and pulled out a holster and gun belt, the leather worn and stained almost black. He placed this to one side before he delved deeper, pushing past the cardboard boxes of cartridges and the paraphernalia of weapon care he had accumulated over the years until his hand clasped around the familiar shape of a revolver. The weapon was kept in a cloth sack, the material soft under his touch. He pulled it out, holding it carefully, then undid the drawstrings and withdrew the battered Navy Colt revolver within.

The weapon had not been meant for him. It had been a gift

to another man, but Jack had coveted it since the first moment he had seen it. When that man had died, he had claimed it for his own. It was not much to look at. Not any more. The metal was dulled, and there was no hiding the scars, scratches and dents that were etched deep into it. The ivory grips had darkened, so they now looked browner than the warm cream they had been when the weapon was new.

He had no notion of how many times he had fought with the Colt, or how many men he had killed with it. Yet standing there in the musty tent, the weight of it in his hand felt reassuringly familiar. He could feel the power in the weapon. It was a reminder of the man he had been, and of the man he could be again.

He placed the Colt on the floor, then delved back into the carpet bag. Lying on the very bottom was his sword. Unlike the revolver, the sword was ordinary, just one of hundreds manufactured at the Nashville Plow Works for the Confederate army before it had fallen to the Union forces as they pushed ever further south into Tennessee. He drew it out, holding it vertical so he could check the blade for damage. Its smell resonated deep within him. There were those who believed the weapon was an anachronism, a reminder of an old way of fighting. Yet he had fought with a revolver in his left hand and a sword in his right more times than he could remember. The weapons completed him. They made him the soldier he would always be.

The blade was fine, but in need of a sharpen. When he could, he would find an armourer and pay for a new edge. But for now, he would leave the weapon behind. He carefully put the sword back into the carpet bag, then picked up the Colt.

'Do you think you'll need that here?' Macgregor was watching him closely.

'You never know.' Jack dug into the bag for a fresh cardboard packet of cartridges and another filled with percussion caps, then sat down and began the process of filling each of its six chambers.

'Oh my.' Watson was looking at him as he loaded the weapon. 'Should I get mine out?'

'Up to you.' Jack pushed in the first of the paper cartridges, then rammed it home with the revolver's loading lever. 'But I reckon you might want it if some Abyssinian fellow comes at you with his spear. Do you remember how to load it?'

'Right, yes, I think so.' Watson tried to find his resolve. He finally chose a place, and put his portmanteau down carefully before opening it and retrieving his own gun, a five-round Beaumont–Adams cap-and-ball double-action revolver that fired a heavy 54-bore bullet.

'It feels strange, does it not?' Macgregor spoke as he settled his belongings. 'I mean, we spent so long getting here. It is hard to credit that we have actually arrived.'

'It's what you paid all that money for.' Jack was nearly done with his revolver. He looked up, shaking his head as he saw Watson working slowly and carefully to load his own handgun. He had trained the academic in its use, both how to load and how to shoot, but no matter how many times they had practised, Watson was still dreadfully slow. Cooper was hardly any better, the Londoner treating his revolver as if it was as dangerous to him as it was to any potential enemy. Jack had done his best with them both, but it did not bode well if they did have to use the weapons for real.

Watson had laid the five cartridges in a neat line on the floor in front of him then pulled out a packet of percussion caps that he placed down next to them. He began working slowly and methodically through the process, his face creased into a frown as he concentrated on the unfamiliar routine. Jack bit his tongue. It would be easy to snap at the man and urge him to speed up. God alone knew what would happen if they ever had to fight and Watson had to reload under fire. But such warnings now would do nothing but put the wind up the academic, who was more used to the quiet, calm confines of a museum than he was to the campaign trail.

'Do you not feel anything, Jack?' Macgregor was looking at him, his eyes searching his face. 'My stomach is in my boots.'

'You're probably just hungry.' Jack met his stare calmly. He would not admit it, but he did feel the first stirring of old emotions deep in his gut. Parts of him that had lain dormant were now awakening.

'I am most certainly not hungry, I can assure you of that.' Macgregor harrumphed at the very idea. 'I could not eat a thing. Quite the opposite, in fact.'

'Then go outside, find the latrine and take a shit.' Jack grinned. He could not help it. Macgregor's discomfort only added to his own feeling of well-being. He was back where he belonged.

'Will you be this dour the whole time?' Macgregor tried to make light of Jack's mood.

'Will you keep asking such stupid questions?' Jack loaded the last chamber then reached for the percussion caps that he began to fit in place.

'I am making conversation.'

'Then talk to Watson. He likes to chit-chat.'

'I am talking to you.'

'In that case, say something interesting.'

'So you feel nothing? No apprehension? No concern? No unease?'

'Of course I do. I worry all the time.'

'Ha! Thank goodness, you are human after all.' Macgregor clapped his hands as if he had just made a great discovery.

Jack shook his head at the display. 'I worry you will slow me down. And I worry Johnny-slow-coach over there will get me killed.'

Macgregor's face fell. 'You are being harsh.'

'And you are croaking like a damned frog.' Jack sucked down a deep breath, then stood up, holstering his freshly loaded revolver. The weight of the weapon sat nicely on his right hip. 'I'm going out for a bit,' he announced.

Without waiting for an answer, he left the tent, followed by Cooper. It was time to learn more about their surroundings and about the campaign they were joining.

The two men walked through the encampment. Neither spoke.

The sun had risen, and although it was still early, it was already uncomfortably hot, the air damp and muggy despite their proximity to the sea. Jack could feel the sweat already starting to run down his spine, and he knew he would honk terribly by the day's end. The thought struck him as funny. He had become soft in London. The years of sleeping in a comfortable bed, with a roof over his head and a good-looking woman at his side, had blunted his edges. Now he would have to become accustomed to his own stink, just as he would have to readjust to the harsh, uncomfortable realities of life on campaign, a life without regular food and dinners in fine restaurants.

The encampment had come to life. Jack looked this way and that as they made their way back towards the piers, not caring that he gawped like a griffin. He did not recall ever seeing such a variety of faces. There were puce-faced English sepoys, their red and grey uniform coats left behind as they worked in shirtsleeves, the fabric of their standard-issue grey undershirts stained with great patches of sweat even though the day was still young. Sepoys from the Bombay Native Infantry regiments worked alongside their white comrades, their constant chatter underscored by the bark of their havildars. Then there were mule drivers and camp followers in their hundreds. The accounts in the London newspapers had talked of people coming from all over the Empire – Persians, Egyptians, Indians and Chinese alike summoned to the great endeavour that Napier had undertaken. The wonderful mix of foreign faces and unintelligible languages washed over him, as he did his best to avoid the working parties that were trying to organise the constant stream of stores coming ashore from the hundreds of ships anchored in the bay.

He paused by a stack of wooden crates. From the stencils and markings on their sides he could see they contained brand-new Mark II Snider Long Rifles, produced by the Royal Small Arms Factory in Enfield. He had heard of the Snider. It was one of the first breech-loading rifles, a converted version of the P53 Enfield rifled musket. The difference between the two was the Snider's new breech mechanism. A side-hinged breechblock was moved to the right to open the breech into which a cartridge was fed. Once loaded, the breechblock was closed and locked. After firing, the same hinged breechblock was opened again then pulled firmly to the rear with the forefinger and thumb to engage the casing extractor. With the now empty cartridge casing sitting in the open chamber, the rifle could be turned to the right and the cartridge shaken out.

It was said that the Sniders were good for ten rounds a minute, which made them an interesting proposition. They would change how armies fought, and Jack could only imagine that the next iteration would fire even quicker. The large, bulky formations that had dominated the battlefield since the days of Napoleon would not stand a chance against lines of men armed with rifles like the Snider.

Yet it was hard to like such a weapon. He could admire it and marvel at the technology that it utilised. But that technology had one purpose and one purpose only: to make the butchery of the battlefield even more efficient. The world of the soldier was changing and it was changing fast. The thought made him uneasy. He knew how to fight. But the rules of war he understood were fast becoming outdated.

'I say, you there. I don't suppose you know where the telegraph office is?' A young man dressed in a cream linen suit tugged at Jack's elbow as he and Cooper passed him by.

'No idea, I'm afraid,' Jack replied. He could not make out much of the man's face, as it was hidden in the shadow of a cream sola topee, though he could see the great sweat stains that had soaked through his linen jacket. It appeared he was not the only one who would stink by the day's end.

'Damnation. I was told it was this way, but I cannot find it for the life of me.' The man removed his hat and held out a hand. 'Armstrong, *Illustrated London News*.'

'Lark.' Jack kept his introduction curt as he shook the rather damp and limp hand. 'And Cooper of the Intelligence Department.' He nodded to his companion, then reached out to take hold of Armstrong's elbows before swinging him out of the way of a fast-moving column of sepoys carrying ammunition crates. 'How long have you been here, Mr Armstrong?'

'Just two days. I am due to depart on the morrow.'

'Then you may well be coming with us.' Jack let go of Armstrong's elbows and dusted something from the younger man's sleeve. He sensed an opportunity to find out more about the campaign. Major Talbot had painted a rosy picture of the opening moves, as he would, given his position, but Jack wanted to know more, and to discover the true state of affairs.

'That would be capital. It would be nice to see a few familiar faces.' Armstrong positively beamed at the news.

'Are you alone here?'

'Some of my colleagues arrived before me, but they are up with the vanguard. I was delayed in Bombay, you see. A problem with my paperwork.'

'It happens.' Jack smiled in understanding. 'At least you are here now. But it appears you have nothing to report on. Everything seems to be well in hand.'

'Oh, all is not as it seems,' Armstrong chimed in, eager to impress. 'Why, I have already filed my first report on the state of the transport animals. When I think of the fate of those poor creatures . . .' He broke off, seemingly unable to say more.

'Indeed.' Jack had no idea what the problem was, but he went along with it nonetheless.

'They are trying to muffle the story, of course,' Armstrong carried on. 'As indeed they should! I heard that hundreds of the poor creatures were left to wander the encampment, desperately searching for water and fodder, whilst the men who were supposed to be tending to them argued for better pay. They say their bodies were left to lie where they fell. You still find their bones all over the damn place.'

'But Napier has it all in hand now?' Jack steered the conversation in the direction he wanted it to go.

'He is certainly doing his best. After all, he had no say in the transport train, so we can hardly lay the blame for that farce at his door. That was down to the officials in Bombay. As soon as Napier arrived here, he brought in some five thousand Punjabis to drive the mules. He also ordered fifteen thousand pairs of army boots to be brought here with all dispatch. Can you credit that? Fifteen thousand pairs! It gives one some idea of the sheer scale of this expedition, does it not?'

'It certainly does.' As a foot soldier, Jack knew the need for good boots better than anyone.

'He has even organised a party of photographers. A group from the Royal Engineers have been given the responsibility of creating a photographic account of the campaign. He wants everything recorded. Can you imagine how thrilling it will be to be able to sit in England and actually see what it was like to be here? We truly do live in a modern world.'

Jack could only agree. He had been photographed just the once, shortly before the first battle at the Bull Run river. It intrigued him to think that Napier had had the foresight to order the Royal Engineers to bring their photographic equipment to join the campaign. It spoke of progressive thinking, something that was so often lacking in the senior officers he had come across in the past.

'What have you heard of the main column?' he asked. The reporter was proving to be a fine source of information.

'There are rumours coming in every day. It is three hundred and eighty-one miles to Magdala, every one of them dangerous. No one expects Tewodros to let us arrive unmolested, but thus far, the only accounts I have heard are of bands of his men roving about the countryside. They are keeping well clear of our chaps, which shows a good amount of common sense on their part. We should expect the first division to do any fighting there is. They are in the van.'

'What of this Tewodros fellow? What is he up to?'

'So far precious little. But it cannot last. He owes his position to his ability in battle. He will not give in. Not without a fight.'

Jack nodded in agreement. Armstrong was echoing everthing he had heard from others. 'So he will make a stand.'

'He has to.' Armstrong's expression turned serious. 'I am afraid Napier will have to fight to secure the prisoners.'

'And you will have a battle to cover.'

'I hope so. I know that sounds terrible.' Armstrong grimaced as he admitted it. 'But it is why I am here, after all.'

Jack offered a smile. 'You and me both.' It was the truth. They were here for very different reasons, yet they both wanted the same thing.

They wanted a battle.

Chapter Twenty-four

───◆◆◆───

The four companions left at dawn.

Jack rode his new horse, a fine black mare with a single flash of white on her neck, trying to get used to its gait. It was a long time since he had been in the saddle, and he could already feel the insides of his thighs beginning to burn. He would be aching and sore by the end of the day, but riding was still preferable to walking, despite the damage it would do to his arse.

The four men had joined a larger group heading towards the front, and together they formed a merry party. They were travelling with two British officers, a company of sepoys, the young newspaperman Armstrong and a naturalist called Beard who appeared to be bringing more guns with him than the entire company of infantrymen. At the rear of the group came a long line of mules carrying supplies for the men of the Royal Artillery mountain battery, which would surely play a key role in the assault on the emperor's fortress if and when it came. Some of the mules were weighed down with wooden cases containing roundshot or powder for the light guns that were being carried all the way to Magdala, but Jack had also seen some transporting small Hale rockets, the weapon the latest incarnation of the Congreve rockets that had seen action in the wars against Napoleon.

The group was departing Annesley Bay around one month behind Napier, and even further behind the advance guard. It would be a long, hard ride to catch up with the column, but the officers accompanying them were confident that it could be done. Their small group would be able to advance much more quickly than the cumbersome army column, which had been forced to halt for several days at a time as supplies were brought up and the ground ahead prepared for their advance. The expectation was, as Jack had heard it, that the main column would not arrive at Magdala much before Easter. That gave them well over a month to complete the long journey south.

It felt good to leave Annesley Bay behind. The encampment had been a miserable place, too full of people for Jack's liking. He wanted to be in the wilds, and it appeared he would get his wish sooner rather than later. They had been riding for barely a half-hour before he saw the first mountains ahead of them. They were shrouded with low-lying clouds that hid much of their upper regions from view. It gave them an un-earthly, mysterious feel. Beyond the mountains, there was nearly four hundred miles of untamed wilderness between them and Magdala. He could not help thinking back to what Macgregor had said of this distant land. He knew that much of it was based on little more than hearsay and the myths that had been perpetuated by newspapers desperate to create a story, but that did not mean it did not hold an element of truth. He could not help but wonder what challenges lay ahead and what tests they would face.

The small column made fine progress through the morning.

Jack rode near the front of the column with Armstrong and Beard and the officers. Behind them the company of native infantry marched easy, the men often breaking into song as they ground out the miles. To the rear of the infantrymen came the artillery train, followed by the officers' servants and a few dozen camp followers, including the three grooms and the mules that would support the group of four on the long march south.

Jack was enjoying himself. His sense of being set free only grew the further they rode into the wilderness. Hawks circled overhead as they followed a dry riverbed to the west, swirling and swooping on eddies of hot air that came down off the mountains before they collided with the cooler air coming in from the sea. The birds would often plunge down, falling at a terrific rate as they dived at a prey they had spotted far below. Jack watched them as much as he could as he rode, his eyes tracking the small winged creatures as they plummeted towards the earth, just as he would trace the path of a roundshot as it seared across the battlefield.

The plan for the day was that they would follow the riverbed all the way to the edge of the great plateau. There they would make the climb to the higher ground before turning south. Their first stop would be the encampment at Koomaylee, around thirteen miles from Annesley Bay, the first in a chain of supply depots Napier had put in place before he allowed the main column to begin its advance. From there they would follow the road laid down by the hard-working Royal Engineers and Bombay Sappers all the way to the town of Senafe, some sixty miles to the south.

Thus far it had been a gentle ride, almost a pleasant one, the path easy even as it ascended the ridge that separated the ground near the shore from the great plateau. Or at least it would have been a pleasant ride, were it not for the hundreds of corpses that lay in every direction. The bodies of the mules and camels had already been stripped of every scrap of flesh by the scavenging animals that would have grown fat on the feast the British army had provided them with. It made for a grim reminder of the realities of embarking on a campaign so far from the main hubs of the Empire. Jack looked at the skeletons and wondered how many men would join the dead animals; how many soldiers would be sacrificed to achieve the aims of the British government.

They reached the plateau itself just over an hour after their departure. A wide, open plain went on for what looked to be a hundred miles, the horizon stretching away in every direction. There was not much for the eye to see. The ground was little more than dust and stone, the only foliage a great number of stunted bushes with tiny leaves interspersed with ferocious-looking thorns. A fresh, dry breeze blew across the plateau, the air carrying with it the smell of mountains and trees. Jack relished it, the wind cool on his face. It tasted unsoiled and crisp, a welcome respite from the muggy heat near the shore. The brisk breeze also scoured away the stink of Annesley Bay that had seemed to linger around them all.

'Do you hear that, Jack-o?' Cooper, riding at Jack's side, called for his attention. The Londoner rode badly, the hasty lesson Jack had delivered that morning the sum total of his riding experience. He sat in the saddle like a sack of potatoes, his back bent forward whilst his legs stuck out at an awkward angle so that it looked like he might fall off at any moment.

Jack cocked an ear. He heard the sound that had caught Cooper's attention almost at once. It was the sound of a loco-motive on the move. He twisted in the saddle and spotted the small engine that followed the tracks laid down by the engineers. It was working hard, every one of the carts it hauled packed to the brim with supplies for the army. It was not the first evidence they had seen of the British endeavour. A telegraph cable had been laid down between Senafe and Annesley, and in the low hills near the edge of the plateau they had seen a long chain of wells dug deep into the ground and capped with pumps. The British were making their mark on this barren land, one that would last long after their aims had been achieved.

They spotted Koomaylee late in the afternoon.

Jack was relieved to see their first stop appear. His arse and thighs were burning and sore, and his spine felt like it had been replaced with a fiery trident whose sole purpose was to lance pain throughout his body.

On the open emptiness of the plain, the white bell tents of the encampment stood out clearly against the pale blue sky. They appeared tiny at first, resembling nothing so much as a child's toy dumped in the middle of an enormous garden. It was only as he rode closer that the sheer scale of this first encampment struck him. There had to be over two hundred tents that he could see, each one capable of sleeping up to fifteen soldiers. Beyond them, great heaps of stores had been piled up in every direction, covered by tarpaulins to protect them from the elements. Then there were the wells. He counted six, each a good fourteen feet across. Huge pumps powered by teams of workers, mostly Punjabis or native infantrymen ordered to the task, spat out streams of clear water into a complex series of wooden troughs that took it away and delivered it throughout the encampment.

'It is nothing short of miraculous, is it not?' Watson had

ridden forward as they approached the encampment. Now he voiced his wonder as he studied the engineering that had somehow managed to conjure clean water from the sandy, stony ground. 'It really is something to behold.'

'It's a bloody marvel.' Jack made no attempt to hide his own awe. He had learned to husband his supply of water years before in the blistering, unrelenting heat of India. It was something he continued to do, no matter the circumstances. To a soldier, nothing was as precious as good water. Yet here, amidst the rocks and the barren land of the Abyssinian plateau, the Royal Engineers had found a way to extract it from the very depths of the ground.

The sappers had done more than just build the pumps and the network of troughs that surrounded them. They had cleared a great area, now strewn with the stumps of a thousand thorn bushes, that surrounded the encampment for hundreds of yards in every direction; they had constructed the road that led all the way back to Annesley Bay; and they had erected long runs of fencing to organise the encampment. The men from Chatham had been busy.

'I do believe those are Douglas pitcher-spout pumps, the so-called American pump. I have read of them.'

'Of course you have,' Jack mocked gently. It was easily done. Watson was a man born to academia. He was as out of place here as a bishop in a brothel.

'You may laugh, Mr Lark, but I am not ashamed of my education. You would think those who are lacking in that regard would seek to hide their deficiency, not parade it to the world.' Watson gave the haughty reply, then deliberately turned his horse's head to the side so that he could ride towards the nearest of the huge pumps.

Jack grinned. He was pretty sure the man's attitude would change when the going got harder. Pretty words and education were a fine thing for a life in London. They counted for nothing here. Watson would learn that, and it would probably happen the hard way.

Yet he would not deny that the six huge pumps were indeed fascinating and worthy of further study. He was not being glib when he had called them a marvel, one that was clearly much needed on the dry, arid plateau.

The pumps were not the only marvel on display that day. As they rode closer to the encampment, Jack was able to see the vast animal holding pens that had been erected. Each contained a huge number of beasts. He saw flocks of small sheep, the animals appearing very thin and bony. They were noisy, each one seemingly intent on bleating louder than its neighbour, but nowhere near as noisy as the goats in the pens nearby, nor as restless. Other pens contained great herds of huge, silent bullocks, or hordes of braying mules. There were ponies by the dozen, and also camels, the strange-looking creatures sitting unperturbed, chewing silently and ruminating on the madness around them.

It took a while to reach the main encampment. First they had to pass the sentries stationed on the engineer's road; then they had to wait whilst the company of native infantry marched past and into camp. Only when that was done did they ride in. The place was busy, like a small town on market day. There was the same bewildering array of faces that had been present at Annesley Bay, every country of the Empire and beyond seeming to have sent at least one representative to join Napier's campaign. But there were new faces too amongst the polyglot crowd, ones that stuck out even to the weary travellers who had been thinking more of a night at rest than an inspection of the local population.

'Would you look at that now, Jack-o?' Cooper was close enough to Jack to call for his attention. He was pointing at a young woman who was walking past carrying a pair of buckets filled to the brim with water. She was dressed in a simple calico dress that went over one shoulder and reached down to her knees. It was prettily decorated with cowry shells, but it was not the design that had captured Cooper's attention. The dress left the woman's chest half naked, much to his childish delight.

'Stop gawping at the poor woman,' Jack chided his companion.

'But still, Jack-o, you've got to admit it's a nicer sight for my poor old eyes than the arsehole of your bloody horse, which is all I've had to stare at these past few hours.' Cooper beamed from ear to ear, clearly well pleased with himself.

'Just don't get any funny ideas,' Jack warned. 'Have you seen those blokes over there? I don't think they'll take kindly to you ogling their bints.' He nodded towards a group of men resting in the shade of one of the many tents.

They sat cross-legged on the ground in a rough circle. The man closest to Jack watched them closely. He wore a long white calico shamma over pale knee-length trousers and matching shirt. At his side lay an undecorated hide shield alongside what looked to be an ancient matchlock musket that would have been out of date on the field of Waterloo. He caught Jack's eye. The two men stared at one another before the warrior looked away, his eyes betraying little more than disinterest and disdain.

Most of the group were dressed the same, the ubiquitous shamma little different from those of any of the peasants that scurried past the group. Their weapons consisted of more of the outdated matchlocks, or else spears that had to be close to six feet long. One warrior, however, stood out. He wore a pale blue cloak in place of the shamma, the cloth clearly of a better quality. On his head he sported a headdress made from a lion's mane, the hairs brushed back so that they stood up to form a kind of hairy halo. His face was scarred, a thick weal running across his forehead like a single worry line, the edges puckered so that they twisted the skin around it.

'They're a lot of dirty-looking beggars, aren't they just.' Cooper ran his eye over the men.

'I bet they know how to use those spears of theirs. Take care not to give them cause to shove one up your arse.' Jack knew Cooper would not heed his warning, but he gave it regardless.

More of the warriors had turned to stare at the new arrivals. They did not look impressed. Jack kept a weather eye on them. For the first time, he spotted that they all wore thick blue cords around their necks, apart from the more finely dressed warrior with the blue cloak, who had a silver cross.

'They can try,' Cooper growled. 'If one of them comes at me with one of those fucking things, I'll shoot the fucker.'

'And you'll likely miss.' Jack had tried to teach his fellow Londoner to shoot accurately on the long journey from London. But no matter what he had tried, Cooper was still a terrible shot and he insisted on snatching at the trigger and jerking his revolver as he fired, as if he had to somehow add impetus to the bullet.

'Then I'll knock the fucker out instead.' Cooper turned to grin at him. 'You know me, Jack-o. I won't get in no trouble.'

'I wish I could believe that.'

They had reached a long hitching rail close to the centre of

the encampment. It was time to dismount and present themselves to whichever officer was in charge of greeting new
arrivals. Jack hissed an oath as he dragged his chafed thighs
across the saddle. His boots hit the ground and he staggered,
his legs almost failing to hold him upright. He would be given
no time to gather himself. Immediately, a great swarm of locals
surged towards him.

'*Christo*?' The first man to reach him started to paw at his
clothing. The heavily bearded face ducked and bobbed in front
of him, whilst all the while the man's hands tried to pull away
the collar of his jacket. '*Christo*?'

'Easy there.' Jack used both his hands to push the man
away. He did not move him far, as more and more men were
pressing close. They swarmed forward in one great mass,
surrounding the four riders in noise and confusion.

'Fuck off!' Cooper was trying to repel the attention of two
other men, to no avail.

Jack had no time to go to his aid. The man who had first
assaulted him was back, this time with a friend. Both men
were clawing at his collar. They were close enough for him to
smell them, the mix of foreign spices and sweat assailing his
nostrils.

'It's all right. They want to see if you're a Christian, that's
all.' Watson's voice carried through the building fracas. '*Tayib*!
Tayib! *Christo*!'

It did the trick. The men pulled away, their faces breaking
into huge smiles. They called to one another as they started to
walk away, clapping hands and hurrahing.

Cooper did his best to resettle his clothing. 'What the bloody
hell was that about?' His face was flushed.

'Damned strange welcome, if you ask me.' Macgregor had

walked over to join Jack. Like the others, he was staring at the crowd of men, who were now slinking back to the shadows of a great bell tent, where they sat down as if nothing had happened. 'Do they do that to everyone?'

'Probably. Their religion is very important to them,' Watson explained. Of the four of them, he was the least flustered. 'They are Christians in a world of Muslims. I suspect that makes them rather sensitive.'

'Doesn't give them the right to maul anyone they fucking fancy.' Cooper was not happy.

'Welcome to Abyssinia, Mr Cooper.' Watson gave one of his odd little smiles at his companion's discomfort. 'I doubt this is the last strange event we shall witness.'

'It had better be. Next time one of the fuckers tries that, I'll knock the bugger on his arse.'

'No you won't.' Jack cut through Cooper's bluster. 'You'll keep your fists to yourself. In fact, you had better keep all your bits and pieces to yourself, you understand me, Coops? No misbehaving here. No fighting. No nothing.'

'Course, Jack-o.' Cooper had the sense to mumble an agreement.

'We would all do well to heed that advice.' Jack looked pointedly at Macgregor. 'Remember why we are here and don't try anything on, with anyone.'

'What are you suggesting?' Macgregor puffed out his chest, as if offended.

'I rather think Mr Lark is suggesting that none of us seek any amorous attention whilst we are here.' Watson had understood Jack's warning well enough.

'Oh, you dog, Watson. Have you been eyeing up the local bints already?' Macgregor twisted his friend's tail.

'Of course not. He was addressing the remark to you.' Watson did not understand the mockery.

'How dare you. I am a gentleman.' Macgregor played to the moment. 'I would never seek the attentions of a local lady. Not unless I was invited, of course.'

'You would, and you know it.' Jack snapped the words. He had tired of the childish byplay. 'While we're here, keep yourself to yourself.'

He said nothing more. His legs were feeling a little stronger, so he hitched his horse and strode off to find whoever was in charge. He hoped his companions would heed his warning.

They did not need any trouble.

Chapter Twenty-five

———◆◆◆———

'Shoot it, you fool!' Jack shouted, then laughed as the troop of monkeys scattered to the wind.

Jonathan Beard was not a good marksman, but he was enthusiastic. The first shot cracked out, the sound echoing and loud. The bullet missed the nearest monkey by a country mile.

'Another one, goddammit!' Beard shouted at his bearer for a second loaded rifle. A few seconds later and another shot was fired. Like the first, it missed.

Already the monkeys were settling down to rest, the animals proving a fine judge of the naturalist's ability and the range of his rifle. There were at least two hundred of them. They came in all shapes and sizes, from tiny babies clasped tight to their mothers to much larger males, their dark faces covered with a thick pelt of hair. Every animal had a great pink backside, many of which were now turned to face Beard, who was berating his bearer, the poor man now forced to carry the blame for the missed shots along with the pair of now empty hunting rifles.

The party had followed another fine road for much of the day. It was smooth and level, the Royal Engineers hacking and blasting passage for the limbers and wagons that followed the route in their hundreds. It made for an easy ride, and if he were honest, Jack had enjoyed Beard's attempts to bag himself a monkey, the sport a welcome respite from the tedium.

Yet that tedium would not last much longer.

'Fuck me,' Cooper breathed as he looked ahead at the pass they would have to traverse as they entered the first mountain range. 'We're going in there?'

Jack left the pointless question hanging as he studied the entrance to the pass. The tales of constant attacks by the natives and the ever-present threat of flesh-eating diseases and face-rotting pestilence might not have proved to be true, but the rumours about the difficulty of the terrain had clearly under-estimated the sheer brutality of the route the army would have to take. It was enough to make him wonder at the sanity of the British government. Sheer-sided mountains pressed close either side, shutting off the light so that the pass appeared to disappear into darkness. A few lone sycamore trees clung to the slopes, their trunks leaning out precariously. Otherwise the place looked devoid of life.

They rode on, heading uphill from the moment they left the road. The going got worse almost immediately, the ground little more than soft sand that shifted under the horses' hooves, making them stumble every few paces. The mountain defile narrowed, the precipitous cliffs on either side climbing ever higher. In a dozen places, they could see where there had been a recent rock fall. The threat of another felt very real, so that every man in the party looked up constantly, anxiously scan-ning the sheer-sided cliffs. The Royal Engineers had done their best to improve the route through the pass. All along the road, rock fall had been blown up, the debris piled and levelled.

Jack did not like to think of the effort it would have taken to climb the pass had the sappers not worked so hard.

The hours crept by slowly. It got darker as they moved through the pass, the high sides sealing them in to what felt like a never-ending chamber. The air turned cold and oppressive, the daylight stolen away, so that to Jack's mind it felt like they were riding willingly into their own graves. The menacing atmosphere was not helped by the dozens of vultures and kites that swirled this way and that in the eddies of warmer air high above the narrow chasm. Not one man spoke as the darkness closed around them, the only sound the scuff of hoof and boot on stony ground. Shadows came with them, fleeting shapes flickering past and up the sides of the chasm, their ominous presence only increasing the sense of danger.

They rode on, cold and silent, every pair of eyes searching the way ahead for the first glimpse of daylight that would signal the end of their journey through what felt to them all like the entrance to hell.

The group was still quiet even when they finally broke free of the oppressive pass, something in the dark, cold air lingering even as they pushed out into the bright afternoon sunlight.

They emerged into a barren rolling landscape. Every one of them searched for anything that spoke of life, but they saw little to reassure them in this unforgiving setting. The ground was rocky, with no soil to speak of, just sand, dust and a million tiny fragments of rock. There were no more of the tiny bushes with their fierce thorns – no trees, no grass, no nothing. They were heading into a desolate wasteland that appeared to possess nothing that would shelter or sustain even a single man, let alone an army.

Jack rode on his own, steering a course that kept him away from the others in the group. He relished the solitude. There was something in the bleak surroundings that he loved. This was a wild, untamed region, untouched by the hand of man, a land unchanged for centuries, or perhaps longer. He was not religious, far from it, but he could not help but feel that he was in a place that was formed exactly as God had intended. It was unforgiving and harsh, but he saw beauty in the barren starkness that he did not want to share with the others.

It took another hour of riding before they saw the first sign of life. The depot at the wells at Upper Sooroo was huge. In many ways, it looked the same as the encampment at Koomaylee, although here there was barely any flat ground, the tents and animal enclosures perched here and there amidst the rocks. In the midst of the lifeless, desolate terrain, the white bell tents of the British army stood out, a very obvious glimpse of the civilisation that had imposed itself on this most inhospitable of lands.

Jack looked at the encampment and felt nothing but admiration for Napier's planning. Moving an army through such country was no easy feat, yet by constructing these depots a day's march apart, Napier had ensured that his forces would be provided for every step of the way to Magdala. It explained why it had taken so long for him to begin the advance. Establishing the chain of supply depots and wells had been no easy task, but they were vital if he was to move tens of thousands of men across four hundred miles of hostile terrain.

Jack kicked back his heels. They had another mile to cover before they would reach the tents at Upper Sooroo. He would enjoy his last moments of peace whilst he could.

Chapter Twenty-six

———◆·◈·◆———

Jack sat outside the tent the four of them had been allocated and began the task of cleaning his revolver. He did it every day without fail, fishing out every scrap of dirt that had worked its way into the weapon's mechanism. The Colt might be getting old now, but he would not contemplate exchanging it for a newer weapon. So he looked after it with meticulous care, even polishing the metal that had once shone as bright as silver, but which now had the dull patina of age.

'It's a wonder that thing still works.' Watson came out of the tent carrying his own revolver. The Beaumont–Adams was brand new and had never been fired in anger. 'May I sit with you?'

'Do what you like.' Jack had to squint as he looked up at Watson, the sky still bright. It was just the two of them. Cooper and Macgregor had taken themselves off, neither man keen to linger near the fetid air of yet another dank tent.

'Thank you.' Watson gave a tight smile and sat down. He spread a handkerchief on the ground in front of him along with his pouch of tools, ready to disassemble his own revolver into its three main parts ready for cleaning. 'I do believe that I shall become used to the routine of these days.' He looked at Jack a little warily as he spoke. 'There is a simplicity to them. We eat, ride, repair, sleep, then repeat. That is a fair description of our time here, is it not?'

'We've barely started.' Jack sighed. He did not relish the idea of a conversation. 'It won't always be like this.'

'How so?'

'It'll get harder.'

'And more dangerous?'

'For sure.'

'I was afraid you would say that.' Watson heaved down a deep breath, then reached for his revolver. His hand stopped short of the weapon as he thought of another question. 'How do you do it?'

'I've shown you how to clean it before.' Jack did not bother to look across.

'Not that.' Watson's hand hovered. 'How do you fight?'

'You close your eyes and pull the damn trigger.' Jack gave the clipped answer.

'Come now, Mr Lark, even I know there is more to it than that.'

Jack sighed again. It appeared the conversation was going to happen, no matter how much he tried to avoid it. 'There isn't. Not really. That's all it comes down to at the end of the day. Pulling that trigger.'

'It cannot be that simple.'

Jack placed his Colt on the ground, laying it down carefully. 'That's it, truly.' He turned his head, giving Watson his full attention. 'But you are right. It's not that simple. It's not that simple at all.'

'How so?'

'Because sometimes you have to look the other bastard in the eye when you do it.' He made sure to fix his stare on Watson's. 'Can you do that? Can you look a man dead in the eye and still pull that trigger?'

Watson tried to meet Jack's gaze. He failed and looked away. 'I confess I do not know the answer to that question.'

'No, of course you don't. You haven't been there.' Jack paused. 'Yet.'

Watson squirmed. But Jack would not let him off the hook so easily. He had summoned this conversation, and so he would have to see it through, no matter how uncomfortable it might be. 'But you will. One day you will be faced with that moment. One day a man will stand in front of you and he'll want to kill you. The only thing that can stop him is that revolver. Will you pull the trigger then?'

'I think I would.'

'You think?'

'I imagine I could.' Watson had to swallow hard as he gave a better answer. 'I am afraid that is the best I can do, Mr Lark.'

'Well, that's just fine and dandy. You imagine that. And whilst you are thinking about it, that man, why, he'll kill you right where you stand. You don't have time to think, not when it comes down to it. You don't have time for anything. Except for pulling that trigger and sending that other bastard on his merry way to hell.'

Watson looked up. As ever, his eyes were rimmed with red, but now they looked moist, as if he were close to tears. 'You have done that?' The question was asked in something close to a whisper.

'More times than I can remember.'

'So it does become simple.'

'No.' The word came out of Jack's mouth wrapped in iron. 'It is never simple. Never.' He shivered. For a fleeting second, he had felt the cold hand of death on his shoulder. 'You pull the trigger. Or you stab the knife. Or you rip the fucker's throat out with your bare hands. You do whatever it takes. Because if you pause, if you hesitate for even one bloody second, he'll do it to you. And then that's that.'

He stopped speaking and closed his eyes. The faces of the dead rushed past in his mind. They were numberless, these legions of the departed. Yet they did not upset him. They were his companions now. They were with him always, the only thing that was.

'I do not think I would be able to do those things.' Watson was watching Jack closely.

'Then you'll die.' Jack opened his eyes. He looked at Watson and wondered if the face he now looked at would one day join the others in his mind.

'Yes.' Watson pressed his lips tightly together as he spoke the word. 'I rather think you are right.'

Jack grunted. It was the honest answer, one that few would ever give. It was to Watson's credit that he could see the truth. Yet it was also the wrong answer. 'Then go home, whilst you still can.'

Watson stared back at him. But he was spared saying another word.

'Jack!'

Jack turned to see Cooper jogging towards him. Despite the heat, his face was the colour of last week's milk. 'What is it?'

'He's here.'

'Who's here?'

Cooper's tongue flickered out across his lips. 'Finch.'

'Finch?' Jack felt a sense of dread settle, cold and lumpy, deep in his gut. He pushed himself to his feet, then grabbed Cooper by both arms, holding him in front of him. 'Tell me exactly what you know.'

'I just saw him.' Cooper stared back at Jack. 'He's here. Got Swan and a whole load of his boys with him. At least six, maybe more.'

'Shit.' Jack was still holding Cooper's arms as the news sank in. He had no idea how Finch had managed to secure a berth on a ship destined for Abyssinia. But for now, that didn't matter. He had more pressing concerns. 'Did he see you?'

'I think so.' Cooper avoided Jack's eyes and stared at the dirt around his boots.

'Cooper?' Jack tried to press. Something was not being said.

Then the question became moot.

'Well, isn't that fucking touching,' a loud voice called. The harsh East End accent was dreadfully familiar. 'At least have the fucking decency to cosy up in private, why don't you.'

Jack dropped Cooper's arms and turned. Finch was swaggering towards him. The strut and the confident air were unchanged. But something was different. Jack had heard it the moment Finch had spoken, and now he saw it. The Londoner's mouth was half open as he harangued them, revealing the gaps where teeth had been; teeth that Jack had knocked out when he had headbutted him all those weeks before.

'Finch.' He said the man's name as if he were speaking to the devil himself.

'Jack Lark, as I live and fucking breathe.' Finch came closer.

He was not alone. He was followed by five of his men, his henchman, Swan, leading the group.

'What do you want, Finch?' Jack glanced around before giving the man his full attention. Their bell tent was surrounded by a dozen others, and a number of soldiers were milling around. He was reasonably sure that not even Finch would attempt to commit murder in broad daylight in the midst of a British army encampment.

'What do I fucking want?' Finch gestured to Swan and the others to hold their ground, then stepped forward. He did not stop until his face was an inch or two from Jack's. 'What I fucking want, chum, is your fucking neck.'

'Well, here I am.' Jack did not so much as twitch. He stared back at the man who had come so far to find him, revealing nothing in his expression. 'You want to kill me, then go right ahead.'

'Oh, I'm going to kill you all right.' Finch lisped over the words, spittle flying from his lips as the missing teeth deformed his speech. 'But I'm going to take my time over it. I'm going to make you wish you had never been fucking born, my lad.'

Jack fought the urge to laugh at the younger man calling him 'lad'. 'You came all this way just to kill me? I'm honoured.'

'You fucking should be. But I ain't here just for you.' Finch took a half-step away. 'I happened to hear there's a fortune to be made out here. And I need a little rhino. It's cost me a fucking fortune to get out here, what with all the palms I had to grease to get on board one of those ratty fucking ships. And of course after you burned my fucking place down, I find myself in hock to them Jewish boys, and let me tell you, that ain't something I'd wish on any man. So here I am, looking to make myself a quick fucking shekel. And it's all thanks to him.' He pointed a single finger at Cooper. 'After all, he put me on to this place. Now I can get what I need to keep them Jew-boys off my back and kill you mealy-mouthed fuckers whilst I'm at it.'

'That's enough.' It was Watson who spoke. No one had noticed what the academic had been up to. Now he was pointing his revolver straight at Finch. 'You have said more than enough, Mr Finch. I must ask you to step away. Rest assured that I have just completed loading this weapon. I shall not hesitate to pull the trigger if you don't do as I say.'

'Who the fuck are you?' Finch's face creased into a scowl.

'I am a friend of Mr Lark and Mr Cooper, and I am the man who will send your soul on its merry way to hell if you do not desist and step away this instant.' Watson glanced quickly at Jack as he made the threat. 'Now do as I say.'

Finch did not move, but Swan did, stepping forward, hands bunching into fists.

'Hold there, Swanny.' Finch turned and raised a hand, then returned his attention to Watson, eyes narrowing as he considered the slight figure waving a gun at him. 'You look to me like you're shitting in your fucking breeches.' He smiled. 'But it's all right, Mr . . .' He paused and held out both hands apologetically. 'Oh, I am getting ahead of myself, ain't I just. We ain't even been introduced.' He bent forward from the waist in a half-bow. 'Mr . . . ?'

'Watson. Horatio Watson.' Watson licked his lips as he gave his name. His nervousness was obvious to all.

'Mr Watson.' Finch beamed as if pleased with the introduction. 'And named after our famous fucking admiral, if I ain't mistaken. Well met, Mr Watson.' He grinned, then turned to look back at Swan. 'Swanny, be a good fellow and mark that name. I rather think Mr Watson needs to be added to our little list. Now . . .' Again Finch paused. He was calm and in control, even with a revolver pointed at his belly. 'Where was we? Ah yes, Jack-o, we was discussing your future, or rather your lack of it. Now don't you worry none, I ain't going to start something, not now.' He pulled a face, as if affronted by the very suggestion. 'No, that's not going to happen, so you can calm yourself the fuck down, Horatio, and put that little shooter of yours away. But you'd better all keep a weather eye out, gentlemen, because I promise you this: not one of you will leave this fucking place alive, you get me?' His face twisted as he made the threat, tongue flickering across the gap where his teeth used to be. 'Still, that's for another day.' He offered a smile, spreading his hands wide. 'It was nice to meet you, Horatio.'

He looked one last time at each man, then turned and walked away, Swan trailing behind him like an extra shadow. His thugs followed, silent and obedient.

'Who is that odd-looking fellow?' Macgregor came striding towards the three men. He was moving quickly, as if he had been trying to reach them in time to be introduced, and now looked disappointed to have missed out. 'A friend of yours?' He addressed the question to Jack.

'Something like that.' Jack shook his head, then looked across at Cooper. 'But I reckon he's more a friend of Coops's.'

'Come on, Jack-o,' Cooper whined as he felt Jack's withering gaze land on him. 'I told you that weren't my fault.'

'No, I know.' Jack took a long, slow breath. It would do no good to blame Cooper for talking. Finch was here. That was that.

'Jack-o, we've got to get out of here,' Cooper pleaded. 'We

can't just hang around the bleeding place. We've got to go whilst we still fucking can.'

Jack nodded. He was right. Finch's arrival changed everything.

'But we've only just got here!' Macgregor was aghast at the idea.

'It doesn't matter,' Jack told him. 'It's time we struck out on our own anyway. We won't achieve anything if we always ride with other people.' He closed his eyes as he thought about what he was saying. His body hurt and his backside was raw. He did not want to ride for another minute let alone another few hours. But he could see no other way. They had to get away from Finch.

'Will you at least tell me why?' Macgregor was staring at Jack, his face creased with concern. 'Am I correct in assuming it has something to do with those gentlemen I just saw?'

'Yes. That ugly bastard is Finch.'

Macgregor's eyes opened wide at the news. 'The man who wants you dead?'

'Yep.'

'And he's come all the way out here to find you?' He was clearly struggling to absorb the news.

'It appears so.'

'How the hell did he know where you were?'

'Cooper told him.'

Cooper shuffled from foot to foot as all eyes turned his way.

'Why?'

'It's a long story. I'll fill in the gaps on the way.'

'You had better.' Macgregor shook his head. 'You can bring poor Watson up to speed too.' He looked across at the academic, who was standing there with his Beaumont–Adams still held at his side as if he had no idea what to do with it.

'Fine. We will tell you the whole sorry tale. But for now, can we at least make a move before that mad bastard takes it into his head to come back and shoot us where we stand? Our only hope is to stay one step ahead of the bugger.'

'If you say we must ride, then that is what we must do.' Macgregor did not look enthusiastic about Jack's plan, but to his credit, he was rallying fast.

'Thank you.' Jack meant it.

'And you're right, we can't achieve anything if we stay with the army all the damn time. We need to take our opportunities as and when we can.'

'Speaking of which,' Watson interjected. He was smiling his odd little smile and seemed well pleased with himself. 'I think I have something that might be of interest.'

'Go on.' Macgregor pushed him to say more.

'There is a little place I have heard of not far from Goun-Gouna. It appears in the accounts I have of this land, and from what I can gather, it is but a few miles from our direction of travel. I took the opportunity to speak to an officer of Engineers before we left the column, and he was kind enough to confirm that this place does truly exist. He was even kind enough to draw me a map.'

'What's there?' Jack asked.

Watson slowly and carefully put his revolver back into its holster before he replied. Only when he was satisfied that it was secure did he look back at the three faces turned his way. 'Treasure.' His smile widened. 'Specifically, a solid gold chalice that is mentioned in several accounts of the place. However, there is one,' he paused to select his next word carefully, 'obstacle.'

'Which is?' Jack tried not to snap.

'If what I have read is correct, and I believe it to be so, then the treasure is held in a church. If we wish to procure it, we will have to rob God himself.'

Chapter Twenty-seven

Near Rayry Guddy, 2 March 1868

ack brought his small party to a halt and looked at the ground that lay ahead. He had never seen the like of it. Not in Europe. Not in America. Not anywhere.

His first view of the Abyssinian Highlands took his breath away. The eastern border of the fabled tablelands was formed of an almost vertical barrier of rock. It stretched across the horizon, blocking the way ahead. The heartland of Tewodros's kingdom was protected by a natural obstacle that secured the boundary more effectively than any man-made defence ever could.

'The Highlands.' Watson made the identification. He spoke loudly, making sure they all heard. 'These mark the start of the tablelands.'

The four men rode close together, with their servants and mules following just behind. They had struck away from the main column within a couple of hours of Finch's appearance, taking all that they needed with them. They would have left sooner. First, though, Cooper had insisted on a last-minute visit to the latrine, something that had taken far longer than it should. Then Macgregor had wandered off to talk to an acquaintance he had spotted. Jack was beginning to think that herding cats would have been easier than getting the three men and a handful of servants to march.

But at least riding in a smaller group made for easier going. Jack set as fast a pace as he thought the horses and mules could bear, and had kept them on the trail for far longer than when they had been a small part of the larger, slower-moving party. They had soon settled into the new routine. They had been alone for just a couple of days, yet already the army, and Finch, had been left well behind.

The view ahead was as impressive as it was daunting. The cliffs that rose out of the plain were smothered with forests of spruce and juniper pine, many easily sixty feet high. The trees were covered with thick bands of creeper vines to create an almost impenetrable barrier of vegetation. High above the tree-line, the cliffs themselves, their slab sides coloured to a warm orange-red by the sun, stood like a stone wall around the heart of Theodore's empire. One that the British army had been forced to break through.

Yet again, the Royal Engineers had been equal to the task. Jack could see the path they had made for the army. It snaked through the forest, then up the cliffs, ascending what he reckoned had to be something close to three to four thousand feet in the space of a few miles. The path was like a scar that ran across the face of the highlands. The comparison made him lift a hand to his cheek. There was something ghastly in the way that the British army had arrived to hack and blast their way through. The disfigurement would last long after they had left, the land forever altered by their touch.

'Shall we make camp here for the day?' Macgregor deferred to Jack. His tone was hopeful.

'No.' Jack pointed ahead. 'There's enough light left.'

'The horses are tired.' Macgregor tried to labour his point.

'They're fine.' Jack dismissed the notion. He looked around him. It was the right call. The ground they were on was dry and barren. The sandy soil had no substance to it, the scarce grass that covered it dry and burned. Over the course of the day, he had seen a few attempts at cultivation, even spotting one or two ploughs at work. In some places, in what he guessed passed as fields in these sterile lands, a large number of locals had been squatting down to work over the ground with sticks. He had no idea to what end. He was no farmer, but he could not fathom what crop they hoped to conjure from the sparse soil. There was nothing here that would help a group of travellers. If they stopped where they were, there would be no wood for their fires, and no shelter from the relentless wind that scoured across the land. They needed both, the nights as unbearably cold as the days were uncomfortably hot.

He saw his three companions share a look, but he ignored it. Instead, he kicked back his heels, and urged his horse back into motion. They could rest when they were dead. Or at least when they had reached better ground.

'So, are we doing this?' Jack had to raise his voice as he asked the question of his companions, who rode around him.

None of the three answered him immediately, each man lost in their own thoughts. They had left the servants and mules behind at the previous night's camp and struck out on their own, following the directions Watson had procured from the Royal Engineer officer before they had left the main column. It was his hand-drawn map that would take them to the church that Watson had read about in the accounts he had studied.

They had left camp with the dawn, riding away as the warm orange and pinks of first light spread warmth through the land. The ground was greener now that they were in the highlands. More than once they heard the sound of water on the move, the local farmers creating a number of channels to irrigate their fields. Once they had even seen a waterfall, the great torrent cascading over the side of a cliff with a thunderous roar. Far off to the south-west, they could see more mountains. Watson confidently named them as the Adowa Peaks, the identification pretty much the only conversation to break the quiet of the early-morning ride. That was until Jack had asked the uncomfortable question.

'It is what we came for.' Macgregor was the first to answer him. He looked across at Jack. There was little to be seen of his expression, his face half hidden beneath the brim of his air pipe helmet.

'If there's stuff we can make a mint on, then I'm all fucking in.' Cooper added a more pragmatic opinion.

'It does not concern you that we will be raiding a church?' Jack did not want any of them to mistake what they were about to do. He had expected Cooper's answer, but he was more worried about the other two. Both men were less inclined to be happy about stealing from a church, least of all one dedicated to the Christian faith.

'I believe it would be preferable if we could find objects of value from an alternative venue,' Macgregor replied. 'But if this is the only option, I do not think we should let it slip past. If we do not do this, then someone else will.'

'Are there any other places?' Jack asked Watson.

The academic winced, as if pained by what he was about to reveal. 'I confess I do not know of another. If the rumours are true, Tewodros has ravaged these lands. If we are to find an alternative treasure, we must find Tewodros himself.'

'And he is at Magdala.'

'Logically, that is where the most valuable articles are to be found.' Watson gave an apologetic smile. 'I fear this church will be our only opportunity before we reach the Gorilla's lair. And who knows how, or indeed if, we shall ever find ourselves there.'

'How does that make you feel?' Jack pulled his horse's head back sharply as it contemplated a scraggy patch of whisper-thin grass that was just within its reach.

'Feel?' Watson raised a single eyebrow as he contemplated the question. 'I feel nothing. I am not a godly man, if that is what you mean, Mr Lark. I prefer to place my faith in history and in science. If my studies have taught me anything, it is that the people who have inhabited this earth have always believed in a god of some sort or another, or even multiple gods, come to that. All have proven to be false. I would not be surprised if in a thousand years from now, historians and academics look back at us and wonder how we could have persisted with such superstitious nonsense.'

'So you're in?' Jack cut through the bluster and sought a direct answer to his question.

'Yes, Mr Lark. I have no faith. I care only for knowledge. If I had to desecrate the tomb of the carpenter himself, I would do so without hesitation or regret.'

Jack nodded. 'There we have it then. We are doing this.'

There was nothing more to be said. The four men would start their campaign in earnest. They would rob a church.

Chapter Twenty-eight

———•◆•———

Jack led them in fast. They raced across the ground at something just short of a gallop, riding in a line abreast. The grass flashed past under their horses' hooves, the speed mesmerising. Jack could feel something stir as he rode, the fast pace pulling emotions from hidden places deep inside him. He felt alive. Resurrected. Powerful.

'There!' Cooper was the first to spot a building around a quarter of a mile ahead.

Jack saw it immediately. It did not look like any church he had seen before. A stone and earth wall surrounded a substantial mud hut with a bushy thatched roof that was supported on a number of thick wooden poles. There looked to be just the one entrance, a gap in the surrounding wall that was left open without gate or barrier.

As one, the four angled their path so that they headed directly towards the simple entrance, holding their mounts in check as they fought the animals' instinct to increase their speed. Yet something in the horses' excitement was infectious, and they found themselves accelerating, the animals' hooves flaying at the ground so that dust and sand was kicked up like bullets.

They came to a noisy halt just shy of the entrance, tackle jangling, breathless horses neighing and snorting.

Jack dismounted first, boots thumping on the hard, sun-baked ground. He could feel his heart pounding in his chest. 'Cooper, stay at the entrance. Keep a sharp eye out.' He gathered his horse's reins in preparation for leading it through the gap.

'Oh, come on, Jack-o. Don't leave me outside.'

'Do as you're bloody well told. Someone has to stand guard. That someone is you.' Jack was unmoved by Cooper's plea. He led his horse on, pulling hard to steer the mare after him through the open entrance.

The ground inside the wall had been cleared, although it was still littered with the stumps of the thorny bushes that had once covered the ground. A few trees had been cut back so that little more than a trunk and a couple of straggly branches remained. There was nothing else to see. And there was no one to greet them, the church seemingly quite deserted.

'Leave the horses.' Jack walked to the remains of what might once have been a handsome tree and tied the reins to its largest remaining branch. He looked around, checking that the others were doing the same. He was pleased to see that Cooper had taken up a position near the entrance that would allow him to warn them if anyone else approached.

Satisfied that he was being obeyed, he turned his attention to the church itself. It stood around twenty yards from the opening to the compound. A square entrance hall stuck out from the round building. He walked towards it, striding across the ground without hesitation.

The building's simple wooden door was unlocked, yet still he paused at the threshold, looking to his two companions. It was eerily quiet, unsettling even. He saw the same uneasy emotion reflected on both their faces. Something in the moment was unnerving, as if they were where they were not supposed to be.

'Jack, I'm not sure about this . . .' Macgregor started to speak.

Jack did not wait to listen to more. There was no turning away from this moment. He had long ago learned to be the one to take the step forward when others hesitated. Sometimes that meant advancing on the battlefield, or moving towards enemy fire. Sometimes it meant pushing back a thin, poorly made wooden door and stepping inside a church.

It was cool inside, but the first thing he noticed was the smell, the air perfumed with a mix of dust, incense and jasmine. He moved forward, treading slowly and carefully, expecting to be challenged at any moment. Yet nothing greeted him but silence.

The walls in the hall were decorated with a series of frescoes. One depicted an Abyssinian warrior fighting a horrific mis-shapen animal that appeared to be a cross between an elephant and a lion. Further on, a knight was captured at the moment of spearing a dragon. A doe-eyed maiden looked on in delighted horror, her hands clasped to her bosom.

'Good old St George,' Macgregor whispered as he glanced over Jack's shoulder. 'That fellow sure got around. There must have been a hell of a lot of dragons to spear back then.'

Jack smiled at the glib remark, then stretched out a hand to hold Macgregor back. 'I'll go first. Stay here with Watson.' He found he was whispering, even though they had still not seen a single soul. He did not know why the air of the church was disturbing him so.

He made himself stride forward, his boots thumping onto the compacted earth that made up the simple floor. He passed more images. One depicted a man he reckoned to be Jesus standing over a table filled with bounty, his hands spread wide as if gesturing to the viewer to step forward and partake in the feast.

The combination of the images was almost enough to make him smile. The men who had decorated the entrance to this church certainly knew what they were about. The images played to a trio of appealing ideas – heroes, lust and feasting. It was no wonder there were so many Christians. But he would never be one of them. He had seen too much of the world, and witnessed too much suffering, to believe in a cosy, beneficent god.

As he reached the end of the hallway, he put all thoughts of faith behind him. He would trust in nothing but himself and the Colt revolver on his hip.

Beyond the entrance hall was a round central chamber. It was quite empty. At its far side stood a simple wooden altar. The smell of incense was far stronger here, as was the fragrance of jasmine, the poles that supported the conical thatched roof decorated with long strands of cut flowers.

Jack crossed the open space, eyes scanning around him, alert for danger.

'Oi! Stop, you bleeding rascal!' It was Cooper who shouted, his voice just about carrying from his watch post outside.

'You two stay here!' Jack snapped the instruction at Watson and Macgregor then moved fast, going back the way he had come, drawing the revolver from its holster on his right side as he went. He emerged from the entrance hall to see Cooper facing down the side of the church, his hands on his hips. From his expression and his posture, it was clear he was not happy.

'What is it?' Jack snapped.

'Some dirty fucking rascal just ran past me.'

'You didn't stop him?'

'I didn't see him until the last bleeding minute.'

'Where did he go?'

'Out the back.'

'Where?' Jack started to walk around the circular building. He had not seen a second entrance in the wall.

'There, by those bushes.' Cooper pointed.

Jack moved closer to the sparse shrubbery. It was only when he was a couple of yards away that he saw the hidden doorway. The tiny door was covered with mud, so that it blended into the surrounding earth and stone wall. Now it was half open.

'Who was he?' He crossed to the doorway and looked out. He saw no one.

'Who fucking knows.' Cooper hawked snot, then spat. 'Good riddance to him, I say. He'd only make trouble if he saw us pinching stuff.'

'Unless he comes back with some friends.' Jack holstered his revolver, then carefully closed the door. 'Find something to block this up. We don't want anyone sneaking back in. Then go back to the main entrance. And this time, try to stop anyone who fancies it wandering past you.'

'Weren't my fault, Jack-o,' Cooper whined.

'I seem to be hearing you say that a lot these days.' Jack shook his head and went to join the other two back inside. There was no point in giving Cooper a bollocking, not now. He just hoped the man would have the sense to shout out if anyone else came towards the church.

Chapter Twenty-nine

———◆·◆·◆———

'We have it, Jack, we have it!' Watson shouted for Jack's attention the moment he returned to the main chamber at the heart of the simple church. He was brandishing a solid gold chalice as if he had just found the Holy Grail itself.

'Where was it?' Jack joined him. The chalice looked a fine find indeed.

'In a niche near the altar.' Watson's face was flushed with excitement. 'It is the treasure I read about, Jack. It is at least one hundred years old, perhaps more, and solid gold. This alone is worth a small fortune.' He turned the chalice around, examining every side. 'It is exactly as it was described. Can you credit that? It is absolutely perfect.' The words came in a reverential whisper.

'What else is there?' Jack pushed past Watson. He wanted to know if there was more to be found.

Macgregor was squatting on his haunches as he delved inside a small compartment cut into the wall of the church. 'Just this.' He handed a silver basin over his shoulder.

'Just indeed.' Jack shook his head as he took the basin. The metal was cool to the touch. 'It's worth a pretty penny.'

He examined the artefact, holding it out then turning it around in his hands. The metal was dulled with age, but it still caught something of the light that was filtering down through openings in the roof above. It had a beautiful quality to it, for all its simplicity.

'Jack, get out here bloody sharpish!' For the second time, Cooper called out in warning.

'What now?' Jack muttered as he moved to answer the summons.

Cooper was rushing into the entrance hall just as Jack reached it.

'A mob of local lads is heading this way,' he reported breathlessly.

'Shit.' They had dallied too long. 'Is your revolver loaded?'

'Of course.'

'Then get back to the entrance. Shoot at the bastards as soon as they are thirty yards away.'

'Shoot at them?' Cooper sounded horrified at the notion.

'You won't hit them, but it might be enough to make them think twice about getting any bloody closer.' Jack turned on the spot. There were good positions in the hall where a man could shelter as he fired on anyone rushing the entrance. He was selecting the best when he noticed that Cooper was still standing there. 'Go! Now!'

But Cooper did not move to obey. Instead, he just stood there. For it was already too late.

A large group of Abyssinian warriors were no more than twenty yards away, heading for the opening in the wall that surrounded the compound. Not one was dressed alike. Some were naked above the waist, their finely muscled torsos shining with sweat. Others wore a shamma, the mix of shades encompassing everything from white to grey, some draped over the shoulders, some tied into a thick band worn across the body. Two were covered in robes from head to foot, their faces hidden away beneath black cotton pagdi. All carried a small round hide shield. Some paired it with a matchlock musket, whilst others carried the long spear that was so commonplace in these lands.

Only one man stood out. He wore bright white robes and a dirty brown animal skin lembd draped over his shoulders, the spotted hide decorated with brass studs. It fell in long panels down his front and sides, the ones over his chest held together with a great brass buckle. In his hands he carried a huge double-edged sabre shaped like a sickle.

'Shit.' Jack took one look at the warriors, then drew his revolver from its holster. He did not think the men now rushing through the gap in the wall would want to parley.

'Put that stuff away, then get out here now!' he shouted over his shoulder at the two men still inside the church, then raised his revolver and fired into the air.

'Stop!' He held up a hand, waving it from side to side as he made a rough tally of the Abyssinians' numbers. There were at least thirteen or fourteen of them, maybe more. Too many for him to fight.

He raised the revolver again and fired a second bullet into the sky. 'Stop there, goddammit!'

'They're not stopping!' Watson's panicked voice came from behind him. Macgregor was there too, as was Cooper, the three bunching around Jack as he tried to stop the small horde rushing towards them.

The Abyssinians spread out as they entered the compound.

They knew what they were about, each man making space for others. In a matter of moments, they formed a rough C-shaped line in front of the four men who stood in the church's entrance, every Abyssinian aiming his musket or pointing his spear.

'Put the guns away.' Jack gave the order. It was the only course of action he could take. He had fought a hundred times, maybe more. He knew how to butcher an enemy, and how to massacre an outnumbered foe without any notion of mercy. But he had also learned the much harder lesson of when not to fight, when not to throw lives away in a futile gesture of soon-to-be-forgotten belligerence.

'Jack?' Macgregor questioned the instruction.

'Do as I say, for fuck's sake,' Jack barked. The tension of the moment gripped tight. He was making the decision and he was making it alone.

The Abyssinians were shouting now. Angry voices filled the compound, echoing from the mud and stone walls. Only their leader was silent.

Jack could just about make out the sound of revolvers being put away. He followed his own order, holstering his Colt. As soon as his hands were free, he raised them to the sky, hoping the universal gesture for peace would be understood.

'Don't shoot.' He spoke in as calm a voice as he could, directing his words at the warriors' leader. 'You understand me? We haven't got anything of yours, okay?' He took a half-step forward, hands spread wide.

The Abyssinian leader shouted an order. It silenced his men in a heartbeat. Yet it did nothing to move the weapons that were being aimed at the four white interlopers.

'We were just having a look-see.' Jack took another cautious, careful step towards the warriors' leader. 'Do you speak English? Do you understand what I'm saying?' He kept his tone soft and gentle.

The leader watched him carefully. Then he barked another order, and his men raised their muskets and spears, readying them for use.

'Jack, he's not getting it,' Macgregor warned.

'I can see that,' Jack snapped.

Again the Abyssinian leader shouted. This time he was greeted by whoops and yells from his men. Angry shouts once again filled the compound, the warriors summoning the courage they would need for what was to come.

'They're going to bloody attack,' Cooper said. 'For Christ's sake, Jack, do something.'

Jack watched the leader closely. He could see the fury in the man's expression, his hatred of the foreigner who now stood in front of him obvious. Cooper was right. There would be no avoiding bloodshed. Not that day.

'Shit.' He hissed the word under his breath. Around him, the shouting intensified, the Abyssinian warriors beginning to chant. Their war cry filled his head, the sound assaulting his senses so that he could barely think. But he had been here before. He knew what had to be done.

The chant grew louder, and the Abyssinians' leader raised his hand. His face twisted into a snarl, then he opened his mouth.

Jack calmed his mind and steadied his body. He would have one chance and one chance only.

He drew his revolver in one smooth, practised motion. As soon as the weapon was level with his hip, he fired.

The bullet struck the Abyssinian warlord in the throat. At such close range, it tore through the flesh and gristle before bursting from the back of his neck.

For one agonised moment, the warlord stared back at Jack, eyes that had been narrowed in anger widening in a moment of pure shock and terror. Then the blood came in an unstoppable torrent, flooding his mouth and what was left of his throat.

Before the Abyssinians could react, a great storm of rifle fire tore into them from behind, scything nearly half from their feet. Men hit by the powerful bullets cried out in anguish, their despairing cries echoing off the walls of the compound.

'Get down!' Jack bellowed the warning, then ducked inside the entrance to the church. Cooper, Watson and Macgregor did not need to be told twice, and all dived out of sight.

'What the hell is happening?' Macgregor shouted the question, desperate to know what had happened to unleash such chaos.

'No idea! Shit!' Jack tried to see who it was who had opened fire, but bullets were impacting into the walls of the church facing the entrance to the compound, and wickedly sharp shards of sun-hardened mud and stone were showering down in every direction.

'Is it our chaps?' Macgregor demanded.

'Maybe. Now shut up and keep down!' Jack had no idea what was happening, but he knew at that moment that it did not matter one jot who had arrived to save their bacon. The one thing that was clear was that the rifle fire was coming from the far side of the entrance to the compound. It came without pause, bullet after bullet hammering into the Abyssinian warriors.

Some of the Abyssinians turned and tried to fight the enemy that had ambushed them from behind. Muskets coughed as they were fired, the defiant return fire filling the open space outside the church with a thick cloud of pungent powder smoke. Most, though, fell where they stood, their white robes slathered in blood as limbs were ripped from bodies and huge gouges were torn in flesh.

As the cloud of smoke cleared, Jack got his first glimpse of the men who had come to their rescue. And he knew their fate was sealed.

'Run!' He turned to bellow the command at the three men still sheltering in the church's entrance hall. 'Run! Now!'

He did not wait to see if he was obeyed. His only thought was to get away.

His boots scrabbled on the dusty ground, then he was running. He heard the pounding of boots on the ground behind him, but he did not look back. Instead he concentrated on reaching the half-hidden exit they had found to the rear of the compound.

'Why are we running?' Macgregor managed to gasp the words as he charged after Jack.

'Finch!' Jack shouted the name.

It was not the British army who had come to their rescue. It was a man who had no right to be there. A man who wanted nothing more than to kill Jack Lark.

Chapter Thirty

---

*J*ack pumped his arms and ran as fast as he could. Already the volume of fire was dying away as Finch and his men ran out of targets for their rifles. Their ambush had been swift, brutal and dreadfully effective.

'Fuck it.' His chest was heaving with exertion, but he still found enough breath to offer the pithy verdict on what he saw as he reached the hidden exit. For once, Cooper had done what Jack had asked. And he had done it well.

The half-hidden doorway was blocked. Cooper had dragged over a small mountain of fallen wood and brush that he had found piled behind the church. The heap of debris now blocked their only escape route.

'Clear it!' There was nothing else for it, not if they wanted to escape from Finch. Jack dived forward and grabbed hold of a splintered and broken branch, hauling it backwards and away from the door.

Macgregor and Watson needed no further urging. Both rushed to help, reaching out to tear away the rough and ready barricade.

'Get on with it, Cooper,' Jack snarled as he dragged his branch away.

'He's not here.' It was Watson who answered him.

'What?' Jack dropped the branch and whirled around. Cooper was still standing near the church's entrance, waving wildly and shouting.

Jack looked across the compound. Finch and his men were rushing forward. Each man carried a brand-new Snider rifle. They ran towards Cooper, ignoring the bodies strewn across the dusty ground. For one moment, Jack thought they would shoot him down where he stood. Then Cooper turned.

The two men were no more than a hundred yards apart. Jack was close enough to make out every detail of the face that had been part of his life for the past five years. He could see fear on the familiar features, but there was something else there too, a peculiar expression that he had only seen before on the faces of soldiers at the end of a battle, in that glorious moment when they realised they had survived and been victorious.

Cooper lifted a hand and pointed directly at Jack. Finch did not need anything more. He shouted an order, setting his men in motion towards their quarry.

In that moment, Jack understood.

Cooper had turned his coat.

He had betrayed them all.

'Go! Go! Go!' Jack turned away. They had no time left. In seconds, Finch's men would start to fire.

'What about Cooper?' It was Watson who shouted the question, his pale face wide-eyed with the stress of the moment.

'He's not coming!'

'What?'

'He's a traitor! Now move!'

Jack threw himself at Cooper's jury-rigged barricade. Only a few branches remained. He grabbed the largest, not caring that a splinter lacerated the palm of his hand. Around him, Watson and Macgregor were doing the same, both men red-faced, sweat streaking their skin.

A bullet snapped past them. It buried itself in the mud wall not more than a yard away from Watson.

'That'll do!' Jack shouted. He darted forward, grabbing at the simple arrangement of planks that passed for a door. He snatched it away, throwing it to one side, then stood aside, his back against the wall. 'Go!'

Watson needed no further urging. He dived for the entrance, stumbling as he bent low enough to get through the small opening.

More bullets spat through the air. Each one made a dreadful whip-crack sound before it thumped into the wall.

'Go!' Jack grabbed at Macgregor's arm, tugging him towards the door.

'No.' Macgregor was staring back at Finch and his thugs. Some were kneeling as they aimed at the men trying to flee. The rest were rushing forward, moving fast. It would not take them long to cover the distance between the two groups. 'We won't stand a chance if they get here.' Macgregor's head darted back and forth as he assessed distances. Then he turned, his left arm reaching out to grab Jack, his other drawing his revolver. 'I'll hold them off. Get Watson away.'

'They'll kill you.' Jack stared back at Macgregor. His friend's face was pale, drained of all colour.

'We have no time to discuss it.' Macgregor snapped the words, then shoved Jack towards the door. 'If we all run, those bloody rifles will cut us down before we've gone fifty yards. So go, goddammit, whilst you still can.'

Jack knew Macgregor was right. There was no cover outside. If Finch's men reached the exit, they would be able to shoot at the three of them as they ran from the compound. It would be as easy as knifing an eel in a barrel. Yet if one of them held them at bay, the other two would at least have a chance of getting away. It was a good plan, a sound one even. Still he hesitated.

'I'll do it!' He shook off Macgregor's hand. He meant it. He would not allow another man to remain behind whilst he ran.

'It's you they want. Not me. If you stay, you're a dead man. Now go! Keep Watson safe.' Macgregor turned away. 'Go on, whilst you can, you dolt.' He fired the words over his shoulder.

Jack was rooted to the spot. Every part of him screamed at him to stay, to stand at Macgregor's shoulder and see it through to the end.

'Come on, for Christ's sake.' Watson reached through the opening in the wall, hands clawing at him, trying to tug him outside.

'Go, Jack. This is it. This is my time.' Macgregor's head whipped around. His eyes caught Jack's own. 'It's what I came for.' He flashed his friend a tight smile. Then he turned away.

There was nothing more to be said.

Jack ducked low, stooping through the doorway. A glance back showed him Macgregor crouching behind some of the branches they had dragged away from the secret exit. Then came the familiar cough of a revolver. He had started to fight. He was giving them a chance.

'Where's Macgregor?' Watson grabbed at Jack the moment he came through the opening.

'He's holding them off.' Jack hissed the words as he straightened up. There was no more to be said and nothing else to be done. It was just time to run.

He took hold of Watson's arm and half pulled, half dragged him away from the opening in the wall.

Watson stared back at him, red-rimmed eyes full of disbelief and fear. But he understood well enough.

The two of them ran, pounding away from the compound, boots thumping into ground baked hard by the sun. Neither looked back, but both heard the sound of Macgregor's revolver firing steadily. Both counted the shots, even as their breath roared in their ears and their hearts pounded in their chests.

By the time Macgregor fired his last bullet, they were a hundred yards away. Ahead, the land sloped upwards. Rocks and boulders littered the ground, offering cover for two men running for their very lives.

Jack and Watson galloped up the slope, feet scrabbling on the broken scree. Neither paused, not even when the rifle fire died out behind them.

It was not until they had scrambled their way close to the summit of the small rise that Jack stopped them. Both were breathing hard. Yet there was no need to run further. They were far enough away to be safe, for the moment at least.

He turned around to look back towards the church. From their vantage point, they could see into the compound. Macgregor was being hauled forward by two of Finch's men. They manhandled him towards Finch and Cooper, who still stood near the church's entrance.

'Did he get any?' Watson asked, the words coming between gasps for breath.

'No.' Jack could see none of Finch's men on the ground. It gave him hope. Finch had no quarrel with Macgregor. There was a chance he would be spared. He would be beaten, but he did not have to die.

He watched as Macgregor was brought to stand in front of Finch.

Cooper was speaking. Jack was too far away to hear the words, but he could see Cooper's mouth moving. Finch stood silent throughout, looking at Macgregor, who remained straight-backed in front of him. He did not flinch or try to run, not even as Finch's right arm rose, a small black object clasped tight in its grip.

He was still standing like that when Finch pulled the trigger.

Macgregor's body fell like a ragdoll, and he crumpled at Finch's feet. He did not move again.

Finch was not done. He lowered the revolver, then fired again and again into Macgregor's prostrate body, which twitched and spasmed as each bullet struck home.

'My God,' whispered Watson. He turned away, bent double and puked.

Jack swallowed his own horror, forcing the bile back down his gullet.

Finch stopped shooting. Macgregor's body lay still.

The group had been four. Now they were two.

Chapter Thirty-one

———◆———

Storm clouds gathered. They moved slowly across the sky, heavy, sinister, ominous. The smell in the air changed. The fresh, clean tang of the mountains was pushed aside by something damper and darker. The air grew thick as the gloom smothered the land, stealing away the sun and shrouding the world in shadow.

Jack walked in silence. It started to rain. It did not start slowly, not like the rain in the English countryside. This was foreign rain. Rain that fell in great thundering torrents. Rain that churned the arid, desiccated ground so that it appeared to boil and bubble, like soup warming on a stove. Rain that pounded into a man's skull, filling it with noise. Rain that chilled a man to the bone in a matter of minutes. Rain that tormented. Rain that filled a man's soul with misery.

The first peal of thunder reverberated across the heavens. It rumbled in the distance like a locomotive leaving a faraway station, and dragged on, heavy and ponderous, the prelude to the storm that was to come.

Their pace slowed as they started to slip and slide, the

uppermost layer of thin soil beneath their boots turned into so much slurry.

'We need shelter.' Watson broke the silence.

Jack looked back at him as if he did not understand. It took him a while to nod by way of reply.

They turned from the trail they had been following, shuffling along like tramps long tired of roaming the lost roads of abandoned souls.

A native house came into view through the murk. It was perched on a flat rocky ledge. It did not look like much; little more than a simple ragged thatched roof on top of mud walls that had long since turned to the grey-brown colour of month-old dog shit. But it would do.

Jack did not bother to call out or shout for attention. He approached the meagre arrangement of wood that passed for a door, kicked it open and went straight inside.

He was greeted by a scream.

The woman moved fast. The moment Jack blundered into the hut, she was on her feet. As he came forward, she backed away, a long knife held in her hand.

There was not much to the hut. It was made up of a single room about fifteen feet in diameter, the conical roof supported by a sturdy post. A hole had been left in the centre of the roof for smoke to escape from the fire pit beneath. The fire was lit, the smoke rushing upwards in a tight column.

'Shit.' Jack swore. He raised both hands, showing them to the woman palm first. 'We're not going to hurt you.'

She crouched low, knife held at her side. She showed no fear.

'Goodness!' Watson exclaimed as he followed Jack inside. 'What are we going to do with her?'

'Shut up.' Jack snapped the words over his shoulder, keeping his eyes on the woman. He guessed she was in her late twenties, or perhaps a little older. She was barely dressed, her upper body naked whilst her legs were covered in a simple wrap skirt. Around her neck was the ubiquitous blue cord along with a necklace of cowry shells.

'We won't hurt you,' he repeated, then took a step forward.

The woman shrieked as he moved, and a torrent of words spewed out of her. Jack did not understand a word, but he saw her jerk the knife forward, its tip held at the same height as his groin. From what he could see in her expression, she would gut him without a qualm.

'For fuck's sake,' he hissed. He slipped his right hand to his holster, his fingers cradling the handle of his Colt. Left hand still held out, he began to draw the weapon, keeping his movements slow. One bullet would end the situation before it became more dangerous. It would be an easy enough shot to make, the woman no more than ten paces away.

'Jack!' Watson spotted the movement and cried out, certain he knew what Jack was about to do.

'Shut your muzzle.' Jack spat the words then drew the revolver. 'I don't have a bloody choice.'

Watson ignored the order. 'Don't do it!' he begged.

Jack took a half-step forward, then crouched down, his left hand held out the whole time. 'It's all right, love. We're not going to hurt you.' He laid the Colt on the ground. 'See. It's all right.' He repeated the same words, keeping his voice calm and steady.

The woman watched him. She fired out another staccato sentence, but her words came out with less force. She understood.

Jack glanced at Watson. 'Put your gun on the ground.'

'Of course.' The relief in Watson's voice was obvious. 'I thought you were going to shoot her,' he hissed as he did what he was told and placed his own revolver on the ground.

'I thought about it.' Jack held both hands towards the woman. 'See. No harm.' He remembered their arrival at Sooroo. '*Christo*,' he said. Using his right hand, he gestured towards his neck. 'We're *Christo*, just like you.'

The woman looked at him, then at Watson. '*Christo*?'

'Yes, love. *Christo*.'

The knife lowered, then the woman directed a fast burst of words at them.

'We don't understand.' Watson spoke slowly, as if to a child. '*Tayib*?'

'*Tayib*,' the woman repeated. She came towards them, then placed her knife on the ground, mirroring their actions.

'Thank the Lord,' Watson breathed.

'I think you should thank me, not him,' Jack scoffed. 'Have you got any money?'

'A little.'

'Get it out. Show it to her.'

Watson dug a hand into a pocket, pulling out two Maria Theresa thalers, which he showed to the woman.

'*Tayib*.' She repeated the single word, then she smiled.

Jack sat close to the flames, savouring the feel of the warmth on his skin. His soaked clothing hung from the hut's central supporting pole, where it steamed gently. His boots were at his side, near the fire.

'When the weather turns, we will head back to Annesley.' He directed the words to Watson, who sat at his side. Like

Jack, he had stripped down to his drawers.

'Why?' Watson was staring deep into the flames. He did not look around as Jack broke the silence.

'I'll make sure you get home.'

Jack glanced over at the woman whose hut they had forced their way into. They had learned that her name was Mazza, or at least something close to that. Watson had been the one to communicate, a protracted exchange of mime and gesture that had allowed them to discover that she was quite alone in the world. From what he could gather from her reaction to his name, she had no love for Tewodros. It was understandable. The emperor had no qualms about purging his own people, and Watson suspected that her family had been victims of his tyrannical rule, her husband and two sons murdered for their overlord's alleged betrayal. Jack was not so sure, but his interest was in more practical matters, and he had been pleased to make Mazza understand that they wanted food. Now she was busy on the far side of the fire, preparing something that looked like a pea soup.

'I don't want to go home.' Watson sounded like a petulant schoolboy ordered to leave a friend's party early.

'What *do* you want to do then?' Jack tried not to sigh. He had a sense that the conversation would be a difficult one.

'Carry on, of course.'

'And do what?'

'And do what we came here for. We find the riches we know are here.'

'You think that's a good idea?'

'I do not think we have a choice. We can't go back to London now. Not after . . .' His voice broke as he tried to speak of the day's horror. 'We owe it to Macgregor.' He forced his wavering voice to harden. 'He sponsored this expedition. Do you not think we should see it through to its completion?' He paused. 'I cannot believe it happened.' The words were spoken so softly that they were barely audible.

'You will in time. But you won't forget it, I promise you that.' Jack knew that that was true.

'Or him.' Watson fixed Jack with an intense stare. 'I shall not forget our friend. I cannot believe he is gone. He was alive just a short time ago. Now . . .' He left the thought unfinished.

'Now you move on.'

'Just like that?' Watson looked at Jack as if he were the cruellest, most callous man in the world.

Jack wiped a hand across his face. 'No, not just like that. But you do it anyway. You cannot help it. Everyone moves on, no matter what. No matter how bad it is or how much it hurts. So just let it happen.'

'You make it sound easy.'

Jack bit his tongue. 'No. It isn't that.' He paused, letting the words settle. 'So, if you don't want to go back, what do you want to do next?'

'Ah, yes, now that is a good question.' Watson was watching the flames carefully. 'It is clear we shall have to avoid Finch.'

'Or kill him.' Jack almost smiled as Watson winced at the very mention of more death.

'He deserves it,' Watson admitted, then grimaced. 'However, I am not sure it is our place to serve such a sentence.'

'Then whose is it?'

'The authorities'.'

'Do you see them out here?' Jack did not bother to moderate his contemptuous tone.

'No. But we could report him. I am sure the British army would not let murder go unpunished.'

'The British army won't give a flying fuck. They've got enough on their plate.'

'So, we are to be judge, jury and executioner?'

'Yes.'

'Does "thou shalt not kill" mean anything to you?' Watson glanced at Jack.

'No.' Jack did not flinch from the accusation in Watson's gaze. He held his stare until the academic broke it and looked away. 'Finch deserves to die for what he did, you said as much yourself.'

'So you would kill him? You would live with that on your conscience?'

'Happily.'

'I could not do that.' Watson settled himself more comfortably. 'I rather think I am learning my limitations. But I do not believe it would be easy, even for a man like you.' His brow furrowed as he pondered the idea. 'He has his men there, and Cooper now, I suppose.'

'We could kill them all.' Jack was deadly serious.

Cooper. Just the thought of the man's name was enough to fire the anger in his belly. As they had walked, the storm lashing down around them, he had tried to puzzle out Cooper's treachery. He could not have been turned until after they had escaped Finch's warehouse; Finch would never have allowed him to set Jack free. So it must have happened later, perhaps when he had first spotted Finch in Suez, or more likely when he had caught up with them at the wells at Upper Sooroo. From there, it all made sense. Cooper had led Finch to them, then encouraged them to flee, effectively separating them from the safety of the army. Finch was no fool. He would not commit murder in front of a hundred watching eyes. But once they had gone off on their own, they were fair game. Cooper had kept him informed of their plans and told him about the out-of-the-way church Watson had discovered. It gave Finch the perfect opportunity to kill them, and to secure himself some treasure into the bargain.

'I'll kill them all.' Jack repeated the bloody ambition in a hushed tone. Cooper would pay the price for his betrayal.

'I think you might indeed succeed in killing every man that has crossed you, Mr Lark. But equally I think you could die trying.' Watson gave his verdict.

'Maybe.'

'And of course, that would leave me in something of a bind.'

'It would.'

'So perhaps there is another plan to consider.'

'Go on.'

'We continue. We secure what we came for.'

'Which is?'

'Funds for us both, naturally. The chance for me to find resources for my studies. But there is something else . . .' Watson gave one of his odd little smiles. 'I also intend to write an account of our time here.'

Jack bit back the urge to scoff. 'You think anyone will want to read it?'

'They will.'

'Why?'

'Perhaps we shall have a tale that will astound.' Watson looked at Jack coyly, as if revealing the first hint of a newly formed ambition.

Jack had no interest in probing deeper. The idea of a book

held no appeal for him. He thought only of the practical, of keeping them both alive. 'Cooper knows where we camped. Even now, he'll be leading Finch there, and as sure as eggs is eggs, they'll take all our gear. If we go back to the army, they'll find us for sure. It's no secret that the whole bloody column is heading to Magdala.'

'Then we don't go back to the army.'

'So we just carry on? The two of us on our own? With no equipment or supplies?'

'We could.' Watson considered the notion.

'What about the locals? You think they'll take kindly to a couple of fellows like us wandering around? As soon as anyone loyal to that mad bugger Tewodros claps eyes on us, we're done for. We'd stand out like a pair of sore thumbs.' Jack sighed. Watson was a man of words and thought. He was clever for sure, but he was as callow as a griffin and about as much use.

'There is another way.'

'There is?'

'Have you heard of Captain Speedy of the Intelligence Corps?' Watson leaned forward and poked the fire with a twig he had taken from the underside of the roof.

'No.'

'He has become rather famous, or perhaps infamous is the right word. He has made something of a name for himself in these parts.'

'How has he done that?' Jack heard something in Watson's tone that made him hold back a sharper retort. He sensed Watson had been preparing this conversation for some time.

'Well, this is the interesting thing. He has a reputation for being able to go anywhere, and I mean *anywhere*.'

'How?'

'It's rather simple. He dresses as a local. Then he walks right into their camps. He has a chat with their leader, or whoever he wants to see, then walks right back out again.'

'Now you're the one making it sound easy.'

'I do not think that is the case at all. It is by no means easy. But this is the remarkable thing. Speedy is something of a giant. The fellow is well over six feet tall, and he has done nothing to tame his red hair and beard. Yet no one stops him.'

Jack grunted. It sounded a ridiculous tale. But something about it rang true, especially in this confusing and chaotic land. Being an impostor was not as hard as some would believe. It required balls, but with the right clothes and the right manner, it was amazing what could be achieved.

'I was rather thinking we could imitate Captain Speedy ourselves.'

Watson stared at Jack, waiting for a reaction.

'And go where?' Jack did not scoff or dismiss the idea.

'We go where the treasure is, Mr Lark.' Watson smiled. For once, it lit up his face. 'We go to Magdala.'

Chapter Thirty-two

'Give her the money.'

Watson did as he was told. The woman took the coins quickly, tucking them away somewhere in the folds of her skirt.

He pulled a wry expression as he glanced back at Jack. 'You look like a footpad, Mr Lark.'

'You think you look any better?' Jack fired back the retort.

The two men were now dressed like locals in white shammas, knee-length trousers and simple white cotton shirts. Mazza had provided them with the clothes in exchange for half the coins Watson had with him. It was the trade of the century, but they had had little choice. They could hardly blunder around the countryside dressed in khaki. Not if they were going to accomplish the plan Watson had concocted. Not if they were going to walk all the way to Magdala on their own.

'It's not too late to go back.' Jack dangled the lure in front of Watson to see if he bit. Once they started out on their long journey, there would be no room for doubt or second thoughts. They had to be fully committed, or else they would surely die.

'No.' Watson spoke the single word with surprising power. 'We cannot turn away now.'

Jack smiled. He could see the change that had been wrought in Watson by the last weeks. He was no longer the timid academic he had been when they had departed London. 'We can wait until the army has defeated that Tewodros fellow and then go into Magdala. You will still be able to write your account of our journey, and it would be a damn sight less dangerous. All we would have to do is avoid Finch.'

Watson grimaced and shook his head. 'But then I would be just one of many. This army is packed full of newspaper-men and reporters, all of whom are already compiling their accounts of the expedition. My story would not be unique. But if we dare to go in now, I will have a tale that will astonish the world.' His face came alive. 'To be the men who were in Magdala *before* it fell. The men who thumbed their noses at Tewodros. Why, *those* men will be known for all time.' His excitement at the idea was palpable, and he grinned at Jack, his expression rife with anticipation.

'What if we die?'

'Then we die trying to be something more than we are. We die trying to be more than ordinary.' Watson had com-posed himself and now gave one of his odd little smiles. 'But I'd rather we didn't die, Mr Lark, if it's all the same to you. I would very much enjoy the chance to return to London and enjoy my notoriety.' He made a play of looking up and down. 'Although I don't fancy our chances if you insist on looking like that.'

'What do you mean?'

Watson pointed at Jack's army boots. 'You cannot think of wearing those.'

'I don't think that's the only giveaway, do you?' Jack indicated the pale, hairy leg emerging from his simple knee-length trousers.

'Nonsense.' Watson fished in the pile of clothing Mazza had produced once she had understood they were in the market to buy. 'Here, we can use these as puttees.' He tossed a long strip of cotton cloth to Jack. 'Then we use these pagdi to hide our faces when need be.' He held up a blue scarf to demonstrate his point. 'No one will suspect us. Unless, of course, you insist on wearing those blessed boots.'

'You really think it will work?'

'I don't see why not.' Watson fished a pair of sandals from the pile. 'These will do.'

Jack looked down at his boots. He was an infantryman at heart. Giving up a pair of broken-in boots that fitted perfectly went against everything he had learned. But Watson was quite right. He could hardly expect not to draw attention if he wore them. 'Fine.'

He sat down and started to unlace the boots. He knew the sandals would be devils to become used to. The thought of the pain to come pulled him up short. For all Watson's confidence, he still had his doubts. He was not even sure he could articulate why he was going along with the plan. He had been rich and he had been poor, and although neither state either excited or daunted him, he supposed he would rather be rich, and so the idea of looting Tewodros's fortress held some appeal. Then there was Watson's hope of writing some sort of account of their adventure. That ambition meant nothing to Jack. There would be narratives aplenty once the campaign was done; more than enough to satiate the desire of John Bull to know more of the demise of the Gorilla King. And even that desire would wane soon enough. As soon as Tewodros had been overthrown, he would likely be forgotten, attention diverted by the next despot to rebel, or by an explorer who found the source of one river or another. The British public was easily distracted and quick to forget.

So why was he going? Was it as some form of legacy for Macgregor? Yet so many people he had known had died over the years, or had left him in one way or another. Macgregor was just one more to add to that extensive list. No memorial could be achieved through risking their lives. To do so was folly, nothing more.

He pulled off his boots and set them to one side. There was another reason for him to go on. The idea of entering Magdala before it fell intrigued him. It was something that no one would believe possible, and that alone made him want to be the man who did it. It was more bloody-mindedness than pride, but the notion was stuck in his mind now, and he knew it would itch there until he had scratched it away.

And there was something else. Something that drove him on more than any desire for riches or yearning to do something thought impossible. If he fled now, he would be leaving this chapter in his life unfinished. He would be leaving with a score unsettled.

He slipped the sandals on, then got to his feet. It was time to make a start. There would be plenty of opportunity to rest when Finch and Cooper were dead.

Mazza came to stand in front of him, something half hidden in her hands. When she held them out, he saw it was one of the blue cords that so many of the Abyssinians wore.

'Christo.' She said the single word, then stood on tiptoe, reaching up to secure the cord around his neck.

'Thank you.' Jack knew she would not understand, but he was pleased to see her smile.

'Now that looks better,' Watson said as she came to tie another of the blue cords around his neck. 'I doubt our own mothers would recognise us.'

Jack grunted at the remark. It was the kind of thing people said. It meant nothing. He reckoned his own mother would recognise him, no matter what clothing he wore. But she was long dead, and all thoughts of her were buried deep in the dark recesses of his mind where he feared to venture.

He turned his attention to his discarded clothes. Hanging from the same peg was his belt and holster. He might have agreed to leave his precious boots behind, but he would be damned if he would leave his Colt. He had no more than a dozen cartridges and the same number of percussion caps, and he had no idea how or when he would get any more. But he had enough rounds to load the weapon a couple more times, and that would have to be enough. He would belt the weapon under his clothing, hiding it from view. He would need it.

For he had men to kill.

Chapter Thirty-three

———◆◆◆———

Outside Magdala, 6 April 1868

Jack stood at the edge of the ravine and stared ahead in
silence. He had never seen anything that compared to
the fortress he was looking at that morning. There were
no walls. There was no glacis to protect against cannon fire.
No ravelins or towers. There was nothing made by the hand of
man to protect this place, but not even the prantara-durga of
the Maharajah of Sawadh or the great walls of Delhi could
compare to the natural defences of the great fortress of the
Emperor Tewodros of Abyssinia. He stared at Magdala in awe
and wondered at the sanity of the British government that had
sent an army halfway across the globe to capture such a place.

It had taken Jack and Watson over a month to reach
Magdala, and it had been a long, exhausting and perilous
journey. They had risen with the sun and walked all day, only
stopping when they could no longer see the way ahead. Their
path had been lengthened as they assiduously avoided the
British army and the many supply depots they had passed along
the way. It had not always been easy. On a dozen occasions

they had seen British patrols roving across the countryside, and once they had almost walked straight into a company of sepoys who were thoroughly lost. But they had avoided drawing attention to themselves. In the eyes of the British and native troops, they were just another pair of locals, and there were enough displaced peoples on the roads to not make them stand out.

Importantly, there had been not one sighting of Finch or his men. Jack had no idea what Finch thought had happened to them after the fight at the church, but he was sure the Londoner would not have quit the campaign. Not with the riches that were said to be in Tewodros's fortress. That idea reassured him. He would get his chance for revenge. He did not know when or where, but he knew fate would not forget him. She would give him the opportunity he craved.

As they had traversed the country, they had lived like locals, passing through dozens of small villages and surviving on whatever they could buy with the meagre funds at their disposal. They had eaten beef and mutton, and the round bread called hambasha, supplementing the meagre diet with a large citrus fruit that was known as terengo and a vast quantity of small tubers about the size of a small pea that the locals consumed at nearly every meal. They had acquired simple cotton sacks to hold their few supplies, and thanks to some quick thinking from Watson, they had pinched a couple of the six-foot-long spears that every self-respecting Abyssinian male carried at all times.

He could scarcely credit that they had walked all the way to Magdala on their own, a journey of over three hundred miles. He glanced across at Watson. The former academic was leaner now, his already sparse frame stripped of any vestige of fat. His beard had grown long and unkempt, and his face had been tanned by the sun and battered by the wind so that his lips were chapped and in places his skin was red and peeling.

The days had ground by. They had bypassed the great British encampment at Adigerat, then walked on, avoiding the stations at Dongolo, Dolo, Antalo and Mashik. They had passed Attala, then crossed the pretty plain near Makan. From there they had carried on, staring in awe at the great lake at Ashangi then continuing to Wofela before reaching the outskirts of the large settlement at Lat, where Jack had let them rest for two whole days before they tackled what had been the hardest part of the journey. Days of marching across a level plain had turned into a brutally hard ascent that had, according to Watson, taken them to over ten thousand feet above sea level. As they climbed, they had been surrounded by soaring peaks and tiny villages perched in impossible positions high on the mountainous slopes.

From Lat, they had walked for several more days before reaching the Jidda river valley, which ran through the patch-work of green fields like a great scar. The sides of the ravine were almost vertical, and fell for something close to three thousand feet. The massive gouge in the earth was some five miles wide at the point they had chosen to cross, and was both impressive and daunting in equal measure. Jack and Watson had stood in front of it and wondered how on earth they were going to get to the other side.

Then they had seen Tewodros's road.

According to Watson, the road had been constructed in such an impossible location to allow Tewodros's beloved artillery to cross the valley on its way to Magdala. From Jack's viewpoint, it was almost as well built as anything the Royal Engineers could have managed. It would have taken a Herculean effort to construct, and Watson had even heard a rumour that Tewodros himself was not above rolling up his shamma and working in the dust with his men.

Even with the road, it had been hard going to cross the valley. At this time of year, it was little more than a wasteland, nothing but a million rocks of every size with just a few scattered pools of stagnant water. That would change in the rainy season that was just a few months away, the dried-up river valley turned into a raging torrent as it drained the rainwater from the mountain ranges that surrounded it. It had taken them two full days to cross, the one miserable night they had spent in the dark confines of the valley passed huddled round a meagre fire. But they had made it out, and now they had reached their final destination.

'It really is everything we were told it would be.' Watson whispered the words as he looked at the great fortress of the emperor.

'It is.' Jack had seen much in his travels, but this fortress was something else. In front of where they stood, the ground dropped away in a series of ledges until it reached the Bashilo river some four thousand feet below. On the far side of the gorge, a succession of rocky outcrops and precipitous cliffs climbed to the foot of a range of lofty mountains. The ground around was a fine rolling landscape. And in the midst of it, about eight miles away from where they stood, was the great flat-topped hill where Tewodros had built his fortress.

'Can we take that in an assault?' Watson was no soldier, but even he could see the harsh reality of attempting to take the place by force.

'Maybe.' Jack could not say more. He understood Tewodros far better for seeing Magdala. Anyone possessing such a fortress would be certain of their power. It would give a man, an emperor, the security to challenge the world, even the courage to stand up to the great queen whose army and merchants had conquered so much of the globe.

He continued to assess the terrain. It was hard to see a way for an army to capture Magdala. The flat-topped mountain on which the fortress stood rose above all the surrounding terrain, the sides sheer, almost perpendicular, drops. From what he could see, there were three separate summits, all with flat peaks. The closest was the lowest of the three. Half a mile beyond and to its left was the highest, the two summits linked together by a narrow wedge of land, so that they looked like the two humps on a saddle. Beyond them was the last of the three summits. It rose from the flat top of the mountain behind a sheer wall of stone. On its top were dozens of native huts, their tall, conical roofs clearly visible even from a distance.

'The closest of those summits is called Fala; the one to its left is Selassie.' Watson named the two hilltops from memory. 'The third, the one furthest from us, is Magdala itself. They all sit on the hilltop of Selamge. We are told that there are just two ways in to Magdala. One, the Kafir Ber gateway, is on its far side. It is reached by a narrow, precipitous path that snakes around the hilltop. The other is called the Kokit Ber, and it opens towards Selamge. That is the only real way in.'

Jack tried to note the strange-sounding names. He was not surprised that Watson knew them all. The man remembered everything he had ever read.

'Do you think Napier can truly take that place?' Watson asked again.

'Yes, but it won't be easy.' Jack shook his head as he pondered the near-impossible task of even getting close to the fortress. 'He'll have to take that closest hilltop first – Fala, did you call it?'

'That's right.'

'Only when he has that secured can he assault the second one.' Jack had already forgotten its name. 'And after that, he can look at attacking Magdala itself. That will still be one hell of a job.'

Each of the three hilltops had sheer sides of black basalt. There was no route around them, or any chance of scaling the cliffs. The only way was along the narrow road that followed a ravine on the far side of the Bashilo Gorge to within a couple of miles of the fortress. From there, the road broke out onto a plain in front of the hilltop, before plunging out of sight as it fell down into the ravine that separated the hilltop from the plain, and eventually rising again, winding its way up the face of Fala. Jack could see that it carried on, crossing the hilltop of Selamge in front of the tall summit that Watson had named as Selassie before narrowing as it made its way towards the gateway of Magdala itself.

'And Tewodros will defend them all.'

'Unless he is truly mad.' Jack looked across at the three summits. The first, Fala, the smallest of the three, looked empty save for a few native huts. The next, Selassie, was higher, and a series of natural terraces made it easy to defend. It would be a terror to attack. For now, it was covered with a large number of tents and a few buildings. It was where Tewodros had encamped his army, and from what Jack could see, he still commanded a formidable force, for all that his power was supposedly waning. There were certainly enough men to mount a strong defence of the two hilltops. But Jack had seen the British army at work and he knew they could be taken, although it would almost certainly be at a dreadful cost.

Then he looked at the third hilltop and the fortress of Magdala itself, and he wondered if it would be possible at all.

'It'll be one hell of a fight.' He made his assessment, glad that he would not have to take his place in the ranks of the regiments sent to make the horrendous assault.

'But Napier will make the attempt, no matter the difficulty or the risk.'

'Yes. He didn't come all this way to sit and look at the bloody place.' Jack shivered. It was not hard to picture what it would be like when the British army set itself to the task of taking Magdala. When it came, the assault would be bloody, and it would certainly claim hundreds if not thousands of lives. But it had to be done. Magdala had to fall to protect the reputation of the British Empire, and to demonstrate its reach and its sheer power. And so men would die. Men like him. Men who were paid a shilling a day to serve their queen. Men who would fight like demons to carry out whatever impossible task they were ordered to complete.

'We can rest now. We'll head over there tomorrow,' he said.

'Are we truly mad to attempt such a thing?' Watson finally turned from staring at Magdala.

'Probably.'

'But we *must* do it.'

They had barely talked of their intention to reach Magdala before the battle that was surely to come, but Jack heard the certainty in Watson's voice.

'We will.' He reached out and squeezed Watson's shoulder. He meant it. He would not let them fail. Not now. 'But we won't linger,' he added. 'We go in, see what's what, then we get the hell out of there. If we can get our hands on something to prove we were there then so well and good, but I won't risk our necks for it. You understand?'

'Yes.' Watson smiled. 'I will not let you down, Mr Lark.'

'Good.' Jack sucked down a deep breath. There was no more to be said. The decision had been made weeks before. So he continued to look across at the three hilltops, his gaze shifting from one to the other until at last it focused on Tewodros's fortress.

It was the final bastion of the emperor's power, and Jack was sure he would defend it with everything he had. It was also where he held his prisoners. The tales of his cruelty to those he had imprisoned had been heard even as far away as London. They spoke of murder and cruelty on an almost imaginable scale. Magdala was a fortress, but it was also a place of death and brutality.

Watson had asked if they were mad to attempt it, and Jack knew that they must be. But it had to be done. Ambition. Pride. Grief. Anger. Sheer bloody-mindedness. They all played a part in his decision. But one thought overrode them all. He would find a way in to Magdala because no one would have believed it possible.

It was time to damn common sense and toss caution to the wind.

They had to enter the Gorilla King's lair.

Chapter Thirty-four

Jack and Watson started out at first light, just as they had every day for the last few weeks. A sharp breeze was blowing, the air chill enough to leave their skin tingling and their faces cold. The sun was slow to warm the sky, but already the palest blue was beginning to show around the edges of the warm ambers and pinks that announced the start of another day.

They took their time, reaching the river running through the centre of the Bashilo Gorge late that morning. It was wide, perhaps eighty yards across, and at least waist deep. The muddy water swirled past as they stood on the bank, neither man keen to plunge into the churning brown torrent.

'Come on.' Jack did not delay for long. He removed his holstered revolver from under his shamma and held it over his head, then took a deep breath and stepped into the water, recoiling and tensing as the water splashed across his legs.

It took fifteen cold minutes to wade across.

For the first hour after the crossing, they followed the dry riverbed of the Wurq-Waha valley. Once again they used Tewodros's road. This was the way his great guns had come, the weapons hauled up the steep path that was just about wide enough for a single gun team at a time. The going was good, the surface hard and compacted, but it was still exhausting, the road climbing for mile after mile.

They rested early in the afternoon at a small pool of drinkable water. Jack reckoned they had covered five miles, even though his body thought it had gone at least twice that distance. Yet it felt like they were still nowhere near Magdala. Now and then they caught glimpses of the fortress sitting serene and untroubled on its mountaintop, the master of all it surveyed. It served as a constant reminder of where they were going, their chosen destination growing more daunting with every passing hour.

By mid afternoon, the sun was roasting them alive. It pounded down, relentless and unforgiving, the only object in a clear blue sky. The going improved as they finally left the ravine behind, the rocky incline replaced by the much flatter land of the Aroge plateau. They should have been able to move faster here, but in fact their pace slowed, both men exhausted. After little more than a mile, the ground dropped away once more, plunging down the almost sheer side of the ravine that protected the approach to the fortress.

Jack held them at the edge of the ravine. It would be no good if they arrived at Fala exhausted. He found them a patch of ground where they could rest, out of sight of the men on the hilltop, and there they spent the rest of the afternoon and the early part of the evening. They saw a good few people in that time, a steady stream of men and women heading towards Fala. Late in the afternoon, a large body of warriors came past, the men loud and brash as they crossed the plateau.

Jack studied them closely. They all looked the part, their

wild hair and confident manner marking them out as fighting men. Yet as he watched them, he felt something close to sadness. Men like this were brave and proud. But bravery and pride would count for nothing when they came into range of the Sniders carried by the regular British army regiments, or the Enfield rifled muskets used by the native infantry. If it came to a pitched battle, there would be slaughter ahead. Tewodros's sole hope lay in a defiant defence of the three hilltops. Only if he held his army behind the formidable defences of Magdala would he stand a chance.

The pair left their resting place as the sun began to set, following Tewodros's road down into the ravine in front of Fala. It grew cooler as they descended, the air in the ravine untouched by the day's sun. Yet the walking warmed them and they pressed on. The road reached the bottom of the ravine then turned sharply upwards as it began to scale the face of Fala, winding this way and that up the sheer sides of the mountain.

They came out of the ravine into a world slowly turning to shadow. The setting sun coloured the sky, the greys of night pushing into the last warm hues of the day. It was dramatic and it was beautiful, the sky turning steadily redder until it was the colour of old blood. It was hard to look at it and not feel a sense of foreboding. It was as if the gods of war knew what was to come, and were foretelling the battle that was soon to be fought.

Jack and Watson reached Fala just as the first shadows of darkness marched across the land. The wind was sharp and chill on their faces, the bone-aching cold of the night beginning to set in. Ahead, all three hilltops were aglow with the lights of a hundred fires as Tewodros's warriors settled down to wait for the battle they all knew was surely to come. The fires would burn all night to ward off the chill of the darkness. There was something benign in the sight, the promise of comfort stealing the edge of the fear that both men felt as they walked towards the enemy's lair.

Neither spoke as they followed Tewodros's road. Both had wrapped their blue scarves tight around their heads, covering as much of their faces as they could. They did their best to ape the gait of the other warriors they had seen, their pace slow and languid, their spears carried with what had become familiar ease.

They were not the only ones heading towards Fala. The steady procession of travellers they had watched through the afternoon had increased as night had begun to fall. Jack had held back until they could join the rear of one larger than average group. Not one warrior noticed as an extra two men shadowed them.

Jack glanced at Watson as they made the last climb. With his pagdi wound tight around his head, he could see little more than his companion's eyes. But they still spoke volumes. They were wide open, the whites bright against the surrounding skin, which had been tanned dark by the sun. There was fear in those eyes. Jack nodded once, the silent gesture meant to offer some sort of reassurance. Watson bobbed his head to acknowledge it. Jack did not know whether his presence offered some comfort to his companion, but he felt something reassuring in the company of another. For once, he was not alone as he stuck his head into the lion's mouth.

They reached Fala without fuss or commotion, scaling the last yards of the road, which became almost vertical as it

ascended the nearly sheer face of the mountain. There were no
sentries posted as there would have been so close to a British
army encampment, and the group carried on, passing a long
line of cannon that were lined up facing towards the Aroge
plateau.

It was Jack's first chance to study some of Tewodros's
beloved artillery. To his eye, they did not look like much. All
were old, and many looked scratch-built. There was no uni-
formity to them, or much precision to their positioning, for
that matter, the guns lined up in a haphazard formation that
would have driven any decent artillery officer into fury. All
were made of brass. Some were plain, others decorated in the
Indian fashion with engraving etched across the barrels. It was
an eclectic collection. He counted two small-bore mortars, and
the cannon themselves ranged from one large fourteen-pounder
to two small guns he reckoned could not fire anything above a
two-pound roundshot. From their condition, he doubted many
would even function when it came to it, and he would not be
surprised if some exploded when they were called into action.

The pair continued to follow the group they had trailed to
Fala as they walked across the hilltop of Selamge. There were
many more warriors there, nearly every inch of ground filled
with either a tent or a group of men sitting around a campfire.
But it was quiet, even with so many men present. If this had
been a British army encampment, or one belonging to either of
the two sides that had fought in the bloody civil war that had
torn America in two, it would have been much noisier, the air
filled with the sound of men talking and laughing. There would
have been music too, a fiddle or a flute playing a familiar song
that would sometimes inspire the men to sing. Yet here, the
warriors stared silently into the flames of their fires, or strolled

around with solemn poise, their dark faces set firm and quite without emotion.

Not one man looked twice at either Jack or Watson. They were anonymous amidst so many. Yet Jack felt something shift as they walked through the encampment. It felt as if they were being watched, some hidden foe fully aware of the pair of impostors in their midst. The feeling was strong enough for him to turn around, his head swivelling this way and that as he sought to locate the source of the disquiet. He saw no one looking his way, or even anyone aware of his presence. Yet the feeling would not quit, so he walked with the sense of another's eyes boring into the back of his skull.

The group they followed peeled off, heading to one of the few areas not yet taken. It gave Jack and Watson the chance to carry on alone, and they took it, staying on the path that led towards the last of the three hilltops. The path that led to Magdala itself.

'You good?' Jack hissed the words under his breath.

'Yes.' Watson's tone was tight with tension.

Jack thought about saying something reassuring, then decided against it. Whatever he said would do nothing to settle the demons he was sure were running free in Watson's mind. It was better to be silent, and to leave the man to fight them alone.

They pressed on, crossing Selamge and passing the second summit of Selassie, maintaining the same languid pace as before. Jack did his best not to gawp, keeping his head still and letting his eyes do the work, but it was hard. He could feel the tension emanating from Watson, and could see the white of the man's knuckles where he was clutching his spear tightly. He felt some of the same tension himself. It was no simple thing that they did. His heart was pounding away in his chest, as if he were running a fast mile and not sauntering along at an easy pace, so he forced himself to breathe slower and to relax his grip on his own spear.

They reached the far side of Selamge without interference then ascended the steep track that led up to Magdala itself. The track was narrow with sheer rock on either side. At the far end waited the gate that led on to Magdala itself. It was unguarded and wide open.

The gateway of Kokit Ber was the first real man-made defence they had seen, and Jack scrutinised it as best he could as they passed through. The heavy wooden gate was surrounded on either side by stone walls that gave way to a thick thorny hedge running around the landward-facing side of the hilltop. But as he looked at the thickness of the walls, some of the first he had seen, he saw nothing that would hold the British army at bay for long. They looked solid enough, but they were as nothing when compared to the great walls of the Red Fort at Delhi, which had eventually fallen to the guns of the besieging forces. Napier had no siege train, but the Armstrong guns he had brought with him would be more than capable of battering a way through Magdala's defences, though he would have to get them close for them to be effective. For that to happen, Selassie and Fala would have to fall, and from what Jack had already seen, that was no sure thing.

On the far side of the gate was a natural scarp, some thirty to forty feet high. There was just one way up, a series of steps just a single yard wide cut into the face. At the top, they crossed through a second, smaller gateway then on to the flat-topped amba at the heart of Magdala. They walked past a raised plateau, where they saw several tents and huts, the area surrounded by more thorny hedges. The only way onto the plateau was up some rough-hewn steps that were guarded by a large number of warriors. It was not hard to work out that this was where Tewodros's prisoners were being held.

They pressed on, passing a large number of native huts, the round buildings with their stone walls and conical thatched roofs pressed tightly together. Every hut was occupied. Jack did his best to observe the men sitting around them without gawping. To his eye, these men looked fitter and better equipped than those he had seen on Fala and Selamge. He saw more firearms here too. The men below had been armed with swords and spears. Here, nearly every man had a matchlock musket, the weapons leaning together in stands near the huts. A few men carried beautifully decorated jezails, whilst he saw at least one percussion cap shotgun. As a display of firearms, it made for an interesting sight. As a show of firepower, it was pathetic. The Sniders and Enfield rifled muskets carried by the British and native infantry regiments were vastly more powerful. In a traditional battle, Tewodros's army would be slaughtered before it could even get into the fight.

'This is too easy.' Watson paused to hiss the words at Jack.

'Shut up.' Jack's reply was snapped. The feeling of being watched had been growing stronger with every moment. He gestured with his spear, pointing the way ahead. They could not stop, not now.

Watson's eyes narrowed as he registered a moment's hurt. Then he turned and walked on.

Here on the amba, there were native huts in every direction, alongside enclosures for animals, but Jack found his eye taken by a great blood-red pavilion positioned at the very heart of the plateau. The ground around it was smothered by hundreds of carpets, so that not a single inch of soil was left uncovered. To the pavilion's front was a huge mortar, the like of which Jack had never seen. He supposed this was the fabled Sevastopol. It was incredible to think that he now looked at it with his own eyes in the heart of the emperor's fabled fortress of Magdala.

Thousands of miles of travel had led to this moment. They had walked into the heart of Tewodros's domain and were standing just a few dozen yards away from the tent where the Gorilla King himself ruled his empire.

Chapter Thirty-five

―――◆·◆·◆―――

*J*ack felt a moment's anticlimax as he stared at Tewodros's great red pavilion. They had done what no sane man would have thought possible. It was laughable. Napier had spent millions of pounds in his attempt to bring thousands of men and animals to this fortress that sat at the very heart of the Abyssinian emperor's domain. It had taken every resource the great British Empire could summon. All so the army could force its way into Magdala, release the prisoners he had dared to take and hold Tewodros to account for his temerity and his refusal to obey. Yet now two European men had achieved a similar feat with no more resources than those they could carry.

He looked around, trying to decide what to do next. Every thought for weeks now had been about how to get them to where they now stood. Now they were here, and he did not really know what they should do.

But Watson did. He looked at Jack, then jerked his head before walking off. Jack followed, for once obedient. They skirted Tewodros's tent, picking a path through the native huts. There was no design to their arrangement; they seemed to have been built wherever anyone fancied. They looked no different to those on the lower levels, even though Jack supposed these had to belong to the officers of Tewodros's army, their proximity to the emperor's tent surely an indication of the importance of those inside. Yet there was nothing to mark them out, no obvious signs of status or power.

Watson increased his pace. Jack would have liked to snap at him to slow down, but he held his tongue. They passed another line of huts, and it was only then that he realised where Watson was headed. On the far side of Tewodros's pavilion were a dozen stone-walled huts, all clearly newer than the rest. Each one looked better built than the others they had seen, sturdier and better maintained.

Watson did not hesitate. He walked briskly towards the nearest one and went inside without a moment's pause.

Jack stopped outside and looked around. It was not totally quiet; no army encampment ever was. There was nothing to alarm him. Yet still he felt a dreadful sense of impending doom. He knew they could not linger. Not even for a moment.

He followed Watson inside, leaving the door open to let in some light.

'Watson,' he hissed. 'Be quick.'

Watson paid him no heed. He had rested his spear against the hut's side and was now peering at something he had picked up.

He turned to Jack. He had unwound part of his pagdi, and Jack could see the look of wonder on his face as he held out the object: a cross that appeared to have been made from solid gold. It was gloomy inside the hut, but Jack could still just about make out that the cross was studded with what looked to be coloured stones.

'I know what this is.' Watson spoke in the hushed, awed tones of the worshipper.

'I don't care what it is. Just take it and let's get out of here.' Jack ignored the cross and stepped towards Watson, already reaching out to take him by the arm. They had already achieved the impossible. It was time to get away whilst they were still alive.

'It is from the coffin of the abuna, the high priest of the church here in Abyssinia.'

'Great. Now hide it away and let's go.'

Watson shook off Jack's hand. He held the cross like a father cradling his newborn son. 'It is worth five thousand pounds, perhaps more.' He spoke without looking at Jack. He had eyes only for the golden artefact.

'I don't bloody care how much it's worth.'

Watson looked up at last, his expression betraying a mixture of confusion and anger. 'Don't you see, Jack? This is what we came for. This alone will make us rich. And it shall stand as evidence of our tale. It will be our proof.'

'It will be our death if we stand here discussing the bloody thing.' Jack made to take the cross from Watson's grasp.

But Watson was having none of it. He pulled it away, clutching it to his breast. 'No. It's mine.'

'Then hide the fucking thing away.' Jack looked around him as if expecting to see someone standing in the open doorway. There was nothing and no one.

The feeling of dread was still there. It was time to act. He had long ago learned to make a decision and see it through. Hesitation and uncertainty were the biggest dangers on a battle-field. Officers who dithered and doubted got their men killed. It was that simple. So they had to go. Now.

'That's enough.' He snapped the words, then stepped forward, grabbing Watson around the upper arm and pulling him close. 'We're leaving.' He reached for the cross again. For a moment, he thought Watson might actually fight him for it. He took hold of the relic, the metal cool under his fingers, and braced himself to tug it forcibly from the other man's grasp.

He never completed the act.

Shadows rushed across the entrance to the hut, stealing the meagre light that had been filtering in. The sound of feet running on sun-baked ground reached his ears, along with the bark of shouted orders.

He turned to see men filling the entrance. He stood there, one hand on Watson, the other on the golden cross, as the first warrior stepped into the hut.

The man was heavily bearded. His shoulders were covered with a fine lion-skin lembd held closed with a heavy brass clasp. In his hands he carried a double-barrelled shotgun that was aimed directly at the two men who stood gripping on to one another, a golden cross held between them.

Chapter Thirty-six

*J*ack walked with his head bowed.

Tewodros's warriors had not taken long to subdue the two impostors. Both had been searched, their hidden revolvers taken. Jack had not resisted, not even when he saw his Navy Colt disappear in front of his eyes. Fighting would have resulted in nothing more than a beating, and he knew they would need all their strength if they were to find a way to escape. So he had watched the revolver that had been at his side since he had quit the battlefield at Bull Run disappear into the hands of one of Tewodros's warriors, and had not done a thing to stop it.

The pair were frogmarched through the growing crowd. Hands reached out to grab at them, fingers jabbing, prodding and grasping. Abuse came without pause, the warriors of Tewodros's closest commanders gathering as the news of the capture of two white farenj spread throughout the encampment.

Jack ignored the jeers, just as he ignored the pummelling and the punching that came from every side. The time to fight was long gone. There was nothing left to do now save to endure whatever was ahead. To resist was to die.

Their journey was mercifully short. The dusty, rocky soil under his boots gave way to carpet, the ground that he stared at decorated with the bright colours and delicate weave of beautiful rugs. It confirmed where he had been taken.

It was a moment in his life when he should have felt nothing short of terror. The tales of Tewodros's cruelty were legendary. The emperor had killed thousands of his own people, and Jack doubted that the fate of two foreign thieves would be any different. Yet for a reason he could not fathom, he felt not even a shred of fear. He felt numb, as if ice had shrouded his soul, leaving it cold and barren.

The men who had taken them were shouting continuously now. He could only suppose they were hooting their triumph. He tuned them out, just as he told his mind not to listen to the bloodthirsty yells and insults that were spat his way.

And then everything went silent.

Jack felt hands press down on his shoulders, pushing him to his knees. Another hand clasped the back of his head, bending his neck forward and forcing it down. The hand stayed in place as his captor kneeled at his side, pushing with enough force to hurt.

Jack kept his eyes open even as he stared at nothing more than the carpet beneath his knees. He saw the shadow of a man coming to stand in front of him. With the sun low in the sky, that shadow was long. And it was quite alone.

The shadow came closer. Jack forced his eyes up. He saw a pair of naked feet in front of him.

The silence stretched thin. It filled the air more completely than even the raucous abuse, more powerfully than the most inventive insult.

'Stand.' The command was given in a clipped tone.

Jack and his captor rose as one, as did Watson and the warrior holding him fast. It gave Jack his first glimpse of the man who ruled the empire of Abyssinia and who had summoned the war that was just a few days away from its brutal conclusion.

The fabled Gorilla King did not look like much, not to Jack's eyes at least. He was dressed simply in a white shamma with a red decorative border, so that he appeared little different to any of the men kneeling at his bare feet. He was well built, his body carrying the muscled build of a warrior. But he also looked old, worn out even. He was well groomed, his long hair braided and smoothed back over his skull. His moustache and goatee were neatly trimmed, and both shone with oil. But all were threaded with grey, the lighter colour standing in stark contrast to the original jet-black. A few rogue ends had escaped the braids, so that they whispered across his face, spoiling the perfection, confirmation that the emperor was not the perfect figure he was meant to be.

Yet it was not all this that captured Jack's attention. It was the emperor's eyes. They were so dark that they looked to be fully black. And they were wild, like those of a cornered animal. They darted back and forth, from Jack to Watson to the warriors around him. They were never still.

'You are spies.' It was a statement, not a question. His English was faultless but heavily accented.

Jack did not see the need to speak, so he said nothing. For a moment, Tewodros's eyes held his own, then the emperor turned away, showing his back to the two men.

He snapped an order in his own tongue. Immediately the area filled with movement. Men who had been kneeling rose quickly and scurried away. For his part, Tewodros did not move. He stood like a living statue whilst all around him was hustle and bustle.

He did not have to wait long for his order to be carried out. Two of his men brought over an old man. He was naked save for a filthy loincloth. Every inch of skin was either marked with welts or bruises or else covered in dirt. What little grey hair he had hung lank from his skull. He was dragged towards Tewodros, his feet trailing across the carpet, his body hanging limp in the grasp of his escort.

Tewodros stopped them with a raised hand when they were no more than a yard in front of him. As they stopped, so the old man raised his head. Bloodshot eyes rimmed with red looked into the face of the emperor. They stayed there for no more than the span of a single heartbeat before they fell.

'This traitor thought to run away.' Tewodros turned to address the two white men in English. 'He was my most trusted servant. I gave him riches, I gave him trust, and yet still he wanted to leave me.' The words were delivered quite without emotion.

Jack glanced at the old man. He looked frail. It was hard to imagine this pathetic creature as a proud member of Tewodros's court.

The emperor looked directly at Jack. 'See what happens to men who defy me.' He held his gaze, then turned away to shout instructions in a language Jack did not understand.

A man dressed in a pair of knee-length white trousers, with a large leather apron across his front answered the summons. His heavily muscled arms were bare, and he carried a large knife in one hand and a huge pair of pincers in the other. To Jack, he looked like a farrier or blacksmith. He came to stand in front of his emperor, then went down on his knees, head bowed. He stayed there as Tewodros gave him his instructions, then got back to his feet, his expression quite emotionless, and turned to face the old man.

Jack was studying the old man's face. He did not see fear there, or even the start of terror. He saw something that he translated as weary resignation, an acceptance of whatever cruel fate he had just heard leave his emperor's lips. That expression did not change even as the man in the leather apron approached.

The two warriors holding the old man knew their role. They forced him to the ground, then held him fast on his back, arms and legs splayed so that it looked like he had been laid on a cross.

Tewodros chose that moment to move forward. He walked slowly until he stood next to the man laid out on the ground. He looked down, holding the old man's gaze for no more than a second, then turned away.

The man in the leather apron came forward then and dropped to one knee, laying his pincers on the ground whilst he held the long knife ready. Without a moment's pause, he sliced the blade around one of the old man's ankles, the skin parting to the lightest touch of the knife.

Blood ran red across the old man's skin. Yet he did not cry out, even as the blade went around again and again, each time working deeper and deeper as it cut down to the bone.

Jack heard Watson gasp. He did not have to turn his head to know that the academic had bowed his head so that he would not see what was to follow. But Jack did not follow suit. He felt he owed it to the old man to bear witness.

He watched as the white shine of bone emerged from amidst the blood and gristle. He did not look away as the man placed his blood-smeared blade on the ground and took up the pincers. He kept watching as the mouth of the pincers was pushed deep into the wound, then clasped tight. With a sharp jerk, the pincers were pulled backwards. There was a sickening snap, then the old man's foot came away from his leg in a single piece.

The old man screamed. It was a pitiful sound, the screech one of pure agony. It died fast, lost in the great cheer that came from the crowd as the man in the leather apron held the detached foot above his head like some sort of gruesome trophy, blood dripping from the cleanly cut end.

In one swift movement, the foot was dropped to the ground and, twisting around, he faced the man's other leg. As before, the knife came first, slicing around the ankle with the neat, practised precision of a butcher. The pincers followed. A moment later, the second foot was snatched from its leg in one short, clean action.

The old man screamed again. Jack wondered how he was still conscious. It would have been a mercy for him to pass out and so be spared the dreadful ordeal. Yet fate was a cruel mistress that day, and she denied the old man the oblivion of unconsciousness.

The man in the leather apron was not done. He stood, gathering his tools, before moving around the old man so that he was behind his head. Again he kneeled, pincers laid down close at hand, knife held ready.

The old man writhed in silent agony, forcing his two captors to lean down with all their strength. He did not cry out, or rage against his fate. Apart from the twin screams torn from his body, he faced his ordeal in silence.

The man worked quickly and efficiently, slicing away the

skin around the old man's right hand, then pulling the hand from the arm with a single sharp jerk. This time the old man did not even scream. The same series of actions were repeated with his left hand. Within the span of a single minute, both had been severed.

Only when the second hand thumped onto the carpeted ground did Tewodros turn back to face his two new prisoners.

'Do you see? Do you dogs see? Do you vile donkeys now understand what happens to those who dare cross me!' He strode forward, face twisted with rage, coming straight for Jack. 'Look at that man. Look at that blood.' He bellowed the words, spit spraying from his lips. 'Look at that man's pain!'

He came closer, thrusting his face into Jack's 'Look at that, you putrid carcass! Look at the fate that awaits you!' His hand shot out, grabbing Jack's chin, his fingers like claws as they forced his head around so that he was looking at the old man. 'Do you see?'

Jack ignored the pain of Tewodros's fingers as they dug deep into his skin. The old man was still alive. His captors had stood back, leaving him lying in a growing pool of his own blood, his arms and legs flapping in a series of ever slower motions. The man in the leather apron had got to his feet and now stood, head bowed, the tools of his trade dripping blood onto the emperor's fine carpets.

'Look at your fate, you dog.' Tewodros twisted Jack's head back around so that the two men's noses were no more than an inch apart. Jack could feel the wash of warm breath on his face as Tewodros panted with rage. He did not flinch or look away. He stared directly into the emperor's merciless black eyes, meeting the glare that bored deep into his skull.

Tewodros's face vibrated with fury. For a moment, Jack

thought he was about to howl, or even to bite like a rabid dog. Then, like a cloud moving away from the midday sun, the fury left him, and his features settled into something like a composed expression. His hand dropped from Jack's face to his neck. There he rummaged around the top of Jack's shamma until he pulled out the blue cord Mazza had given him.

'*Christo?*' The question was asked quietly.

Jack did not understand the sudden change in the man who could order his death with a single crook of a finger. But he managed to nod.

Tewodros's expression revealed nothing. He rolled the blue cord around in his fingers, then placed it carefully back under Jack's clothing.

He gestured to the man in the leather apron and gave a short command. The man nodded, then strode forward. An assistant came to his side carrying a heavy wooden crate.

Jack looked down as the man in the leather apron kneeled at his feet. The crate was placed at his right hand and he reached inside it, pulling out a length of chain followed by two manacles. Only then did he look up. Jack tried in vain to read the emotion he saw in the man's eyes. He could not imagine what it would be like to serve a ruler like Tewodros.

The man gave the slightest shake of his head, then looked down to begin his task.

Jack felt the touch of strong fingers around his ankle, then the cold, remorseless grip of the first manacle. The man at his feet reached into the crate for a small hammer. He worked quickly, landing two blows squarely on the bolt that held the length of chain to the manacle. Jack felt a moment's pain, then the ring closed tight. The action was repeated, the chain secured to a second manacle fastened around his other ankle. The whole process was done swiftly, the man in the leather apron clearly an expert.

With Jack done, he turned to Watson and the process was repeated. Watson looked down the whole time, as if assessing the man's skill. Only when the chains were attached did he glance across at Jack, an expression of relief on his face.

The pair were chained and manacled, but they were still alive. They had come face to face with the Gorilla King himself, and had lived to tell the tale.

At least for the moment.

Chapter Thirty-seven

Magdala, 8 April 1868

*J*ack woke to greet the day shivering and chilled to the bone. That he had slept at all was a miracle. The manacles had chafed the skin so that it was raw and bloody. It felt like two red-hot bands had been clasped around his ankles. It was impossible to find even a moment's respite, the pain burning, fierce, constant.

'What is his plan for us?'

He blinked, quite unready for the question, then raised his head, the movement sending a lance of pain shooting down his spine. Watson was sitting in one corner of their small hut, his legs straight out in front of him. He was staring directly at Jack. Clearly he had been waiting for his moment for some time.

Jack cleared his throat, which was claggy and sore. 'I have no idea.'

'Why not kill us? Or maim us as he did that poor man?'

'Because he didn't want to.' Jack could no more explain the actions of the Mad King than he could explain why the sun rose each day no matter how much misery engulfed the world. Yet the answer seemed to satisfy Watson.

Jack raised himself slowly, using his hands to lever himself into a sitting position. The pain in his back was worse than ever. He had slept on his back, and now his spine felt like it had been crushed all along its length.

He took a moment to look around their meagre quarters. The hut was no more than ten feet in diameter, with an empty fire pit in the centre. The roof was thatch and filled with a dense network of spider webs. He could see dozens of the tiny creatures scuttling back and forth. They made a gentle scratching as their minute feet scraped across the thatch, the sound enough to make his skin itch.

He had done his best to keep his head up as he and Watson were frogmarched away from Tewodros's pavilion the previous day and taken to an area of raised ground towards the rear of the hilltop fortress. It had been no easy thing to ascend the steep set of steps leading to the prisoners' compound with a set of chains around their ankles, their gait reduced to little more than a shuffle, but the point of a spear held near their kidneys had given them enough incentive to make it.

The prisoners' compound consisted of dozens upon dozens of huts, the whole surrounded by a dense hedge of thickets so that it was fully enclosed, with just a single, heavily guarded, way in and out. They had glimpsed a few other prisoners as they were led to their hut. Some had looked back at them with blank eyes, but most had ignored their arrival. They saw no white faces, their fellow prisoners other Abyssinians who had fallen foul of Tewodros's ire. Jack could only assume that the Europeans who had inspired the whole campaign were held in the other compound they had seen closer to the Kokit Ber gateway.

'Surely he will kill us.' Watson broke the silence.

'If you are certain, then why ask?' Jack's reply was waspish. 'Is there water?'

'No.'

'Bugger.' He rolled his tongue around his mouth in a vain attempt to summon some moisture. It felt like a tramp had slept in it.

'Perhaps he just plans to leave us here to die,' Watson suggested.

'Perhaps.' Jack sucked down a deep breath, then forced himself to rise. He hissed as the pain raged up and down his spine before rushing down both legs. Yet he pushed through it, and shuffled towards the open door. A chilly breeze whispered in, but he barely felt it, his skin already frozen.

Outside, the compound was quiet, even though dawn had fully broken. Only birds were abroad, and he saw red bishop birds and flycatchers darting this way and that as they chased the first of the day's flies. All was peaceful. With the sky coloured orange and amber, there was even beauty in the moment.

He savoured the peace. There was something calming in the stillness of the morning. And he needed to be calmed. For he had awoken with a fire deep in his belly. It was contained, just as he contained all his emotions, but it was there. It would not take much to stoke it into fury. And he knew there would soon be a time when it would be released. He would not shuffle to his fate like a man without hope. He would hold his anger in check until the moment was right. Then he would let it go in all its wild madness. He would fight, and he would maim, and he would kill, until he was either free, or dead himself.

He looked at the warming colours of the dawn and thought only of the fight that was to come.

The peace of that early morning was not to last. The first guards swarmed up the steps as the sun rose high overhead. More followed, warriors with spears and swords storming into hut after hut, the prisoners inside waking to chaos.

'Get up,' Jack snapped at Watson, then stepped outside. He would be damned if he was going to allow either of them to be dragged out.

Shuffling forward, he forced his aching spine straight. All around the compound, men, women and children were being hauled out of their huts and forced towards the steps. He spotted a lone white face amongst them. A man with a long grey beard was being given his own personal escort towards the stairs, half a dozen warriors surrounding the pitiful figure that crabbed along, back bent with pain.

His view of the action came to an end as he saw two guards carrying spears walking towards him. It seemed that none of Tewodros's prisoners was to be left behind.

He stepped forward decisively. He would not wait. He would face his fate with his head held high and his back as straight as he could manage.

Jack and Watson were standing shoulder to shoulder in a great press of bodies. The prisoners had been led down from their compound then herded together not far from Tewodros's blood-red pavilion. They had been guarded every step of the way, the men with spears cruel and spiteful. Any who stumbled or delayed were beaten, be they man, woman or child. Those that fell were thrashed even more cruelly, the ends of spears used as clubs. More than one man was beaten unconscious, their bodies left to be dragged along by their fellow prisoners.

All the captives were in a terrible state. Few were wearing anything more than rags and most were skeletally thin. The men were all shackled, and some could do little more than crawl, their broken bodies no longer strong enough to support even their meagre weight.

'What the hell is happening?' Watson whispered the question directly into Jack's ear so that only he could hear it.

'Just be ready to do whatever I tell you,' Jack hissed. He would not waste his breath on pointless speculation.

They were not left to wait for long. Tewodros came out of his pavilion flanked by dozens of his commanders. Today he was dressed as a king. The simple shamma he had worn the previous day had been replaced with a silk one decorated with a network of golden threads woven through the cloth, with still more gold in the fringing. He wore white fringed trousers, the material catching the morning light so that it glittered and shimmered as he walked towards the great crowd of prisoners summoned at his command.

'He looks like a bloody magician,' Jack muttered. Hyde Park was filled with Indian magicians dressed like Tewodros was that day. There they delighted the crowds with tricks and sleights of hand. Jack wondered what sort of evil magic Tewodros was about to demonstrate.

He looked up as the emperor's retinue approached. Around him, the crowd shuffled, a low-pitched murmur spreading fast. The fear was like a living creature, lurking in and around them, whispering in ears and filling men, women and children with dread. Jack felt it, and it raised the hackles on the back of his neck. It was like nothing he had faced before: standing there still and silent, part of a great throng waiting patiently for death or torture to arrive.

He looked away from Tewodros, searching the faces of those around him, seeing the terror on every one. He was still searching when he glimpsed a white face staring back at him. It was the same man from before. His pallor was grey and he was painfully thin, but his eyes were alive and they met Jack's, holding his gaze for several seconds before they finally looked away. Jack wondered who he was. Was it Rassam, the foreign officer who had delivered the British government's ultimatum to Tewodros? Or was it perhaps Consul Cameron? Jack had no idea which of the prisoners this man might be, and he wondered if the man knew of the great endeavour that had been started by his incarceration, or if he was unaware of the trial being endured by the thousands under Napier's command.

Tewodros arrived in front of the crowd. Without a word of command, every prisoner kneeled, heads bowed low. There was absolute silence.

Jack kneeled with those around him. But he kept his head up. He wanted to see.

Tewodros raised his eyes to the heavens, then lifted his hands until they were shoulder high. He stood like that without moving, holding the pose as the seconds stretched, time dragging by with excruciating slowness. When he eventually looked down, his face was filled with sadness.

He spoke then. Jack did not know what was being said, the foreign words meaningless, but as the emperor addressed his prisoners, great fat tears filled his eyes and ran down his cheeks, falling to the ground, where they dampened the dry, sandy soil by his bare feet.

His sad speech concluded, he bowed his head. He stayed like that as the first guards came forward.

Jack tensed, bracing himself for the first scream.

There was silence.

Around him, the crowd started to fidget. Whispers came, fear spreading fast again. All knew Tewodros. All knew he could kill them without a qualm.

'Jack—'

'Hush.' Jack cut Watson off. He strained his hearing, trying to read the situation.

The whispering intensified. Those near him started to shuffle on their knees, as if they were fighting the urge to flee. The tension crackled through the packed ranks. It would only take a single spark to set the crowd's fear aflame.

Then someone cried out.

Jack started, his body flinching before he could register what the noise was.

It was not a shriek of terror. It was one of joy.

Tewodros's guards had laid down their spears. Instead of killing, they were stepping into the crowd, helping men and women to their feet, leading children away by the hand.

Blacksmiths came forward carrying hammers and chisels. Moments later and the sound of hammering on metal came clearly as the first shackles were cut away.

The crowd did not press forward – there was still too much fear left for that – but hope grew until it hummed around the great throng. At the front, more and more people were being released from their shackles. It was a slow, laborious progress, but already a steady stream of people were heading towards the trail out of Magdala that would start them on their journey to freedom. A few fell and had to be helped to their feet, their fellow prisoners supporting those who could not walk.

Jack stood and felt the anticipation in the air. The unthinkable was happening.

Tewodros was setting his prisoners free.

The blacksmiths worked solidly for an hour. The pile of discarded chains grew steadily, and a near-constant procession of withered souls made their way towards the gatehouse.

Jack stood amidst the crowd and waited. Every few minutes, he shuffled forward with those around him, inching across the dusty soil towards the small group of blacksmiths charged with setting them free. Not one person spoke. There were no cheers or cries of excitement, just the mute, patient expectation of those whose hopes had long ago been extinguished. It was as if they could still not believe what they were seeing.

Tewodros stood alone, his back turned to the crowd, his face raised to the heavens. Jack looked at the ruler of the Abyssinians and wondered what it would be like to wield such complete authority. He had never craved that kind of power. It was true that he had started out with a thirst to be an officer, but that was something different, at least to his way of thinking. Officers wielded power, there was no denying that, and at times they gave orders that would lead to a soldier's death or a life-changing mutilation. Yet they were not rulers.

As much as he had wanted to lead men into battle to prove that a boy from the meanest streets of the metropolis could do it as well as someone born with a silver spoon in their muzzle, he had never wanted to lord it over the men he commanded. He wanted to serve them by giving them the best officer they could have, something that rarely seemed to happen in a world that looked to a man's birth and the size of his family's fortune as the sole criteria for awarding responsibility and power.

He had lost something of that ambition over the past years, the bloodshed and wholesale slaughter he had witnessed crushing the desire to serve anyone other than himself, but as he looked across at Tewodros, he wondered what had first fired the emperor's desire to rule, and how much of that motivation remained in his blackened, bloodied soul.

A distraught wail came from the front of the crowd, recapturing Jack's attention. The slow, shuffling progress had come to a stop, and he immediately saw why. The blacksmiths were leaving. Men with spears took their place, the weapons once again held out ready to be used.

Tewodros walked away from the crowd. The time for mercy was over.

The wails and moans intensified. Those close to the front wept as they saw their chance of freedom disappearing in front of their eyes. The first angry shouts came, those towards the rear of the throng venting their distress.

The crowd started to surge forward. Men at the front raised their chains, shaking them at the guards as they cried out, fury and frustration released. The noise rose to a crescendo, metal clashing on metal, voices raised in rage and despair.

The guards held their ground. Their leaders bellowed at the crowd, their threats and orders adding to the chaos being unleashed.

Still the crowd bayed for their release. More shuffled forward, brandishing their chains as if about to use them as makeshift weapons.

The guards stood firm, spear points lowered.

It was enough.

Fear returned quickly, the silent threat of the weapons quelling the sudden anger that had intoxicated the crowd.

Slowly, reluctantly, the prisoners turned away and began to trudge back to their compound. Jack and Watson went with them. Neither had even come close to the men removing the chains. It appeared their freedom, if it was to come, had been postponed.

Chapter Thirty-eight

———◆•◆•◆———

The guards woke the prisoners at first light. Just as on the previous day, they were herded together then led out of the compound.

Jack shuffled along with Watson at his side. The pain of the chains around his ankles was worse that morning. He could feel the trickle of fresh blood, and the metal grated on the raw skin with every step he took. He was not alone in suffering. Most of the men in the crowd were shackled, and Jack knew that some would have been held that way for months on end.

He could feel that the crowd was on edge that morning – a strange combination of expectation and excitement at the thought of freedom. They shuffled, crawled and staggered under the command of their guards, some jostling to get closer to the front of the throng. They had awoken with hope in their hearts, and now they were doing their utmost to make sure it would be they who were released that day.

They did not go far. They were gathered together towards one side of the amba, away from the warriors' huts, where the ground was flat and level. To the west, the land sloped downwards until it stopped at the very edge of the amba. The drop beyond was sheer, a great void all that existed once the earth came to an end.

Jack attempted to tally the number of prisoners being herded together that morning. He failed, but it was clear that there were many more than there had been the day before. He could only guess that Tewodros was emptying both compounds and gathering together for the first time all those he had incarcerated. He saw more white faces than yesterday. Grey-bearded men walked with their families and what he guessed were their servants. He recognised one face from Watson's papers: the missionary Stern. He looked thin and fragile, his body reduced to little more than bones held together with skin. His beard was long and unkempt, and his clothes appeared to be little more than rags.

More and more prisoners were brought out. Some were dragged to one side of the crowd. Many could not walk, and were dumped without ceremony on the ground. They looked half dead in the morning sun, their emaciated, battered bodies little more than sacks of flesh and bone.

The crowd had stood for no more than a dozen minutes before the dour-faced blacksmiths came forward. Once again they started to remove the shackles and chains from around the legs of the prisoners. Once again the pile of discarded metal began to grow, and a thin file of men, women and children headed for the gatehouse, taking their first steps towards a freedom not one of them would have expected to see.

'I do believe he plans to release us all.' Watson had to speak loudly to make sure Jack heard him. The crowd was no longer silent, and chatter rippled back and forth as the excitement grew in their ranks. 'Do you see him anywhere?'

Jack shook his head. Tewodros had not appeared. 'If he

doesn't release everyone, there'll be trouble.' He could sense that the mood of the crowd had changed. The previous day had seen fear, then disbelief, then hope. Now there was expectation and growing signs of impatience. In the hearts of those who had anticipated nothing but a slow and painful death, the prospect of being released mixed with the fear of being one of those left behind produced an intoxicating and volatile cocktail.

'He must do it.' Watson spoke with the same hope as any other man there.

'I don't think that mad bastard thinks he *must* do anything.'

'But he must, he must.' Watson repeated the words as much to himself as to Jack. He was looking around, his head turning from side to side.

'Just stay calm.' Jack saw that his companion was agitated. The mood of the crowd was infectious.

'I am calm,' Watson snapped.

'Then bloody act like it.' Jack reached out and clasped the other man's shoulder. 'Look, who knows what's going to happen. So just be patient, all right?'

'That is not so damn easy.' Watson shook off Jack's hand. 'We must be freed.'

Jack studied Watson more carefully. There was strain on the younger man's face. He was craning his neck, trying to see to the front of the great crowd in an attempt to judge how close they were to being freed. He was not alone. All around them, the crowd was shifting this way and that, men who had stood the previous day in mute, silent expectation now more eager and alive.

A man far to Jack's left was haranguing the guards. Jack did not understand the words, but it was clear from the prisoner's hectoring tone that he was making some form of demand.

Other voices chimed in. They were quelled almost instantly, the guards shouting orders of their own, their words reinforced with threats and spears thrust forward. It was enough to quieten the crowd instantly.

Time passed slowly. Jack did his best to find some patience. The sun climbed higher, the heat increasing as the minutes crawled by. At the front of the crowd, the blacksmiths worked away, but their pace flagged as their arms tired. The stream of released prisoners was reduced to a trickle, the pile of discarded chains growing at a slower and slower pace.

After what Jack judged to be a good two hours, the blacksmiths stood and laid down their tools. The act was greeted with a howl of disappointment from the crowd. Men near the front pushed forward, voices that had been held silent wailing in distress as they saw their chance of freedom sliding away. The lament spread fast, dozens of voices crying out in protest as the exhausted blacksmiths started to back away.

Jack saw one old man step out from the front of the crowd. He was little more than a skeleton. He wore a filthy loincloth and his body was covered with open sores. Yet from somewhere deep in the desiccated husk of his body, he found the strength to confront the closest guard. He shuffled forward and cried out, moving with an awkward, shambling gait, the chains around his bony legs dragging in the dirt. There was little force in his reedy, frail voice, but there was no mistaking the plea he made.

The guard was clearly a warrior, his tall, powerful frame standing in stark contrast to the pathetic frailty of the old man. He jabbed his spear forward threateningly, the long weapon held firmly, and shouted two words. Every person in the crowd heard them and understood the threat that came with them.

But the old man took no notice. He continued to hobble forward, his voice pleading.

The guard did not hesitate. He lunged, thrusting the spear with all the force he could muster into the old man's chest. It exploded out of his back, the spearhead coming clean through, then was withdrawn a heartbeat later with one short, sharp motion.

For a single drawn-out moment the old man stood there, his skeletal fingers clawing at the cavernous hole ripped in the centre of his body, before he crumpled.

The silence that followed was deafening.

Then the crowd erupted. As if at a hidden signal, every man, woman and child started to cry and yell and shout. The noise exploded out of them, the force of it shocking. Jack was enveloped by the roar of the mob and felt the anger he carried in his own belly shift. It would have been so easy to release it then, to let it build into the unstoppable rage that he knew would follow. Yet he held it in check. To release it now was to die.

He reached out, taking firm hold of Watson's arm, and took one step backwards. Watson whirled around, his face alive with the madness of that moment. One look at Jack's expression quelled that madness.

Together they wove back through the crowd as quickly as their chains would allow. They were the only ones moving away from the confrontation. The crowd had begun to surge towards the blacksmiths. Arms were raised, fists waved at the guards. Angry shouts filled the air, the prisoners' rage beginning to spew forth, growing in power with every passing moment. The mob released a visceral, primeval sound that came from deep within each of them. It was the anger of those who had been afraid for too long, the rage of those who had waited for death for so many days and nights that it no longer held any terror for them.

The chaos summoned Tewodros.

Jack could just about make out the emperor as he emerged from his great red pavilion, flanked by his retinue, the small group of trusted advisers and commanders who clung to him day and night. He was too far away to make out Tewodros's expression, but he did see the sharp gestures of command as the emperor gave his orders.

'Whatever happens, stay with me.' He hissed an order of his own. He still held Watson's arm, and now he shook it vigorously to reinforce his words.

Watson licked his lips nervously, then nodded his understanding.

It was enough for Jack. He looked back. Tewodros was striding towards the crowd. He carried a sword, the blade glinting in the morning light. He had not left his men to deal with the anger of the prisoners. Instead, he faced it himself. And he faced it with rage.

Without pause or delay, he rushed at the crowd, legs moving fast, his sword raised high above his head. As he came closer, Jack saw wrath on the emperor's face, his lips pulled back in a bestial snarl.

He lashed out. The blade cut through the air and slammed into the closest prisoner, cleaving deep into the side of his naked chest. The man fell, his anguished scream lost in the flood of terror that had swamped the throng the moment Tewodros struck.

The emperor recovered his blade, then swung again, the sword moving faster than the eye could track. Blood flew bright in the morning sunlight as he hacked another man down, the blade half severing the prisoner's head from his shoulders. Still the sword moved on, the weapon never still as Tewodros flailed it this way and that. Some prisoners tried to run, their only thought to get away. Few made it more than a few yards before they were cut down by Tewodros's guards. Others tried to defend themselves, lifting their arms in a desperate attempt to ward off the blows that came without pause. But flesh and bone were no defence against the steel blade of the Gorilla King, and more prisoners fell as he cut them down without mercy.

The crowd's anger died. Those who had been pushing forward, faces flushed with rage, now turned to flee. Shouts of fury turned to terrified cries as fear took hold and spread fast.

'Stay close.' Jack held Watson's arm tight, tugging him backwards, keeping bodies between them and the slaughter.

Tewodros came to a standstill. He was surrounded by those he had slain, his bare feet paddling in blood. Yet he was not done. Even as he gasped for air, more orders were shouted. At once, his men plunged into the crowd, grabbing at anyone they could reach. Men, women and children were all taken in that first wild rush, their emaciated and weakened bodies unable to resist. They screamed as the guards dragged them towards the sheer cliff away to the side of the amba.

'Good God.' Watson saw what was intended.

Jack ignored him and increased his pace. He was not alone. Those near the back of the crowd were starting to flee. Some ran, or at least tried to, their shackled legs moving as fast as their chains would allow. Most just shuffled, their bodies too withered and frail to do more. Jack went with them, heading back towards the compound. In that moment, it was the only destination he could think of, the only possible sanctuary from the slaughter.

The guards reached the edge of the amba. They did not pause, their obedience to their emperor complete. Those prisoners they held were pitched out over the edge and into the void.

'The bastard.' Watson stumbled along in Jack's grasp, tears flowing freely down his face.

Around them, men clawed and grabbed at one another as they fought to escape, even as Tewodros's guards returned to grab hold of more prisoners. Dozens upon dozens were taken, victims chosen quite without thought of mercy. Screams came without pause as prisoner after prisoner was pitched into oblivion, the terrified shrieks of the lost echoing across the mountains before they were cut off abruptly as the bodies broke on the rocks far below. Through it all, Tewodros stood there watching, his bloody sword held at his side.

Jack pushed on. His skin burned from the iron grasp of the manacles, and his chest heaved with the strain of trying to run with his legs chained tight. His rage grew with every awkward, painful step, yet he choked it down. He could not fight back. Not without a weapon. Not against so many. So he led Watson on, elbowing his way past those around him, his only thought to get them away from the murderous Abyssinian king. He did not look back again. He did not have to. The constant screams told him that more prisoners were being taken as the guards warmed to their gruesome task.

At his side, an old woman fell. With his free hand, he hauled her to her feet then pulled her along with him, refusing to let her stop.

Those who had been able to get away stumbled on. They entered their compound and ran for their huts. There they hid, praying that the emperor's lust for blood had been satiated.

At the top of the steps, Jack let the old woman go. She fell to her knees, face buried in her hands. But it was enough to have got her there, and he left her, dragging Watson inside their hut. There he bent double, hauling air into his tortured lungs. Watson staggered for another few paces, then sat down heavily. He curled into a ball, hugging his knees to his chest and burying his head before rocking back and forth, his half-muffled sobs of distress coming between gasps for air.

Jack said nothing. There were no words of comfort he could offer that would ease Watson's anguish. There was nothing to be done save to endure.

And to pray that Tewodros stopped short of slaughtering them all.

Chapter Thirty-nine

Good Friday, 10 April 1868

Jack woke to the call of a bugle sounding the reveille. It came from far away, but it was clear enough for him to recognise the series of rising notes that summoned soldiers from their rest.

'Do you hear that?' Watson was sitting near the door to their hut, facing outside.

'Napier must be close.' Jack eased his pain-racked body into a seated position. 'Any water left?'

'Some.' Watson answered without looking around. The prisoners' compound had a simple well near its centre. They had not been fed, but at least they had water.

Jack kept his body moving, ignoring the shooting pains in his back and the red-raw welts around his ankles that burned like they were on fire. They kept the water in a simple clay gourd they had found in another abandoned hut, and he made his way over to it and drank a mouthful of the brackish liquid.

'Do you wonder why they didn't come for us?' Watson asked.

'No.' It was a lie, but Jack did not want to debate the

pointless. After the slaughter the previous day, they had fully expected Tewodros and his men to sweep into the compound, killing any prisoner left alive. It had not happened. For some reason, they had been left in peace. 'Maybe he saw Napier was close. Or maybe it was enough that we were all back in here. Maybe the sick bastard had just murdered enough defenceless old men for one day.'

'We should be grateful.'

'Maybe.' Jack limped his way to the doorway. 'Here.' He handed over the gourd.

Watson took it and drank whilst Jack sat down at his side. Neither said anything more as they looked out at the rising sun that marked the start of another day. The sky glowed red, the horizon touched with the colour of fresh blood.

The sun rose slowly. The vibrant colours of dawn faded into the pale blues and golds of morning. No one came to disturb the prisoners' compound. Jack watched a few other prisoners scurry past as they went for water or to the latrines. But most of those that were left stayed in their huts. Hiding from the day as best they could.

'Do you think you have enough material for your account now?' Jack could not resist the barbed comment.

'Oh, I don't know. Perhaps we can be a part of another massacre. That would add some spice.' Watson gave one of his odd smiles. 'Although I doubt anyone will credit the tale I already have.'

'You will be the toast of London when it is published.'

'Ha!' Watson snorted at the line. 'I doubt anyone will read it.'

'It will sell in the thousands. Maybe Vicky will even invite you to the palace to tell your tale in person.'

'I like the sound of that.' Watson grinned at the notion. 'However, I must conclude that there is one small flaw in your vision of such a rosy future.' He looked outside. 'We have to be alive and in London for any of it to come to pass. And that must start with us getting out of here.'

'We will. But for now, we need to wait.' Jack voiced the plan that was forming in his mind. 'If we leave now, I don't think we'll get far. Some bastard or other will stop us. We need to wait until Napier attacks. It'll be chaos then. That's when we'll have the best chance of escaping.'

'I'm sorry to nit-pick, but again I see a small flaw in that plan. You are suggesting that we escape when battle has begun. From our current location, that will mean moving *towards* and perhaps *into* the battle. Now, from what I have heard of war, I suspect that might not be the safest option.'

'It's better than sitting on our arses waiting for that mad fucker and his bloody minions to top us all when they realise the game is up.'

'Ah, yes.' Watson gave a little grunt at Jack's choice of words. 'Perhaps there is a certain logic to it after all.'

'Of course. I'm always right.' Jack had meant to sound glib, but it came out as a flat statement of truth. 'And I know battle. I'll keep us safe.'

'Then I shall not worry.' Watson resumed his former posture, his eyes scanning outside. 'So for now we have to wait?'

'Yes. We wait.' Jack felt the decision settle. He could feel the anger squirming deep in his belly. It would soon be time to let it have its head.

But not yet.

*

The world grew progressively darker as the day dragged by. Heavy grey clouds filled the sky, shutting off the sun and casting the earth into shadow. Jack sat in the doorway to the hut, staring upwards. He saw no sign of a storm, yet he could feel one coming – one created by man, not by the gods.

The prisoners had been left in peace. Once they had heard distant shouting, the commotion lasting for no more than a few minutes. But there had been no cannon fire, or sounds of an army on the march.

'What is taking so long?' Watson asked, breaking the silence. He sat at Jack's side.

'Napier is getting ready,' Jack explained. For once he did not mind talking. He was bored. He found it laughable, but it was the truth. He was sitting there, unarmed and defenceless, in the heart of the Gorilla King's lair, just a few hundred yards away from where he might have been one of hundreds slaughtered in the emperor's name. And yet he was thoroughly bored. 'He needs to get his guns in place first. I cannot imagine that is easy, given the terrain.'

'What will happen then?' Watson pushed for more.

'A bombardment first. If I were him. I'd flatten this whole damn place before I sent the boys forward.'

'The boys?'

'His men. The poor bloody infantrymen who'll be told to take the fortress.' Jack could picture the red- and grey-coated ranks rushing forward, their formation tight. Their colours would lead them. He knew what it was like to follow his regiment's colours through the confusion and slaughter of the battlefield. They acted as a beacon, a visible emblem of the regiment's pride. If he was right and Napier did attack, then that day he would once again see the British regiments' colours on the battlefield. And this time, he would be on the wrong side.

'I am glad that I am not one of them.' Watson gave his honest opinion.

'Me too,' Jack agreed. 'It won't be easy.'

'But they will succeed?'

'Yes.' He did not have one shred of doubt that the British would take Magdala.

'And when they come, we leave.'

'Yes.'

'I hope I do not let you down.'

'Why would you?' Jack looked at his companion. He could see the worry and doubt in his downcast expression.

'I do not think I am cut out for battle.'

'You'll be fine.'

'How can you be sure?'

'You got this far, didn't you?' Jack offered the reassurance he felt was needed. 'When I first saw you back in London, I thought you'd surely quit as soon as the going got tough.'

'I am glad to disappoint.' Watson's voice quivered as he replied.

'Of course, you only managed it thanks to me.'

'Yes, I think you have that right. I would not be here without you,' Watson replied earnestly.

'And I'll see you right.' Jack tried to put Watson's mind at rest. It was all he could do. No one knew what fate had in store for them, not when battle started. Only time would tell if they would make it away from Magdala with their lives.

The sky darkened further. The air became heavy as more clouds gathered over the hilltops. It was oddly silent, as if the world was drawing one last breath before hell was unleashed.

Jack pushed himself to his feet. He had not moved for some time, and his body protested as he forced it to obey his command.

The faintest hint of a breeze whispered across his face as he stepped outside the hut. From there he could look down on the entrance to the prisoners' compound. Normally there were at least half a dozen guards stationed in the area beneath the steps. Now there were none.

It was too good an opportunity to ignore.

'Come on.' He looked down at Watson. 'I've had my fill of sitting here.'

'Are we leaving?' Watson scrambled to his feet.

'Yes,' Jack called back over his shoulder. He had eyes only for the compound and the series of steps that led down to the main encampment.

A few other prisoners were around, but most peered anxiously from their huts, eyes wide with fear. From what he could see, the steps were unguarded. If they wanted to leave, there was no one to stop them.

'Come on.' He gave the order again as he crossed the ground between the hut and the top of the steps. Others followed, perhaps a dozen prisoners trailing him. Most still hid away, reluctant to leave the dubious safety of their huts, even though they were no longer under guard.

He reached the steps. He was the first there, but he did not hesitate and plunged down them, increasing his speed without thought.

There was no one waiting at the bottom.

He did not have to wait long to discover where everyone had gone.

A great cheer sounded from the far side of Selamge, near the hilltop of Selassie. It was a feral sound. The war cry of men about to be sent onto the battlefield. The last hurrah of men about to die.

Military sense dictated that Tewodros stay behind his defences and wait for Napier to attack. Instead, he was gathering his army around him.

He was the Gorilla King. And he wanted to fight.

Chapter Forty

‘Get on with it, boy.’ Jack stood over the young lad they had found lurking in the corner of the blacksmith's hut and snapped at him to work faster.

The lad could not have been more than ten or eleven years old, and he spoke not a word of English. Yet he had understood the threats that Jack had delivered, and even now he was attacking one of the manacles around Watson's ankles with a hammer and chisel.

The sound of metal on metal rang out.

‘Oh, thank God.’ Watson could not hold back the relief as the first manacle fell away. ‘Thank God.’ He reached down, fingers probing gently as they massaged at the broken and bruised flesh.

Jack bit back an urge to snap at the lad to go faster as he started to work on Watson's other ankle. He could feel his impatience building. He wanted to be away. But nothing could happen until the shackles were released, so he did his best to hold his temper in check.

He could hear Tewodros's army. Their war cry called to him. Battle was coming, and he wanted to be a part of it. He had been away from the battlefield for five long years. Now he wanted to fight – no, he *needed* to fight.

'Hurry up,' he hissed. The lad was hammering away at Watson's ankle with enough force to send out a shower of sparks with every blow. Jack raised a bunched fist. He would not hold back the blow if it were needed.

The lad saw it and flinched, attacking Watson's second manacle for all he was worth. Moments later it fell away, the metal jangling as it hit the ground.

'Hellfire and darnation.' Watson hissed in pain as the metal scraped his raw skin.

'Shut up,' Jack snapped, then thrust his own leg in front of the young apprentice blacksmith. 'Get on with it, boy.'

The lad obeyed, placing the chisel then starting to hammer away. Each blow sent a judder running up Jack's leg that set his teeth on edge. Every impact of the hammer hurt, each one driving the metal into the raw wound beneath. He ignored the pain. It meant nothing.

'Find weapons. Anything will do.' He fired the instruction at Watson, who was hobbling around the hut like an old man.

'Are we going to fight?' Watson turned to look at him.

'Yes.' Jack hissed the word through gritted teeth. 'Oh, sweet Jesus.' He could not help the cry as the first manacle fell away.

'It feels good, does it not?' Watson gave a fleeting smile as he saw the relief flood across Jack's face.

'Get the weapons,' Jack barked as the lad began to attack the second manacle. Again, the pain came on strong, but he set his jaw and ignored it. He watched Watson shuffle awkwardly out of the hut, his legs still not able to understand that they could move normally once again.

It took a few minutes, but eventually the second manacle was released. Jack felt the pain fall away with the remorseless metal clasp. The sense of freedom was intense.

'I found these.' Watson returned to the hut carrying two spears. They were shorter than the ones the warriors usually carried by a good foot, but they would do.

'Good.' Jack stepped forward. It hurt to try to take a full pace. But he took the spear, hefting its weight in his hand. It felt good to hold a weapon again. It was no rifle or revolver, but it still lent him power.

He glanced at the lad who had freed them. The boy was scurrying back into one of the hut's corners, where he hid away from the two white men now carrying spears. He was no threat, so Jack gave his full attention to Watson.

'Are you ready?'

'Yes.' Watson sucked down a deep breath. 'How will we get past?'

'We won't.' Jack took another tentative step forward, stretching his tendons and muscles as he did so, trying to loosen them.

'So how are we getting out of here?' Watson reached out to hold Jack in place.

Jack shrugged off the hand. 'We're going to join them.'

'Join who?'

He paused to smile wolfishly. 'We're going to join Tewodros's army.'

'Are you mad?' Watson's mouth gaped open.

'No, it's the only way. No one will notice us.' Jack fought the urge to laugh. Perhaps he was mad to suggest it, but he could see no other choice. Every instinct told him that Tewodros was going to fight. No matter how that played out, he was sure

they could use the chaos that would follow to their advantage
and find a way to get out of Magdala.

They moved slowly. Neither man could walk with freedom,
their legs still tight and painful, but at least they looked the
part. They were still dressed in the clothes they had been captured in, and now armed with the spears Watson had found,
they appeared little different to any of the dusty warriors
moving to join their emperor.

They were not alone. A steady stream of men moved across
the amba towards the Kokit Ber gateway, all heading for
Selassie, where Tewodros was gathering his army. It was easy
enough to join them, and not one warrior gave them a second
look.

Ahead, thousands of warriors were already gathered. There
was no order to be discerned, the men bunched together any
old how. Tewodros might have been forced to retreat to his
final stronghold, but he still commanded a great host, one that
surely outnumbered the battalions Napier had marched
hundreds of miles across country.

The emperor had positioned his artillery on Selassie. The
mismatched collection of cannons was lined up on the western
edge of the hilltop, standing wheel to wheel. Even the great
Sevastopol was there, the enormous mortar in pride of place at
the centre of the line.

'There!' Watson tugged at Jack's sleeve, then nodded off to
the right.

Jack saw Tewodros immediately. The emperor was mounted
on a great bay charger, looming large over the heads of his
warriors. To Jack's eye, he looked like an ancient warrior, a
man from the distant past, when men fought with sword and

shield. The London papers might have titled him the Gorilla King, and Napier's men might believe they faced a madman, but here, in all his pomp and majesty, was a warrior who had made himself an emperor. He had bound men to him, so that even now, with a British army at the gates, he commanded a host of devoted warriors willing to fight, and to die, in his name. This man, this cruel, spiteful, malicious ruler, was no ordinary enemy, and Jack prayed that Napier was not under-estimating his foe. For Tewodros was not beaten. Not by a long way.

The emperor was addressing his men. He stood in his stirrups, his long hair blowing back in the sharp breeze that whistled across the hilltop. With the darkened skies at his back, he cut a magnificent figure, and his men responded, the chilled air resounding to thousands of voices that cheered in unison as they returned their leader's exhortations. The wild sound rolled across Selassie. Intense, deafening, maddening.

Jack waited on the fringe of the crowd, the hairs on his arms and neck standing to attention as the warriors of the Emperor Tewodros screamed their defiance to the gods above.

And they were heard. Thunder rolled across the heavens, the low rumble spreading far and wide so that it was as if the gods themselves were replying to the cries. The sound goaded the warriors to even greater frenzy. Their yells and bellows increased in volume and intensity. There was insanity in the air then. Madness and anger. Tewodros fanned the flames of his army's rage, adding fuel to the fire that was spreading across the hilltop.

Jack stood amongst that great horde and felt some of the same madness. And he understood it.

Tewodros's best hope of victory lay in a stout defence of his fortress. With his cannon, and with so many men at his command, he could defend Magdala for days, even weeks, forcing Napier to launch a series of bloody assaults that would see many of his men left dead and broken. The British general might have no choice but to fall back on his lines of supply and wait for reinforcements, or perhaps even for the order to retreat. If the emperor could hold on for long enough, and if he could kill enough of Napier's men, then he stood a chance of snatching victory from the very jaws of defeat.

But no one on the chaotic hilltop entertained such a notion. There was no thought of a protracted, drawn-out, defiant defence. There was just fury and a wild, searing desire to fight. These men were Tewodros's finest and most loyal warriors. They had all fought before, and had killed in his name. They had earned their master the title of emperor, and they had cut down all who tried to take it from him. Now they saw the approach of the British army, and they thought only of battle. They would take their spears against this new enemy, and they would send them running back to the coast and to the ships that had brought them here.

Jack did not see the signal, but from somewhere the great horde started to move. It shifted slowly at first, the men dancing and stamping as the searing madness set their souls aflame.

And then they charged.

Chapter Forty-one

———◆•◆•◆———

The horde moved as one. Jack and Watson went with them. It was the opportunity Jack had hoped for. Tewodros's army was attacking. In the havoc of battle, he would find them a way out.

He caught a glimpse of Tewodros as the great charge began. The emperor rode steadily through the horde he had released, making for his precious cannon, his wild exhortations replaced by an eerie, detached calm.

The horde crossed onto Fala. They shouted their war cry as they stormed forward, their wild yells echoing from the mountains so that it sounded like the whole world was crying out in anger.

They made a fine sight. Jack looked at the mass ahead even as he advanced with the men around him. It seemed as though the entire Abyssinian army had joined the charge. Most men wore the white shamma, the bright robes vivid in the darkness that had engulfed the world. The horde flowed across Fala, then on down the steep path that scaled its almost vertical face, and up and towards the great plain beyond.

Their chieftains led them, mounted on horses, their bright

red shirts marking them out against the white-clad masses. They shouted their orders, daring their men to follow.

There was something wild in that charge. Something primeval. Something even glorious. Jack felt it. There was joy in this moment. He had experienced it before, this madness of battle, this lust to fight. He tasted something of it then, even though his own emotions ran cold. This was not his moment, but still he felt the lure of the fight.

He caught the first glimpse of Napier's army on the great plain to the front of Magdala. He had expected to see a long line of artillery, the cannon grouped into their batteries, or the tight, ordered ranks of the red- and grey-coated regiments as they advanced on the fortress. He had expected to see the regiments' colours unfurled and splendid, the flags bright even in the gloom. He had expected to see a British army ready to fight.

Instead he saw a baggage train.

The long line of carts and mules was trundling along the same path he and Watson had taken when they had arrived at Magdala just a few days before. They were spread out in the order of march, the wagons moving in single file. If they saw the Abyssinian horde coming towards them, they gave no sign of it, the carts rolling on just as they had for hundreds of miles now. Jack had no idea what they were doing there, or how they could have got so far away from Napier's main column, but he knew they were in terrible danger. Napier's soldiers were equipped with the most modern weapons of war, but that firepower would not help the men in the wagon train. They would not stand a chance against the spears and swords of the Abyssinians charging towards them.

Tewodros's warriors ran hard and fast. They flowed across

the rocky terrain, fleet-footed and nimble. The air resounded to almost constant peals of thunder, the sound echoed in the wild war cry coming from the throats of the warriors. The twin sounds pulsated, the noises intertwined, at times fading then increasing in both volume and tempo so that it sounded like a denizen of some other realm had been released. There was no order to the rush. Men jostled and shoved at one another as they raced to get ahead and be the first to slake their spear with blood.

Jack pushed his tired, aching legs to keep moving. He and Watson were far to the rear of the massive horde. He had little in the way of a plan, save for a vague notion of getting close to the British lines and falling down to play dead. Then he and Watson could wait until the Abyssinians had been pushed back before revealing themselves to the nearest friendly troops. It was a plan fraught with danger, not least as it meant advancing alongside men who would delight in killing a white-faced foreigner. It also involved rushing the British line, which at some point would surely flay the charging Abyssinians with volley fire. But it was all the plan he had, and he could not think of another.

He raced on, glancing over his shoulder every few moments to check that Watson followed. He was doing his best. Like Jack, his legs would surely be on fire, and the muscles and tendons would be in agony as they were stretched and strained after days held chained. But despite that pain, Watson stuck doggedly to Jack's tail, following him through the rear ranks of the horde.

Together they did their best to get on. The rear of the Abyssinian horde was the domain of the old, the slow and the cowardly, and the pair made decent progress, forcing a path so that they got somewhere close to the middle of the charge as it flowed onto the plain that led away from the three hilltops of Tewodros's lair. It was only then that Jack caught his first glimpse of the second, larger British column.

The leading regiments were only just advancing onto the plain. All were in column, the formation in which they marched. They would need time to re-form into the two-man-deep line of battle in which they would fight, time that was in short supply as the Abyssinian horde rushed across the plain.

He was not alone in seeing the column. The horde started to break up into two groups, one heading for the wagon train, the other charging at the bulk of Napier's army, which was only now shaking itself into order of battle.

Jack saw the horde start to split and made his choice. From what he had seen, the wagon train was doomed. With at least half the Abyssinian horde heading its way, it would be cut apart in minutes. But the main column was a different prospect. Spears, swords and matchlocks could not compete with the rifled muskets and Sniders carried by Napier's troops. The mob of which he was now a part would not stand a chance against them. It would be a meeting of the old world and the new: sword and spear against bullet and rifle. And it would be a massacre. So he angled his path, trusting Watson to follow as he lumbered after the body of men charging towards Napier's infantry. For only in the slaughter that was to come would there be a chance to feign their deaths. Only in death was there hope.

The sky turned to the colours of night. Grey clouds became black and thunder boomed across the heavens, as if the gods themselves were beating a drum to inspire the warriors in the world below.

The Abyssinians charged. No one had told them that they would find only defeat in this uneven battle. No one had told them that they would die, their bodies torn apart by the heavy bullets sure to come their way. They thought only of seizing the opportunity to drown their land in the blood of the invaders. And they had a chance. It was a race now. If they could hit the British column before it re-formed, then they could still taste victory. In a hand-to-hand fight, the swords and spears held by men trained in their use almost since birth would have the advantage.

On the other side of the battlefield was another race, one that the Abyssinians would surely win. The wagon train was finally alive to the danger. Jack could not make out much, but he could see the men of the wagon train rushing this way and that as they prepared for the fight that was coming their way. Batteries of cannon were deployed, the gunners rushing to be ready to open fire on the horde charging towards them. A handful of infantrymen stood with the guns. No more than two companies of Punjabis against more than two thousand Abyssinian warriors. Yet the men from the Punjab stood their ground, their thin line forming up as the first cannon deployed, facing the advancing mob.

Jack ran hard, forcing his body to obey. Around him, Tewodros's warriors shouted their war cry, their rage sustaining them as they ploughed on. The distance between the two armies closed fast. Jack caught fleeting glimpses of the first British battalions reaching the plain. All were rushing to re-form. It was the moment the infantrymen had trained for. On parade grounds and practice fields from Hampshire to Bombay, they were drilled in the art of moving from one formation to another. Now they were doing it on the battlefield, and they were doing it quickly. The great lumbering columns of march were breaking up, and already the first firing lines were formed across the face of the Abyssinian horde.

Tewodros's men saw only their enemy. They saw densely packed formations breaking into fragile thin lines. They saw victory. They gave it everything, racing forward, war cries turning into screams of delight. The enemy was disordered and vulnerable. Their triumph was at hand.

Then came a great roar of cannon fire, and everything changed.

Chapter Forty-two

---◆◈◆---

*J*ack flinched as the guns of the baggage train opened fire and the air filled with a thunderous roar. It was a terrible sound to hear, as if the very heavens were being ripped apart by the gods.

He tried to watch what was happening even as he ran with the men charging the larger British column. He saw the first roundshot scythe into the Abyssinians attacking the baggage train. The fast-moving shot ripped through the mass, tearing men apart. Shells followed, the lighter British guns firing rounds that exploded in the air over the heads of the Abyssinian warriors, showering them with musket balls and fragments of red-hot shell casing. With the artillery fire came the unmistakable crackle of rifle fire, the two companies of Punjabi infantrymen firing their first volley, the roar of their Snider rifles adding to the storm of sound that filled the world with a never-ending cacophony.

Screams rang out. Men torn apart by the roundshot died without a sound, but those hit by shrapnel yelled out in horror as the wickedly sharp shell fragments ripped into their flesh.

A dreadful screeching came hard on the heels of the first

roar of artillery. Jack heard it and twisted around as he ran, his eyes searching for the source of such an unearthly howl. He saw great streaks of smoke scorching across the sky before they slammed down into the Abyssinian warriors charging the baggage train, bursting through the ranks like solid roundshot, showering men with eruptions of sparks and flame.

He knew what they were. He had seen the small Hale rockets carried on the mules of the Royal Artillery. Now he saw them in action for the first time and he knew that he had been wrong. It was no baggage train that half the Abyssinian army was attacking. It was the artillery column. The gunners of the Naval Brigade and the Mountain Battery had no right to be so far in front of the main infantry column, but that had not stopped them from making a stand. It was bravely done. Jack knew it was no small thing to stand your ground whilst a couple of thousand wild-eyed, spear-toting warriors charged towards you. Yet the gunners were holding fast. Even as he watched, they fired a second salvo. Roundshot, shell and rocket tore into the mass of Abyssinians running towards the stranded artillerymen, the barrage striking men down in mid stride.

It was carnage.

Tewodros was not to be outdone. Even as half his army was being savaged by the British gunners, he ordered his own guns to fire. It was the moment he had waited for. Years of work and cruel exploitation had fabricated the Gorilla King a great battery of guns, and now they slung their own roundshot and shell towards the British infantry as they re-formed in front of the second half of his army. Even the great Sevastopol was brought into action, the explosion of sound the mortar made as it was fired in anger for the very first time echoing off the mountain ranges that surrounded Magdala.

Jack heard the roar as the guns on Selassie boomed out. He tried to see the path of their shot, but in the press of bodies charging the British infantry he could catch no glimpse of them as they slashed through the sky.

The first roundshot fell short, smashing into the leading ranks of Tewodros's own warriors. Men screamed as they were cut down from behind by their emperor's opening salvo. A flurry of shells exploded far in front of the British ranks, where they did nothing more than churn the ground and throw great shards of broken rock into the sky. Tewodros had worked for years to build his artillery, and now, on the battlefield, it was clear that it had been years of folly.

Still the Abyssinian warriors charged on. They pounded across the rocky ground, callously ignoring those already struck down. Jack ran with them. He no longer tried to look across the battlefield to see what was happening to the half of Tewodros's army attacking the baggage train. Everything he had was focused on the British line to his front. Watson was at his side. He saw the academic's mouth moving as he shouted something, but the words were lost in the storm of sound that surrounded them.

Ahead, the men of the 1st Battalion, 4th King's Own Royal Regiment formed the foremost British line. The four hundred and forty-six men had moved quickly, and they now stood in a loose formation that screened the men behind them.

Jack saw the men standing in their skirmish line. He saw the steady ranks, and he could just about make out the snap of orders as their officers prepared them for what was to come. He knew how they would be feeling. He had stood in the line of battle when the enemy charged. He knew the fear of that moment, the pounding of the heart and the dry mouth; the terror of standing still and mute as the enemy raced towards you. The great mass of Abyssinian warriors would seem un-stoppable to the men in that line. There would appear to be too many to be turned, the unequal fight seemingly unwinnable. Yet there was nothing to do save to stand there, impassive and silent, waiting for the horde to come into range.

The Abyssinian warriors were just two hundred yards away from the first British line. They saw their enemy waiting for them. From somewhere they found the strength to increase their speed. They powered forward, spears and swords held ready. Jack did his best to keep up, pushing his floundering body to its limits. He saw the British line standing steady and knew what was to come. It took all of his willpower to keep moving. Every instinct begged him to stop, or to dive to the ground. Yet he kept moving, running as hard as he could. Waiting for the first volley. Waiting for his chance.

Two hundred yards became one hundred and fifty. The pace of the charge increased again, the ground flashing past. Jack sucked down a last breath and reached out, taking hold of Watson's arm. He was ready. If he lived, he knew what he would do.

If he lived.

Fifty more yards passed in a flash. Ahead, the British line raised their rifles. Nearly five hundred Sniders were aimed at the Abyssinian charge. Jack saw the steady barrels and steeled himself for what was to come.

The British line fired.

It was a battalion volley. Every one of the four hundred and forty-six men standing in the line snatched back his trigger and fired at the same moment. The best part of five hundred heavy Snider bullets tore into the leading ranks of the Abyssinian charge. Every one found a mark.

The men leading the charge were scythed down like wheat before a threshing machine, bullets cutting through bodies, tearing away limbs, ripping flesh apart.

'Down!'

Jack had flinched as the volley gutted the Abyssinian ranks, a cry of pure terror torn from his lips as he heard the dreadful wet slap of bullets striking flesh. Yet still he managed to bellow the command as he dragged Watson down with him, throwing them both to the ground.

They hit the rocky soil hard, breath driven from their bodies.

Around them, the Abyssinians surged on, pounding over the bodies of the dead and the dying. They had fought men with muskets before. They knew that to survive the first volley was enough. Now their enemy would be defenceless. It was time to carry the charge home. It was time to slake their spears and their swords with blood. It was time to fight and to earn victory for their beloved emperor.

But the British infantry did not carry muskets. They carried the most modern rifles that the British factories could make. Their Sniders could fire ten rounds a minute, and now a second volley followed hard on the heels of the first. Another storm of bullets tore into the front of the charge. Men who had yelled in relief as they survived the first volley screamed as they were cut down. Bodies fell in every direction, the warriors toppling like skittles at the fair.

A third volley fired just seconds later.

In that moment, the charge died. The ground was spread thickly with broken bodies, creating a barrier that no man would cross. Those still alive came to a horrified halt, the fury that had driven them so far gone in an instant. It was replaced by terror.

The British poured on the fire. More bullets tore through the now stationary warriors, killing and maiming with wanton cruelty.

Jack lay on the ground and tried to bury himself in the rocky soil. He had never heard anything like the British volleys that day. They came with a speed that was mesmerising. It was a demonstration of modern military power, and the Abyssinians never stood a chance.

Chapter Forty-three

―――•◦•―――

Tewodros's warriors broke. Jack did not know of any army that could have stood its ground at that moment. The British continued to fire without mercy, heavy Snider bullets tearing into the packed Abyssinian ranks even as they fled.

Bodies thumped into the ground all around him. Some still lived, their desperate, anguished sobs echoing in his ears. Most crumpled and lay still, blood gushing into the barren soil.

The storm of fire stopped abruptly. Orders rang out, crisp and clear.

Jack sucked down a deep breath, then pushed down with his hands, forcing himself to his feet. 'Get up!' The words rasped out of his dry mouth as he called to Watson. This was their moment. It was time to get to safety.

It took a second for him to find his balance. As he steadied himself, he saw the bodies strewn around him. It was like nothing he had ever witnessed. The dead, the dying and the broken smothered the ground. They lay so thickly that it was as if the battlefield had been covered with a great carpet made from red and white cloth. But it was a cloth that pulsated with the remnants of life. Here and there bodies moved as men tried to rise. Pitiful moans came without pause, along with the screams of those in agony and the sobs of those facing death. Jack stood in the midst of that sea of suffering, for a moment quite overcome with the sight of so much horror.

'There!' A loud English voice rang out. A moment later, a bullet snapped past his head. 'Shoot the Johnnies down!'

He faced the British line. Two officers stood in front of their men. He was close enough to see that both were impossibly young, no more than boys dressed in uniforms. Both held revolvers.

'Hey!' he shouted. 'Stop!'

He was ignored. Both officers fired again.

'Stop!' He called out once more, then lifted his arms to wave. He had no idea if the men even saw him.

Another bullet zipped past. It was close enough for him to feel the snap in the air as it missed him by no more than a foot.

He turned around, head swivelling this way and that as he tried to find somewhere they could hide away until the shooting stopped. But he was short on time. The Abyssinians were massing again. They had been mauled and they had lost hundreds of men, but they were proud warriors all. They had not carved out an empire by fleeing at the first taste of defeat. Even now their commanders were rallying the broken ranks, their shouts and yells of encouragement stirring their men.

More shots came. Another bullet buzzed past Jack's head.

'Shit.' He hissed the single word.

'What the hell are they doing?' Watson had lumbered to his feet, but now ducked down again, squatting low as more shots whipped past them.

'The stupid bastards.' Jack hunkered down. His plan was

failing. Time was slipping away. Shouts and yells came from the Abyssinian warriors as they regrouped. He could scarcely credit it, but he saw the first of them start to move forward once more. A second charge was coming.

'Fuck it.' He cursed, then stood tall and waved at the British ranks. 'We're English! You hear me, you bastards?' He shouted as loudly as he could, waving his arms back and forth to draw attention.

He succeeded. Heads turned his way.

But it was not to call him in. Instead, rifles and pistols were raised, their barrels pointing directly at him. The British ranks did not see two desperate fugitives. They saw two men dressed as warriors in Tewodros's army. They saw targets.

'Shit!' He swore again as he threw himself to the ground once more, dragging Watson down with him. Bullets zipped past above his head. They could not reach the British ranks, not dressed as they were. If they tried again, they would be shot down.

'What the hell are we going to do?' Watson plucked at his arm.

Jack had only one idea left. 'Play dead.'

Watson's eyes widened. 'What?'

'Do it!' Jack snapped the words then went still. There was no time for anything else.

For the Abyssinians were charging for a second time.

And Jack and Watson were trapped between the two armies.

The second Abyssinian charge was quieter than the first. Tewodros's depleted army no longer cheered or screamed their war cry. They came on in silence, breath saved for the task ahead.

It was bravely done. The warriors knew what was to come. They had seen the power of the rifles their enemy carried, and they knew the fate that awaited the men who dared to go against the frail line that snaked across the ground. But they had pride, these men of Abyssinia, so they charged for a second time, the great mass still outnumbering the lines of redcoats and sepoys that stood in front of them.

One of Tewodros's generals led the attack, mounted on a fine white charger. He wore a bright red shirt over his white trousers, an animal-skin lembd decorated with brass draped across his shoulders. His headdress was made from the mane of a lion, the hair arranged so that it stood up in a great crescent over the general's head. He looked every inch a warrior; a man who would inspire others to follow.

The charge flowed across the ground. It moved fast, the warriors advancing with loping strides, crowding together in one great mass.

Jack did his best to lie still. It was not easy. Every instinct screamed at him to run towards the British line. But to move was to die, and so he forced his head down, fighting the urge to watch.

He knew the charge was coming. He could feel it in the ground, which vibrated from the thump of hundreds of pairs of feet running fast.

Then the British line opened fire for the second time.

The delay between the two charges had allowed other battalions to join the 4th's line. Thousands of rifled muskets and Sniders now faced the Abyssinian horde. They fired as one.

Hundreds upon hundreds of bullets tore into the advancing warriors, cutting men down in droves. Jack lifted his head, unable to resist. It was as if the Abyssinian charge had run into the jaws of some hideous creature. The leading ranks had been shredded by the dreadful storm of bullets. The general was down, his broken body thrown to one side as his charger fell, the brave animal struck by at least a dozen bullets, its white coat sheeted in blood.

For a second time, the Abyssinians turned and ran.

'Come on!' Jack saw his chance and took it.

He pushed down, then stumbled to his feet. This time he did not pause and began to run, forcing his legs to find every scrap of speed. He heard Watson behind him, his companion's pants and whimpers loud enough to be heard in the quiet between volleys.

They ran together.

And they ran towards the remains of the Abyssinian charge.

Another British volley crashed out. To Jack, it felt like the very air itself was torn apart around him as the bullets seared past. Then it was over, the only sound the roar of his breath in his ears and the thump of his heart in his chest.

The British did not let the Abyssinians retreat in peace. Another volley came, and then another, redcoats and Indian sepoys firing quite without mercy. Bullets struck home, knocking men over. The retreat turned into a rout, the warriors of the emperor fighting and jostling as they tried to get away.

'Come on!' Watson was flagging, and Jack cried out, trying to force him on.

Another volley flayed the air. Bullets snapped past. Away on the other side of the battlefield, the British gunners and rocketeers fired without pause. Jack saw the other wing of the Abyssinian horde running in disorder, their ranks blown apart by the vicious close-range volleys of the British guns and the brave Punjabis who guarded them. Rockets still seared through the sky, the red and gold fire that spat from the fast-moving projectiles colouring the air above the retreating Abyssinian ranks. Like the infantrymen, the gunners fired without thought of mercy, shot, shell and rocket ploughing through the retreating warriors, striking men down even as they ran.

It was carnage and slaughter on an industrial scale.

Jack put his head down and ran, Watson just behind him. There was nothing else to be done.

They raced through the sea of death, their boots thumping down onto the blood-soaked ground. Both tried to avoid the corpses smothering the ground, but there were too many of them, the bodies lying in the twisted, broken shapes that only the dead could make.

Jack's boot caught on something and he stumbled forward, the spear he still carried lost as his hands reached out to break his fall. He struck the ground hard, teeth jarring together at the brutal impact.

'Get up!' Watson reached out, taking firm hold of his robes and hauling him upright.

Jack staggered to his feet. He saw what had tripped him. A severed head rolled to a stop where he had booted it across the ground. Sightless eyes stared back at him from above a grotesque tangle of bloody offal and gristle.

More bullets scorched past. The range was long now, even the high-powered Sniders becoming ineffective, but enough still snapped by to remind Jack that he could not linger. He put his head down and forced his legs to carry him on, chest heaving, breath burning as he hauled it down into his tortured lungs.

They reached the broken ranks of the Abyssinian charge.

No one noticed them, those around them intent only on reaching safety.

The pace of the rout slowed as the British guns finally fell silent.

Those of Tewodros's warriors that had survived filed back towards Fala. They were pitifully few now, the massed ranks reduced to a huddle of tired, scared men. They hobbled back onto the hilltop. Many were wounded, their white shammas stained with great patches of blood. Some limped or dragged damaged limbs. All bore the same wide-eyed stare of terror.

A moment's sunshine broke through the grey. The thunder that had underscored the battle died out, the sky falling silent.

It was over.

Chapter Forty-four

Jack climbed onto the hilltop of Selamge. His legs were cramping, and it was all he could do to put one foot in front of the other. Everything hurt, yet he knew he was one of the lucky ones, one of the few who had come through the great charge unscathed.

It had begun to rain as the remains of Tewodros's army filed away from the battlefield. Now it came down in a great torrent, as if the sky wept for the dead. It soaked the tired and bloodied warriors, heaping one more misery on the heads of men cowed and broken by the scale of the defeat that had been inflicted upon them. The survivors of the charge sat on the ground in small groups, heads bowed, weapons lying beside them. All were silent.

With Watson at his side, Jack crossed the hilltop, then passed through the Kokit Ber gateway and onto the amba of Magdala. He picked an empty hut and headed towards it. He thought only of rest and getting out of the rain.

Watson had other ideas.

'Look.' He tugged at Jack's elbow, turning him away from the hut.

'What?' Jack was crabby, and he snapped as his chance of rest was delayed.

Watson pointed at a man sitting on a rock not more than twenty yards away. It was Tewodros, Emperor of Abyssinia, and he was quite alone.

Jack could not recall seeing a man look so dejected. Tewodros sat hunched, his head buried in his hands. If he noticed the rain pouring down upon him, he showed no sign of it.

'Give me your spear.' Jack held out a hand. He had lost his own spear when he had fallen and so was unarmed.

'What's that you say?' Watson prevaricated, holding the spear away as if Jack was about to snatch it.

'I'm going to kill the bastard.' Jack tasted a moment's anger. He was hurting, bruised and exhausted. He had been shot at by his own side and forced to return to the enemy's stronghold, one he had risked his life to escape. Now he peered through the rain and saw the man who had imprisoned him, and who had killed and murdered countless innocent people in front of his eyes. He had just one thought in his mind.

It was time to kill.

'No.' Watson read his intention easily enough.

'Give me the fucking spear.' Jack spat the words out. 'Or so help me, God, I'll kill you too.'

Watson's eyes widened at the naked threat. But he did not give in or turn away as once he would have done. 'Do this and you'll die.'

Jack held out his hand impatiently. If he was going to strike, then it needed to be now, whilst Tewodros was alone. He looked across at the emperor, plotting the path he would take. He saw no one in a position to oppose him. It would be easy.

Watson stepped in front of him. 'Think about it. Did you really come all this way to die now?'

'If I kill him, I end this. Do you see?' Jack did not have time to explain properly. But he knew that if he killed Tewodros, the defence of Magdala would be over. There was no way the Mad King's warriors would stand without their beloved leader. The British would be spared a bloody assault. Countless lives would be saved.

A servant approached Tewodros. The man was bowed so low he could only move at an awkward shuffle. He held a sheet of paper that he sheltered from the rain as best he could with his shamma.

'The spear. Now.' Jack held out his hand and looked deep into Watson's eyes. He thought only of taking the weapon and burying it deep between Tewodros's shoulder blades. It would take a single death to save dozens more.

Watson held his gaze for one more moment, then lifted his chin. 'No.'

'What?'

'I will not let you do this.' He held the spear out of Jack's reach, half hiding it behind his body. 'I will not let you die.'

'Give me the fucking spear.'

'No.' Tears formed in Watson's eyes, yet still he stood firm. 'If you try this, they will kill you.'

Jack felt the first burn of anger. He looked at Watson and saw his defiance and his determination. 'Don't test my bloody patience,' he growled.

Behind Watson, Tewodros took the paper from his servant's hand without looking up. He read it slowly, not caring that the rain soaked the single page.

'We need to rest. Then we can plan what we do next.'

Watson swiped a hand across his face, dashing away both rain and tears. He spoke slowly as if to a difficult child as he sought to deflect Jack's anger.

'You need to give me that spear then get out of my fucking way.' Jack stepped forward, hand snatching for the weapon. 'If I kill that bastard then I end this.'

Watson twisted away, still shielding the spear with his body. Jack grabbed at him, grasping his shoulder and trying to spin him around. Watson fought back. 'It doesn't have to be you,' he spluttered. 'Let someone else do it.'

'Give me the spear.' It was all Jack could do not to lash out and hammer his fists into the man who was stopping him.

'No.' Watson struggled out of Jack's grasp. He stood there, hair plastered to his scalp, the precious spear held away. 'I won't let you die. I won't!'

'For fuck's sake.' Jack moved quickly. His left hand shot out, grabbing Watson's robes near his throat and hauling him forward, whilst his right reached for the spear.

Even as he was tugged forward, Watson twisted around, moving the spear away so that Jack snatched at thin air. They wrestled then, hands grabbing and grasping. Somehow Watson kept the spear out of Jack's reach.

The anger came fast. Jack no longer saw the man he had travelled with for so many hundreds of miles. He saw an obstacle, and his hatred flared bright and hot. Control fled. His right hand bunched into a fist, and he punched hard, slamming it into the centre of Watson's face.

The blow snapped Watson's head back. Blood already pumping from his nose, he thumped down onto the ground, landing heavily on his arse, the spear falling from his grasp.

Jack did not pause. He bent down and scooped up the

weapon, then stepped forward. Not once did he look at the man he had knocked down.

Behind Watson, Tewodros jumped to his feet. For one heart-stopping second, Jack thought he had spied the short fight and was about to unleash his guards. But the emperor stood still, his head bowed. His body was vibrating with emotion, every muscle stretched tight. He stood like that for the time it took Jack to take half a dozen steps, then he lifted his head to stare at the sky and started to rage.

Jack could not understand the cries. But he understood the man's emotions well enough. Wrath and fury spewed out of the emperor, his shouts increasing in tempo and volume as he stamped his feet and howled at the sky. Jack felt the same anger burn deep in his own soul. He too wanted to unleash it, but he would not yell or scream. He would find his release in killing.

He stalked forward, scanning his surroundings. There were plenty of servants nearby, but none brave enough to approach their master. Most stood with their heads bowed, arms tucked against the front of their bodies. It made Jack's task simple, and he plotted his route, his eyes assessing the distances and placement of anyone who might try to stop him. He planned his murder even as he moved to commit it.

No more than twenty yards away, Tewodros tore the paper into shreds and tossed them to the wind. Only then did he fall silent. Rage spent, he sat back down on his lonely boulder. This time his back was towards Jack.

A servant came forward, a glass held in his hands. Jack could see the man's fear as he approached his lord. He shook as he took hesitant step after hesitant step, closing on the emperor slowly.

Jack himself felt no fear. He knew Watson had been quite

correct. He did not doubt that he would be killed moments after he had thrust his spear home; there were enough warriors in the vicinity to make that certain. But he vowed he would go down fighting. At the last, he would kill as many of Tewodros's men as he could. He was destined to be here, to administer this justice. It was why fate had led him to this moment.

It was meant to be.

The servant reached his emperor. The glass was placed carefully on the rain-soaked ground near Tewodros's bare feet, then the man stepped away, his pace increasing as he scurried backwards.

Tewodros's head came up. He stared at the glass, then reached out to pick it up. He sipped at it just the once, then placed it carefully back on the ground.

Jack came forward. The spear was heavy in his hand. He liked the feel of it, the wood smooth and warm against his palm. No one moved to intercept him, or even noticed his slow, measured approach.

The ground slipped by under his sandalled feet, foot by foot, yard by yard. He closed the distance slowly, planning every pace. When he was close enough, he would strike and it would end.

The rain started to slow. What had been a torrent became little more than a few spits. The sky had run out of tears.

Tewodros slipped off the rock on which he sat, falling to his knees. He stayed in that pose, head bowed.

Jack heard the murmur of prayer as he approached the man who had murdered and killed without a qualm. It would not stay his hand. He came on, keeping his pace steady even as he felt his heartbeat start to race. He could hear his own breathing and did his best to slow it. There was no need to rush. He had just the one chance. He could not waste it.

Tewodros lifted his head. As he stared at the dark sky, one hand delved beneath his robes. It came out a moment later holding a small revolver.

Jack stopped in his tracks. For a moment, he thought Tewodros had sensed his approach. Every muscle tensed, and he sucked down a last breath as he prepared to throw caution to the wind and gamble everything on one last rush.

Then he saw what the emperor intended and he froze.

Tewodros raised the pistol and aimed it at his own head. Then he pulled the trigger.

The crack of the small handgun's retort was loud in the silence of the mournful encampment. The bullet exploded from the barrel, grazing the side of Tewodros's skull, then flew on to bury itself in a rock ten yards away.

Tewodros howled then. With blood pouring down the side of his skull, he screamed in despair and rage, the sound torn from deep within his being.

Jack held his pose. All around him, servants and warriors swarmed forward, weeping and lamenting as they saw what their beloved master had tried to do.

In that moment, the emperor's cries changed, his anguished howls morphing into a roar of belligerent triumph.

His servants surrounded him. They fussed and wailed, engulfing him so that he disappeared from sight. Jack's last glimpse of Tewodros was of his face. One side was sheeted in blood, but there was no mistaking the ecstasy he saw reflected in his expression at that moment. The Mad King had tried to take his own life. And he had failed. Yet from that failure he had found strength. He had gone from despair to elation in the time it took a single bullet to be fired.

Jack turned on his heel. His chance to be the man that ended the Gorilla King's bloody reign had been snatched away.

Ahead of him, Watson had got back to his feet and now stood still, rain-diluted blood running freely down his face. He looked utterly bereft.

Jack lost sight of him as more men ran towards the emperor. He pushed against the tide, his only thought to get to Watson. Bodies thumped against him, elbows and arms battering him out of the way as Tewodros's men rushed to his side.

The crowd thinned.

Watson was gone.

Jack staggered forward, his head turning this way and that as he tried to locate his companion. For one dreadful moment, his mind turned to Finch. He had not thought of his enemy since they had arrived on Magdala, but now the spectre of the Londoner loomed large. First Finch had taken Cooper from him and then he had killed Macgregor. Now Watson was gone too. Jack was quite alone.

He searched the press of warriors for Watson, but it was impossible. There were too many men, the single gunshot bringing every warrior in earshot to their lord. Behind him he heard the fuss and commotion as they surrounded the bleeding, barefoot emperor. Cheers came as Tewodros exhorted his men, his rage replaced by a passionate fervour.

A deep, visceral chanting started. Tewodros's warriors had been slaughtered by the British rifles and pounded by their artillery. They had been utterly defeated, but now their beloved master stood in front of them and promised them a victory. They responded by chanting his name over and over, the sound filling the fortress hilltop. Tewodros tapped into their last vestiges of defiance and they answered him, their cries and shouts a promise that Magdala would be defended to the last man.

Jack walked away from the chanting mass. It was as if they were mocking him for his failure. Fate had brought him here, and had presented him with the opportunity to slay the Mad King.

He had failed.

Now he had no purpose. He was alone and surrounded by an enemy that would fight to the death for the man he should have killed.

The battle for Magdala was far from over.

Chapter Forty-five

Easter Sunday, 12 April 1868

Jack awoke to the sound of church bells. He lay on the ground in the abandoned hut he had chosen and listened to the distant sound, wondering who was still going to worship this day. It was a reminder that he was in a Christian country. But a shared religion was no defence against the might of the British Empire, not for a murderous king who had dared to flout the queen's will. Tewodros and his people might worship the same God as their invader, but that would not stay Napier's hand.

He sat up slowly, feeling the pains and aches ripple through his body. He did not want to move or do anything much at all. The previous day he had done his best to find Watson. Exhausted after the battle, he had still searched across the hilltops, moving from one empty hut to another whilst doing his best to avoid the warriors that remained. There had been no sign of Watson anywhere.

A wave of despondency washed over him. It was new, this feeling of hopelessness. Despite everything he had done in the past, he had never lost faith in himself.

Doubts flooded his mind. He tried to recall why he was there, why he had placed himself at the heart of the enemy's strength. He failed. There were half-remembered reasons, half-formed notions of revenge and treasure, but none made sense. Not now. Not now he was alone.

He lay down again and closed his eyes. For the first time in many years, he tried to summon the faces of the lost into his mind's eye. Yet even they hid from him. They had haunted him for more nights than he could recall, yet now, when he needed them, they too had abandoned him.

The sound of movement came from outside. He did his best to ignore it, closing his ears and letting his mind drift.

He did not know how long he lay there. But he did know that the sound of movement came without pause. It was the sound of people on the move. A lot of people.

The urge to see what was happening grew until he gave in and pushed himself to his feet. The cause of the noise was immediately obvious. A great column of people stretched from the Kokit Ber gateway all the way to the prisoners' compound. At the last, Tewodros was letting the rest of his prisoners go.

For a moment, Jack was tempted to join them. There were no guards on the column, the prisoners left to find their own way across the hilltop. He could slip into the throng, taking his place amongst the other lost souls. Then all he had to do was walk. Within an hour, he would be in the British lines. And it would be over.

Except that he knew it would never be over. Not until he found Watson and made sure his friend made it to safety. It was the one purpose he had left.

Jack remembered Watson's excitement as he had made his

plans. He recalled the way his face had lit up as they conjured an image of his future, one that placed him in front of John Bull as the man who had dared to enter the Gorilla King's fortress and survived to tell the fantastical tale. It was a future that could still come to pass, and Jack was determined to make it happen. He would search all three hilltops until he found Watson, and then he would ensure he made it safely to the British lines, where he could start the process of writing up his tale.

He took a deep breath, forcing air into his lungs. It had a peculiar taste, the breeze carrying with it the taint of death. The corpses from the battle would still be lying where they had fallen. The flesh would rot quickly, and he knew that by the day's end, the foul miasma would permeate every inch of all three hilltops. It would linger there long after the bodies had been buried. Magdala had become a place of death, a mausoleum to the ambition of one man.

The sense of purpose lent him strength. He would find Watson. Then he would leave Magdala behind. Beyond that, the future would take care of itself. It always did.

Jack stood on the edge of Selassie and stared out over the plain beyond. The fires of the British lines stretched across the far side. There were hundreds of them. To his eye, they promised warmth and companionship. He did not know how many nights he had spent at campfires just like the ones he was looking at. They had not always been joyous places. At times, they had been mournful, the men sitting around them looking at the spaces that had once been taken by those who had died. At other times, they had been places of fear, shrouded with a silent terror as the men contemplated their fate in the next day's battle. But they had also been places of friendship and comrade-ship, and as he looked at them now, the night breeze cold on his skin, he felt nothing but a sense of being utterly alone.

It had been a fruitless, tiring and irksome day. He had searched for Watson across all three hilltops. Twice he thought he had spotted his companion at a distance, and on both occasions he had lost sight of the figure long before he could get close. For the rest of the day, he had trudged back and forth, checking the many empty huts and tents. His search had only stopped when the sun had set.

Now the moon was up. That night it was the oddest colour, its contours shaded with more orange than white or grey. To Jack's eye, it looked like a white shamma slathered with blood. Like the hundreds of campfires on the far side of the plain, it was a warning of the fight that was still to come, and the blood that would be spilled before the Gorilla King was finally brought to account for his actions.

Napier's men were in position for their assault on Magdala. That assault was sure to come, and when it was unleashed, it would come with the full force of the British army. It would be terrible to behold, the fury and might of the modern weaponry Napier had brought to this place certain to end even the most stubborn resistance.

Tewodros's reign would come to a bloody end, but Jack had to track Watson down before that happened, or else the pair of them would be caught up in the chaos that was sure to follow the fall of Magdala.

He had to find Watson, or risk them both being killed by their own side.

Chapter Forty-six

Easter Monday, 13 April 1868

Jack awoke long before dawn. He had slept badly, his rest broken by a procession of nightmares. All had been fuelled by memories of his past. In his dreams, he had once again climbed the slope below the Great Redoubt at the Alma river, the ranks of red-coated soldiers advancing with him disordered and confused as they braved the dreadful storm of cannon fire that shredded their ranks without mercy. He had stood once more on the blood-soaked battlefield beyond the Bull Run river, the thin line of blue-uniformed soldiers around him torn apart by the Confederate reserves, who had arrived just in time to turn the Union flanking attack. His mind had replayed the bitter street fighting at Magenta, and he had heard again the thunderous roar of the Maharajah of Sawadh's army as it charged the cantonment at Bhundapur. Watson had been at every fight and every battle. Every dream had Jack chasing after his friend. Not once had he got close.

He would resume his search on the main amba of Magdala itself. It was where Watson could most easily hide away and it seemed the most logical place to start, even though he had searched it three times the day before.

He was not the only one on the move. Even though dawn was still far off, large numbers of men were gathering their possessions and preparing to leave the fortress. As Jack started to head towards the rearmost sections of Magdala, he saw the first group depart. Most were warriors, but he saw at least two finely dressed commanders in their midst. Heavily laden donkeys and mules were led towards the Kokit Ber gateway along with small herds of oxen, sheep and goats. The few women and children left on Magdala followed their menfolk, each one burdened with possessions. The warriors themselves carried nothing but their weapons. At the last, Tewodros's army was deserting him.

The sun rose quickly that morning. It pushed away the darkness and burned away the early-morning clouds. The sky turned from grey to orange to a brilliant blue, the sun relentless and powerful as it reasserted its dominance over the world.

Not all of Tewodros's men were abandoning him. Jack passed through a few groups of silent warriors. They sat in small huddles, weapons at their sides, or else prowled across the hilltop in armed groups. All were waiting. These were Tewodros's most loyal men, and they gathered on Magdala, the hilltops of Fala and Selassie abandoned to the British.

These warriors remained to mount one last defiant defence of the emperor's fortress. Tewodros and his warriors might be facing certain defeat, but they would still fight. It would be a fitting finale to Tewodros's empire, a tale that would resound through the centuries that followed. All would learn of the Emperor Tewodros and his defiant stand against the Great White Queen. For years to come, children would be told the tale of Magdala and the small band of warriors who had refused to bow the knee.

Jack searched the amba throughout that long, tense morning. The clouds gathered, the sky once again filled with foreboding. He could feel a storm brewing, the air heavy and charged with tension. A tempest was coming to Magdala.

Around mid morning, he watched a small band of warriors march out of the Kafir Ber gateway on the far side of the fortress. He had no idea what they intended, but they returned shortly afterwards. Others went to try to retrieve a few of Tewodros's precious cannon. He heard the sounds of gunfire, and even the telltale boom of cannons firing, as the British soldiers tried to stop the emperor's men carrying off the artillery pieces.

He ignored it all, his mind focused solely on the task at hand.

He spent a long time searching the second prisoners' compound on the far side of Magdala. There were still people there. Men too sick or too weak to make the journey down the mountain sat forlornly in their huts, a few women and children remaining with them. All looked at Jack, a flare of hope arriving in their eyes as they saw a white face. But he was no saviour, no deliverer of freedom. That would come later, and only when the fortress had fallen.

Twice, he heard the sound of a British regimental band, the martial music caught on the breeze and reaching all the way into the heart of the fortress. It was the overture to the main act that was sure to come later that day. Even as he searched for Watson, the British troops would be readying on Fala and Selassie. They had their guns and rockets with them, the final assault on Magdala sure to be presaged by an artillery barrage. It was just a matter of time until they were ready.

*

By early afternoon, Jack had finished searching the amba. He had entered every hut in both prisoners' compounds. He had even been able to survey the tents and huts of the treasury, the men who had once guarded them abandoning their posts as they too prepared for the final battle for Magdala. The treasures of Tewodros's reign had been there for the taking, but he had left them to lie where they were. He had no need of such trinkets. They had never been what he had been looking for, not really.

But he would not quit his search for Watson. Not even now.

That decision was to be taken out of his hands.

He was walking down the steps from the prisoners' compound when he ran into trouble. Two warriors were coming up. The first passed him by, his head bowed as he watched his footing on the uneven steps. The second paused, as if to let Jack slide past. His head lifted and he looked Jack dead in the eye.

For a moment, the two men stared at one another. Then the warrior's eyes widened.

'Shit.' Jack hissed the word as he saw the rush of surprise register on the warrior's face.

The warrior's mouth started to form a cry of alarm. Jack lashed out, punching the warrior in the face, ramming the words back down the man's throat.

The warrior reeled backwards, blood pumping from his nose. Jack stepped after him, hands reaching up to seize him around the throat. He grabbed tight, fingers clawing into the soft flesh.

The warrior jerked as Jack took hold, then lashed out, trying to punch his attacker in the head. The blow missed, his reach too short to get at Jack, who angled his head back even as he tightened his grip, straightening his arms and pushing downwards, forcing the warrior to the ground. The man fought to get free, flapping his hands at Jack then grabbing at his forearms, trying to prise his hands away. But Jack was bigger and stronger, and he kept up the pressure, his arms aching with the strain and his fingers cramping.

As soon as the warrior was on his back, Jack pulled up with all his might, then slammed the man's head down against the rock of the step with a sickening crunch. Eyes bulging, the warrior still tried to fight. But his blows lacked strength, and his flailing arms bounced off Jack's shoulders. Again Jack forced the man's head up, then crunched it down onto the blood-splattered step.

This time he let go. The warrior lay still.

The other Abyssinian had reached the top step and now turned to see what was delaying his friend. There was time for him to shout out in horror as he saw the white-faced foreigner step away from the body of his comrade.

His cry was lost as a dreadful roar filled the sky. The sound rolled on and on, as if the gods were tearing the very heavens apart in a sudden outpouring of rage.

Napier's bombardment had begun.

The first roundshot landed ten yards beyond the Kokit Ber gateway, hitting the ground before skipping back into the air and rushing on, the heavy projectile moving at an impossible pace.

The second scored across the prisoners' compound. It gouged through the earth, throwing up soil, and hit the warrior staring down at Jack, tearing him in half, a brief explosion of blood and bone showering the ground.

Jack turned and began to run. These first shots were range finders, nothing more. Even now, the officers of artillery would be making their corrections. Gun crews would be standing ready, the cannon that would fire the bombardment lined up wheel to wheel on the hilltops of Selassie and Fala. Every barrel would be aimed at Magdala.

He ran as hard as he could, paying no attention to the warriors who rose to their feet as the barrage began. He ignored the looks of surprise and fear that he saw reflected in their expressions. He thought only of finding a place to ride out the bombardment that was to come.

There was a pause, the air suddenly quiet and still.

And then the storm hit.

Roundshot after roundshot slammed into Magdala. Some crashed into the outer gateway itself, or crunched into the walls and hedges that surrounded it. Others had been aimed higher, the fast-moving shot blazing over the scarp before burying themselves in the ground of the amba or hitting the huts beyond. Shells came with the roundshot. Napier's gunners knew their trade, and the first shells exploded in the air all across Magdala, showering the warriors below with red-hot fragments of casing, or the deadly musket-ball hail that had been contained within the shell itself.

Warriors still in the open were cut down, heads and shoulders gouged by the lethal shower of metal. Some were hit by the roundshot. The iron balls seared along at a dreadful speed. When they hit a man, he ceased to exist, his body shredded into a thousand gruesome fragments.

Jack kept running. A roundshot punched through the air not more than two yards away, and he could not help ducking away, even though the missile was already past. He heard screams and shouts all around him as Tewodros's warriors ran to take up their positions. Orders came fast, those left to command the final defence summoning more men, or else sending others to defend elsewhere. One commander bellowed at him as he ran past, the unintelligible order cut off abruptly as a shell exploded right over the man's head. The full casing's worth of shrapnel cut him down, his body lacerated by hundreds of fast-moving fragments of razor-sharp metal.

More shells came without pause. Hut after hut was hit, the air around them filled with jagged splinters and shards of wood the length of a man's arm.

Jack pounded on through the chaos. Dust and debris choked him. To his left, a man fell as a foot-long splinter of wood speared through his chest. Another went down no more than two yards away, his face pounded into offal by a chunk of stone torn from the gateway. Jack nearly fell as he tried to avoid a corpse that had been eviscerated by shrapnel, the warrior's guts torn from his belly and left lying on the ground beside him, the blue and red offal still connected to his guts by long, bloody strands of sinew.

A shell hit the ground to his front. Soil and rock were thrown high in a great fountain, the explosion both spectacular and terrifying. He ran through the falling debris, his arms pumping hard, ignoring the patter of dirt and earth that rained down around him.

The bombardment carried on without pause. Rockets joined the salvos of shot and shell. They seared through the air with a terrible screeching sound, their tails on fire, showering sparks.

Jack reached the upper gateway that led onto the amba and slid to a halt, falling to his belly then scrabbling forward.

Shells, roundshot and rockets continued to rain down. The

air was filled with dust. Screams came every few moments, men who had tried to shelter from the lethal storm cut down in their hiding places.

Jack's fingers clawed at the dirt in a pathetic attempt to dig some sort of pit into which he could crawl, his body flinching at every shell or rocket that came close. Around him, the air itself vibrated, the ground he lay on shaking with each concussion, trembling as if terrified by the onslaught.

As he lay there, choking on the dust, his body curling tighter and tighter, his mind emptied. He no longer thought of Watson, or of leading his friend to safety. He did not think of the future or of the past. Every thought, every emotion, every hope was scoured from his mind, save for one. Only the terror of that moment was alive, and it filled every fibre of his being. As the bombardment went on and on, the fear burrowed deeper, pushing down into his bowels so that his guts churned and his backside puckered and quivered. Yet he could do nothing but lie there and endure, existing in the hell of the moment, hoping to live.

Chapter Forty-seven

———◆·◆·◆———

The bombardment stopped.

At first, Jack did not dare to believe it. He stayed curled in a ball, every muscle clenched tight. But the silence stretched on, and so he made himself move.

He did not go far. He knew what the silence meant. The British gunners would only stop for one reason. The assault was coming.

He crawled to the edge of the scarp beyond the Kokit Ber gateway. It offered the perfect vantage point. He could see the approach to Magdala.

The British army came on in fine style, their officers leading the way. The field officers were mounted, the commanders of the battalions and the two men who commanded each wing advancing on horseback, whilst the company commanders and subalterns kept to their allotted stations in front, to the side of and behind the formed ranks. At the centre of each battalion was the colour party. For the first time in the long campaign, the bright flags had been removed from their protective leather casings and unfurled. Now the colours led the men forward, each regiment's own distinctive flag carried next to the queen's colour of the Union Jack decorated with the regimental badge.

Behind the colours came the men who would be expected to fight. These were the men Jack knew best, the non-commissioned officers and the poor bloody infantrymen who would be ordered to carry their rifles and their bayonets towards the enemy. These were the men who had won the queen her many victories. The power of the artillerymen and the rocketeers was terrible to behold, the modern rifled cannon and rockets they fired capable of wreaking havoc on any enemy standing against them. But in the end, and just as it would be on that fateful day, the guns would always fall silent, and it would be down to the men in those long ranks to carry the fight to the enemy. Only the infantry could win a battle. And now they came forward, colours unfurled, the tight, ordered ranks marching on Magdala.

The end was in sight.

Jack stared at the advancing ranks, mesmerised by the spectacle. His eyes roved along the line, picking out the regiments he recognised. He saw the 33rd Foot in the van, their distinctive grey jackets so dull and drab compared to the scarlet he had worn when he had stormed the Great Redoubt at the Alma. With the 33rd came the men of the 45th Foot. Like those of the 33rd, they wore grey uniforms with white shoulder belts and air pipe helmets. As he watched, the 33rd took the lead. They came on fast, ranks tight and ordered, Snider rifles loaded and ready, advancing as only the British army advanced. There were no war cries or roars of excitement. The men in grey marched in silence, the only sounds the occasional bark of a sergeant demanding that order be kept in the files.

It was time for the last defenders to stand and fight. Tewodros's warriors still held the Kokit Ber gate. They had done their best to strengthen the position. Boulders and rocks had been piled up behind the gates, so that even if the British sappers and engineers managed to force a way through the gates themselves, they would still have to find a way through the temporary barricade.

Then there was Tewodros himself. Jack saw the emperor at once. He stood ten yards behind the gateway. Once he had commanded an army one hundred and fifty thousand strong. Now he had just a handful of men left. No more than a dozen men had stayed at his side to defend the gate, with only the most loyal warriors, ministers and senior commanders holding fast to their oaths this close to the end. All were armed, and even as Jack watched, they took up firing positions, their ancient muskets aimed through the loopholes prepared for this moment.

If they stood steadfast and resilient, then the men of the 33rd would still have to fight hard to force their way into Magdala. Many would die, the men from Yorkshire falling thousands of miles from their homeland.

Jack watched the 33rd advancing along the road below the Kokit Ber. In a matter of minutes, they would reach the gateway itself. With pitifully few men standing against them, they would surely fight their way into Magdala. Then the real chaos would be unleashed. Jack knew the British army. He knew the men who marched in those neat, ordered ranks, and he knew what they would do when confronted with an undefended and largely abandoned enemy fortress. It was one of the unwritten rules of war, and nothing would hold them in their ranks after they had forced their way inside. These men, paid just a shilling a day, would ransack every inch of the fortress, taking anything they found of value and drinking anything they could lay their hands on.

He got to his knees and started to remove his shamma. It was time to shed the last of his disguise and once again look like an Englishman, even if a raggedy, threadbare one.

Below the gateway, the British soldiers formed their line. Their orders carried clearly to Jack's ears, giving him warning of what was to come, and so he dropped to the ground and covered his head with his hands.

The men of the 33rd fired one volley. Seven hundred Snider bullets tore into the gateway. The sound was dreadful. Hundreds of the bullets were wasted, the heavy rounds punching into solid stone. But enough tore through gaps or sent wickedly sharp shards of stone slashing through the air. Some defenders fell, their bodies lacerated by splinters or hit by one of the few bullets that had found a path through. Others ran, their desire to stay and fight at the emperor's side failing at the last.

Beyond the gateway, the 33rd gave three great cheers that they had saved for this moment. Then they were released.

Jack heard the men storm forward, the sound of hundreds of boots pounding on the rocky path that led up the Kokit Ber carrying clearly in the silence that followed the volley. The few defenders left opened fire. The matchlocks gave a strange double cough, the powder in the pan firing just before the main charge behind the musket ball. Tewodros was still there. He stood a few yards from the boulders that barred the gate. He was quite alone.

The 33rd reached the gateway. Jack expected to hear the detonation of a powder charge as the engineers and sappers with the infantry blew a way into Tewodros's fortress.

None came.

He lifted his head. He could see a few of the gateway's defenders firing again. The sound of their volley was pitiful, the smattering of musket shots as nothing compared to the massive volley fired by the British Sniders. But the range was short now, and even the ancient matchlocks could wound. Jack heard the first cries as men in the leading ranks of the 33rd were hit.

The infantry outside started to fire back. Shots came at the gateway without pause, driving the defenders to ground. A brave few dared to thrust a musket through a loophole and return fire, but most just cowered away.

Tewodros stood silent throughout the exchange of gunfire. He did not flinch even as bullets snapped past. He did not cry out or encourage his men. With his face turned towards the heavens, he stood silent, even as his world was thrown into chaos and destruction.

Jack heard a new sound from the far side of the gateway. He did not know why there had been no powder to blow the gates open, but now he could hear that the British were going to do it the old-fashioned way. Axes thumped into the wood, each heavy blow loud enough to be heard even over the rifle fire that came without pause.

At the same time, grey-clad figures emerged from the hedge-line a few dozen yards from the gate. Some men from the 33rd had tired of waiting for the sappers to force the gates open and had found another way inside, scaling the rock then clawing their way through a gap torn in the hedge by the British bombardment.

There were not many of them, barely a dozen infantrymen led by a single officer. As Jack watched, they formed a thin skirmish line, then fired. The bullets cut down Tewodros's men, the defenders hit from the side. No more than five remained standing.

Volley fired, the party from the 33rd charged. It was bravely done. It was no small thing to be the first into an enemy fortress, and the Yorkshiremen stormed forward, teeth bared, bayonets lowered, courage screwed tight.

Tewodros saw them coming. He shouted something at his last companions. The five took off at once, fleeing for their lives.

At the last, the Emperor of Abyssinia stood alone.

Jack had a clear view of the scene from where he lay. He saw the emperor turn and flee. Even as the men from the 33rd ran towards the Kokit Ber, Tewodros galloped up the steps that led up the scarp and to the smaller gate that led on to the amba itself. The emperor tore through the gate then stopped. Jack saw the emperor's hand move to the pistol holstered at his waist. The weapon glinted as it was drawn, the polished metal catching the sun as it was raised one last time.

Tewodros did not hesitate. He opened his mouth wide, then pushed the barrel of the pistol deep inside.

The men of the 33rd ran hard towards the scarp. A young officer led them, his sabre drawn. None of them would reach the emperor in time.

Tewodros, Emperor of Abyssinia and descendant of the great King Solomon and his Queen of Sheba, pulled the trigger. This time he did not miss.

And so Magdala fell.

The reign of Tewodros II was over.

Jack crossed the amba. The ground was littered with rubble and debris from the bombardment, along with dozens of discarded matchlock rifles, some with fuses still aglow. Nearly every hut had been destroyed, and now the British soldiers rampaged through the destruction, all intent on finding some-thing of value. It was time to take a reward for the weeks of slogging across the godforsaken country.

'Hold there, pal.'

Jack did as he was ordered. He had left his spear with his discarded clothing and so was unarmed. He was dressed in a grubby undershirt over knee-length peasant trousers that had once been white but which were now a dirty shade of grey, the cloth stained and ragged. He could not have looked less of a threat, but still the soldier from the 33rd presented his bayonet-tipped rifle, the steel blade aimed directly at Jack's chest.

'Where do you think you're going? All you darkies should be heading back down the hill.'

The soldier's accent was broad Yorkshire and it made Jack smile. It had been a long time since he had heard any English voice save for Watson's. 'It's all right, Private. I'm English.' He addressed the soldier just as an officer would, identifying the man's rank and adding the clipped tone of command to his words.

The soldier did not look convinced, but he lowered his bayonet. 'What you doing looking like that then?'

'I was a prisoner here.' Jack answered honestly.

'Shit. Sorry, mate. I didn't realise.' The soldier's rifle lowered completely. He looked shamefaced. 'Our Ruperts are over near the gateway, if you want them.'

'Thank you.' Jack had no intention of going to find the officers. He wanted to make one last circuit of the battered fortress to look for Watson before he quit the place once and for all. As far as he could guess, Watson must have left Magdala with the other prisoners the day before the bombardment. It made him feel rather foolish. He had risked his life by staying when there had been no need. Once again, he questioned his own judgement. It was another mistake, another bad decision to add to many others. They stretched in a long line all the way back to that night in the Babylon when he had allowed a hidden revolver to slip inside.

'Off you go, lad. Join your mates.' He almost smiled as he gave the command. The soldier was still standing awkwardly in front of him, his eyes darting back and forth as he looked longingly at his comrades, who were running past as they searched for loot.

'Aye, sir.'

The man did not linger. He was on his toes the moment Jack released him. Jack did not blame him. Opportunities like the one presented to the British infantrymen that day were few and far between, and normally only followed a bitterly hard fight.

More and more men were arriving in the fortress. The first of the native infantry regiments entered through the gateway. They needed little invitation to break ranks and rush forward. With them came the 33rd's bandsmen. Unlike their comrades, the band stayed together and set up a post not far from the great red pavilion. Once settled, they began to play 'God Save the Queen'.

Jack stood back as a file of babbling sepoys rushed past. Only when they were gone did he move on. He took his time, avoiding the men who were ransacking the ruined huts. Abyssinian spears and shields were favourite finds, and many of the soldiers walked past carrying the local weapons. A few even traded blows, the air filled with their laughter as they pretended to be the warriors they had vanquished. Others came out of the huts carrying gifts from the European powers that Tewodros had once hoped to make his allies. One sepoy pranced past carrying a fine telescope, whilst another hooted with glee as he laid out a set of toy soldiers on the ground. Jack walked past them all and headed for the great red pavilion that had been Tewodros's home.

He was not alone. The red tent had drawn men in from all over the fortress. As he came closer, he saw the first spoils of war being brought out. One man emerged dressed in a fine scarlet robe, the seams decorated with golden fringing. He paraded past his fellows, his arms waving this way and that, much to his comrades' amusement. They bellowed and cheered as the mock-emperor demanded they bow to him, the air filled with laughter.

Other men came out carrying golden or silver figurines, fine leather-bound books, rolled rugs or bundles of robes. Some worked in groups, bringing out large chests that they then hacked open with their bayonets, their finds greeted with huge cheers if they contained something of value, or groans of despair if it was something less interesting. Many of the chests contained nothing more than manuscripts, which the disgruntled soldiers tossed into the air so that the fortress was soon filled with a thousand discarded sheets of paper that caught on the breeze.

Jack skirted the pavilion, heading round to the back. He was not there for loot. Once he had finished looking for Watson, he would be on his way.

A sepoy staggered past, his arms stretched round an enormous ceremonial drum that was almost too heavy to carry. Jack ducked past him, then slipped down the side of one of the tents behind the great red pavilion, thinking to bypass the steady stream of soldiers following the main thoroughfares that wound around the amba. He was nearly done. He would make one last search of the prisoners' compound where he and Watson had been held, then he would quit.

He stepped around one of the smaller tents and found himself in a narrow stretch of ground with the backs of the tents on one side and a line of broken huts on the other. To his relief, he was alone. It would take a while to pick his way along the alleyway, the ground littered with thatch, sticks and mud from the huts that had been hit by the British gunners, but at least he could move without being barged into.

He had taken no more than half a dozen steps before a figure stepped into his path ten yards ahead. Jack recognised him in a heartbeat. It was Swan, Finch's enforcer.

He had been so intent on finding Watson that he had forgotten all about Finch and his men. But it appeared they had not forgotten about him.

Chapter Forty-eight

'My, my, Jack Lark, as I live and fucking breathe.'

Jack stood still. He did not turn as he heard the familiar voice behind him. He did not need to. He knew who it was.

'What's a fellow like you doing skulking around dressed like a fucking darkie?' Finch addressed Jack's back. 'Have you got yourself a little box of matches with you? Are you going to set another fucking fire?' The questions came one after the other. 'You like a fine fucking fire, don't you, Jack-o? Nothing like a nice blaze to put you in a great fucking mood.'

Jack held his tongue. He had no doubt now that his time was up. He had presented his enemy with the perfect opportunity. He wondered when Finch and Swan had first spotted him. Had they come up with the 33rd, or had they held back and advanced with the second wave of native infantry? Either way, they must have been delighted to spot him in the fortress, and even more pleased to see him slip out of sight behind the line of tents. Now they had him penned in, one ahead and one behind. The murder – and it would be murder, he was sure of that – would be carried out quickly and quietly.

But Finch wanted to enjoy his moment.

'You thought you was so fucking clever, didn't you, Jack-o? Sneaking off after I found you at that fucking church. It was clever, I'll give you that. And you was right to do it. I was going to do you in right there and then, you and that skinny streak of shite with you. Just like I did for your chum.'

Jack felt the first burn of anger at the mention of Macgregor. It came hot and fast, rising from deep in his belly, where it had been contained so long. He fed the rage. He pictured Bella lying on the floor of the Babylon, her face covered with the waxy sheen of death, and he thought of Macgregor walking to his death. The images fuelled the anger, mixing with his hatred of Finch. The volatile cocktail started to surge through his veins, and he closed his eyes as he savoured its touch. He wanted it. He needed it.

'That poor fucker pissed hisself at the end. You should know that. That posh prig chum of yours died with pissy trousers.' Finch barked a laugh. 'You going to piss yourself, Jack-o?' He paused, giving Jack a moment to think about the question. When no answer came, he spoke again. 'Course you won't, not a tough bastard like you. But you're all the same at the end. You all bleed. You all cry. You all die. Doesn't matter how hard you think you is. You all die just the fucking same.'

Jack heard the change in Finch's tone. The talking was done.

He opened his eyes.

'Swanny.' Finch called out to his henchman.

Swan had stood silent throughout his master's speech. At the command, he straightened up, a hand swiping across his head to control the errant flap of hair that half covered his bald scalp and which had lifted in the breeze.

Jack faced Swan. He balled his fists. There was time for him to suck down one last breath.

Swan dropped his hand from his head. It moved to his waist and to the revolver that was stuck into the band of his trousers.

Jack saw the movement. He knew what was to come.

Swan drew the weapon. It stuck for a moment, the barrel catching at the top of his trousers, and he glanced down, a moment's anger flickering across his weathered features.

In that moment, Jack charged. Fury filled his mind, gloriously all-consuming, thrilling, powerful. It surged through him, sending its wild strength rushing into every fibre of his being.

Time slowed.

He rushed forward, boots barely touching the ground.

Swan freed the heavy revolver. He looked up.

Jack saw the surprise register on his face. Then a flash of fear. But Swan was no griffin. He raised the revolver, barrel still, nerves banished.

Jack strained every muscle to find more speed. Yet he was still five yards away as the revolver levelled out.

Swan fired.

Jack felt the punch as the bullet snapped past. In that moment, he bellowed the rebel yell, the madness taking him. The wild cry that had so terrified the Union soldiers five years before rang out, the yips and yells quite unearthly. He felt no fear. Only white-hot rage. And joy.

Swan fired a second time.

Jack felt the bullet hit him. His right arm was thrown back as the bullet cut through the flesh above his elbow. The pain was sharp and instant. Then it was gone, lost in the tumult of emotions that scoured through him. He ran on, closing the gap, everything he had focused on the man to his front.

He saw the confusion on Swan's face as he realised that his first two shots had failed to strike Jack down. He held back the third, straightening his arm, holding the revolver stock still as he lined up another shot. Taking his time. Making sure. Jack knew he would not miss a third time.

This was it. Everything he had been, and everything he had done, had led to this last moment, this moment of his death.

He threw back his head and gave the rebel yell one final time as he charged at Swan. He did not care that he would die. For he had found what he had been looking for. He was who he was meant to be, and his killer would strike him down with the defiant cry of a fighter ringing in his ears.

Jack Lark would go to his death shrieking like the devil.

Jack did not see the bullet hit. The rebel yell filled his head so he did not hear the revolver fire, but he saw the front of Swan's chest punched outwards as the metal tore through him.

Swan's eyes widened in shock. The revolver that had been aimed at Jack fell from his grasp, the weapon tumbling to the ground. Blood surged from the hole ripped in his chest. It came in a great torrent, sheeting down his front.

A second bullet was fired. Another gruesome exit wound was torn in his chest.

Swan crumpled, his body appearing to collapse around itself.

It was then that Jack saw Watson. The former academic was standing still, his Beaumont–Adams revolver held out in from of him. His face was pale, every vestige of colour drained from his skin. But his red-rimmed eyes looked at Jack. Then he smiled.

Jack skidded to a halt in front of Swan's corpse. There was

no time to feel the relief of still being alive. That would come later. For now, the rage was everything.

He reached down, snatching Swan's revolver from the ground. He could feel blood on the weapon, the metal slick and warm. The moment he had a grip on it, he turned round, facing back down the alleyway between the tents.

He saw Finch for the first time. He was not alone. Cooper stood at his side, a silent, treacherous companion.

Finch raised his revolver.

Jack saw the gun come up. There was no time to fire back.

'Get down!' He turned as he bellowed the order, showing Finch his back.

Watson was rooted to the spot, staring at Swan's body, his mouth open as he contemplated the first man he had killed.

'Down!' Jack cried out again as he lurched into motion. He jumped over Swan's corpse, arms outstretched.

Finch fired.

Jack threw himself at Watson. He had acted fast, his instincts propelling him forward. But he was slower than a speeding bullet.

A bullet that struck Watson in the chest.

Watson's shamma twitched as it reacted to the impact. Then the blood came. Jack was still moving forward, and he collided with his friend. They fell together, arms and legs thrown this way and that. Watson hit the ground first, thumping down onto his back. Jack landed a second later, his painful contact with the ground barely registering. Swan's revolver was lost as he crashed down.

He did not lie still. The moment he hit, he scrabbled forward and threw himself on top of Watson, covering his body with his own, shielding him from the bullets that came searing through the air as Finch fired twice more.

He felt the blood then. It was pumping from Watson's chest, staining the white of the shamma red.

Jack twisted onto his side, then pressed his hands down, trying to hold back the flood. The blood was warm on his skin and his hands slipped across Watson's chest, so he was forced to push down hard to keep them in place.

Finch fired again, a fourth shot snapping past Jack's head before burying itself in the back of a nearby hut.

Watson stared up at Jack. His mouth opened and closed, but no sound came out.

A fifth bullet seared past, buzzing like a fat, angry insect.

Jack heard a shout as Finch cursed his poor aim. He heard the demand for Cooper to hand over his revolver, but he paid it no heed. That would come later.

'It's all right,' he whispered to Watson. 'It's just a scratch.' Both men knew the comforting words were a lie. 'You're going to be fine.'

Watson's hand flapped at Jack's arm, trying and failing to take hold. Blood dribbled from the corner of his mouth as he tried again to speak.

'Here, hold here.' Jack pushed Watson's hand down onto the wound. 'Hold tight.'

Watson grimaced, his lips pressing together with the pain of the wound. Yet he did as Jack told him, his hands moving to cover the rent in his flesh.

'That's it. Press hard now.' Jack had no idea if it would be enough, but he did not think Watson would die, at least not immediately.

'Jack?' Watson's voice came in no more than a whisper. It was the first time he had used Jack's given name.

'Stay quiet.' Jack clasped his hands over Watson's own, pushing them against the wound. Already the flow of blood was slowing.

'I did it.'

'Did what?'

'I pulled the trigger.' Watson's voice quivered.

'Yes, you did. Now bloody lie still.' Jack clenched his jaw tight. He remembered challenging Watson, doubting that the academic had the balls to kill a man. He had been wrong. Watson had what it took. He had it in spades.

'No.' Watson's voice hardened. 'It's time.'

'Time for what?' Jack could feel the warmth of his friend's hands underneath his.

'Kill him.' Watson hissed the words. 'Kill Finch.'

Chapter Forty-nine

—◆◆◆—

J ack stayed where he was for one more moment, making certain that Watson's hands were clasped tight to the wound to his chest. Only when he was sure that they were in place did he move.

He reached out with his left hand, taking up Swan's revolver from where he had dropped it when he had knocked Watson to the ground. With his right, he picked up Watson's own weapon. Blood ran from the flesh wound to his upper arm and both hands were slick with Watson's blood, so he took a firm hold of the two revolvers as he pushed himself up, making sure neither would slip from his grasp.

He turned the moment he found his feet, revolver in each hand.

Finch was still there. He stood little more than twenty yards away, another revolver held out ready to fire. Cooper was at his side. He stared as Jack rose from the ground, his eyes widening as the blood-splattered figure came up with a gun in each hand.

Finch fired.

The bullet flew past at least a foot over Jack's head.

There was time for Jack to smile. Finch was scared. And he was a terrible shot.

Jack took a single pace forward. He knew both weapons he held had already been fired. He had counted the shots, instinct kicking in without thought. Both were five-shot weapons, so he knew there were three rounds left in each. Finch had taken Cooper's own Beaumont–Adams revolver, which would surely have been loaded with five rounds. One had just been fired. That left four. It was almost an even contest.

Almost.

He took another step forward, closing the distance, holding his fire. He wanted Finch to see him. To fear him.

Finch fired again.

The bullet zipped by, closer this time, but still missing by half a foot.

Jack felt the snap in the air. There was not even a flicker of a flinch. He paced forward, both guns held out. But still he held his fire.

Finch fired again. His third bullet passed an inch over Jack's head.

Jack was close enough to see the man's fear. It was so strong he could almost smell it. Yet Finch was no coward, and he screwed his courage tight, then twitched his revolver lower, a final correction made.

But it was too late.

Jack fired Swan's revolver first. He held it in his left hand, as he did in battle when he fought with a sword. He did not miss.

The bullet struck Finch in the gut.

Simultaneously, he fired Watson's revolver, the shots coming so close together the sound of the discharges blurred into one.

The second bullet hit Finch no more than an inch to the

right of the first. As the twin strikes tore through him, Cooper's revolver fell from his hands and he clutched at the dreadful wounds ripped in his belly.

Jack was not done. He fired both weapons again. The two bullets cut deep into Finch's chest with enough force to make him stagger. Then he collapsed, his body curling over his pain so that he fell twisted at the waist.

Cooper had not moved. He stared back at Jack, eyes wide in terror. He was unarmed.

Jack came on with even, measured steps. He could hear Finch sobbing.

'Jack-o.' Cooper spoke for the first time. Both his hands came up, palms held towards Jack as if they would somehow ward him away. 'Don't you do it, Jack-o.'

The words meant nothing to Jack. He stalked forward. Each of his two revolvers held a single bullet.

'Please, Jack-o.' Cooper's face crumpled as he saw his death walking towards him. 'Let me go, I beg you. It weren't my fault. None of it. He made me do it. You know that, don't you, Jack-o? He was going to kill me right there and then, back at them wells at Sooroo. I didn't have a choice. He said it was you or me.' The words tumbled out, one after the other. 'I had to do it, I had to do what he wanted. And I'd already saved you once, hadn't I just? Back at Finch's warehouse. I got you out. He was going to kill you. But I got you away, didn't I, Jack-o? I fucking saved you.' Cooper wept as he blabbered, great rivers of tears and snot running down his face.

Jack stopped. He was close enough.

'No, Jack-o. No.' Cooper's legs could no longer hold him up, and he fell to his knees, face twisted with fear. The words stopped, and great sobs racked his body as the terror took hold.

'Don't kill me.' His last words came out in a whisper.

Jack aimed both revolvers. But it wasn't Cooper he saw. In his mind's eye, he pictured Macgregor and Bella standing together, their faces coming to him with utmost clarity. Both were laughing.

He fired the guns.

Chapter Fifty

Jack stood over Finch. The man was still alive, but Jack knew he would not linger for long, not with four bullets buried in his body. The blood was flowing fast. There was a lot of it, and it pooled around Finch's curled up figure, soaking into the dry, barren ground. Jack reckoned he had a few minutes left before he bled out. He was glad. It would be a slow death.

He felt nothing in that moment. No remorse. No thought of pity. No sense of mercy. He looked down at a dying man and felt only a sense of satisfaction at a dirty job well done. He had killed more men than he could count, but he could not think of a single one who deserved it more than this one. So he would leave Finch to die, no matter how long it took.

He turned towards Cooper. The man who had come with Jack from London still knelt in silence, his thin frame shuddering and shaking with barely controlled fear.

Jack had twitched each revolver before he fired, making sure that neither bullet would hit. At the end, he had chosen to let Cooper live.

Finch convulsed, his body clenching tight. Jack watched,

emotionless. He kept watching as Finch convulsed once more, then lay still.

It was over.

'Go.' He said the single word, then turned on his heel. He did not look back, even when he heard the sound of Cooper scrambling to his feet, followed by the scuff of his boots on the ground as he fled the scene.

He hurried back to Watson. It was quiet now, peaceful even. The fortress still resounded to the sound of its ransacking. Cheers came as soldiers made one fine discovery after another, and there were peals of laughter alongside shouts of anger as men fought over the best trophies. But in the narrow passage where two men had found their deaths, all was still and hushed.

Watson lay on his back, his eyes flickering back and forth as they studied the sky. Jack sat down next to him and placed the empty revolvers on the ground.

'You're still alive then.' He leaned forward so that Watson would see him.

'It appears so.' Watson winced as he spoke, the words coming out in little more than a hoarse whisper. 'Did you do it?'

'Yes.' Jack's tone was flat and quite without emotion.

'Cooper?'

'Cooper's gone.'

'That's good.' Watson let out a long breath. 'So it's over?'

'Yes.' Jack slipped a hand onto Watson's, which were still clasped to his wound. He heard orders being shouted nearby, as officers began the long and difficult task of bringing their men back under control.

'I have something for you.' Watson spoke quietly, his voice quivering slightly. 'You should take it.'

'What is it?'

'In my waistband. I rather think you must get it yourself. I don't think I should move my hands.' He gave a sickly smile as he made the wry remark.

Jack studied Watson's face, his eyes searching his friend's gaze. Then he did as he was told. As he gently pulled back Watson's shamma, he saw a flash of gold. It was the cross that Watson had stared at in such wonder in the minutes before their capture by Tewodros's men. It was a beautiful object, and a valuable one, made from solid gold, every surface decorated with precious stones. He tried to recall what Watson had said about it. It had come from the grave of some priest, he remembered that much. But more than its history, or its value, he remembered the look of awe that had spread across the academic's face as he held the relic for the first time. It had been more than excitement at how much it was worth. It had been something more reverential. Some things had more value than their price.

'It's for you. A payment, if you will.' Watson's gaze was locked on to Jack's face. 'For all you have done for me.'

'No.' Jack's reply was firm. He did not want it. He had not come here to steal away the fallen emperor's wealth. He was back to being the man he was meant to be, and he would take that with him. It was worth more than any shiny metal. 'I think you should keep it.'

'Are you sure?'

'I have never been more certain of anything. Now let's get you sorted.' He grinned at his friend as he planned his next move. He would use Swan's shirt as a temporary dressing for Watson's wound, then he would find some soldiers to help carry the academic to the nearest surgeons, who would surely have been prepared for a large number of casualties and would now be standing idly by with few men to treat.

He straightened up. His arm throbbed and his back ached, but he would not complain. He knew he had been lucky to come out of the fight with his life intact. And on top of that, he had found what he had come all this way to find.

He had found a man he thought he had lost.

He had found Jack Lark.

Epilogue

British headquarters, Dalanta plain, 15 April 1868

J ack sat outside the tent allocated by the station officer. It was cooler out here, the air inside the tent hot, stuffy and filled with the ripe stink of sun-warmed canvas and another's man feet. It had been a short day's walk from Magdala to the British headquarters on the Dalanta plain. It was just the first of many as he began the long march back to Annesley Bay and a vessel that would start him on the first leg of his next journey. At that moment, he did not know what he would do or where he would go. But he was certain that it would not be London. He was still a fugitive, wanted for the killing of a rich man's son. Yet that alone would not have stopped him from going back, not if it was what he truly wanted. The other threat to his life was gone, but there would always be another enemy like Finch, or another friend like Macgregor, and Jack had no desire to encounter either. Life was simpler only when he was alone.

Watson was alive. With the assistance of some soldiers from the 33rd, Jack had carried his friend to their regiment's surgeons, the men with the knives and the saws only too happy to have a casualty. They had given Watson their fullest attention, removing the bullet from his chest then doing their best to stitch up the wound so that it would not fester. When Jack had last seen him, he had been sitting up in a cot, his upper body swathed in bandages. Their final conversation had been brief. Jack had left with a promise that he would return the following day – a promise that he had never intended to honour. Watson had what he had come for. He had a tale that would make him the talk of London and perhaps beyond. He no longer had any need for the services of a battered former soldier. So Jack had walked out of the surgeons' tent and not looked back.

A company of sepoys marched past. He could not help running his eye over their ranks, checking their order, the habit deeply ingrained. They looked smart, even to his critical eye. The period of indiscipline that had followed the fall of Magdala had not lasted long, the officers bringing their men under control within the hour. That had not stopped the soldiers from ransacking the fortress. From what he had heard, they had done a fine job of it, gorging themselves on the treasures Tewodros had accumulated from across the empire he had forged. So much had been taken that Napier had felt compelled to issue a general order for its return. Many of the items that had been looted had little in the way of monetary value, but they would be of much interest to the waiting public back home, who would want to learn and see more of the reign of the Gorilla King they had read so much about.

Jack knew many soldiers would tell Napier to go whistle, and he doubted that any of them would part easily with anything they thought could be turned into money or drink. He was not alone in thinking that the men would be reluctant to give up their ill-gotten gains, and twice he had seen whole companies of men paraded so that their haversacks could be searched. He had little pity for any soldier foolish enough not to have hidden their stuff away. They deserved to have it taken, especially as so many of their officers were more than willing to buy up anything their men fancied turning into ready cash.

He pulled out his revolver and laid it on the ground, ready to begin that day's routine cleaning. It was the Beaumont–Adams he had taken from Swan, the weapon he had used to murder Finch. It was a production-line model without the customisations that had made his Colt stand out, but it would do for now. He missed the Colt, but he did not lament its loss. Weapons were tools, nothing more. They came into his life and went from it whether he wanted them to or not. Just like people.

He pulled open a leather pouch that held the cleaning tools he would need. Like all his current possessions, it had been pinched. After his time as Tewodros's prisoner, he had been left with nothing of his own, and so a few officers from Napier's column would soon notice that one or two of their belongings had gone missing since the fall of Magdala. He hoped it would serve as a warning to take better care of their kit. He did not think any would mind, every one of them sure to be made richer thanks to the success of the campaign.

Not that the campaign was done. Before the army could depart, they had one last task to perform. Jack had heard that Napier would raze Tewodros's fortress to the ground, but there was no talk of attempting to colonise the emperor's lands, or to hold the ground they had taken. Tewodros's prisoners had been released, so Napier had got what he had come for. Now he would take his army home, just as he had always planned.

Abyssinia was weaker and more divided than ever, but it would be left to find its own future without the interference of the British. Tewodros's son and heir, Prince Alamayou, would go to Britain, where he would be educated and kept safe, far from the lands that his father had claimed for his own. The Gorilla King would become a footnote in the history of the British Empire, his demise an example to any tinpot ruler who ever gave thought to the idea of rebelling against their Great White Queen.

Jack would not wait to see Magdala thrown down. He would leave with the first party heading towards Annesley Bay. There was no reason for him to linger.

It was time he took the first step on his next journey, one that had no destination. At least not yet.

But he would find one. He always did.

Historical Note

———◆◆◆———

The tale of Tewodros II, Emperor of Abyssinia, has largely been forgotten, and like many of the British army's campaigns of this period, so has the costly expedition that was mounted to secure the release of the prisoners he had the temerity to take. It has always been one aim of this series to throw some light on those campaigns that have fallen out of our collective memory, and by doing so honour those from both sides who fought and suffered in the name of the British Empire.

I faced one challenge right from the get-go. So many different names were used for both places and people that I must confess I found it all rather confusing. In many accounts, Tewodros is named Theodore, especially those accounts written for the contemporary British public, who may have struggled with the name he had chosen for himself as a nod to the short but golden age of Tewodros I, back in the early fifteenth century. I preferred the slightly more colourful version of his name and so stuck with that. Ever one for simplicity, I chose to use the place names from the map produced by the artists accompanying the campaign, using one version for each name and place throughout the novel. I hope that this approach makes sense and is clear enough should you wish to read more about this astonishing campaign.

The Reverend Henry A. Stern's desperate encounter with Tewodros is loosely based on Stern's own account of the event, as written in his history *The Captive Missionary: Being an account of the country and the people of Abyssinia*. Using Stern's account allowed me to bring in his own words and those he recorded of Tewodros himself. Of course, as with any first-hand account of an event, it should be taken with a grain of salt, but I wanted to set the scene for the events taking place in Abyssinia at that time, and Stern's account gives us a superb insight into what it was like to be faced by the Gorilla King himself. I have added some colour to the event, and those additions are completely of my own making. I hope Stern will forgive me.

Stern was released by Tewodros on Saturday 11 April and by the end of Easter Sunday all of the emperor's European prisoners, including the Consul Cameron and the envoy Rassam, had been released in a doomed attempt to curry favour with Napier and secure Tewodros favourable terms of surrender. However, the last-minute release of the prisoners was not enough for Napier to grant Tewodros his terms, although he did urge the emperor to accept an unconditional surrender. When he did not, Napier, beholden to the alliances he had formed on the way to Magdala, had no choice but to order the assault. Thus, ended Tewodros's reign.

There were a number of journalists covering the campaign, and their accounts are a wonderful resource for a writer like myself. George Henty, who would go on to become a historical fiction author of great renown, was there, as was Henry Morton Stanley, the man who would make his name as the explorer who found Dr Livingstone (and whose account of the Battle of Shiloh has already featured in the historical note to *The Rebel Killer*). Another journalist, William Simpson of the *Illustrated London News*, was present, and I recommend his book, *Diary of a Journey to Abyssinia 1868*, as a great place to start if you would like to read more of this campaign. None of these journalists were brave or foolish enough to try to enter Magdala before it had been captured, but I wanted to thrust Jack and Watson into the heart of the action, and so like many fictional heroes they followed a path entirely of their own making. The pace and plot of this novel also required some other changes to the events that occurred in the last, chaotic days of Tweodros's reign, and of course much more was going on than Jack could possibly see.

As well as reading about the campaign, it is also possible to see some of the treasures that were brought back to these shores. I shall not argue the right and the wrong of that here, but I will say that the V&A in London has a wonderful display case under the title 'Magdala', whilst one of my favourite museums, the Royal Engineer Museum in Chatham, has its own collection of items brought back from the campaign. The REM also houses Wellington's map of Waterloo, which they exhibit in a brilliant interactive display. They also have a number of items from the Zulu War of 1879, including the revolver that Lieutenant Chard used at Rorke's Drift. As many of you will know, the film *Zulu* is my all-time favourite, and so you can imagine how exciting it is to see such things!

For those who wish to read more of Tewodros himself, as well as the detail around his final days, I would recommend Philip Marsden's superb *The Barefoot Emperor*. This is a wonderful and very accessible account of Tewodros's reign and one of the very best histories I have read of any period. There are plenty of other resources available; the peerless Osprey series has some wonderful books that cover the British soldiers of this period, as well as the Abyssinian warriors they faced at Magdala.

So what is next for Jack? Well, he now finds himself on a new continent, one that offered plenty of opportunities for men of action. It is the age of the great explorers. Burton and Speke have discovered Lake Tanganyika and Lake Victoria. Sir Samuel White Baker has found and named Lake Albert. And the most famous of all these Victorian explorers, David Livingstone, has already crossed Africa from coast to coast, and by the time Magdala falls is deep in the wilds on his quest to find the source of the Nile. Against this backdrop of exploration and adventure, I think there could well be a role for Jack to play. Let's see where fate takes him next.

Acknowledgements

Fugitive is the ninth Jack Lark novel, and to be honest I never thought I would ever reach such a milestone. Yet here we are, and for that I have many people to thank. David Headley, my superb agent, started me on this road some eight years ago, and I know I would not even have a single book to my name were it not for him. The team at Headline are as brilliant as ever, and I have to thank Frankie Edwards and Bea Grabowska for their insightful comments, bottomless patience and unwavering support. Jane Selley, my copy editor, has done a superb job on *Fugitive*, as she has on so many of the Jack Lark novels, and I am very grateful indeed for her help. I must also thank my colleagues at work for putting up with my tendency to bore on the subject of my books. I would also like to take a moment to express my sincere gratitude to all those who have read any of my books and especially to those who have taken the time to contact me. It really is much appreciated. Finally, the biggest thank you of all goes to my wife Debs, and my children, Lily, Will and Emily.